H

KILLING STATE

JUDITH O'REILLY is the author of *Wife in the North* (a top-three *Sunday Times* bestseller and BBC Radio 4 Book of the Week) and *A Year of Doing Good*. Judith is a former senior journalist with the *Sunday Times*, and a former political producer with BBC 2's Newsnight and ITN's Channel 4 News.

JUDITH O'REILLY

KILLING STATE

HEAD
of ZEUS

First published in the UK in 2018 by Loughman Press

This hardback edition first published in the UK in 2019
by Head of Zeus Ltd

9 7 5 3 1 2 4 6 8

A catalogue record for this book is available from
the British Library.

ISBN (HB): 9781789542684
ISBN (XTPB): 9781789542677
ISBN (E): 9781788548922

Typeset by Divaddict Publishing Solutions Ltd

Printed and bound in Great Britain by
CPI Group (UK) Ltd, Croydon CRO 4YY

Head of Zeus Ltd
First Floor East
5–8 Hardwick Street
London ECIR 4RG

WWW.HEADOFZEUS.COM

In memory of Frank O'Reilly,
who loved a good thriller.

Prologue

This morning for Honor Jones MP was unremarkable, except in one respect. She was going to die.

In a dark fleece and trainers, a black Dockers cap pulled over his ears, her killer looked like any other jogger as he waited. It wouldn't be long now. She liked to run when the streets were quiet and the park was empty.

The day before, he watched her as she stepped out with her shiny blonde hair in a ponytail and white earbuds. She was alone. He could have told her that was dangerous. When there's a predator about, you're safest in the herd.

She'd eased the door shut behind her – a considerate neighbour – and, yawning, she fiddled with the iPod. He could have told the Tory MP for Mile End that she should vary her habits. That routine would be the death of her. Down the short herringbone path, through the cast-iron gate which creaked, and onto the street. Stretching out her quads, her slim leg doubled as she pulled her foot up behind her. She did the same with the other leg and then set off. Running steadily down her street, across the road, ducking under the railway bridge, into the park where small-time dealers did small-time deals, by the canal, past the graffitied lock and right into Majesty Park. By the time she was round the far edge of the lake, she was breathing hard but even.

It was there he planned to move in behind her, and, with her listening to her music, he hoped she wouldn't hear him. He would slide the blade once through the heart, and once through the wall of the stomach, aiming to catch the artery so she would bleed out before help came. Precise. Efficient. Professional. He had been through it in his mind a hundred times, counting it out: she would die forty-two seconds after she first felt his breath on her neck under the swing of that blonde ponytail. He would be careful not to get blood on his running shoes.

After yesterday's run, the banker who lived in the flat above hers came out as she left for Westminster. She smiled, her hand on his forearm as she said something that made him laugh, leaving him staring after her as she headed for the tube station. The police would question the city boy after the body was found. Had he found her attractive and did she reject him? Did that make him angry? He'd be appalled at her death, distraught, and then outraged that anyone would think that he could do such a thing.

Across the road, Honor pulled the front door behind her, and the watcher felt the oak thud of it. She yawned as she opened the creaking gate, and behind the privet hedge, in the shadowed doorway, he flexed his muscles. He let her go, drawing out the two purple horse-pills from his fleece pocket, chewing them, swallowing. He could hear the sound of her trainers against the wet pavement. And then he moved out from the shadows.

*

At first, he kept his distance.

She was a quarter of a mile ahead of him, then five hundred paces, then four hundred. As she breathed in, so did he, and out again, in and out, drawing the air down deeper as she did. Her stride was shorter than his, but across the water, he knew the exact moment her breath grew ragged and a light sweat broke out on her forehead. She wasn't as fit as he was but she was fitter than most. Fifty paces between them, she kicked up her heels, pushing herself and forcing him to move up a gear. She was flying.

She was in sight until the moment she disappeared into the trees. A less experienced man might have panicked, but the run through the woods took two and a half minutes, time enough to catch her, and he had the knife ready. Six inches, serrated, he would make it quick, make it a mercy.

His pace was fast and steady. But as he entered the woods and rounded the bend, she wasn't running ahead of him but sitting on the park bench alongside the path. Smoke curled up from her mouth and for a moment he thought she might be on fire, till he realised there was a cigarette between her fingers. The burning tip the sudden centre of the world.

He broke his stride, hesitated, stopped.

Honor Jones had eyes which were sea-glass green and gold close up and there were smudges under them that looked like bruises. She'd been crying. She pulled first one bud and then the other from her ears, watching him all the while.

"I have to finish the cigarette," she said, and with the tip of her thumb nail flicked ash from the barrel onto the damp ground.

From behind the trees, there was a squawking and a clatter as four Canada geese rose from the lake up into the air. And it came to him that she knew what he was. She'd known he was there all along. Waiting for her. Pursuing her.

Which meant that she knew what he was there to do. But why wasn't she screaming?

His right hand lay alongside the knife, the thin polyester tracksuit the only thing between his cold flesh and the warm blade.

He was still six feet away from her, and she could run. Twenty feet beyond the shadowed bench was open ground and she might be lucky. A man might be walking a dog. It might have been a dog which spooked the geese. An Alsatian lapping at the water's edge between the concrete and the slime. He didn't think she would run though, her muscles weren't bunched and ready for flight. Her left arm was stretched out along the bench, and he imagined her sitting relaxed on the green benches of the Commons chamber waiting for her turn to speak.

Her chest rose as she inhaled again. He moved closer and her jaw tightened.

She flicked the cigarette onto the ground and stood with a sigh. "I was warned you'd come and I didn't believe it," she said, using her trainer to grind the cigarette end into the path.

The blade was cold now – enough to burn through the muscle down to the bone. She tilted the blonde head to one side.

"Have you been sent to kill me?"

There was a note of enquiry to her voice rather than panic. Curiosity rather than fear. She took a step closer into the silence between them, and North smelled the Chanel on her skin. She reached for him, but didn't touch him.

"Where's Peggy?"

Honor's voice was soft – persuasive.

He had no idea where Peggy was. No idea who she was.

All he knew was that when he broke into the MP's flat yesterday, Honor had scrawled the name Peggy in scarlet lipstick over and over again on her bathroom mirror.

She dropped her attempt at persuasion, glaring at him, her hands on her hips. "You're going to kill me because I'm looking for her aren't you? That's the only possible explanation."

Her friend Peggy was missing and she was trying to find her. Someone didn't want Honor to find Peggy.

He wasn't a murderer or a mercenary. He was duty-bound to follow orders, and this was nothing personal. The MP was a target, and she was dead already if only she knew it.

His weight on the balls of his feet.

Honor's death would happen in seconds. Merciful. She wouldn't suffer more than she had to. North made a deal with himself.

1

London

He heard the messenger slide the black envelope under the door during the night, but he ignored it. An exercise in discipline.

Sun fought against charcoal clouds through the window of the Marylebone flat as a scowling Michael North emerged from the bedroom. His head pounded. He ran through in his mind the fight a week earlier: several sledgehammer punches to his temple and jaw before he closed the guy down. Not clever bearing in mind his situation.

And it was too bright in here. He pressed a button and the Venetian blind slid halfway down the glass. For a split second, he glimpsed a figure on the street gazing up at the building, but the falling wooden slats moved too quickly and, when he checked again, the figure had gone.

He popped the blister packet he pulled from his back pocket, chewing the two purple tablets en route to the kitchen, the taste bitter on his tongue. He didn't know what

7

was in them – the Harley Street medic prescribed them. "In the circumstances, Michael…" that is to say *"bearing in mind you'll be dead soon, you can have these experimental drugs"*. He didn't ask the medics questions but sometimes they told him anyway. Things like *"Watch for an escalation in the insomnia and migraines or any obsessive behaviours – that may well mean the bullet has shifted"*. And when the bullet in his brain shifted, he didn't need anyone telling him – he was a dead man.

He was shot on patrol outside Lashkar Gah in southern Afghanistan five years ago.

The sniper made his own ammunition and the doctors told him he was "freakishly lucky" in the bullet's trajectory and position – just short of the posterior parietal artery in the right temporo-parietal junction. North didn't feel lucky. Neurosurgeons removed fragments of bone but couldn't extract the bullet without further catastrophic damage. They were sorry. Instead they induced a three-month-long coma and let the inflammation of the brain subside. Would he like them to operate again? He'd said no but he often thought he should have said yes. Because what the doctors didn't know was that he suspected the bullet was driving him mad.

On the upside, there was as yet no sign of the loss of cognitive and motor decline they warned him of. And he doubted he would live long enough for the epilepsy and dementia to kill him.

On the downside, the bullet affected his brain processing – new neural pathways establishing themselves, heightening his intuition when it came to other people, a sixth sense so to speak. At least that's how he rationalised it when he left the hospital and did the research. Neuroplasticity it was called. The brain's ability to heal and to compensate. He trawled through academic papers, medical journals and books he barely understood till it didn't frighten him. Till he could make himself believe it was possible, probable even. Till he could comfort himself that he was as normal as the next person. Though the next person didn't have a bullet in the brain.

If he was wrong about the re-wiring, then he was suffering from the hallucinations and delusions common after traumatic brain injury and the bullet had triggered full-blown psychosis.

He didn't know which was worse.

With a boost like someone knocking him sideways, the drugs kicked in, spangles and the sensation of annihilating pain fading, and North relaxed.

He crossed to the door and picked up the black envelope, and with it copies of the day's papers. Scanning the front pages as he switched on the coffee maker – interest from the Balkans in the New Army, Friday's G8 summit in London, and a Newcastle barman who threw himself from Westminster Bridge, killing himself and a tourist on a Thames cruise. He read the suicide story twice against the racket of steel blades grinding single estate beans.

Something rankled.

There was a prolonged and dangerous-sounding hissing, and a solitary stream of espresso poured into a white cup.

Edward Fellowes jumped from the bridge late on Thursday night. But there were any number of bridges along the Tyne, why would a twenty-one-year-old Geordie travel three hundred miles to jump off a London bridge? North shrugged. The problem with his job was he couldn't read about anyone dying without wondering who killed them, and whether he'd have done it better.

He carried the cup across to his desk, and sat staring at the envelope.

There was no name on it, but then there never was. The name that mattered was inside. Who was it this time? Would he recognise the face? He felt the familiar rush of adrenalin.

North never liked to hurry opening his orders. There was, after all, a man's life at stake. It merited some ritual – a degree of reflection. He sipped the scalding coffee, savoured the earthy roast, tasting the promised notes of dark chocolate. He put down the cup, then slid the butcher's knife under the flap, opening its crimson throat in one smooth sweep. There were no ragged edges.

The dozen 10x8s were snapped in a hotel foyer. An oversized lamp was on, so it had to be late. He lifted the first photograph. It was of a couple and he scrutinised the man. Twenties. Denim jacket. Full-blown hipster beard. His phone must have rung at some point because he took a call, turning away from the coffee table to face the camera. But instead of closing in on him, the pictures were suddenly all about the woman. Confused, North fanned them over the table looking for more close-ups of the man, but photo after photo was of the woman. She was dressed in an evening gown, and even in the black and white of the photography, it shimmered. The draped folds of its cowl neck exposing the elegant shoulders, chin resting on her fist, slim fingers covering her mouth as she listened to her companion. Her glance to one side, a slight smile. Even in two dimensions North felt the pull of her.

North flipped the photos with the knife – reluctant suddenly to touch them. On the reverse of the best one was a label written across in cramped moss-green ink. "Honor Jones (31), Tory MP for Mile End, East London. Extreme security risk. Status: critical. Termination: essential. Proposed disposal: random/sexual attack in public space. Deadline: one week. Authorisation: Tarn."

The iPhone lay on his desk.

North had worked for the arms-length, extra-judicial, extra-governmental agency known as the Board for four years. He was going to die young – the bullet guaranteed it. He told them he wanted to do something useful with the time he had left. And they took him at his word.

He scrolled through his phone to tap the Crypt app with its skull and bones icon – a series of numbers and letters spun out through space then lined up, one banging into the next, shuffling and jumping, till the tail-end Charlie arrived and they shuddered to a stop. His private key – good for a 60-second window to break the encryption of the incoming email. He pressed his fingertips together as he swung gently on his chair, waiting for the ping of an incoming email. The digits and letters crumbled to dust in the silence. He refreshed the inbox but it stayed empty.

In the email he expected a briefing on his target of between two and thirty pages – aliases, addresses, known associates, places frequented, crimes, convictions, employment records, recreational activities, usernames, passwords, bank accounts, more photographs and videos, private surveillance and acquired CCTV. Nowhere in the encrypted text would it repeat the instruction to kill – that only came written in moss-green ink in a tar-black envelope. Perhaps there was a change in procedures and they'd sent a hard copy instead, along with the commission? He turned the envelope upside down and shook it to make sure, then peered into its emptiness. Perhaps intelligence on her came in late? More likely the threat was so immediate there wasn't time to do the background breakdown – but he couldn't leave it like that.

Pulling the laptop towards him, North took a DVD from a drawer, sliding it into the slot to load the virtual machine he used for sensitive work. These days you couldn't be too careful. When he finished the work, and closed down the laptop, everything would disappear with it. There was a microsecond pause while he wondered if the Board hacked his computer despite his best precautions. He shrugged – he didn't have anything to hide from them. But without the email's unique digital signature, he had no authentication of the handwritten instruction. Unless you count money.

The manager of his account at the Austrian bank spoke English with only the barest trace of an accent. Yes, £100,000 was paid in late last night. Yes they were sure, Mr Wilde (the name in which he kept his account). The normal reference code. Could they help with anything else? Unctuous. Smooth. Unless they could explain why he was paid before rather than after the job, he didn't need their help. He shouldn't complain. He had his orders, and he would earn the money.

On first sweep, Honor Jones MP appeared to be a model citizen – a law degree from Oxford, Fulbright scholar, pupillage, tenancy in a leading Chambers specialising in criminal and regulatory law, with a special interest in domestic violence and child protection. Ambitious, smart, connected and charming – no great surprise when a London Tory constituency association selected her for a safe seat. Since then, four years' steady media-savvy work, tipped for promotion at the next reshuffle, even mentioned by futurologists as a Prime Minister-in-waiting.

He almost missed it.

An online interview in a newsletter for a children's mental health charity in North London. The article introducing the charity's new trustees. A chartered accountant, a clinical psychologist and lawyer Honor Jones. *"What's your interest in children's mental health?"* the journalist asked. "Let's say I have a special interest in resilience. How children who've been the victims of domestic violence or witnessed that trauma close up are affected long term." *"May I ask is that something you have personal experience of?"* "Unfortunately, that would be correct."

She could have capitalised on it but she never mentioned it again. Not in any speech. Not in any national interview. Though there were traces of it. A radioactive legacy if you knew what to look for. He went back into her parliamentary record. A hardline speech in a Commons debate on sentencing in cases involving domestic violence. An amendment to a housing bill to make it easier for victims to retain benefit when they moved into a refuge. Written questions on the value of psychiatric counselling for the families of murderers.

Whatever had happened to her as a child, she'd survived. Thrived. Gone into politics, and made a difference.

He'd gone into prison. The Army. Almost died, and killed people for a living.

They had their "resilience" then in common, aside from the fact he was going to be there at her death.

His mind turned to his mother. His drug-addled, booze-soaked, ruinous mother. Neglect. Bruises. Willing to sell herself for a wrap of heroin or a can of strong lager – the fact North loved her, never enough. She loved him too, he supposed, as much as she was capable of loving him. Just not enough.

Honor's face in the photograph looked different to him now he could read the past in her. The smile still a thing of wonder. But once he looked harder, he thought he could see the hurt in her don't-touch-me eyes. Harm that couldn't be undone.

He was curious.

Not professionally.

Personally.

Looking in on her life from the outside, Honor was living up to her name. She was working to make the world a better place. Just like he was.

So what turned her from a public servant into an imminent danger to the security of a nation?

Status offered no defence, he knew that. Power. Wealth. Nothing could protect you if your name came up. He'd taken out a philanthropist-cum-arms-dealer at a black-tie charity ball – a tiny injection as he shook the man's hand, solid gold cufflinks in the shape of guns, a heart attack, "terrible" everybody said. A corrupt chief constable – driving too fast, narrow road, knew it like the back of his hand but the shame of it: no seat belt, and he was "normally such a stickler". Logically, killing an MP was not such a stretch, was not so very different. Forget the fact she was a beautiful woman. Forget her childhood. Fixate instead on her adult guilt, on the wrong she had done. But he had no idea what she'd done – why should she be terminated?

He leaned back into the oblique angle of the chair – staring at the laptop, willing it to explain something to him. He just didn't know what.

Occasionally on an operation in Iraq, hair would rise on the back of his neck as if the air itself carried a message, an electric charge. On those days, at those moments, he stepped more lightly on the sandy roads under his boots.

Something was off.

His bosses thought he could improvise – and he could. When he needed to. But North liked routine, because routine minimised the scope for error. The messenger brought an envelope with photos and a name in green ink and an order to execute. An email spelled out the reason and the details. An unfortunate death came about – restoring a sense of how-it-should-be, of the world brought back into alignment. Only then did the noughts on his bank account ratchet up.

He had a code. He didn't kill women. This time, worse yet, the Board wanted it to look like a "random/sexual attack". And that left a bad taste, because there were things you didn't do, even for King and Country. Remorse and shame weren't feelings he ever experienced. Not as a child and not as a soldier. Not now. Never. But he feared Honor Jones was a game changer. Honor Jones would haunt him.

Only hunger made him realise the best of the day was gone. Sirens blared, the noise falling away as quickly as it came. His eyes snagged on the crucifix hanging on the wall before he closed them. After five years, North was used to his insomnia. Daylight torpor, night-time fading in and out of reality, and, when he did sleep for an hour or so at a time – the shuddering and falling through space into nightmares of blood and sand and fear. He let out a breath and, as he did, every page he'd viewed downloaded again in his brain, one after the other. Twelve hours. Hundreds of screens. Headlines. Photographs. Hansard reports. Local press. Shaking hands. National stories. Helpful speeches. Maverick blogs. Honor's smile. The line of her cheek. North's brain shuddered as if caught in an earthquake. He felt it like a stroke coming on him. Once. Twice. Three times. The sensation of flat moving silver sweeping over his consciousness, his memories, coming fast like the sea over a causeway, covering everything. He fought it and he lost; his last thought was Honor, killing her, and then he slept.

2

London

6.32pm. Saturday, 4th November

Londoners passed – this way and that, the city hazy and splendid on the horizon. A cold front was moving over the country from the Arctic, a warning that winter was closing in and it would be hard.

Nobody noticed North standing looking over Blackfriars Bridge into the Thames, thinking about where the moving water might take him.

North never met the Board's other operatives. He presumed like him they'd signed the Official Secrets Act, and were well rewarded for their lonely service. Occasionally, he recognised their modus operandi. One favoured intricately plotted deaths of mid-ranking types that exploded across the papers and were never resolved – attributed to professional Eastern European gunmen, overshadowed by talk of serious financial or criminal interests – the type of murder investigative journalists chased down for decades, never getting anywhere. Another preferred "assisted suicides" – all "he-seemed-so-happy" and "we-never-thought-he'd-do-such-a-thing". They generally used North when they needed someone who could think on their feet.

He took a breath – the air sharp and painful in his lungs. He hazarded that no one would pick up the phone so late on a Saturday night.

"Chalfont Securities. How may I help you?" The voice was chilly, well-bred.

"Please tell Mr Chalfont…"

That he hadn't received the email.

That he needed authentication for the order to kill.

To send it and he would kill her. Chip-chop and sharpish.

He raised his fingers to the ridged dip where the bullet had torn through his skull.

"I can't make the meeting."

Please tell Mr Chalfont that he wouldn't kill Honor Jones. Couldn't.

Because Michael North didn't have much. But he had his code and it didn't include killing a woman unless she was physically holding a gun and pointing it at his head. Unless Honor Jones was doing that – and she didn't look the type – the Board would have to find somebody else.

More than that. The touch of his scar under his fingertips. He couldn't trust himself. What he believed he knew. Did his mind fill with other people's thoughts and voices, or his own complex delusions? Freak or lunatic? He had no idea which he was. But he knew this. He'd done too much, killed too many, and he wanted it over. He wanted his freedom. It came to him suddenly, a neural snap, an instant of electricity re-routing his soul – like falling in love.

The certainty shocked him. He wanted to be a good soldier, to follow orders and get the job done. Not least because doing his duty was the only peace he'd ever known. Up to this point, he read a name on a page and followed through without hesitation. The problem was this time the sight of Honor Jones's face made him ask "Why?" And instead of anticipation as he considered the photograph of the woman who was to be his next target, all he felt was profound dismay.

There were limits, and he'd reached them. Whatever time he had left, he wanted to live it differently. To stop the killing. To be honest. To connect. Not to be alone.

Beneath him, a Thames barge loaded with rubbish passed through the bridge on its way to the sea. It would be an old-fashioned way to die, he thought, drowning in a river. A Victorian death meant for lost women and foundlings.

"How very...unfortunate." A note of surprise, disapproval, at the other end of the phone. As if no one had ever cancelled a meeting with Mr Chalfont before. "Are you sure," a pause, "Mr North?" How did she know his name, he wondered? The number? He used a disposable pay-as-you-go. Different every time. Voice recognition? Or was his the only job out there at the moment?

He left the question out there. What happened when you said no to people who didn't take no for an answer? He wasn't at all sure, but she didn't need to know that.

"Mr Chalfont will be in touch." She disconnected the line.

Mr Chalfont didn't exist of course. Neither did Chalfont Securities. Nor was there a frosty PA tapping at her computer with polished nails. Or maybe she at least existed – not so much a PA as an officer in an organisation whose only business was killing.

He dropped the phone on the ground, covering it with his right shoe, feeling the mobile give under his sole. Honor Jones was safe – at least from him. He'd made his decision. The phone splintered, the display cracking into a spider's web, the back popping to reveal the guts of a tiny sim card. He picked out the sim and dropped it over the parapet into the Thames. A fierce eddy swirled around the supports of the bridge, the water a muddy brown, the tide high and choppy. The glinting sim rested on the surface for a second, before it sank. He once read a story about a fisherman who caught a fish, and when he gutted it, he discovered the fish had eaten a gold ring. North thought about the fisherman, how if a fish ate the sim card, he'd have to find the fisherman who'd caught it and kill him. Stone cold dead.

A yell of protest from further along the bridge brought him back to reality. A shaven-headed lad in New Army uniform staggered along the pavement – high on something cheap and potent. Behind him, an elderly vagrant, his skinny dog on a string, was limping away as fast as he could.

Months ago, as an isolationist US under President Donald Trump slashed its defence spending on Europe, the UK Government privatised the Armed Forces.

Reports about the nascent National Defence Force warned that thousands of experienced soldiers, sailors and airmen had quit overnight. In particular, traditionalists slammed the fact "New Army PLC" soldiers swore no oath of allegiance to King and Country. But the move was already saving the country millions in salaries and pensions, and recruitment – particularly straight out of prisons – was booming. No one could argue with the figures. Indeed, any opposition was branded unpatriotic as private investors brought market efficiencies to defence, re-invested savings into equipment and training, then sold back the services of the streamlined Armed Forces and procurement to the government. All the while making a neat profit and preserving national security in a post-NATO world. The term "nasty boys" to refer to the new recruits was unfortunate, but the New Army admitted there were still a few branding issues to work through.

North figured he was well out of it.

A bitter wind sliced through him like razors as he looked away, moving the pieces of the phone with his foot, letting them fall into the gutter. He started walking. He could afford to turn down this one job.

But they would never let him quit. There were no gold watches in this business. No, if he really wanted the killing to be over, he'd have to disappear – start over in some other place. Somewhere warm? Freedom. He raised his head. Pursed his lips to whistle. He liked whistling, though he couldn't hold a tune.

When the nasty boy smashed hard into his chest, North used his own bulk to ward him off – careful not to meet his eye. But the lad wanted more respect.

"Mind yourself, cocksucker," he snarled – the heady smell of lager and piss, grabbing hold of North's arm to spin him round, spittle spraying his face. Like an old-fashioned boxer, the lad's knuckles and the gaps between them were tattooed. Instead of LOVE and HATE though, it was with the New Army motto BRITAIN across the right fist and FOREVER on the left. "Britain Forever". Patriotism made easy for those who didn't have to live by it. This swaggering, vicious thug claiming to defend a country which was nothing like him.

The Board would come for him, thought North. Not tonight. But soon. He gave a quick look-round, checking the solider wasn't a diversion, that an attack wasn't coming hard and fast from somewhere else. But the street was quiet.

North held the struggling nasty boy away by the lapels of his serge jacket. The outraged solider pushing in towards him keen to do violence, spitting, cursing, small eyes bulging either side like those of a reptile – primed to survive, threaten, intimidate.

"You dropped something," North said and spun him to one side, pushing the shaven head closer to the ground and raising his knee at the same moment to smash into the lad's face. He brought him up again. From a distance it would look as if North steadied a drunk against the stonework of the bridge. Up close, he flattened one hand against the crushed wreckage of the cartilage and pressed hard. The nasty boy shrieked in a rising note of pain, his voice muffled by North's other hand, and blood spurted from between the fingers.

He released the weeping nasty boy who reeled and staggered across the road, only stopping to spit and curse from the safety of the other side of the carriageway. And North admitted the truth to himself. Somewhere, the small print of his unwritten contract carried the warning that refusal was prejudicial not just to your career but to your own prospects of survival.

3

London

5.50am. Sunday, 5th November

The vintage Bentley moved alongside him like a shark scoping a surfer. Occasionally the driver revved the engine; once the car mounted the kerb behind him – its steel bumper almost catching his heels, but North kept his pace steady. His trainer had a hole in the bottom – London rain filling the fabric shoe so fast he might have been barefoot in the roll and broil of the sea. He never gave much thought to his own physical comfort. If anything, he enjoyed the soft smack of the rain on his face – first this way, then that – puddle-damp feet, breathing in bus diesel and city dirt, the bite and push of the north-easterly wind through his sodden hoody bringing him back to a sense of who he used to be, distracting him from the conviction that something bad was about to happen. He just wasn't sure what – or whether it was going to happen to him.

The Bentley bumped back onto the road.

At ten to six in the morning, the shops along Marylebone High Street were still shuttered and dark inside; bundles of bulky Sunday newspapers tied up like prisoners outside the newsagent.

Beside him, the rear nearside window cracked, and cigar smoke crawled out and up around the roof, eager to escape.

"Come in from the rain," said the voice.

North stopped running, and turned on his heel towards the car.

"We can't have you catching a chill, darling boy."

A stranger might have termed the traveller's voice engaging, but even a stranger would have recognised an order rather than an invitation.

A teardrop of rain trickled down North's velvet nape and bumped along the bones of his spine before plunging into the warmth he'd been hoarding between hunched shoulder blades. Someone, somewhere, had been telling him what to do since he was born. A man could tire of it.

"North," the voice warned, and with a sigh, North reached for the handle of the Bentley.

He hadn't closed the door before the car set off, veering to the right. The door swung away from him, his body shifting outwards with the weight, dipping over the rapidly moving ground before he managed to pull himself upright again and slam it – his heart banging in his chest.

In the front – the driver's head almost touched the roof of the car; the back of a familiar fat neck, the folds of flesh red and hanging over the shirt collar. North found the rear-view mirror, a razor flick of the driver's pouchy eyes rewarding him for his effort, before they went back to the road.

"North, you look well."

Lord Lucien Tarn, former Justice of the Supreme Court, himself looked like nothing more than a death's head.

"Doesn't he, Bruno?"

"Peachy," said the driver, loading the word with contempt and ill-will. There was the sound of rods tumbling into a lock and Tarn spoke again.

"Not like a man with a bullet in his brain at all." The judge sucked hard on the stub of a cigar as he regarded his reluctant passenger, its tuck flaring crimson and white, the acrid tang of it hot and dry. "Good enough to eat." Under the cheekbones, smoke and words came out of the judge's mouth, both together. "As Bruno says."

During the trial at Southwark Crown Court for the manslaughter which left his mother's pimp dead, thirteen-year-old Michael North learned to be wary when the judge's sunken gaze met his; when the lawyers argued self-defence and those gimlet eyes told the boy that he already knew his absolute guilt, presumed his murderous intention, understood, and didn't blame him. North resisted the sudden smell of blood, the shattering of bones. The judge never saw him without thinking of who he was as a child and what he did. Or he never saw the judge without guilt – one or the other. He forced himself to stare back; the skin beneath the judge's clipped hair on the skull so white it was as if the stubble grew straight from the bone.

"Your call last night hasn't been well-received, darling boy." The judge shook his head in fond rebuke.

Bruno swung the car left on to Wigmore Street, clipping the pavement, and North braced himself against the seat in front.

"What can I say? It didn't feel right." How to begin to explain the deep sense of unease triggered when he stared at the photograph? His recognition that Honor Jones had survived who knows what. His sudden yearning for a life which was clean and free of the need to kill. It was a simple thing to write a name in green ink. It was altogether harder to draw a line through it.

"Exactly who is the Board?" There were times when it was easier to attack rather than defend a position.

Tarn frowned, and the atmosphere in the car chilled. A sudden memory came to North – one that was all his own. His mother, drunk, and shivering on a stained mattress. Gripping his hand. Blaming the future. Mortality. *"Someone walked over my grave,"* she said, blessing herself over and over. Father, Son and Holy Ghost. Before letting go, to reach for the nearest bottle.

"Why ask?"

"I woke up curious."

He'd always thought it better that he didn't know. But who were these people who decided who should live and who should die, while other men did their killing?

"I'm intrigued, Michael. Perhaps you consider you have the luxury of free will?" Bruno's eyes met his. Envy. Anticipation. Loathing. An appetite to do bloody violence. The sound of the car locking as he climbed into it.

"Because you made your choice when you signed up," the judge spoke with deliberation – as if he were explaining due process to the accused child still standing in the dock. "You swore an oath to protect your country against its enemies, and it does have enemies. Are you paid enough for what you do? These questions, this virginal hesitation – is it a matter of money, dear-heart? Because as I understand it, you've already been paid?"

The implication he could be bought devoured North – anger growing and writhing and filling the world, filling him, before he sensed Bruno move in his seat, two massive hands gripping the wheel going to one, the other sliding into his jacket pocket. What did the big man have? A gun? Bespoke knuckle-dusters for those immense hands?

North exhaled, letting go the violence he wanted to do. The exchange was designed to provoke. He was back on trial.

He didn't do what he did for money. Never.

As if he had been teasing all along, Lord Tarn laughed, his voice loud in the confines of the car, and patted North's knee with bony fingers. The flick-knife eyes in the rear-view mirror widened in surprise, but Bruno took his hand from his jacket pocket again and moved it back to the wheel, then the gearstick, taking the Bentley up to sixty in what had to be a restricted zone. The car hit a speedbump – lifting and dropping back onto the road, and the impact travelled up through North's spine and into his head. Another razor flick, as Bruno made clear the punishment was intentional. Tarn didn't seem to notice, his hand still on North's knee. He moved, and the judge remembered the hand, removing it with the kindest of smiles.

"Without my intervention, the Army would never have taken you. I spoke for you on your release from custody, because I saw something of myself in you. I always have. I understood what you'd done as a child and the great man you could be. And five years ago, when you were wounded, I sat at your bedside every day willing you out of the grave. Your own father couldn't have done more."

The memory of opening his eyes to the buzzing strip lights of the military hospital, of crushing pain, and of the judge's face leaning in towards him. The shock of the other man's pity. The judge's desire smashing its way into North's own mind. Before he worked out what the bullet did to him.

Tarn stared at the length of ash ready but not yet falling from the tip of his cigar. "Once you recovered, I assured people that you could be relied upon – and they took me at my word." The judge pushed out his pale lips in distaste. "You have a purpose, my darling – don't throw it all away on a whim, because it could be the last thing you do." His eyes met North's. "And nobody wants that. I wouldn't want that."

Rain skidded and careered down the passenger window. The car slowed. Photographs of a woman burning in the sink. North knew London well, took a pride in it. Fire devouring the woman's beautiful face, turning her to ash. And he knew where this journey was heading because he bought the ticket a long time ago. There was no going back. No freedom.

But the judge was still talking.

"You and I, North, we share a belief in real justice and in our sacred duty. Our political system is dying from the inside out. We can trust no one. We have no one. The Board is necessary – now more than ever – because we keep things safe."

"...*Cannot be allowed to live...*" he heard the judge as clearly as if he'd passed down a verdict in open court. "*She's dangerous and she's too much of a risk to leave out there. Honor Jones threatens to bring down everything.*"

There it was. Whether he was mad or whether he had a skill he didn't want. Here was the truth of it. The beating heart. This man he trusted – a judge who dedicated his own life to public service – believed Honor Jones had to die. Or, North's own subconscious knew that as a fact.

But it was hard. The taste of stale cigar smoke filled his mouth, furring his teeth as he made one last attempt at escape.

"I'm tired, Tarn." His voice came out louder than he expected. The car had stopped. A beat.

"Aren't we all? But we carry on. Regardless. The death of Honor Jones is regrettable, I agree, but it is necessary." The judge reached out to a silver ashtray in his door and dropped the tiny body of the almost-dead cigar in its belly, its ash finally breaking apart.

"There's a greater good," the judge said as if it were the answer to everything.

It was over. The endorphin release of his run gone, North admitted the truth to himself – he wasn't free. He would have to kill her. Honor Jones MP RIP. His gorge rose. Queasy from the cigar, the confinement, the job, he fought the urge to retch.

The door on his side opened onto the backstreet. He was somewhere in the furthest stretches of South London. Bruno would have made sure it was as inconvenient as he could make it.

"Don't be distracted by a pretty face. Remember, without Eve, there would have been no Fall."

North climbed out – and, as he looked back into the car, Tarn took hold of a newspaper, settling into his morning routine. "Latest hack embarrasses social media giant…" He couldn't read the rest of the headline.

"You have till Tuesday. Let's get it done." Tarn's teeth were blinding white, his smile charming. "You're beloved by the gods, North, as well as me – few among us are given a second chance."

As the Bentley drove away, the dirty spray from a gutter puddle drenched him. He stepped back, but too late, and swore. Through the side mirror, Bruno watched him, grinning.

North hoped Honor Jones was ready to die.

4

London

12.32am. Tuesday, 7th November

The photograph was a good one, their hair everywhere in the wind, blonde and black mixing together, pink cheeks and noses, laughing. When she printed it out, she wrote a reminder on the back in pencil like her mother used to do – *Hermitage Island, February.*

Bleeding cold!

Honor slid it back under the portcullis fridge magnet alongside the postcard quoting Winston Churchill – *Never, never, never, give up* – and reached for the merlot to pour a glass. Still standing up, she drained it, before she checked the phone. Peggy's last text from three weeks ago. "Working on something big sweetie. Need headspace. Will be in touch soon as I can. Peggyx."

Honor didn't see it at first. She was too furious.

She didn't see it till she got home after meeting Ned Fellowes in the hotel foyer, and read it over.

Peggy never called her "sweetie", only ever "sweetpea".

She'd never have used the term "headspace".

And she never signed off her messages "Peggy". She signed them Px, or didn't sign them at all.

Despite the fact they lived in different cities, they talked every day without fail, sometimes two or three times. Things became real once she'd told Peggy. Events mattered more. Jokes were funnier. Most days they texted. Occasionally they emailed. At night, one or other would call and they'd talk through their day before sleep. Even on the nights she spent with her partner JP in Knightsbridge, she talked to Peggy at some point. JP sulking with silent fury till she wound up the call. Peggy maintaining it was good to make him wait.

What they never did was go to radio silence.

Honor checked the phone again, but there was nothing more from Peggy. No new email. No text. No call missed. By now, she'd have been surprised if there were.

It took her a long time to get back to any sort of normality after her parents died. For the longest time afterwards, Honor jumped at the slightest noise. Insomnia, nausea, palpitations, flashbacks.

They all came back sitting across from poor Ned Fellowes the exact moment he told her that Peggy's text message was a fake.

Ned was one of Peggy's misfits. Honor didn't use the term misfit in a critical way. She was one herself, so how could she? He was on the spectrum, which wasn't unusual, Peggy said, for someone studying astronomy. It wasn't the reason he had to drop out of the undergrad course at Newcastle. But despite living with family, he couldn't cope. *Too fragile*, Peggy said. The last thing Honor heard was that Ned was working in a bar. Till he turned up in London last week telling her Peggy was missing and that he needed Honor's help finding her. Honor was an MP, and that was "useful in the circumstances" he said, not least because he believed Peggy wasn't the only person missing.

Even as Honor heard herself reassuring him, her heart began to pound and she felt the old loneliness inside her open up and threaten to swallow her whole. Honor hadn't believed a word about Ned's conspiracy. But, the truth was, Ned got something right – Peggy would never disappear, because she knew what that would do to Honor.

Honor prided herself on being a rational creature. Sitting at the kitchen table, she moved the vase of stocks to one side, and drew a piece of paper and pen towards her. These were the facts.

1. Peggy had not communicated with her for three weeks.
2. Ned said Peggy was in trouble. That she had disappeared and he didn't know why or where to.
3. He said that he was looking for her.
4. And that she wasn't the only one to go missing.

Honor had been cleaning her teeth on Friday morning, her eyes still closed as she listened to the local radio news. The presenter made a misjudged remark about a Kamikaze Geordie killing a Japanese tourist on a dinner cruise. *And now, the weather.*

She'd known in her bones it was Ned. Before she'd opened her eyes. Had thrown up before she'd even confirmed the details with the Metropolitan Police. A friend of the family.

An MP. They'd been very helpful. Ned Fellowes jumped to his death from Westminster Bridge less than an hour after Honor said goodbye to him. Did he seem upset about anything, they'd asked, but she hadn't answered.

Honor wrote the number "5" and then the words "Ned" and "suicide" before surrounding the word suicide with question mark after question mark.

She'd known about Ned for three years, she'd met him herself on trips to Newcastle, and she didn't believe for one second that he killed himself.

a. He wasn't the type.

The scratch of her pen was the only sound in the flat.

b. She'd seen his return ticket to Newcastle upon Tyne.
c. She'd overheard him making plans to meet a girl called Jess the next day.

And you don't accidentally trip over a paving stone and plunge to your death from a London bridge. Which made it murder.

She paused – her pen over the paper. Red ink bleeding into the white page. Was that possible? Honor ringed "murder" over and over till the point of her pen tore through the paper.

Within the hour of hearing the radio report, she'd bought her own ticket to Newcastle. Checked Peggy's home. Her work. Chased down contacts in the UK and abroad. Getting more frustrated – more desperate with every hour. A job in Chile, they said, but Honor didn't believe it.

She stopped writing. Her head in her hands. Fingers in her hair.

She'd failed Ned – she admitted it. Utterly. Peggy would be furious. He came to her because she was Peggy's best friend. Because, naively, he presumed she was important. And, selfishly, she walked away – panicking and angry with him because he was saying the un-sayable. That something was wrong. But Honor would feel guilty about Ned later. Because one thing was for certain, she wasn't failing Peggy.

She took the memory key in its plastic wallet from her handbag. She'd watched the video Ned had uploaded onto it as soon as she got back from Newcastle. Again and again. Surely he had it wrong? But he'd said to hide it, and now he was dead. She slid it between the flower stems, hearing it clink as it hit the china base.

It was a primitive response to patrol the flat – checking the doors and the windows. Walking through to the bathroom – her eyes on the mirror. Peggy's name written over and over in lipstick when she'd been drunk. JP had once accused her of being obsessed with Peggy. But then JP came from a big Irish-Catholic family who loved each other as much as they drove each other crazy. He didn't know what it was to have no one to love you, no one to love. Honor did though, and it was a lonely place to be. Peggy mattered. She was the only family Honor had. Her chosen family, and without Peggy Honor had nothing to hold her together. It had taken her years to get past the tragedy of her parents. Suffering. Tears. Choosing to smile and nod, all the while feeling like she'd been obliterated. Like she wasn't even there. Peggy saw past all of it, reaching into the cold darkness and bringing Honor back to life. Yes, Honor owed Peggy a great deal. She thought back to the video – she couldn't help herself. Ned's rodent teeth and auburn hair. Like a red squirrel. His self-conscious, self-important warning. His final words. She'd barely registered them at first.

That if he himself disappeared, she should run.

Because Ned Fellowes was dead. And Peggy Boland was gone.

So where did that leave Honor Jones?

Only then did she think to look.

In the darkness of her bedroom as next door's baby wailed behind the party wall, she stayed at the window for three hours before she sensed rather than saw his shape in the shadows of the empty house opposite and two doors down.

There was a man outside her flat – standing in the lee of the doorway where it was darkest. And Honor was of the opinion he intended to kill her.

Her iPhone in her hand, she almost gave in then, almost pressed 999. An intruder. A burglar. A stalker. The call in from a lone female – an MP no less. The police would come, but as soon as the watcher heard a siren, glimpsed a blue light, he would melt away, disappear into the shadows and the brickwork. And if she called the police, she would lose the only clue she had – the stranger waiting for his chance to kill her.

He was good. She was prepared to admit, even admire, the killer's patience and professionalism. But she could be patient too.

For years she played chess against her father.

And Honor Jones possessed an advantage the stranger knew nothing about, because Honor Jones never saw the world as a safe place. For her, it had always been a place of monsters.

Only when she decided her plan of action did she take a blanket from the bed and go back through to the lounge, switching off her lights, to stretch out fully dressed on the couch.

★

As the mantelpiece clock ticked away the minutes, she could feel him out there – waiting.

She feared him. Of course she did. He was a stranger who meant her harm and she wasn't a reckless fool. The urge came on her again to call for help. Was this too much for her to handle alone? She pulled herself up, balancing on her elbow, her hand reaching out for the phone, then flung herself down, clutching the blanket, dragging it up to her chin, burrowing in it to try and warm herself and stop the shivering. She was made of sterner stuff – wasn't she?

Then again, she could go to her upstairs neighbour, Hugh. Naked. Dishevelled. A maiden distressed. In need of comfort. Knock on his door, slide into his bed. His surprise. Warm reassuring hands over her body. Ensnaring him. Hugh looked like he could handle himself. The broken nose, the broken little finger cocked at some bizarre angle which he'd explained away to her one day, boasting of schoolboy rugby and glory on the field. But no, it would be wrong to put this on him.

JP Armitage was older than Hugh, older than her, but she didn't mind that. He had a personal trainer, worked out to keep his belly flat, watched what he ate – high protein, low carbs, barely any alcohol. However youthful JP kept himself though, Peggy warned her that sleeping with him was a mistake. But it was such a little thing to do for him and he was so keen, so extraordinarily grateful for her attention. He worked her, she knew that, over the years: pulling her in with his devotion, his power and status. The alpha-male. The ultimate father figure, but one she could control this time. One who loved her more than she loved him, because it was altogether safer that way.

Strange what your mind turns to, sliding between sleep and wakefulness, when death looms. The fact she should write a note to Ned's family, and what to say. Peggy, of course. Where she was right this second, and what else she could do to find her. If she only had the time to do it. And she thought about her mother. Her smile. When she woke the last time, she was suddenly awake, fully awake, aside from the fact she thought her mother called out her name in warning.

5

London

5.32am. Tuesday, 7th November

It was damp and bitter – the street lights still on – and Honor yawned as she walked down the path, but it was out of fear rather than tiredness. A cigarette and matches were already tucked into the sock. Earbuds hung from her ears, the wire taped to her skin under the running vest, and the jack unplugged so she could hear him coming. She kept her gaze straight ahead, resisting the impulse to stare into the doorway where she knew he stood. If only Hugh had done what he always threatened to do: got up to run with her. If she turned back, if she screamed, Hugh might hear and the watcher would go away. Surely it was better to live another day?

But then again, the watcher might harm Hugh, and she didn't want that. This was her fight – not his.

As much to convince herself as because she was ready, she pulled open the gate and set off. There was no point running away from danger. Her mother taught her that much, because you never could run fast enough.

For the first hundred paces she allowed herself to hope, allowed herself to think that she called it wrong and that Ned's hysteria had infected her, when not a noise so much as a vibration across the water brought her back to reality.

It was hard to tell without looking back, but she judged him to be a quarter of a mile behind her, and closing in. She could feel the blood pump faster in her chest, and as she breathed in she imagined him breathing out, in and out, drawing deeper as she did. It was too intimate, and she hated him for it.

She felt him close again. Her stride was shorter than his and timing everything. Her breath grew more ragged and a sweat broke out on her forehead. She wasn't as fit as he was but she was fitter than most, fitter than he would expect.

He was almost on her, fifty paces between them, she reckoned, when she kicked up her heels, pushing herself. Flying.

Briefly, she considered hurdling the railing and disappearing into the undergrowth, but he'd catch her and strangle her in the dank foliage amid the tinnies and used condoms. She resisted the temptation to hide from him. Committed. Focused. Locked on.

The bench stood further down the path than she remembered, the seat lichened green and slick with dew, and as she sat the dampness ate through her jogging pants and settled in the marrow of her bones. She pulled the cigarette out of her sock and struck a match. He wasn't a stalker or a psychopath, she reminded herself. He wasn't deranged and this wasn't personal. Honor was relying on the fact that civilisation was built on reason. Reason and money. She fought the urge to shake compulsively.

Smoke filled her lungs, curling up from her mouth as she watched the path. Bring it on, she thought.

He was bigger than she expected – taller and broader – in a dark fleece and jogging pants. From last night, she thought he'd be a small man made for cracks and shadows, but he was huge. He broke his stride, stopped. His eyes locked onto hers and she felt a moment's electric triumph at the dumb shock in them. Hunter and hunted. Which was which?

She pulled first one bud and then the other from her ears. If she was going to die, she chose to die on her terms – facing him down. Nobody's victim. But she didn't want to die. Not today. Not this morning. Because there were things she had to do – like find Peggy.

"I have to finish the cigarette." With the tip of her thumb nail she flicked ash from the barrel onto the damp ground, and behind the trees there was a squawking and clattering, as birds rose from the unseen lake up into the air.

He stood still – his left hand bunched into a loose fist, the right flat along his thigh. She couldn't see a weapon but she knew he carried one.

He was six feet away and it came to her that she could still run. Twenty feet beyond the shadowed, mossy bench lay open ground, and she might be lucky. A passing policeman? A dog-walker? But she wasn't going to run. That wasn't the plan. Instead, Honor stretched out her left arm along the bench, studiedly casual. It was important not to show fear, because fear invited violent men to do their worst – excited them to frenzy – she'd known that since she was a child.

Inhaling. Fire devouring the fragile paper and packed tobacco. She didn't want him seeing the tremble in her fingers so she flicked the cigarette onto the ground. Vile habit – smoking – she should give up before it killed her. Peggy was always telling her.

With a smoky sigh, she stood to face him. Younger than she'd expected – younger than her anyway – with a powerful jaw, his face chiselled but brutal. Was he too young to put any value on life?

"I was warned you'd come and I didn't believe it," she said. Her executioner was all she could see now, all that was left of her world. "Have you been sent to kill me?"

It was strange to think she could be dead within seconds. She wondered if Ned had known he was about to die. Hoped not.

But Honor wasn't Ned Fellowes, and she wasn't an innocent. Her killer might not realise it yet but she was his opponent, his enemy in whatever game they were playing. Control had slipped from his hands to hers. And she was playing her hand to win. Because if she was right, Peggy needed her and Peggy was worth the risk she was taking. Worth any risk.

Honor took a step closer. Her hand reaching out to him. If she could only make a connection.

"Where's Peggy?"

A reasonable question, but the stranger didn't respond and his silence infuriated her. She put her hands on her hips – her feet apart. Filling the space. Owning it. Making herself bigger.

"You're going to kill me because I'm looking for her, aren't you? That's the only possible explanation for you standing here. Which means you must know where she is. Tell me. Please."

She tried to reach into him for what she needed.

Peggy. North had seen the name written on Honor's mirror. Was Peggy the reason he had to kill her?

He didn't know.

All he knew was that Tarn needed Honor dead. Tarn's hand on his knee.

"She's dangerous and she's too much of a risk to leave out there. Honor Jones threatens everything."

Why come out all alone into the deep, dark woods?

Because of Peggy.

Because she wanted to ask him that question.

Need, he thought. What it must be to need someone enough to stake your own life on it. He hadn't needed anyone in the longest time.

"Where's Peggy?" He didn't mean to, but he thought she saw it anyway, the tiniest shake of his head, a flicker in the downturn of his mouth. He had no idea where Peggy was. He had no idea who she was. Honor Jones took another step closer to him. She wasn't trembling any more. Her pupils were wide and black.

"Whoever you are, mister." She jabbed the air. "Whatever this is. It's wrong, and you must know that at least."

She gathered herself, and he had the impression she was reining in an impulse to take hold of him and shake him apart till he bled, or wept, or disappeared to nothingness. She was tiny – there was nothing of her – and he beat back his own instinct to smile.

Tiny beads of perspiration on her upper lip. The scent of fresh smoke and mint on her breath. She was near enough for him to take her and kill her where she stood. But he wanted to hear what she had to say.

"Don't kill me. Do the right thing. Maybe for the first time in your life." She didn't like him. "Help me find her."

He'd sworn an oath.

He'd killed any number of bad men. Often they knew what was coming. Sometimes they didn't. But at the point of death, they thought only of themselves. They knew their crimes. Honor Jones thought only of her friend, and he sensed no guilt.

But that didn't mean she wasn't going to die. It was an order, he told himself. And he was duty-bound to follow it. Tarn made that clear.

His fingers found the ridged handle of the knife.

The bullet in his head would kill him sooner rather than later, North knew that. He didn't know if the fact he believed Honor was innocent was down to his intuition or because the bullet had driven him mad. She was frightened but not for herself, and she was grieving.

As North heard the birdsong, a fragile pink and pale gold streaked the London sky and the dusty blackbirds and mottled thrushes seemed to wake at the same moment.

His weight on the balls of his feet.

Forty-two seconds.

He sensed Honor brace, steady herself, and he felt her sigh, smelling the citrus notes of her mixed with smoke, only after he'd passed her by.

He released his grip on the knife.

Intuition or insanity? North wasn't killing Honor Jones MP today or any other day.

6

Westminster, London

9.10am. Tuesday, 7th November

God, she needed a cigarette. Every time she thought about that man, she started trembling. Honor took a sip of the black coffee which she'd let get cold and glanced towards the entrance.

No pass-holder walking in off the Embankment gained access to the foyer without holding a lanyard against the electronic reader which released the revolving glass doors. Through security – the X-ray machine, bodily pat-down and physical inspection of bags – no visitor gained access to the bustling atrium without a pass-holder on the other side of the glass doors ready to meet them. She could see some young guy now, patting his pockets, gesturing with his hands. She was guessing he'd lost his official pass. They wouldn't let him in – he would have to call a colleague down to vouch for him, before they wrote him out a day pass. Yes, she made the right call – she was safer in the Commons than at home, and safer again in a public space than in her office.

In the open-plan café, Honor shifted the table so that it was set square on to the knee-high wall rather than on the diagonal like all the others. Next to the tables, a bank of fig trees shaded customers as if they were in a Paris park instead of under the arching glass and ironwork dome of the MPs' offices at Portcullis House.

She settled her MacBook towards the edge of the wood, her cup to one side, and her iPhone on top of a pile of Commons papers she'd picked up from the Vote Office. She nudged everything again, and only then did she settle.

This morning was a Hail Mary and it hadn't worked. Stake herself out in a clearing to see what terrible beast came out of the jungle to devour her. Then catch it and tame it.

Shaking her head, she stared at the laptop's blank screen. What was she thinking? She was lucky he hadn't torn her limb from limb.

Or did she get it wrong?

Honor stared up into the canopy of leaves as she considered the idea the runner this morning was just that. Blameless. Some young jogger who headed into the office with a tale of escaping a lunatic woman who accosted him in the park.

But if that were the case, wouldn't he have run past her? Before she started talking?

Honor struggled to remember if she blocked his path while she fired her questions. Tried to recall the look in his eye as she challenged him to kill her. Did he even speak English? He hadn't said a word. Was the entire encounter a hideous overreaction to Peggy going off-grid, and poor Ned and his conspiracy theories?

The police believed her for all of five minutes. The sergeant frowned with concern that she'd been followed on her morning run. He scribbled away. The time. The park. The description. But his writing slowed when she mentioned Ned being murdered. Stopped when she talked about Peggy disappearing. Eventually, he took her in to an interview room, provided her with a polystyrene cup of sugary tea and, twenty minutes after that, a hard-faced detective came in to inform her that Ned left a suicide note. In his pocket. No, there was no return train ticket. Only a single – Newcastle to London. Honor was confident that she wouldn't have been told that much if she weren't an MP. As for Peggy, yes, their Northumbria Police colleagues had Honor's concerns on record up in Newcastle. Was there anything else they could help the honourable member with? The detective glanced at her watch as she asked.

But it was real, she knew it.

Ned wasn't suicidal. She had seen the ticket and she'd heard his plans to meet a girl called Jess the next day.

She shuddered as she thought back to the runner who'd followed her into the woods, the set of his jaw, the narrowed eyes. He was going to kill her – she knew it. But for some reason, he changed his mind.

And if the stranger came for her this morning, time was running out.

Ned said there were others missing. Not just Peggy, and she dismissed it as a paranoid delusion.

He also said don't search the internet.

The green light of the camera flickered above her screen as she booted up the laptop. Did that usually happen? She couldn't remember. Her fingers went to her lips. Hesitating.

7

London

9.10am. Tuesday, 7th November

If he didn't kill Honor, someone would – and soon. He hadn't rung in to confirm the termination.

Plus they would be all over her laptop and phone.

As North watched, occasionally the MP for Mile End picked up her cup as if it didn't have a handle, and took a mouthful of coffee. North knew it was cold because she wrinkled her nose every time. Once or twice, a researcher or a fellow member glanced across from the snaking queue at the café bar, but he figured the tension, the concentrated way she leaned her head on her hand, her elbow on the table, walled her off from casual approach. She raised her head to look up into the trees as if she was thinking hard, then went back to staring at the computer screen before closing the lid to draw a pile of paperwork closer. North didn't think she was reading it.

From his corner vantage point he walked softly, his leather-soled shoes barely touching the marble floor, the authentic

Commons pass he'd pickpocketed in Westminster tube station swinging on the lanyard round his neck. The gun with its silencer, which he'd smuggled through security in 15 pieces distributed between an umbrella and a briefcase, was complete. The umbrella turned inside out and discarded in the same gents where he'd assembled the gun. The briefcase open and abandoned in an unoccupied office as if left behind by a visitor. The gun itself he'd covered over with order papers and a folded newspaper held close to his chest.

He estimated there were nineteen steps between them.

At the entrance, he counted eight policemen, two of them armed, and four New Army soldiers, all of them cradling machine guns. Did they know he was here? Was it a trap? It was simple. He wanted to break free of the Board, and rules and blood. To be himself. Why then was he walking towards the complication that was Honor Jones when he should be running in the other direction?

He thought back to the park. The faint sweat on her upper lip. The smell of smoke on her breath. The black pupil widening in the pale green iris.

And here she was again. His breathing quietened. The pulse in his blood hesitating, dropping away – his heartbeat slow. If she saw him too soon, if she opened her mouth to shout, he would have to kill her. He should have killed her this morning.

Fifteen steps.

As he kissed her cheek, he would settle her in the chair, tip and rest her head on the palm of her hand. A still life. No life at all.

Nine.

It would be some time before anyone thought to interrupt, and sit in the seat opposite her hoping for a quick word.

Five.

Then the screaming would start, the terror and panic – policemen pushing and crowding their way through the doors. And he would be long gone.

One.

Tarn would be delighted.

She didn't look up until he pulled the black padded chair out from the table.

"Do you think they miss the rain?" He gestured towards the spreading trees and the dried and shrivelled leaves shrouding their soil, palming the gun with his other hand before she could notice it. "It seems cruel to make them live this way."

He sat down across from her and Honor flung her body against the back of the seat, putting space between them, the chair screeching backwards at the force of her recoil.

No panic, though she checked the state of security at the entrance. Too far. Their attention was focused on the comings and goings of MPs and constituents, lobbyists and schoolchildren. The unarmed and innocent. Her best chance of help would have to come from someone much closer to hand. The portly Tory gentleman? The twenty-something secretary? The nine-year-old child on a school trip from Bolton? Honor was doomed. He watched as she reached the same conclusion.

She swallowed hard, and he sensed her fight back a cry of protest as he used his right hand to slide her phone from the table, burying it in the loose earth next to them, tamping it down, covering it over with dried leaves – all the time looking at her.

"They're recording audio and video remotely," he said as he extracted a vial from his top pocket and swivelled the laptop towards him. "They've copied every text, document and contact you have." Opening up the lid, he snapped the glass with his thumbnail and poured its contents over the keyboard. "There's no one to go to, and no one to call without them knowing." Tiny twists of smoke emerged as he closed the lid again, sliding the laptop off the desk to rest between the table leg and the wall before it could attract attention.

Her eyes darkened to the green of a jade tiger he'd once seen in the penthouse apartment of a Chinese industrial spy he strangled. The tiger was snarling, he remembered, with razor-sharp teeth and curved claws. It made him bleed when he picked it up to admire the workmanship.

"You're the one who should be worried about cameras," she said.

"Cameras don't bother me." He pushed the clear-glass designer frames up onto the bridge of his nose. An affected gesture of an attractive man who wore a bespoke suit and Gucci glasses all the better to find his way up the greasy ladder.

She leaned in towards him. Her look hating. "Why didn't you kill me this morning?"

He'd asked himself that question a dozen times before he'd cleared the park.

He didn't kill her because she was innocent and he'd had enough of killing. Because as a dying man he didn't want to make a mistake he would regret the rest of his short life. And because, maybe, he could save Honor Jones from herself. All she had to do was take a hint. Freedom, he thought. Even the taste of it in his mouth felt right. Freedom and white sands and warm sunshine and smooth, bronzed skin against his. He had this one detail to sort, and it could all be his with a clear conscience.

He drew out the envelope from between the folds of the newspaper and pushed it towards her. He shook it and bundles of red £50 notes and a passport slid out. He eased back the money into the envelope as she picked up the passport – her fingers moving to the photo ID page. Checking that it was indeed hers – the one she kept in the locked filing cabinet in her garden flat under Personal Papers (Passport. Expiry: 2025). Processing the fact North broke into her flat within minutes of her leaving it this morning in order to rifle through her files.

"The best flight for you is a Virgin out to Washington at 11.25am. It's tight but you might make it. There's a Delta out to New York at noon but that's half an hour waiting to get picked up if they put an alert out for you. If you have any kind of luck though, you'll have landed by the time they wake up to the fact you've gone."

She was letting him talk, and North decided that was a good sign.

"The trick is to dig yourself as deep into the city as you can and disappear. Don't reach out to anyone you know over there, and if you want to carry on to Boston or Chicago or anywhere else, catch a bus or a train, and use cash. There's £10,000 here. No more flights. No more credit cards. Make the money last and when you need more, get a job cash-in-hand. Waiting-on – something like that."

"Or sex work, maybe?" she said.

She wouldn't starve, he figured. But she wouldn't get many tips for her congenial disposition.

He stood up, smiling. His good deed was done and his conscience clear. It was up to her now. Live or die. She could take her chances along with everyone else.

"If you don't sit down," she smiled at him in turn. "I'll have to scream."

"And then I'd have to kill you." He had stopped smiling.

"True." She nodded towards the armed police at the doors. "But it will all get terribly messy, terribly fast."

He contemplated walking past the schoolchildren and the policemen out into the damp November air. Despite the threat, he guessed she wouldn't cry out, that she'd allow him to slink back to the shadows and lose himself there again.

Or she might not. Honor Jones was the all-or-nothing kind.

The berry-red sheen of her lipstick was wearing off, he noticed, and kisses tattooed the coffee cup. Shrugging, he sat back down, leaned over, picked up her cup and drained it, pressing his own mouth against the shadows of hers. He was right. It was cold.

"I'm supposed to believe you're trying to help me?"

"I'm a boy scout."

"Why?"

Because if he didn't, Bruno or someone just like Bruno would put his hands around that slim neck and squeeze the life out of her.

She didn't seem to expect an answer.

"Are you in trouble after this morning?" she said.

He was in enough trouble to last a lifetime – especially his. He had refused to follow orders, thereby turning his back on a man who saved him from the gutter. And by warning a target who posed a possible threat to the security of the nation he was making it worse.

He wasn't going to kill her, she'd decided. He could tell by the loosening of her shoulders as she sat forward, closing down the space she first made between them. Her voice dropped. Intimate. Persuasive again. They were on the same side now.

"I can help you if you help me find Peggy."

He laughed, a brief explosion of air, and the frown line between her eyebrows deepened.

"I know you want to."

"I lied when I said I was a boy scout. They wouldn't have me."

She waved her hand, pushing to one side his comment.

" 'Peggy' is Dr Margaret Boland. She's an astronomer – a genius. She's disappeared and I've no idea where she is."

North turned over the name in his head. Boland? Had he ever heard it? Read it? He didn't think so.

"I'm marrying one of the richest men in the country. I can pay you hundreds of thousands of pounds. Half a million. A million?"

"But as you can see," he glanced at the glittering diamond on her ring finger, before tapping the envelope between them, "I don't need your money."

"Please."

He didn't doubt her sincerity, but she had bigger problems than finding her friend. Like the fact she should already be dead.

"Honor, I don't know anything about anyone called Peggy."

A light went out in the green eyes. A closing-down.

Sighing loud and hard, as if she'd heard out a troublesome constituent but now had better things to do, she gathered up her papers. She was finished with him – he felt the dismissal in her, the disappointment. He'd yielded nothing. He could live with disappointing her. But would she do the sensible thing and run?

When he first awoke in hospital and the voices came at him, he raved at the doctors and nurses who warned him that "severe loss of cognitive function" should be expected, bearing in mind the nature of the head wound. They sedated him. When he came round the next time, he knew better. He blamed the drugs for the confusion, said he felt surprisingly well considering. They were all delighted.

He didn't reveal that the senior nurse planned to leave her husband for the neurosurgeon, and the neurosurgeon was having second thoughts. True? Or a bizarre construct around a lingering smile between the two, the sexiness of the nurse, the arrogance of the neurosurgeon, the wedding bands of both.

As time passed, it became less of a distraction, though if his own emotions were heightened it got worse – voices grew louder, pictures sharper. But hour to hour, like finding a pirate station on a radio, the signal came and went as he moved the dial.

He believed Honor was thinking about home. About the flat. Peggy's picture on the fridge. Flowers in her kitchen. She wasn't thinking about planes or New York City. North caught her hand as she made to stand, and it was warm.

"Forget Peggy for now. Catch a cab, and a plane – somewhere far away. You have one chance to stay alive – maybe. If they aren't watching you. If they are watching – then it's already too late."

She pulled her hand out from his and he let her.

He had done what he could. Honor Jones was guilty. Tarn said so and the Board ruled on it. Summary justice was still justice.

And Honor was nothing to him. Innocent or guilty.

Peggy. Whosoever Peggy was – astronomer, genius, best friend – was nothing to him either, however vital she was to the woman across from him.

Honor's face was the shape of a heart drawn by a child with two fingers in the air.

A note of pleading entered his voice. "This isn't your world, Honor. I don't know what your friend did or if she's alive. But if she's dead, you're already too late. If she's alive, the very fact you're looking for her might make them kill her. But if you keep looking, what will certainly happen is that you will die."

Honor dropped the passport into her handbag, and her tone was almost friendly. "I'm an MP because Peggy told me that I could make a difference. I don't by the way. Politics isn't who I am, it's just what I do. And it has its downsides, like these loony-tunes who arrive in Central Lobby with shopping bags bursting with papers, raving about conspiracies. No one warns you about that on election night."

She stood up from the table, still talking. As if he were a colleague.

"Ned was like that. Peggy attracts waifs and strays. Right now there's a Chinese girl who's a force of nature. There's a traumatised family over from Syria. Ned. Me. He dropped out of uni but Peggy refused to write him off. She visited him in the psych unit and when he got home, she helped him out with money. We took him out for Sunday lunch together, walks in the park. I like him. I should say I 'liked' him.

"But the other night, to be truthful, I wasn't all that pleased to see him. In my defence, I'd a lot on my mind with Peggy gone and I kept thinking 'get to the point, Ned baby'." North strained to make out what she was saying, the hubbub in the café rising around them as the need for morning coffee intensified. "I didn't listen hard enough. And I should have. He was a clever guy and I should have given him more credit, because Ned is why the two of us are here."

She put her hand on North's shoulder, and the immediate shock of her touch coursed through his bloodstream.

"Did you throw that boy off the bridge? Did you kill Ned Fellowes?"

Her voice invited confession – held out the prospect of full absolution to the repentant sinner, as the warm, expensive scent of her wrapped round him.

Ned? North racked his memory. Ned. Ted. Ed. Edward Fellowes. The headshot published in the newspapers had him clean-shaven, younger, but when he met Honor Jones in the hotel, he sported a hipster beard. The "jumper" off Westminster Bridge. That's how Honor knew to watch for him. How she'd known she was a target. The guy drinking wine in the photos with Honor Jones was the guy who leapt from Westminster Bridge. Except he didn't leap to his death. North did the sums. He suspected it as soon as he read the piece.

Someone pushed Ned Fellowes to his death, and since he didn't favour coincidence, North presumed that it was an agent of the Board.

Peggy disappeared. Ned was dead. Honor was next.

"You didn't. I can see that much and I'm glad." She lifted her hand, freeing him and he felt the loss of her. "But even if you didn't kill him, someone just like you did.

"I kept hoping Peggy would reach out. Even when Ned died, part of me believed it had to be a mistake. Even when I went up to Newcastle. But then, there you were – standing in the dark. Ready to kill me. I'm not brave – or reckless – but if I don't find her, Peggy isn't coming back. And you can tell whoever you work for that is simply not acceptable to Ned or me."

As she walked away from the table with its manila envelope of money, away from the cover provided by the trees, and the stranger trying to help her, out into the bustling foyer, he kept watching, but Honor Jones didn't look back.

8

"Are you in trouble?" Honor said it and she got that right. One thing was for certain, North didn't need her dragging him any further into her mess.

He warned her.

If you disregarded a warning, that was on you. Caution saved lives. Fact. Surveil the territory, assess the risk, decide your next action accordingly. Advance? Retreat? Dig in and send for reinforcements? If you were outnumbered and outgunned and there were no reinforcements a-comin', it was sheer stupidity to advance. Retreat was not dishonourable when it was a strategic necessity. It was required.

North was leaving her to her fate.

The black cab was parked up on a quiet Westminster backstreet along from a think-tank. Black cabs attracted no attention wherever they were parked. He'd called the cabbie an hour ago. Keys under the front wheel-arch on the driver's side. Usual deal. A mutually beneficial arrangement that had served him well over the past five years. He bought the discretion of a cab and an official green badge to hang round his neck, while the divorced cabbie enjoyed three weeks in Florida with his new partner and both sets of kids. Win-win.

The key turned clockwise in the ignition and the engine caught. For an intelligent woman, Honor Jones behaved like a no-brain fool.

He glanced at the clock. The flight to Washington would have landed at Heathrow by now. Cleaners would be going through it for the turnaround flight back. If she'd listened to him, he could be driving them both to the airport instead of driving away and leaving her to certain death.

He turned the key again, anti-clockwise this time, and the engine died. What would she do?

He rested against the cabbie's wooden-beaded seat relief. It annoyed him. He'd ask the guy to take it off next time. He was paying him enough. He checked himself – there wouldn't be a next time. He was out.

Would Honor stay in the safety of Parliament?

He shifted around trying to get comfortable.

Impossible.

He just demonstrated safety didn't exist in Parliament or outside it.

He gave up on the beads, sliding off the suit jacket and undoing the silk tie, rolling up his white sleeves, before tossing the clear-glass spectacles out of the window.

Honor Jones MP. He wished he'd never heard her name. Or seen it, written in green ink on the back of a black and white photograph which showed her sitting with a man who was already dead. Never think of them as real people. Only as targets. Too late now.

A small groan escaped him.

She must have gone to the police about Peggy and got nowhere. Otherwise there'd be a hue and cry all over the news. He wasn't surprised. The Board had centuries of experience at covering up their operations.

He pulled out the pay-as-you-go he'd picked up an hour ago. Margaret Boland.

Astronomer. 302,000 results. Newcastle University physics department. A professor with a list of incomprehensible publications to do with cosmology. Honor appeared to be right. Peggy was a genius. The professor stared out from his phone screen. Not to-die-for lovely like Honor, but striking enough with dark eyes, wild black hair and high cheekbones. The strong face of a capable woman who regarded life as a serious business. And if she didn't before, she did now. He hesitated over a TED Talk she'd given a year ago – *Listen: the earth is singing*. She bowed her head as the applause started. Tall. An hourglass figure in a plain grey marl T-shirt, jeans and a dark jacket. Excited. Pleased to be there. Moving from foot to foot. She lifted her hand. Enough applause. North pressed the off button. What did it matter if the Earth sang and Peggy Boland heard it? He didn't need to listen because he was a free man.

He'd park the taxi up in long-stay. The darkest, furthest corner he could find in the most distant, shabby carpark. He'd wipe it over, get a message to the cabbie. He never left it at Heathrow, and the cabbie wouldn't be happy but he'd leave an extra grand in the glove compartment. For his time and trouble. The cabbie would get over himself. If he was lucky he'd get a good fare out of the airport back into the city. North himself would break up the gun and dump it in several bins. Then he'd catch a flight to Singapore and onwards where the spirit moved. With a passport in the name of Philip

MacDonald, and with one flight out of Changi airport every ninety seconds to three hundred cities in eighty countries and with more than fifty million people through there a year, he had a good chance of getting lost, which sounded like a great destination in itself right at this moment.

Eventually, he'd go to ground in the Caribbean, he thought. One of the smaller islands that attract enough of the affluent and idle to blend right in. White rum daiquiris and cracked ice? Too sweet. Whisky then. Yamazaki single malt, aged and almost, but not quite, ruined with ice. Ice in a ball this time. And the whisky not drunk alone, but in an infinity pool with a giggling woman with a heart-shaped face.

Freedom. It was within his grasp. He'd earned it. Several times over. He saved enough lives when he was in the Army – walked through a minefield to reach a wounded mate and got shot in the head in return. He was leaving Honor to it, and starting over.

He rested his head on his hands as they moved to grip the top of the steering wheel. He should strap himself to it, tie himself with thick jute ropes. Let the storms rage. If he waited here, quiet and peaceable, in this street with its pretty Queen Anne houses, in an hour or maybe two he'd hear the sirens. The metropolitan equivalent of the tolling bell marking the death of Honor Jones MP. Because that was about how long she had left to live. He should sit here, mourn briefly – he barely knew her after all – and drive into an apricot sunset and just reward. Wispy clouds scudded over the roofline as he peered upwards through the windscreen. There was enough in his account to buy a boat and sail between the islands. A ketch – something with good lines that handled like a dream. He'd carve the name into a piece of wood and hang it on brass chains from the stern. "Honor". Twists and ringletted oak blowing away in the trade wind. No – that was a terrible idea. He would call the ketch "Liberty".

He turned the key in the engine.

Surely Honor was too smart to stay. She set herself up this morning for a particular reason – to catch him. She wouldn't do it again because she was on a mission – to find her friend – and dying would put a real crimp in that.

No. She would run. Hide out while she kept looking for Peggy. However reluctant she was to follow his advice, it was her only real option. He ran through the encounter in his head. The sweep of the passport into her handbag as she kept talking. If she caught a plane to the US, she could have a Cosmopolitan in her hand by nightfall. She could drink a cocktail and thousands of miles away he would drink whisky and rest easy, with a soft woman who looked nothing like Honor Jones. Freedom could still be his.

He pulled out, ignoring the crunch as the hard-rubber tyre caught the arm of the discarded spectacles, crushing them, plastic and glass splintering, the frame left mangled in the gutter.

The problem was the only thought in her head when she walked away was going home. And if there's one place you don't go, when people are trying to find you and kill you, it's home.

9

As he leaned in to Honor's front door to pick its lock, North glanced across at the house for sale where he'd watched for her this morning. He should have texted an acknowledgement that he did the job. How long would they wait before they sent someone with fewer scruples? Bruno wouldn't have any problem with a murder disguised as a random sexual attack. He'd relish it.

He was putting her on the first flight out of Heathrow – Destination: Anywhere. Short haul was better by this point. Less time for the Board to organise any sort of pick-up at the other end.

The tumbler retracted under the pressure of the pick and North felt the lock give.

He had his story ready for "Chalfont Securities" to buy them both time. He would watch her plane take off from the observation deck and explain he'd tried to take her out in the park and again in the Commons, but there were always too many people around for what they wanted. Thirty thousand feet up in the sky as she opened a foil packet of peanuts, he'd explain that he must have spooked her because she fell down a crack in the pavement. He'd hang up all "count-on-me" and "any-minute-now", and catch his own plane, slip down his own crack in the pavement, to start over.

Behind the door to flat 21A as he stood in the narrow hallway she shared with the banker upstairs in 21B, he could hear her moving around.

He changed his pick, tripped the lock and eased his way into the flat.

Her court shoes were neatly aligned by the door.

He tracked pale grey footprints over the cream carpet of the hallway, into the lounge and beyond. She was in the kitchen. He could see her from the doorway.

Picking up a vase, Honor carried it from the table over to the draining board. She extracted the flowers and plunged her hand down the narrow throat, but whatever was in there she couldn't reach it. Her hand emerged dripping; cursing, she smashed the vase hard against the butler sink – a large crack opening up in the ceramic wall. He moved forward as she leaned over the sink, sorting through the pieces, raking over the broken china, till she found what she was looking for.

"Shame about the vase." His tone was hostile.

Honor jumped. Swore.

"It looked pricey."

"I wouldn't know." Turning to face him – her back to the sink, her white-knuckled hands gripping the laminated wallet. "It was a gift."

"And the memory stick in your hand – was that a gift?"

Honor slid the wallet into the side-pocket of her dress, and he recognised his mistake. Whatever was on that stick was part of the reason the Board judged Honor Jones a security risk. The Board didn't make mistakes – they'd have thought hard about killing an MP not least because the publicity would be brutal. Her friend Peggy was involved in something bad, and it had corrupted Honor.

"All right – Ned gave it to me." With her free hand she reached for his arm and gripped it, wetting his sleeve. "I need it."

North shrugged. It wasn't his business. All he wanted was Honor Jones the other side of the world, and his life back.

"And I need you on a plane before you get us both killed, because, trust me on this, they're coming for you."

She stared at him, as if she were deciding something.

"Trust cuts both ways," she said, raising her chin as if in challenge.

Her palm was warm on his bare arm. Electric.

Trust me – I'm a politician.

Her fingers touching North as she touched the banker yesterday morning before she walked away, as she touched him this morning. Coming into his space, invading it, connecting – knowing the effect. Her touch was her weapon of choice as much as a gun was his.

"I don't even know your name."

North hesitated. A name gave her power over him. He could still walk – leave her to her fate. Maybe he would take the memory stick with him as leverage to keep himself alive? He didn't think she would last long on her own – but if the police got involved along the way, perhaps she'd live long enough to tell them his name. He shouldn't tell her anything.

"North."

It came out despite himself – as if it were waiting for her to ask.

"OK – North." His name sounded different on her lips. "Give me two minutes in the bathroom and then I'll catch a plane. Though I'm going to Chile not America."

She walked past him, across the lounge and over to her shoes before sliding them onto her bare feet. A thought appeared to come to her.

"You should come with me," she said and smiled. Shy for the first time since he met her.

He knew she didn't trust him. Her gestures. Her smile. The shy invitation. They were lies. He knew it, and he didn't care because he wasn't a weak-chinned, gooey-eyed banker. He glanced across at the flowers which didn't yet know they were dying, the remnants of china, the damage she'd done. The mixer tap needed a washer. The drip pulled at the tap till gravity did what gravity does and the water smashed into the cracked bowl, echoing the tick tock of the kitchen clock as the seconds passed. *You should come with me.*

He turned over the offer in his mind.

Why would he?

Because she was stop-your-heart beautiful.

Then again, the world teemed with beautiful women.

Because he wanted to know how it ended.

Badly, he predicted.

Because if she came back for that memory stick, she intended to keep looking for Peggy.

You should come with me.

Enough women found him attractive for the invitation to make sense, but Honor Jones didn't want him as a sexual diversion – she wanted him as a weapon in her armoury. As hard muscle and a source of information.

Even so, he considered Chile. The weather in Santiago in November. Mild, he guessed. Springtime. New life. Fresh starts. She could forget Peggy. He could make her forget, and she could make him forget he used to kill people for a living.

She was taking too long.

Two thoughts slammed into his brain at the self-same moment.

She intended to use the bathroom window as her way out.

And she wasn't the one to walk the dirt into her new carpet. He tracked the dirt through the living room and down the corridor.

From under the bathroom door, water seeped slowly into the sodden cream of the wool. With a roar he kicked the door open.

Her attacker kept her under the water, his enormous hand forcing the blonde head below the seething surface, pressing down, the other holding her two ankles together, stretching her out the length of the bath. A cut-throat razor lay in the blood-splattered sink, blood from her right arm writhing and turning and spinning in the water as she struggled to break free, her hands reaching out towards her attacker's face, fingers scrabbling for a hold on his sleeves. North threw himself against the man, smashing him into the sink and against the tiled wall. The sound of water rising and falling as Honor made it to the surface, gasping and retching, blood pumping from the wound.

North was big but the intruder was bigger. He snarled as he steadied himself against the sink then rounded on North, slashing in front of him first one way then the other, the razor in his left hand making a swooshing noise as it cut the air into ribbons. North leapt back, slamming his spine into the half-open bathroom door, groaning with the pain of it, as the man – his teeth bared in a grim smile – closed in for the kill. If you can't run away and you don't want to stand still, the only way is forward, a grizzled Army instructor once told him. The Charge of the Light Brigade he called it. Into the jaws of death, into the mouth of Hell. North stepped in towards the flailing razor, both hands reaching for the man's wrist. The intruder reached his right arm across North's body to keep him away but North took out his right leg and the man tipped, falling wildly, heavily – the razor still between them – into the bath. Curled up at the other end, half over the edge, bleeding still, a white-faced Honor moaned as the man's head and chest hit the water, a pinkish wave rising and falling against her with a crash. The human body carries an average of nine pints of blood; you can lose around forty per cent before shock sets in. She would die if he didn't stop the bleeding. She was already dying.

Inch by inch, North forced the razor closer and closer to the man's straining neck – the weight of his body now against the intruder's legs, pressing his lower half against the side of the bath. The other man's fear, his desperate urge to suck down oxygen, almost made North let go, as below the water the attacker's face smashed against the bottom of the bath, the jaw working furiously, chewing the water – air bubbles rising to the surface and popping. As the blade bit the skin, sinking through the cartilage and larynx, under North's body the man's struggle grew more ferocious – then less, and less again, till the panic went out of him and he stopped fighting altogether.

North sat back on his hunkers.

Honor's mascara-swept eyes blackened the sockets, her face whiter than the tiles behind her. She lay back against North as he dragged her from the water onto the black and white linoleum floor, grabbing for a towel to hold against her wrist, arterial blood saturating it within seconds – white turning to crimson.

The Board knew. Tarn sent the attacker to do what North didn't do. Kill her. Instead, North killed the attacker, and saved her. It was a topsy-turvy world. He could feel her shallow breaths through the wet clothes. Hours ago, he should have slid his knife into this flesh because green ink and powerful men told him to. She was too easily broken, too small and vulnerable. He didn't want her dying in his arms because the world would be a colder and less interesting place without her in it.

With his free hand he dragged the corpse along the bath closer to them. The nearside jacket pocket was empty. The same on the other side. He found it in the inside jacket pocket. Folded over twice. The same picture of Honor sitting across from Ned. Her name on the reverse, smudged and running from the bathwater.

At first he didn't see it, the water sticking the photographs together, but as he peeled them apart he saw his own face folded into quarters. Snapped one morning running. The morning Tarn caught up with him. The Bentley coming up behind him in the rain. Bruno at the wheel staring down the lens – as if he knew the cameraman was there, which meant Tarn knew the cameraman was there. Few of us get second chances Tarn told him. North was nobody's dear boy. Nobody's darling. If he didn't take the job, they were going to kill him.

"The mirror." Honor's voice rasped, her eyes fixed on the wall behind him, and North turned.

There was nothing to see. The mirror was clean and sparkling. It took him a second. No lipstick scrawl. No "Peggy" written over and over. The attacker made sure of it. Wiping away the name like the genius astronomer herself was wiped out of her life. In the same way they wanted to wipe away the bleeding woman in his arms. If he didn't believe there was a link before between the disappearance of her friend and the death sentence over Honor's head, he believed it now. The lip sticked name of Peggy written across her bathroom mirror was a loose end and the Board made a point of avoiding loose and messy ends. They wanted Honor dead with good reason. She was tugging at the thread, refusing to let go, intent on unravelling some meticulously crafted creation.

North had no doubt they would keep coming for her till they could draw a black line through the green-inked name. Except he couldn't let that happen. He travelled light. He'd never wanted the responsibility for someone else weighing him down, slowing him down.

Except here she was in his arms.

10

University of Oxford

Sixteen years earlier

The girl in paint-on blue jeans was drunketty-drunk-drunk
as her dad used to say. Blonde silky hair framing a heart-
shaped face, and small tip-tilted breasts. No one had to
imagine their perfection because the girl's top was off as she
danced on the bar. She danced well, her tanned arms lifted,
but the baying members of the college hockey club weren't
showing their appreciation of any sense of rhythm. As the
girl swayed, almost toppling, and the reaching hands went
up to pull her down, Peggy Boland in her solitary corner
of the college undercroft bar put down a half-finished
pint on the sticky table. She closed the ring-binder file and
slid it under the bench, before pulling on the sheepskin
jacket.

She'd had enough.

She stood up, remembering too late to duck to avoid
concussing herself on the stone arch. She should have stayed
in the library. But it was Friday night, and she thought – this

once – she would finish her work while enjoying a drink in peace. Thanks to these braying, lecherous toss-bags, she was managing neither.

Cursing under her breath, she stood on the chair to rescue the T-shirt dangling from the candle light fitting, before pushing and shoving through the outlying ranks of the cheering rabble.

The team captain, his cheeks bumpy with purpling acne scars, was holding the dancer upright against his chest, his meaty arm around the golden skin.

Peggy moved with the crowd, using her own height and weight to intimidate the middle ranks. She needed full-ticket access. She caught a glimpse of the blonde's bleary-eyed face, as the bruiser half carried and half dragged her through the crowd towards the doorway. A dozen others followed him, whooping their encouragement.

He didn't notice Peggy at first.

"You're in my way, Chewbacca." His breath reeked of stale beer and spicy kebab. The colour rose in Peggy's cheeks as she held out the girl's discarded T-shirt. "You'll catch your death. It's perishing out."

The blonde's green eyes attempted to bring Peggy into focus as she patted herself down to check the exact state of her undress. The small hand went to her mouth in exquisite confusion at the nakedness it discovered, and blushing, she shrugged herself into her top as the mob booed its disapproval.

"Come on with me, sunbeam," Peggy said. "It's past your bedtime."

She was even prettier close up, Peggy thought. Smiling hazily, the girl took a step towards her. Two steps.

"You're not her effing mother."

The meathead jerked the girl back into him, holding her forearm tight enough to make her squeal. She slapped the palm of her hand against his barrel chest in feeble protest.

"Bugger off, Lurch." The voice of entitlement – the result of hundreds of thousands of pounds spent at the right sort of school with the right sort of people. Not that of a man used to disappointment or refusal. "If anyone's seeing her home, we are. Aren't we, boys?"

The captain leaned down to slam his wet lips against the girl's, forcing open her pink lips and pushing his tongue into her mouth to the raucous cheering of his team mates. She reared back, the blonde head moving from side to side as she tried to squirm away, but he held on, sliding his muscled thigh between the slim legs.

One of the team held his hockey stick in his hand, the curved head balanced on the floor as if it were a rifle and he were a solider on guard duty. He took the kiss as his cue to shove Peggy hard in a bid to get her moving, but she held her ground. It helped to be a big lass sometimes.

"Touch me again and I will deck you," she said to the rifleman, and there was a roar of laughter and jeers from his teammates.

Why wait? It was inevitable.

Peggy slammed the heel of her hand into the soft tissue of the Roman nose on the right and heard it break.

Her dad, a roughneck on the oil rigs, taught her never to wait for the lummocks to catch up. It was a waste of your valuable time and evolutionary advantage.

"Peggy, lovey, when it's going to end badly, be sure to get your retaliation in first," he'd told her. *"Don't ever think you have to play nice. Trust your instincts and play by your own rules – not theirs."*

Blood gushed from the Roman nose as she wrested the hockey stick from the rifleman's shocked grasp, driving the stick end into his belly and the wooden head into the jaw of the man on the left, raising her leg in the same moment and kicking him full-on in the crotch. Shrieking, he staggered sideways, bent over, his hands clutching his groin. If she were lucky she'd broken his jawbone and front teeth, as well as dispatching his bollocks to his chest cavity.

She had seconds.

She grabbed the blonde's wrist, hauling her away from her captor, taking a step backwards and then another, her eyes still locked on the shocked face of the team captain. The dancing girl moved as Peggy moved. Sobering up fast. Heat coming off her. The smell of blackcurrant and cider.

There, Peggy saw it.

A white-hot flare of outrage.

The big lump had disrespected him. In front of the boys. Failed to pay due deference. Worse yet, she was stealing his prize. His beautiful piece of flesh.

As the meathead rushed at them, Peggy used the stick as a scythe, shin height, forcing their attackers into reverse, tipping a chair, another, and then a table, glass shattering against the paved floor, before slamming the stick at an angle into the narrow doorway, creating a barricade between them and the rats' nest of boys.

The meathead shouted – hurling aside a broken chair, his teammates piling in behind, as Peggy shoved the blonde out into the corridor, slammed the huge outer door shut and rammed home the bolts. There was a moment's silence as the two girls leaned their backs against the door.

It was cooler in the stone corridor. The air fresher without the fug of cigarette smoke and the heat of sweaty, compressed bodies.

There was a crashing noise as the ancient door juddered in its frame as if a bench were being used as a battering ram.

"Nice stick work," the blonde said, as she smashed the glass case of the fire alarm with her elbow and pressed the button. "But how fast can you run?"

11

University of Oxford

Sixteen years earlier

The vomit came fast and violent, surging out of her stomach and up her oesophagus to splatter into the metal waste bin, pinging and humming as it hit the sides and bottom. Honor collapsed back onto the bed, but the arm behind her forced her up again. Sure enough, the vomit hadn't finished with her. She retched, and felt a cool hand sweep back her hair, hold it behind her ear, and some part she hadn't anaesthetised with vodka and tablets called out for her mother and the pain of missing started over.

Whoever was holding her must have decided Honor was done. She felt herself lowered back into the pillows and a cold flannel wiped over her face then laid across her pounding forehead.

Should she look? If she opened her eyes, it was going to hurt. Darkness was safer. Closer to blessed, longed-for oblivion. But she wasn't being given a choice.

"Honor. Do you think you can drink some water?"

She opened her eyes. Bright sunshine. Agonising. Sweeping off the flannel, she squeezed them tight shut, turned over in the bed despite the shattering pain of it, face to the whitewashed wall. Leave. Her. Alone. For God's sake.

It was night when she woke again. The headache there but dulled and, self-pitying, she groaned, opening her eyes just a fraction. All right, she was ready for that water and paracetamol.

But this time the figure by the lead-paned window didn't move to her aid. She was gazing up into the stars.

"The strangest thing happened."

Warm breath clouded the cold glass.

The figure turned, as if sensing Honor's eyes on her. It was Peggy. The northern nerd studying physics. Again. It was bad enough the other night when they did a runner from the bar. She was grateful. Obviously. Apparently, there'd been trouble with the hockey club before and it hadn't ended well for the girl, which is probably why they didn't bring in the police or the college authorities this time. Still, ever since, Peggy kept turning up. Knocking at her door with that smile where she never showed her teeth. Her eyes crinkling as if she had never seen anything better than Honor in her entire life. And Honor telling her things to fill the silence as they drank instant coffee together, before she could make her excuses and throw her out. Knowing Peggy would come back. Didn't she know anyone else? Didn't she have any real friends? She was like a stray dog. Honor didn't need another friend. She had plenty of fun people to hang with. Admittedly, they weren't here right now, and she didn't feel like being alone. Plus, if her memory served, she'd been sick, so poor old Peggy might well have been on puke patrol. An unfamiliar sense of shame crept over Honor, settling somewhere in the pit of her bilious stomach. It was a bad one yesterday – the anniversary. That excoriating loneliness. The noise of the shotgun firing over and over. Blood everywhere. The wreckage of her mother's face. Her father. She flung an arm over her eyes, willing herself back down into sleep, but it wasn't there.

Peggy was talking again. Her voice flat and mellow, easy to listen to. Where was she from?

"I was out at the observatory a while ago and it was a clear night."

The thrumming in Honor's ears was loud but she held onto the words to pull herself through the noise and nausea, climbing hand over hand up from the solitary darkness where the only company was bleeding, worm-eaten corpses. Normally Peggy didn't talk – she listened. Honor found herself wanting to hear what the other girl had to say.

"A right good night for watching. And what I'd wanted to see was the Crab Nebula because that's my favourite. It's what's left after the explosion of a supernova nearly a thousand years ago – 6,300 light years away from Earth, and I check on it every now and then, to make sure it's still there."

Tentative, Honor used her hands to lever herself up onto her pillows, resisting the sensation that meteorites were falling on her head, one after the other, from an immense height.

"I've heard of it happening, but it's never happened to me before." She turned towards Honor. "I found it all right, the nebula, and then out the corner of my eye there were all these other stars, other galaxies, and it was as if the night sky were swallowing me. It was so immense, so infinite, and I was this itsy-bitsy little thing."

Peggy smiled and Honor smiled with her at the thought the huge girl at the window could ever be itsy-bitsy, but Peggy's eyes remained serious.

"I realised I was nothing, and out there," she gestured to the window, beyond the glass, "was everything, and that I didn't matter."

Honor lay still in the bed. She didn't need to look into the stars to know she was nothing. Peggy left the window and walked towards the bed. It wasn't far. Four steps. Three. But to Honor it seemed to take an age before the other girl sat down.

"The thing is, just for that solitary moment, I forgot that I do matter."

"You don't." Honor's voice to her own ears was ugly from the retching of earlier. "None of us do."

Peggy drew herself back, reaching out her hand to turn on the bedside light, changing the room from bluey darkness to a golden yellow, and the pain was back. Honor shielded her eyes from the worst of it, blinking, adjusting to the brightness, before she took away her hand.

Peggy waited.

"There's the thing, Honor Jones. Look again, because you're absolutely, bollockingly wrong. We do matter. All of us. Especially you and me."

In the college room at the top of the winding staircase, they talked most of that night. Peggy drinking builder's tea, Honor sipping water and then a weak cup of peppermint tea. Eating toast and anchovy butter. They talked through that weekend and, by tea-time on Sunday, they had it all worked out. Honor was studying law. She would be a lawyer. Right wrongs. She'd go into politics and become Prime Minister. While Peggy found new worlds, Honor would change this one into something altogether more marvellous. Peggy had no doubt it was an excellent plan and Honor was prepared to believe her.

12

London

1.30pm. Tuesday, 7th November

Names were scrawled in blue and green marker pen on a whiteboard behind the nurses' station on Ward 23 at St Thomas' Hospital. He'd followed the housekeeper through the door to avoid buzzing for entry. And as two nurses passed, their heads close together, he willed them not to look up. There was a moment's panic as he scanned the board for "Honor Jones". No such patient. No HJ. No MP. No Jane Doe. No Jane Smith. Perhaps someone advised discretion – who? A hospital consultant? A call from Downing Street?

How would you keep things discreet in a hospital?

In red pen, Room 1, marked "isolation measures".

He pushed open the door, checking the corridor as he closed it behind him, the squeaky wheel of the housekeeper's trolley receding into the distance. Honor lay in the hospital bed, unmoving and whiter than the sheet which covered her.

He'd watched the paramedics arrive at her flat, the blue

lights of the police shortly afterwards. He wondered what they would make of the corpse. Exactly how the Board would erase it from their statements and memories.

When they stretchered Honor out, he slipped away. He did what he could. It wasn't enough to keep her safe, but she was at least alive. He was keen to stay that way himself – to disappear and to believe that there was an outside chance that the Board would let him. That Tarn would argue he had served them well. That his discretion could be relied upon and that savage dogs should be left to sleep. But it wasn't happening – the photograph proved as much. Tarn's concern – telling him he mattered, that he could be a great man – all of it relied on North being the obedient son. Step out of his prescribed role and the sanction was ultimate and bloody. Bruno was probably pleading to be the one to deliver the coup de grâce.

She sensed him rather than heard him, and her eyes fluttered and opened – widening at the sight.

"...*killer*..." he heard. A rabbit punch. What did he expect? That she'd see him and think he was a hero? She didn't trust him, he reminded himself, and that was okay.

"You look better," he said. "Better" but still too pale. "Better" but a saline drip stood by the bed, its tube strapped to the right arm which lay above the sheet, a tight bandage around the wrist and up her forearm.

"Better" as opposed to exposed and ridiculous, which was how he was feeling. Her one-time murderer dropping by her bedside to visit. He should have brought black grapes and barley water.

She tried and failed to sit up straighter in bed, her head falling back onto the pillow at the effort.

She eyed the small rucksack on his back.

"I didn't figure you for a rambler, North."

She hadn't forgotten his name. He didn't know whether to be flattered or worried.

In the rucksack was Honor's ten thousand pounds and passport, and fifty thousand in sterling and dollars of his own, along with a selection of credit cards in a brown Smythson wallet, passports and driving licences – in three different names – a couple of boxes of the purple pills and a SIG Sauer P226, collected from a safe in Hatton Garden, where an Orthodox Jewish jeweller made discretion another god. North believed in escape routes.

"I owe you an apology. I didn't believe you when you said they'd send someone else so soon." She wrinkled her nose. "I didn't want to believe there was some assembly line of sociopaths, all of them out to kill me."

"If that's you saying thank you, you're welcome."

She frowned as if she were thinking hard about something unpleasant – him probably – but as she opened her mouth he raised his finger to his lips. Voices outside the door...

"she's resting...shan't disturb her...just need to..."

The visitor had no intention of being stopped.

North moved fast, easing the bathroom door in the far corner of the room all but closed, as the visitor pushed open the ward door, crashing it against the wall.

Honor raised her head, her arms reaching for her visitor, and in the windowless, antiseptic-smelling bathroom, North felt a flicker of envy.

North recognised the visitor because he read the papers. JP Armitage: fifty something communications billionaire, Conservative Party donor, philanthropist and major shareholder in the country's New Army.

"What on earth were you thinking, Honor?"

The tycoon threw down the swag of tiny pale-green and crimson-throated orchids across the bed as if they embarrassed him. His craggy face was set, his lips a line as he dragged the moulded-plastic chair closer to the bed, his powerful legs tucked under him – a big man sitting on a chair meant for a smaller one.

He gave up trying to keep his temper. He was incandescent. "You should have come to me."

JP Armitage – rumoured to keep a black book of grudges that went back to his childhood in the cobbled back-to-backs of the roughest streets in Leeds. The third richest man in the country according to the Sunday Times Rich List – his wealth founded on his scrap metal company which had long since evolved into a transnational empire of communications and IT, real and cyber security, and high finance. The New Army just one more way to make money.

Armitage bent his head over the bandaged hand he held between his, and North sensed the tycoon attempt to master himself.

"I told you Peggy was missing," Honor said.

"Peggy is in Chile – the university told you that. Or New Mexico. Star gazing in some desert. Her mind's full of pulsars and quarks – whatever the hell they are."

"I only wish that were true."

"I've set good people in both places looking for her. They'll find her. Her brain doesn't function the way your brain works or mine. She'll be horrified when she gets home and sees what she's put you through."

So Peggy was some absent-minded professor who might forget the fact her friend worried about her? That might well be true, thought North, but it didn't explain the death sentence on Honor.

"JP, you don't even like Peggy so don't pretend you care."

"What do you mean 'I don't like Peggy'? She makes it perfectly clear she can't stand me. She as good as accused me of grooming you when you were a kid. It's hard to spend Christmas with someone after that."

JP knew Honor as a child. North re-evaluated the relationship as Honor narrowed her eyes.

"She's important to me."

"I respect what she did for you when you were younger," JP's tone softened. "But you're all grown up."

"Then stop telling me what to think. And what about that poor boy who died on the bridge?" Honor never lost focus, North realised. Even when it appeared that she might be on the defensive, that she was distracted or changing course, in reality, she never lost sight of her primary target.

Armitage waved, dismissing the boy on the bridge and his leap into oblivion, keeping hold of Honor with his other hand as if she might slip away. She was off-message. From his vantage point, North could see Armitage's foot bouncing up and down. He was working hard to control his anger.

"Ned wasn't your responsibility. He was unbalanced. He needed a psychiatrist, Honor – not a bloody MP." JP's voice was loud. This wasn't their first argument about Peggy, North guessed. "I know you want to, and I know why, but you can't save everyone."

The colour in Honor's cheeks rose as she made to draw her hand away, but the tycoon refused to let go, moving his chair closer to the bed.

"You think that you have to be perfect, Honor, but this isn't a perfect world. I blame myself – this affair dragging on when we should be married. You need stability in your life and I've been too distracted by work."

"JP, you flatter yourself." Finally, freeing herself from his grip. "Someone tried to kill me – that's not on you."

A flicker of puzzlement crossed the craggy face before he smoothed it out, but Honor caught it anyway. She considered her bandaged wrist, and as she turned back to him her voice rose – an anxious child, one who can't sleep because of the bogeyman under her bed. "Ask the doctors. They'll tell you. Ask the police."

Desperate for him to believe her. Desperate to sound normal. Failing.

The tycoon sat back in the too-small chair, one arm dangling, and the hand Honor couldn't see bunched itself into a tight fist.

"Depression happens to the best of us. It's not something to be ashamed of." Coaxing. Charismatic. Armitage could be all of those – his worst enemies said as much. And he was working hard.

She slowed her delivery. Spelling it out. Keeping it simple and hostile. "A man. Attacked. Me. In my bath. I was fully dressed. He cut me," she brandished her wrist at him, "and did his level best to drown me. I did not do this to myself."

North sensed Armitage's surprise – he guessed not many people challenged the tycoon on anything. Sensed escalating anger and fear for Honor's state of mind.

Honor took hold of his lapel, plastic tubing flapping, the drip teetering on its casters with the movement, to bring Armitage closer. "JP, there's a dead body in the flat." Her voice trailed off into confusion. "Isn't there?"

As she let go, JP reached out to steady the drip, his face expressionless – that of a tycoon who did business deals and never allowed himself to be second-guessed, used to hiding his feelings from partners, colleagues and observers, maybe even from himself. North listened, but all he could catch from Armitage was concern for Honor.

"And someone else attacked me this morning in the park when I was running...except..." She trailed off, hearing herself, disbelieving her own claims as if North might not be there behind the flimsy bathroom door, as if she needed to call him as a witness and prove something to herself if not to Armitage. Goosebumps rose on North's arms as Honor contemplated the bathroom door, and JP half turned. North held his breath. If she betrayed him, if she told Armitage he was there, it was over.

Honor opened her mouth.

But Armitage spoke before she could.

"Honor, I love you, but life's complicated for you and you put too much pressure on yourself. And that's the truth."

His rugged features, the broken nose and flattened vowels – North thought how much conviction he carried, this hard man whose good opinion others sought, a self-made, bottom-up success.

"You don't believe me." She gave him one last chance to contradict her.

"I'll be back in an hour." He glanced at the heavy sparkling watch on his wrist as if when he said "an hour" he meant one hour and not one minute longer.

"And we'll take you somewhere lovely to rest up. One of my companies owns a place in Suffolk. The best people. Superlative care. More like a spa than a clinic. Everyone goes there. Then when you're better, if Peggy still isn't back, I'll take you to New Mexico and on to Chile myself. We'll visit every telescope out there till we find her. And as far as this 'incident' goes, my crisis management team is all over it.

They'll handle Downing Street, the constituency, the press. You just have to rest up."

He made it sound easy, thought North. Leave it to JP and he'll make everything right again. Throw money at it. Pull strings. Bring in the spin doctors. A debilitating viral infection. Acute exhaustion. Physical collapse. Normal service will be resumed. Meanwhile, get his unbalanced lover into the best place with the finest head doctors and use some high-priced corporate security firm to track down her missing friend. If all else failed, charter a private jet or fire up his own. He was the type to have one on stand by.

Even so, JP's brows were drawn together as he stood. He didn't seem convinced by his own plan. Perhaps he doubted that they could keep it quiet? Or that Honor's mind could be pieced back together?

"You aren't to do anything. You aren't to talk to anyone. Your worries are mine, sweetheart, not yours."

Honor lay back on her pillows, her eyes unfocused, hands hidden under the sheets – a picture of defeat and pretty acquiescence. And North had a sudden urge to warn the tycoon that she was lying. JP's good opinion, his approval, had ceased to matter. Her face closed in on itself as she gamed her next move. Rebooting her system. She wasn't checking herself into any clinic. In her mind, the tycoon wasn't even there anymore.

JP bent to kiss her, but instead of kissing her cheek, his lips found hers and North closed the door just a fraction so he didn't have to watch.

An aroma of citrus, cinnamon and money lingered as North emerged from the bathroom. Honor ignored him, reaching for the TV remote and pointing it at the corner of the room. It went through North's mind that she was trying to turn off her life, but then the TV blared.

"...Reports are emerging that leading Tory backbench MP Honor Jones is today recovering in a London hospital after a failed suicide attempt." The presenter's face contorted itself into an expression of saccharine concern that such a terrible thing might happen.

The assassin in him, the trained killer and professional soldier, admired the Board's ability to pull together such an effective cover-up out of his own treachery, but he didn't think it was wise to voice it.

Away from the studio, the pictures cut to distant scenes outside Honor's flat – blue lights, an ambulance at the kerbside, paramedics carrying a stretchered body, then grainier archive of the Honourable Member speaking in the Commons, on election night, beaming, youthful, happier than he'd thought she could ever look, with a blue silk rosette pinned to a figure-hugging dress. Hectic with excitement, a skinny young woman stood outside the doors of the hospital – its name visible over her shoulder, her words tripping over themselves: "...set for a brilliant career...tipped to be a future Prime Minister...apparent history of psychiatric problems, including a diagnosis of bipolar disorder. Parliamentary colleagues are understood to be deeply concerned. Honor Jones appears to be an unfortunate victim of her own tragic family history. Older viewers might remember..."

Throwing the zapper at the screen, Honor let out a stream of obscenities. An impressive, imaginative, curated collection for a civilian, thought North as the remote smashed against the wall, plastic shrapnel, batteries and plaster dust exploding across the room.

North unbuckled the rucksack. She had JP, but he was leaving the envelope with its cash and passport just in case. And he was going – he'd already been here too long.

"Where's the body of that animal who tried to kill me?"

A long way from her flat by now. Another loose and messy end tidied away.

North had left the front door ajar, before he laid her gently on the bathroom floor and slipped out the French windows into the garden at the last possible minute. He'd hopped the fence and, from a little way up the street, he'd watched like any concerned neighbour as paramedics carried Honor out. Aside from the ambulance, there was a solitary police car and a handful of passers-by, but no TV cameras. He guessed that the TV pictures, shot from the far end of the street, showed the disposal of one dead assassin minutes later, rather than the rescue by the genuine emergency services of an apparently suicidal MP. Use the enemy's own momentum against him. Use Honor's injury and her personal history to demonstrate her mental state.

"They've cleaned up," he said.

"By destroying my credibility?"

He felt the loss in her. He didn't know how ambitious she was, but a media firestorm about her mental health had to be a blow. Honor Jones wasn't heading for political glory any more. Political comebacks were always possible, but even if she made it out of this alive, suspicions would linger that she wasn't tough enough for the top job. That she wasn't made of the right stuff. Politicians were flawed creatures when it came to drugs or drink or unsuitable bed fellows. They were venal, grasping and morally dubious, and the public expected no less.

But suicide?

There was no recovery from that virus, however good JP's crisis management team were.

Eyes shining, Honor blinked several times, forcing back what he took to be unshed tears as he shifted from foot to foot. Sympathy wasn't his speciality. He should go.

With a grimace, she tore away the tape attaching the saline drip to her arm, ripping the cannula from the vein, to fling back the sheets from the bed, smothering the crimson-throated orchids without a thought.

As she clambered out of the bed, she pulled at the ties at the neck of the hospital gown, which fell to the floor, before reaching naked into the wardrobe, regardless of North's presence. Like Armitage moments before, he had stopped existing.

He drew out of the rucksack the passport he'd rescued from her bag, and the envelope with its bundle of money which he'd already given her once.

"I'm not getting on any plane if that's why you're still here," she said, drawing up a pair of white lace pants.

A few hours ago, she was about to leave her flat by the bathroom window – she never intended on getting on any plane, then or now. Not to Chile. Not anywhere. With him or without him. He didn't need telling, but he wanted her to have the cash anyway.

The corner of her lower lip was caught between white teeth as she fiddled with the clasp of her white lace bra. He felt her recalibrate – the vibrations, the complex shifting of finely engineered machinery as pistons moved up and down, crankshafts turned and sparks fired. Who stood where? Which pieces were lost and whether the game was over. "But I'll take your guilt money." She said it like she was doing him a favour. "I'll pay you back when this is over."

She took out a dress on a hanger and threw it onto the bed to unzip it, and he placed the envelope on the bedside locker next to a plastic jug of water.

"Don't go home, Honor."

Home to her blood-spattered bathroom. The home where they had already come for her twice.

The third time they'd use pills and a note – or that's how he would do it. Give her something to make her sleep, then wake her up and force her to take more, let her sleep, wake her up. She would need less persuasion each time.

She faced him, the dress bunched in her hand, the hanger back in the wardrobe.

Easy. Natural. Oblivious to the effect she was having on him.

"I'm not an idiot. I'm not going home. I'm going back to the start."

She meant Newcastle, where Peggy lived and worked. The Tyne Bridge. The river. Peggy's smile.

Holding out the dress by its shoulders, so that it pooled on the floor, she stepped into the emptiness, pulling it up in one smooth movement, its silk lining whispering against the length of her.

"The last time we talked she said something strange."

He could hear her, but it was as if she were talking to herself.

"She said that politics was my game of choice, but her favourite game was hunt the thimble." Honor slid the zip up her spine to her shoulder blades, wincing as she reached down an arm to pull it the rest of the way. The dress was still damp – it clung to her.

He couldn't help but notice.

Was that a strange thing to say? He had no idea. All he

knew was that the body underneath the dress was exactly how he thought it would be.

"Peggy's favourite game is Risk. It's been nagging at me ever since I saw it on her shelf at her place. I didn't think anything of it at the time, but she's hidden something for me to find. Maybe at hers. Or in the university somewhere. But it has to be in Newcastle."

Honor Jones was a woman who leapt from A to B to Z without once looking down into the abyss.

He was at the threshold, his hand on the handle ready to press down, pull open the door, walk out into the corridor and leave Honor behind.

He wanted his boat.

He wanted to see that body again. See the naked woman in the tangle of sheets that JP Armitage knew.

He turned a fraction and her eyes held his. Dressed, hands on her hips, as she'd stood in the park.

He fought the urge to walk across and strip the dress from her body. To hold her.

"You should come with me." Classic misdirection. Lying to him, on her way out of a window to get as far away from him as she could. But that was then.

He owed Honor nothing. But she stood there like she thought otherwise. The urge to see her naked again left him.

"Honor, I am not coming with you. We'll both end up dead."

"Did I say you were invited?"

On his back was a rucksack of plausible IDs and ready cash. In Vienna, an account with more money than he had time to spend. She had her own means of escape – a sugar daddy with his very own army, once she could persuade him she was sane, and she was persuasive enough. She'd be fine.

North was walking away and living happily ever after for as long as he had left. He shouldn't even walk. He should run. She could chalk up two corpses already – a conspiracy theorist called Ned and a nameless trained killer. Three, if you counted the unfortunate Japanese tourist who broke Ned's fall. Proof, if anyone needed it, that she was dangerous to be around, helping her: reckless, treasonable, and liable to get you killed. He wished JP Armitage all the luck in the world.

Tarn said he cared about him. North thought he did. But Tarn cared much more for power and his role within the Board. He'd sacrifice North and not lose a moment's sleep: lay lilies on his grave, but he wouldn't mourn him. In the Army North made friends, good friends he'd have died for without hesitation, and they'd have done the same. He'd barely talked to them since he left the Army, and couldn't say why. Because he wasn't the same man? Because he didn't want to be exposed to how they really felt and who they really were? Because he wanted to keep them decent and honourable and courageous like they were in his memory? But Tarn was a friend. No – more than that. A mentor. A wise man, and the closest thing to a father he'd ever known. And Tarn's betrayal hurt when not many things hurt North any more because he didn't let them, and he preferred it that way. Clean and cold and clinical.

She was moving again. Her fingers combing her hair at the mirror over the sink, pinching her cheeks to put some colour in them, biting at her pale lips.

But he did hurt. He admitted the truth of it as he watched Honor ready herself for the fight.

There was hurt and there was anger.

His name was written in green ink. *Michael North. Extreme caution advised. Disposal: any way possible.* Who was he trying to kid?

He was in this till the end. Locked in at the very moment he realised how precious freedom was. It all came back to Peggy. And if Peggy locked him in, then Peggy was the key to his freedom.

"I've never been to Newcastle," he said, and she paused – her right foot hovering half in and half out of its shoe. Like the dress, the shoes must still be wet. Her eyes widened as she completed the motion, before sliding the left foot home.

"You should get out more."

Did he want to meet the woman who was the roundabout reason for Tarn writing his name in green ink and sealing it in a black envelope?

Yes he did.

North had no idea what time he had left. Not enough. But he wanted to do one thing before it was all over: he wanted to find Peggy Boland and ask her what she'd done that made her so damn dangerous to know.

13

A West London Hotel

A few days earlier

Honor slipped out of the function early on. She had had her fill of strangers for one night. Had enough of JP and his relentless networking of contacts over this New Army business. Frankly, JP wasn't in her good books about Peggy. He didn't even pretend to like her. He was probably delighted she'd disappeared off the radar.

Anyway, it was cooler out of the crush and she preferred the space, the marble floors, the vaulted ceiling with its ironwork, even the huddles of Middle Eastern businessmen crouched over tables too low for them.

One glanced in her direction as she passed. At the navy silk column dress with the cowl neck, the exposed back and shining blonde hair, and she smiled vaguely but didn't make eye contact. In a chair in the far distant corner, she slipped off the silver mule and slid a bare foot under her as the waiter approached. It was wasteful to pay for a drink when they were free in the function room yards away, but she ordered a glass of Pouilly-Fuissé and a black coffee.

Her slim fingers unclasped the crystal-studded clutch bag and extracted the phone, pressing Peggy's mobile number again. The call rang out as a long-stemmed glass appeared, a pot of coffee. She raised her hand in thanks to the waiter as she imagined Holst's *The Planets* ringtone blaring out in Peggy's bag. Imagined Peggy reaching, pulling the bag up onto her lap, fumbling through papers and books and scarves to answer it. But the call went to answerphone – again. "Hey, this is Peggy. Time may be infinite but speak now."

Honor frowned.

As she sensed movement, she glanced up. But it wasn't the waiter. A bearded young man in skinny jeans and a denim jacket stood by her. He moved from foot to foot as he glanced around the foyer – his eyes flicking between the tables, across to the reception with its glass bowls of spiky tropical flowers, the gold braid of the concierge, the ornate doorway through to the fundraiser. Anywhere but at her.

She was excellent with names, but it took her a second. The beard.

The fact he was in London. Out of place.

Ned Fellowes.

What did Peggy say about him? That was it. *"He's always turning up. It's downright uncanny."*

Still without meeting Honor's eye, Ned held out his hand. But when she attempted to take it, he slapped his palm against hers – once, twice – before curling his fingers into hers, then breaking away to snap them with a small click. He glanced in her direction, waiting. Normally he reserved his special handshake for Peggy. Honor clicked her thumb and middle finger, and the snap made the waiter turn and frown in their direction. She shook her head, waved him away as he started towards them, and Ned sank into the wingback chair opposite. There was a sweet smell of the deodorant meant for adolescent boys as he placed his canvas shoulder bag with due ceremony on the floor.

"Are you planning to drink that?" He pointed at the silver pot, gnawing at the bed of his devastated thumbnail as Honor poured him a coffee. She was thankful he hadn't claimed the glass of wine.

"You're a long way from home, Ned, honey."

Over the steaming cup, his nose twitched at the mention of home. His eyes were a clear amber peeping out from under his russet hair. He had waxed the tips of his moustache, she realised, the curling ends spiralling in on themselves like an old-fashioned strongman.

There was a chink as he put the cup back in its saucer. He'd drained it.

"Two hundred and eighty-three miles." He grinned at her and then looked away – the grin quick and furtive behind the beard, one front tooth lying over the edge of the other. "It took three hours and thirteen minutes. That's eleven minutes longer than the average journey. I asked the guard, whose name was Peter, and he attributed the difference to 'signalling at Peterborough'."

There was an old-fashioned ringing which got louder as he pulled his mobile from his pocket, and his train ticket fluttered to the floor.

"I'll be back tomorrow, Jess. I told you."

Honor bent to pick up the ticket, sliding it back across the table to him.

Silence.

"Leave it up there. I'll clean down the whole thing when I come in." Silence. "I know you do."

He put his phone down and shook his head as if to clear it of the distraction that was Jess, before reaching across to grip Honor's forearm.

She bit her tongue to stop herself from yelping in protest.

"Ms Jones, you're an important person."

Close up, his crossed-over teeth looked sharp and the twitching nose reminded her of a rodent.

"No." With her free hand, Honor removed Ned's hand from her forearm. He sported a thick red rubber band on his wrist, she noticed. "I'm an MP – a public servant. You're every bit as important."

"But you know the Prime Minister. You talk to her. You meet with her. You need to tell her that citizens are disappearing. She'd want to know." Ned sat forward on the edge of his chair, his hands clasping and unclasping. Long, bony fingers with bitten-down nails. "Every day. There. Gone." Ned snapped his thumb and middle finger together as he had before, and this time there was a loud, dry report like gunfire.

What had Peggy said about him? He'd been sectioned because he posed a risk to himself, not to others. Please, God, he was harmless.

Honor gestured at a passing waiter that she wanted the bill, scribbling in the air with an imaginary pen, and Ned's voice became more urgent. She took a mouthful of the flinty wine as she glanced at her watch – calculating when she could leave. Five past ten – she'd give him another five minutes. Was he having another breakdown? Should she persuade him to ring back this Jess person, and then talk to Jess herself?

Evidence compelled him to the conclusion, he said, that thirty-three citizens had disappeared. Honor could help.

She was part of the Establishment, and that was useful. It might make all the difference. He needed official protection, and he knew he could rely on her. Meanwhile, he would do everything he could to find the disappeared, and he would keep in close touch with Honor and the Prime Minister – provide them with regular reports. Oral or written, whichever they preferred.

"Trust no one, Ms Jones." His hand rose to his beard and he pulled and tugged it, glancing about. The Middle Eastern businessmen long gone. "Don't talk to anyone about this apart from me. It's not safe." He placed a memory stick in a plastic wallet on the table between them. "This explains everything."

Poor, sweet Ned. Was he down in London on his own? Did he have anywhere to sleep tonight? His family was in Newcastle. Why was he even down here?

"Ned, can I call someone for you? Jess maybe? Is Jess worried about you?"

He looked at her – stricken. There was a pause. A heartbeat. Two, before, wailing, he slammed the heel of his hand against his temple. Honor pulled at his arm, rocking the table as he struggled to hit himself again and again, and the empty wine glass crashed to the ground, smashing into a million pieces.

"Stupid Ned," he whispered. Dropping his head, curved over on himself, he rocked back and forth before his fingers went to the rubber band on his wrist. He snapped it – once, twice, three times. And again – three times. A red line appeared on his pale skin as he lifted his head to lock eyes with her.

He was calm. At peace.

The waiter hurried towards them. A brush and pan in one hand, the bill in the other, but she held up her palm to stop him coming further. The waiter glanced towards the uniformed concierge standing behind the desk, and the concierge moved out.

"I haven't made myself clear, Ms Jones. Peggy is in trouble. She's been taken. They have her. She's one of the disappeared. I should have said that at the start."

A hole opened up at the centre of Honor. In her chest cavity she could feel the pounding beat of her heart.

"Ned, Peggy is working on something and is off-grid so she can concentrate. She sent me a text."

The text leapt into Honor's mind as she picked up her bag. *"Working on something big sweetie. Need head space. Will be in touch as soon as I can. Peggyx."*

The dismissal.

Loss.

Ned's hands flapped in denial. "That's what they do." His nose twitched and his voice grew louder in the sudden quiet of the atrium. "What they say. 'I'm away'." He snapped at his band. " 'I'm on holiday'." He kept snapping. " 'There's been a bereavement in the family'. 'I'm on a deadline. Sorry to cancel'. 'Will get back to you. It might be a while'. That's 'Them'."

Finally, the band snapped, the two pieces flying in opposite directions. But Ned didn't notice. "Did you see Peggy? Did she ring you after the text? I know she didn't, because I'm telling you, Honor – she's gone."

Ned was a paranoid lunatic. Honor's heart started to race. She couldn't draw breath. Had forgotten how. She needed air. She had to get back to the reception and JP, almost stepping on the silk hem in her haste to stand. Poor Ned. He had to be off his meds.

He slid the small plastic wallet over the table towards her. Afterwards, she thought she picked it up because he used her name. For the first time. Used it as if she were a friend who owed him that much courtesy. She opened the sparkling evening bag, tossing in the wallet. Nauseous. Irritation rising hard and fast. Not at rabbity Ned with his rubber band and his twitches and his Asperger's. At bloody Peggy. Needing space to work on something big. It was the most inconsiderate thing she had ever done, because it wasn't just Honor she'd abandoned – it was everybody. It was Ned. She wanted to scream. To weep. When Peggy did make contact, Honor was going to bollock her from here to kingdom come.

14

Westminster

A little later

He was being followed. By the Embankment, Ned was convinced of it. A tiny woman in a camel coat sliding out of a doorway to trip-trap behind him, but as Ned slowed his pace, considering his options of escape, she lunged past him, almost running, into the open arms of a beaming overweight man in a pin striped suit.

He'd relaxed then. Stopping to watch the fat man lift his companion, swinging her round, the coat flying out behind her, one heel falling to the ground. The camel-coat woman picked up the shoe, leaning on the fat man to slip it onto her foot before tucking her hand into the crook of his arm. Together they walked to the river's edge. Whistling, Ned climbed the concrete steps. As his reward, he would find a Domino's and order a hot chilli beef pizza with mushrooms and smuggle it through the hotel reception to eat while he watched the news. He'd ask them to leave it uncut, because he preferred to cut it himself.

Nine identical slices. Otherwise he couldn't eat it. Yes – the trip down had been hard, but he'd done what he'd set out to do. Asked Honor Jones MP for help. Told her what was going on. Given her the memory key. She didn't believe him at first, but that was all right. He didn't expect her to. He got upset, but he calmed himself the way he'd been taught to. When he told her about Peggy, she left straight away to take action. He made the right decision talking to her. After he had eaten the ninth and final slice of pizza, he'd ring Jess. Tell her all about it.

He was still thinking about Jess when the man barged into him, knocking him against the stone wall of Westminster Bridge. Still thinking of her smile as the world turned upside down and he was falling. Still thinking about her till he stopped thinking at all.

15

London

1.55pm. Tuesday, 7th November

Settling into the tan leather seat and snapping the seatbelt into place in the silver Porsche Carrera GT, Honor ran her fingertips along the shining dashboard.

North revved the engine, whistled in appreciation, and Honor groaned.

"This isn't your car, is it? You stole it." She pulled her hand back like the dashboard burnt her.

In the scheme of everything he did before, during, or since leaving the Army, stealing a car was the least of it. She must know that.

"And you're an accessory." He glanced across at her, raising his eyebrows as they swung out from the gloom of the hospital's underground car park, up the ramp and into the heavy traffic, all without stopping or his hand leaving the ball-topped gear lever. "Plus, you are suicidal and mentally unbalanced. It was all over the news."

The hospital wasn't happy when she discharged herself

– the panicking nurses summoned a consultant. North told them he was her brother, which was the only thing stopping them from barricading the door. He was as dark as Honor was fair and twice her size – they made for an unlikely brother–sister combo, but he put his arm around her and she laid her head against his chest as if posing for a picture for the family Christmas card. *"My brother and me on suicide watch – Merry Christmas and festive greetings."*

The bow-tied consultant arrived at a trot, spluttering about psych evaluations and "systems" to put in place. Honor heard him out, asked his opinion on the new health insurance system, shook his hand and walked out anyway – North lifted his electronic key fob first. They'd passed a couple of New Army soldiers as they'd slipped out of the door the ambulances used in A&E. North couldn't prove it, but he was willing to bet they were heading for guard duty outside Honor's ward. There had to be some perks to being a major shareholder in the New Army. Even if he didn't believe a word Honor said, JP wanted journalists kept out and visitors kept to a minimum till he claimed her.

With three times the horsepower of a normal car, the Porsche could do more than two hundred miles per hour. North pressed his foot lightly against the accelerator and the racer responded immediately with a throaty roar. He was tempted to keep it. If he had to die, behind the wheel of a Porsche Carrera seemed as good a way as any. But an alert was probably out on it already. Even if the consultant didn't yet know it was missing, the Board would check the CCTV in the immediate aftermath of Honor's discharge from the ward.

No Porsche then – but he still had options. There were three cars in lock-ups around London, a turbo-charged Mini Convertible in Stoke Newington, a Jaguar XJ Supersport in Notting Hill and a V8 Range Rover in Rotherhithe. The Jaguar? Too flashy. The Mini wouldn't do. Which left the Range Rover.

Hands on the wheel, not too fast, not too slow, his eyes watching for pursuers, North did the calculations. The Board was looking for him. He was reluctant to take the job – only agreeing under pressure. They knew he didn't kill Honor – worse yet, their other operative ended up dead in her bathroom. Honor was a good talker, but it was doubtful she talked a fifteen stone goon into drowning himself and then cutting his own throat. Which meant she had help. Plus, they knew he'd found his own photograph and his own green-inked name. So the Board wasn't just looking for her. They were looking for him.

The lock-up down the cobbled alley and just off the main drag didn't look much on the outside – it didn't even merit a padlock. But in this part of London a padlock proved as much an invitation to the criminally minded as a deterrent. It did, however, possess a state-of-the-art nine-pin lock.

The pounding beat of gangsta rap started up somewhere close, the bass rumble loud enough to shake windows out of frames; cursing, North leaned in to the damp wood of the double doors, bracing himself against the puddled road for purchase. Along the alley, a figure appeared, then another, the hoodied silhouettes lit by the orange flare of flames from a metal brazier. A grinding as the doors gave, frayed and splintering hems scraping against the broken-up concrete floor and splintered glass.

On Jamaica Road, the lads gathered in the rain, readying themselves for a night of trouble ahead. North didn't know the cause. Joblessness? Anti-immigration? Islam? Anti-Islam? No one needed a reason these days.

North risked a quick look towards the end of the alley. They needed to leave before the boys got down to the serious business of burning out corner shops and lobbing bricks at riot police. As one of the lads turned his head and shouted, North pushed Honor into the darkness of the garage and half threw her into the Range Rover. Rounding the bonnet, his hand against the cold, smooth metal, in the lit-up interior behind the glass of the windscreen, Honor sat complaining at his rough handling – her mouth opening and closing. Politicians – they never knew when to shut up.

The gang appeared in force, skidding to a halt, swinging themselves around the open doors as he slid the key into the ignition and pressed the accelerator to the floor, flinging Honor back into the passenger seat, her arms spread either side of her, the youths scattered. Who doesn't like a few easy pickings? But they weren't going to get themselves run over before the fun began. In the rear-view mirror, the lads were turning their attention to the Porsche. To steal or to burn? To drive or to destroy? Everyday dilemmas for the modern delinquent. He hoped for the car's sake they would drive her, because if they did, surely they wouldn't be able to stick an oily rag into her petrol tank, light it, and watch her burn?

"You nearly killed those boys."

He fought an urge to stop the car, open the door, and push Honor out. Smiling at his irritation, she settled into her seat, angling it so that her body turned towards him, folding one bare leg under her, stretching out the other – he tried not to look. Theirs was a professional dynamic, he reminded himself, unusual but professional.

"Tell me about Ned Fellowes," he said.

"I told you."

"Did he really give you this?" He pulled the memory key out from his pocket and she snatched it from his fingers. "I didn't steal it. You dropped it when you took your early bath."

She quietened, either at the reassurance or the mention of her near-death experience. He didn't know which. He had killed a man for her. Given up his way of life, because she stood in a park and made him believe she was an innocent. Surely he was entitled to know what this was all about.

"A woman I once met told me trust cuts both ways."

He gestured to the glove compartment and she opened it. Inside was a small computer.

Her fear of letting go, her suspicion flooded him. His own face staring at her as he'd stared in the park, ugly, cold, ready to kill her. But that was then.

"How do I know this isn't some long con you're playing, North?" Her eyes were enormous in her face. "You could be using me."

"Back at you."

She studied the key in her hand. Ned's earnest face. Russet hair. *"Don't trust anyone.*

Apart from me." But he was dead.

She pushed the key into the tablet. The screen went from green to black and finally to a small box, antennae waving on top of it like an old-fashioned TV, the white Play arrow obscuring the face behind it. Honor clicked on it.

The young man's voice was scratchy. A Geordie accent. North recognised him immediately – Ned Fellowes. He slowed, turning his head to avoid a roadside camera. The rain was heavy and set to get worse. According to the forecast, winds would kick in around Yorkshire and travellers were advised to stay at home unless their journeys were strictly necessary. He counted staying alive as entirely necessary.

Honor sat without moving, but on screen Ned couldn't sit still – his rabbity nose twitched every few seconds, as if he scented danger. His hand went up to his beard, which he stroked. Attempting to self-sooth, North judged.

"To my certain knowledge, Ms Jones, thirty-three people are missing."

North grimaced and the young man twitched furiously as if sensing his scepticism.

"I say thirty-three because I have proof of it, and I include, of course, our mutual friend Peggy Boland. I suspect, however, there are more." The nose twitched again. "I know for a fact Peggy is missing, because I was across her emails and, indeed, all communications."

Ned did not appear embarrassed at this confession. As far as he was concerned, this was objective evidence in his case.

"Dr Boland had no plans to travel. Indeed, she had fifty-one commitments, including teaching, research and social events that she failed to honour on, or after, the ninth of October. Among them a doctor's appointment and a dental check-up, four choir rehearsals and a trip to the theatre. She offered no explanation, gave no notice, sent no apologies."

Honor's finger pressed pause, and Ned's rodent face stalled.

"He was stalking her."

"I got that," North said.

As if he heard them, Ned leaned in towards the camera.

"Dr Boland is my friend. Friendship is a responsibility I take seriously, as I know you do, Ms Jones, which is why I hope you'll understand. Why you won't think badly of me.

"Three weeks ago, Peggy's email password changed. Indeed, all her passwords changed. Peggy hasn't changed her password for two years, four months and six days. Naturally, I wondered why she'd do such a thing, and it occurred to me Peggy had found out I'd taken what she might regard as too close an interest. When I attempted to make contact with her to explain, I was told she'd left the country. This struck me as – unlikely. Peggy's absence..." He hesitated as if reluctant to say the word. "...disturbed me. Lowered my mood. Doctors tell me in these circumstances that I have to take action to bring myself round rather than become 'overwhelmed'. The action I decided to take was to find Dr Boland."

"He should have gone out and got drunk," North said.

But Honor's attention was fixed on the screen.

"This is no longer an analogue world, Ms Jones. We're connected. Absence is noted. Felt. But we don't search the streets. We don't ask God. We search the net because that's where the answers are. The truth.

"I went into the latest social media data dump. Normally there's a delay of years, but I hit lucky – this dump was immediately after the hack."

It was North's turn to press pause.

"I checked it out," Honor said, and North remembered that she must have watched the video before. That none of this was new to her, only to him. "When hackers breach security, they can dump all the usernames and passwords out there for anyone to see. But the companies have 'hashed them'. They've converted the passwords to a string of letters and numbers and symbols which the hackers have to break to get to the personal info. Sometimes the hackers can't break them and they can't sell them, or they're making a point about what they can do, so they leave them out there for all comers."

On screen, Ned was talking again.

"Peggy was there in the dump. It was a big one – thirty million users. I identified her from her username, which is her email."

He held up a piece of paper between both hands. On it was a line of characters, numbers and symbols written in black marker.

"This is Peggy's new password. I can't break it, but that's irrelevant."

He let go of the paper and leaned in to the camera so closely his breath fogged the screen.

"It is also the password for thirty-two other people within the dump. The chances of two people sharing the same hashed password of twenty-three characters is less than one in ten to the forty-six. That's less than one in ten septillions. That's less than one in a thousand million." Ned counts them off on his fingers, "million million million million million million million. That is to say, it's never going to happen. And this is thirty-three people. Not two."

North pressed pause. "This guy was a barman?"

"He used to be Peggy's student, but his brain blew."

"I can see how that would happen."

Ned was still talking: "Furthermore, twenty-five of them with any kind of on-going social media presence had all signed off from the real world in broadly the same ways – an extended holiday, sickness in the family, bereavement, a new job."

Ned held up a snap of two freckled identical girls. Leaning in to each other, they looked as if they were trying hard not to laugh as they pouted, their eyes huge with winged eyeliner and their hair draped over their shoulders. It reminded him of the photo of Peggy and Honor he'd seen on her fridge door.

"Emily and Gemma Dolan from North London. They're seventeen-year-old twins. Studying for A-levels. Their entire lives are online. Friends expressed concern that the girls had disappeared from their social networks. One week later, a message goes out that the girls are in Bali. But no photos. No updates. Emily and Gemma Dolan – each with the same hashed password as each other and as Peggy. Or, Bunty Moss from Surrey." The photo held close to the camera was of a smiling older woman with a strong jaw. Her bobbed hair white and perfectly cut. "A retired ward sister, and Captain of Ladies' Golf, she sent out a general message with apologies days from a big tournament. Sickness in the family. She'd be in touch in due time. The same hashed password. Anthony Walsh, eighty-three, a retired union official, went missing in the Peak District. The exact same day his password was changed."

Honor's face was set. North took time to glance at her. Ned chose his words with consideration.

"Their closest family believe or purport to believe these explanations, and there are no ongoing police investigations into these disappearances." He isn't surprised, as if he doesn't expect much of the police and has yet to be disappointed.

The picture shifted, chopped off Ned's head, as the camera filming him shifted. There was noise and movement and skinny fingers as Ned settled it back on the laptop.

"Sorry," he said, grinning somewhere behind the beard – young and vulnerable, not at all like he was going to be dead within a matter of hours.

What did Honor say at Portcullis House – North tried to remember – that she hadn't believed Ned? Had she let it show? Had he gone to his grave disappointed? In her? In himself?

"One last thing, Honor. Do you mind if I call you Honor? You did once tell me it would be all right and it's how I always think of you. On no account search these names on the net. There'll be an alert out on them. Whoever is behind this, you don't want them knowing you're looking. Okay? Don't write anything down. And if anything happens to me, if I disappear…" He shook his head in denial at the prospect, but North knew that Ned believed it might, "tell my mum and Jess I love them, and you need to run. I'm telling you that when we meet, but I mean it. Don't trust anyone."

He smiled, one front tooth crossing over the other.

"Apart from me."

And this time there was shyness around the eyes. He was excited at the predicament he found himself in, North thought. Excited at the prospect of meeting Honor face to face again. Of finding Peggy and being a hero.

The video crashed to black and faces filled the screen. Men, women, children, all ages.

Names and addresses. Photos. Job descriptions. A jumble of the retired, professionals, students and babies. Sixty-three-year-old Bunty Moss, teenage twins Emily and Gemma Dolan. Eighty-three-year-old Anthony Walsh – a union leader. Jasmine Ramesh. Richard Patterson. Alex Hill. Angela Baxter. Marmaduke Pennington-Ward. Johnnie Cooper. Maisie Trumpton. Julia Morgan. It went on. Both sexes. All ages. All ethnicities. The names meant nothing to North.

It didn't make sense. Whatever this was, the Board was involved. Honor was a target because she was looking for Peggy, and if Ned were right then Peggy wasn't the only one to disappear lately. But why Peggy? And why these others – some of them children? The Board guarded the integrity of the state. North knew the Board would take action – even drastic action against individuals – if they judged it necessary, but at first sight these "disappeared" seemed downright ordinary.

Honor switched off the machine and turned her head to stare out of the window. The sound of rubber against wet tarmac.

"Is he right?" She turned back to face him. "Or crazy?"

"Both? Neither?"

He couldn't tell her the truth. That if Ned were right, that was bad news for Peggy, because it meant this was deeper and more complex than he'd thought at first, and Peggy would be all the harder to find.

"What do we do? Do we start looking for these other people?"

"She's still the best way into this."

He glanced across. Honor's body had quietened again. Holding itself ready for flight, but there was nowhere to go. They were trapped in a car, travelling faster than they should be, as far away from London as they could get.

"Are your parents alive, North?"

He was silent, but she didn't wait for an answer.

"Mine died when I was young."

He was cold suddenly. And frightened. Staring out of Honor's eyes into a bedroom with a locked door. The handle turning. The door rattling as whoever was on the other side threw themselves against it over and over. Yelling Honor's name. Shouting at her to come out. Or else.

A horn blared behind him. The car was drifting over the line into the other carriageway. He swung the wheel. A lorry driver wagging his head, mouthing obscenities as he overtook, keeping the flat of his hand pressed against the horn – spray from the wheels thundering against the glass and metal.

Did it happen? Was that true? Or was he constructing a narrative for her based on little more than guesswork and what he'd read when he researched her? She'd said she had personal experience of domestic violence when she was a child, hadn't she? He gripped the wheel, steering himself back to the certainties of the present.

Slipping back again. Struggling to stay focused on the fog lights of the lorry in front.

But it was no good.

Worse than the shouting was when the man's voice dropped. Soft, coaxing. Telling her Daddy wasn't angry. To come out. That her mother needed her. Couldn't she hear her mother calling her? She was to come out like a good girl and do as her father told her.

He dragged himself back to reality. At this rate, he was going to do Tarn a favour and kill them both in a car smash.

He should ask her what happened. And know for certain and all time whether the bullet had added something to his cognitive function or taken away his power of rational thought.

But if he did that, she too would know. She would know he had a skill no one would want, and that she had no privacy or hope of it. That he belonged in a laboratory where white-coated scientists would use him up like one of their pink-eyed rats. Or that he belonged in an asylum for the criminally insane.

Either which way, she would know he was less than the sane, normal, everyday assassin he tried to be.

He chose discretion.

Fact: Honor Jones had strangers chasing her wanting her dead.

If he weren't mad, if he were right, someone wanting her dead wasn't a new experience for her. She'd known terror before, but she wasn't ready to admit it.

"JP wanted to take me in, but I refused. I moved in with a cousin of my mother's but she was old and sick, already dying really. At sixteen, she paid for me to go away to school. I can't say I made friends, which was on me, not the other girls. I was a neurotic, toxic mess. When my cousin finally died, she left me enough to cover the end of school. No one knew. I didn't tell them – I'd had enough of other people's pity. Holidays I'd spend alone in a scummy hotel in some dying seaside resort eking out the money. I'd dress up so I was old enough to pass as a grown-up and sleep with waiters. There was no one to care who I was or what I did. And I did a lot. Until Peggy." Her sigh was loud but she didn't appear to notice.

"Peggy 'fixed' me. That's what she does – fixes what's broken."

He had a lot that needed fixing. Too big a job even for Peggy Boland. "What's she working on? Is it something that would get her dead?"

"I honestly can't see why." Honor frowned. "She's an astronomer. She's involved in setting up something called the SKA – the Square Kilometre Array – which is going to be the world's largest telescope. It's not literally one big telescope. There's an 'array' of antennae – hundreds and hundreds of dishes in South Africa and a million dipoles, which look like TV aerials, as well as some dishes in Australia. They're linked by optical-fibre cabling."

"And what will the SKA do?"

"Detect radio signals billions of light years away. Tell us how the universe was formed. Whether Einstein's theory of relativity was correct. What dark matter is."

"What is it?"

"I'm not Brian Cox."

He slid a finger round his collar. Dipoles. Relativity. Dark matter. He had the growing sense that he wasn't the best qualified person to be having this conversation.

"She wouldn't have walked away from it." Honor was adamant. "I don't pretend to understand all of it, but she keeps it simple for me and it's her life so I keep up as best I can. I know this much. The signals from space are really weak."

North could understand that much, although his temples felt tight.

"And there's two problems. One is handling the sheer amount of data the SKA will bring in. But Peggy was more interested in the other problem, which is cutting the interference coming out from Earth so that you can hear the cosmic signals better. It's not like she's developing biological weapons."

Honor maintained her friend was a genius. North didn't know much about geniuses. But he imagined they could get themselves into a mess like anyone else. Bigger maybe. The wrong decision. The wrong turn, and whosoever you were, life got shunted off course all too easily.

"The SKA operates from Jodrell Bank and the team there were the first ones I rang, in case she said anything to them about moving abroad, but she didn't. Peggy and I talk – all the time. It doesn't matter she's there," Honor gestured with her hand, to outside the car, up the road, "and I'm here. It's like she's in the room next door and I only have to raise my voice and she'll reply. There's been nothing from her for three weeks."

"You must have been making a lot of fuss for me to have been brought in." "Brought in" to kill you, he meant. She raised an eyebrow but didn't comment.

"I kept calling her mobile but there was no response. Her office number rang out. The home number was dead from the get-go. I rang the university and they stonewalled. Then Ned cornered me, and I got a bad feeling about it. The next morning, when I found out he'd 'jumped off a bridge', I panicked and got on a train to Newcastle."

North felt the desolation as Honor went back to staring out of the car window. A carriage window of a train – the world moving faster and faster while she sat still.

16

Newcastle Upon Tyne

A few days earlier

Honor's phone rang just as she was about to knock on Peggy's front door.

The Whips' Office. Again. She let it go to answerphone, and three seconds later it buzzed with a text.

"You missed the vote so you'd better be dead. Where on earth are you Honor? Ring in. NOW or yesterday."

If she called, she could explain. But whatever the explanation, the Whips would tell her to get back, and she was hardly caught in traffic on the Embankment. She was in Newcastle upon Tyne nearly three hundred miles from any place she should be. She typed, "Sorry. Family emergency. Back tomorrow."

The Whips had to be furious. She tried to care.

As she shoved the phone back into her coat pocket, she shuddered at the thought of Ned's death, of his warning that Peggy was in trouble. It was no use thinking about Ned

– what she had or hadn't done. He was gone. She had to focus on Peggy.

The lace curtain upstairs twitched, and a still, small hope ignited that it was all a mix-up. Peggy would be astonished to see her when she opened the door. Contrite. Over a glass of red wine, they would mourn poor, deluded Ned together.

Even so, Honor kept up the knocking, and the door opened a crack. The chain on it.

Whoever had opened it was standing too far back to make out.

She smiled into the gloom. Peggy's houseguests were called Rahim and Sonja, she reminded herself. They had two children and they were refugees from a Syrian–Turkish border camp.

"Is Peggy home? I'm a friend of hers."

Rahim opened the door just wide enough for Honor to slide through, before slamming it again behind her.

Peggy took in the family two months ago and the house smelled different already. Instead of lemons and fresh linen, the air was altogether richer and warmer – cumin and cinnamon and roasted chicken in there somewhere.

"No Peggy. No here," Rahim said, shaking his head.

He was in his early forties. Spectacles. Dark-skinned and slight. In the doorway of the kitchen, a woman who must be Sonja broke off from washing up. She started nodding, as if she'd been expecting Honor, waving sudsy hands at Rahim to take their guest through to the lounge.

Peggy's books were piled two deep on the shelves. More books stacked horizontally in the space between the books and the shelf above, which carried Peggy's old, battered board games of Monopoly, Scrabble and Risk. Rahim went straight to the middle shelf.

The purse he handed to Honor was a burgundy embossed crocodile Mulberry.

Inside were Peggy's credit cards, her driving licence, her departmental ID and £80 in cash, along with a crumpled receipt. Slippers. Knickers. Socks. Vests. Trousers. Jumpers. Coats: £238. Peggy had gone shopping for the kids in town. But wherever she went, she was without any means to draw cash or prove who she was.

Rahim's eyes were on Honor's face. He didn't like the fact Peggy left her purse behind.

Crumpling the receipt in her hand, Honor took out the £80 and placed it on the small table next to her. Whatever was going on, Peggy would want Rahim to have it.

She shivered as she sat back into the battered purple cord sofa, hugging herself, though the room was warm.

There was the sound of soft steps along a corridor. The smell of fresh coffee getting stronger as Sonja pushed open the door and the overhead light went on. Small, a shy half-smile. Sonja was pregnant, Honor registered somewhere in the back of her head, the other woman's belly button pushing against the thin wool jumper she wore. An old one of Peggy's, Honor realised.

Behind her mother, a twelve-year-old girl with a plait down to her waist held the hand of a toddling boy, who clutched a toy lamb. What did Peggy say the girl was called? Honor struggled to remember. Amira? The child acted as the family translator, and Peggy said her English was getting better every day.

Honor dipped her head in thanks for the coffee.

"Amira, do you or your parents know where Peggy is?"

"Dr Boland hasn't come back to the house for twenty-one days." The girl was nervous of the stranger, and formal.

"My father..." she gestured, her voice defensive, "visited the university, but they were not helpful or kind. Also, he went to the refugee council and told them, but they said it's okay we stay here. Dr Boland is happy with us. She invite us and it's official. They said she must be on holiday and we hadn't understood she was going away. But my parents are worried for her."

The mother sat cross-legged on the floor, the toddler in her lap now, his tiny hands pulling at hair under its gauzy scarf. She said something and the girl argued with her briefly.

"My mother wants to leave." Breath escaped from Amira's lips in irritation at her mother's weakness. "She says if we may stay tonight, we will leave in the morning. Early."

Honor reached across the table for the mother's hand and clasped it between her own. She could feel the bones.

"Peggy wants you and the children here, Sonja. Don't be going anywhere. She'll be back – I'm sure of it."

Sonja bowed her head and her hand slipped away from Honor, her index finger blotting tears, not allowing them to fall. The toddler's arms around her neck, his cheek against hers, and across the room Honor bit the inside of her lip till it bled.

It was Rahim who ushered her upstairs after she'd finished her coffee, as if he wanted her to see for herself that Peggy was gone.

On the landing, Honor emptied out her own pockets. Mac. Jacket. Jeans. £150. The parents were sleeping in the study, the children in the guest bedroom where she herself normally stayed. Honor pushed open the door, and left the notes on a pillow. She'd have to figure out what more she could do for the family when she got back to London.

Holding her breath, she entered Peggy's bedroom. *Please, please let her be there.*

Sweetpea!

But the room was empty.

Honor sat down on the side of the bed and there was a bark as a scrawny greyhound shot from under the bedframe, heading for the door, his frantic claws scrabbling against the floorboards.

"Jansky," Honor called, but he wasn't stopping. Her heart pounded. He was a rescue greyhound. Kept hungry so he'd run, all set for the knacker's yard when he stopped catching the hares. A neurotic bag of bones, Peggy said, but she loved him all the same. She took him everywhere. Even to work.

Peggy's office was on the third floor of a massive concrete and glass building that housed the physics department of Newcastle University. Honor knew that much from a previous visit. Ned was dead. Peggy wasn't home. But perhaps she was on a simple study trip, and perhaps her work would know all about it?

The departmental secretary seemed as good a place as any to start.

The door was open. Almost hidden behind a towering wall of paperwork, a pinch-faced woman in a knitted tabard and a matching olive-green blouse hammered at her keyboard. Smaller piles of paperwork were stacked on the adjoining windowsill, along with an ugly cactus in a chipped mug without a handle. Teetering on the edge of the desk as if considering whether to jump was a brass nameplate engraved with the words *Anne Craggs*.

Over thirteen years, Honor had never heard Peggy express dislike for anyone – with the singular exception of JP. Peggy had made it very clear she had no time for JP Armitage. The most she said about the secretary was she thought she had a *difficult home life.*

Honor attempted to channel Peggy's patience as she explained who she was and why she was there as the woman continued to type.

"Professor Boland upped and left." Sniffing, the secretary reached for a handkerchief tucked into the sleeve of her blouse, the corner just visible like the nose of a white mouse. "No notice. And a great deal of work for everybody."

Especially her, she meant.

" 'The 'department' " – the woman said it as if it were a sacred thing – "had to pull together. I was required to redraft timetables. There was – disruption."

A second, greyer handkerchief appeared and, sniffing again, Mrs Craggs mopped at her nose as it ran with clear water, before crumpling it and stuffing it back up the other sleeve.

"Do you have any idea where she's gone?" The cactus was dying, Honor noticed.

"Chile."

The secretary spat the word out. Heat. Glamour. Advancement. Exoticism. None of which could ever be hers. Honor understood the other woman's envy, but it didn't make her want to slap Mrs Craggs any less – violence flaring like a lit match tossed into a pool of petrol. Honor's own anger frightened her – making her think of her father.

Honor kept her voice relaxed. Smiled. Charming. Perhaps she could see the letter of resignation?

Mrs Craggs moved aside a photograph frame of three weasel-faced children to paw at the stacks of paperwork on her desk. Slid open a drawer full of sinus medication and chocolate wrappers. Closed it again. She didn't think so. That would be against departmental policy. Sniffing, she offered Honor the suspicion of a smirk and Honor fought the temptation to embrace her genetic heritage, take hold of the letter opener on the desk and stab her to death.

But she had come for more than Mrs Craggs.

Honor started at one end of the corridor and knocked at every door. The first four were empty.

Emeritus Professor Dr John A. Swann's door was already wide open, a frail voice instructing her to *Come right in, fear no evil* as she raised her fist to knock. Behind an immense iMac, the professor's head tilted to one side to peer at her with interest – his spine curved over into the shape of the letter C.

John Swann. *Johnny is my darling,* Peggy said once. *If he was seventy years younger, I'd marry him tomorrow. Why – how old is he?* Honor asked her. *Big Bang old,* Peggy said.

Beckoning Honor in, the tiny professor reversed away from his desk, his right hand on the gearstick of the motorised wheelchair, the arthritic fingers gnarled and set at a forty-five-degree angle.

"What an unexpected delight."

As he manoeuvred himself around the desk it was hard to see the professor's face in full, but he appeared to be beaming. Puttering to a halt in front of his desk, he reached out to close the door with a slim rubber-tipped cane.

"I have the advantage, Miss Jones, because I recognise you from the news, and because Peggy so often talks about you."

Honor blinked back at the kindness. It wouldn't do to cry. She wanted information rather than comfort.

Dr Swann raised his eyebrows and they disappeared into his dandelion hair. The position of his head gave the academic the appearance of acute shyness, as if he couldn't bring himself to look directly at the world. But Honor didn't think he missed much.

He pointed at a tub chair in the furthest corner.

"Did she forget something? She didn't need to trouble you. I'd have sent it on."

"I haven't heard from Peggy, Dr Swann." Honor sat down. The chair was low slung to give its occupant a better angle on the academic's face, she realised. "Your secretary tells me she's taken a job in Chile."

The light went out as the professor's already corrugated brow folded over and over on itself.

"Apparently so. All very spontaneous." Trying and failing to sound joyful. In his lap, one hand nursed the other as if one or both hurt. "It's selfish of me, the elderly get that way I'm afraid, but I was so sorry to see her go. Without even the chance to wish her well. I miss our morning coffees together. I even miss Jansky." He reached over to Honor – his palm warm and papery on her arm. "But lately she's seemed preoccupied. Not happy, and she's always such a positive person. I've been worried about her myself – I'm hoping the move restores her."

Anxiety shut down Honor's throat.

"Where would she go in Chile, Dr Swann?"

Behind them, the door slammed against the wall and Honor jumped.

"You always attract the glamorous visitors, Swann. They must feel sorry for you."

The speaker held out his hand and Honor stood to shake it, trying not to stare at the intruder's shining pate or notice the acrid scent of an unwashed body, or that flakes from his pink skin fell off in her grip.

"Dr Walt Bannerman. At your service, Miss Jones."

From his leer, Dr Bannerman believed himself to be a desirable man, although Honor had no idea why.

He let go of her hand with apparent reluctance, as his lashless eyes slid down her body, resting on her mouth, her breasts, beyond, and back to her breasts.

There was a buzzing noise as Swann reversed and turned his wheelchair, his colleague forced to step away from Honor or risk being run over, and the elderly don retreated behind his desk.

Bannerman made no effort to hide the fact he knew who she was. The secretary must have called him on an internal line or scuttled round to his office, sniffing all the way.

Honor disliked her even more.

"I brought you something." With some ceremony, he drew a thin wallet from his mustard-coloured tweed jacket pocket, fishing in it to pull out a scrap of card. He held it just out of her reach. Even so, Honor could read "Professor Peggy Boland" written in Peggy's angular script. The nameplate from her office door.

"I always envied Peggy her view over the city," Bannerman explained, "so when she left, I claimed it."

"Her office was virtually identical to your own," said Swann.

Bannerman ignored his colleague, but his lips thinned to nothing.

The nameplate was only a ruse, thought Honor. An excuse to be nosy. She reached for the card and he twitched it away. Incredulous, Honor glared, and, the picture of benign condescension, Bannerman brought it back within reach. Another flare of anger as she took the card from his fingers. Why had he kept it? A souvenir of Peggy?

A souvenir from her office. This oddity with his turtle nose and flaky skin was working where Peggy should be working, sitting where she should be sitting.

"What happened to her books and papers?" The question sounded abrupt, accusatory even. But Bannerman didn't take offence, merely waved his hand, and flakes of skin filled the air between them.

"Everything was picked up by courier. I boxed them myself. A personal favour." He gave a bow from his scraggy neck as if waiting for applause at the generosity of his nature.

Honor let out the breath she'd been holding. What did she think? That Peggy would have left behind directions as to where to find her?

"Did the courier say where they were going?"

Bannerman shrugged, his shoulders rising and falling against the sound of crunching bones.

Utter indifference. He looked over to his colleague behind the desk as if for affirmation. "Word is Chile. Isn't that so, John?"

The elderly professor nodded.

"It's not my field. I'm the history of science discovery. My concerns are the past rather than the future, but I did wonder if she had perhaps gone to ALMA?" Swann proffered the thought as if he didn't believe it.

Honor screwed up her face. Did Peggy know an Alma? She'd never mentioned her.

"The Atacama Large Millimeter/submillimeter Array," said Swann. "They're building it in the Atacama Desert in northern

Chile. Sixty-six high-precision antennae. She'd wanted to visit for a while."

Had she? thought Honor. Why didn't she say? They could have gone together.

Bannerman's arms wrapped themselves around his own scrawny body. Loving himself.

"Old Man Swann's in shock at the loss of his pet. One more reason to retire, old man. They must have made her a great offer. And money in UK universities is so tight these days. I do know she was struggling to pull together all the funding she needed to progress her research. Good for dear old Peggy striking out for Chile. A one-woman brain drain."

He pulled out a scrap of paper and a cheap orange biro from his pocket and scrawled something.

"Chilean universities – in case she isn't at ALMA. Give her my best when you talk to her. Swann here would get his wheels stuck in the sand, but tell her I'm open to offers."

She checked into the first hotel she came across. Cheap. Cheerful. A high street name. The greasy-faced porter leering at the single woman without luggage. She blanked him. Who cares what he thought?

Honor spent three hours emailing the three Chilean universities which Bannerman named: Universidad de Chile, Pontificia Universidad Católica de Chile, and Universidad de Concepción. She allowed herself the thought that when she found Peggy she'd catch a plane. Visit her in the desert. Drink tequila together. Then she widened the search to include Universidad de La Serena, Antofagasta, Católica del Norte, Valparaíso and Andrés Bello. Finally, she hit the phones to the people at ALMA. Nothing. No Peggy. No tequila. Only rising panic.

And later, on the lumpy mattress in the trough of strangers' bodies, her hands cradling her head, she listened to the raucous nightlife and disco beat of the bars below and opposite. Then to the departing drunks, and the hour of silence before the birds woke and the rattle and rumble of traffic started up again. She forced herself to drink a cup of tea and chew her way through the toast she'd ordered on room service. Sip. Chew. Swallow. Till it was done.

She didn't believe Peggy was in Chile.

And it was impossible to escape the fact that Ned Fellowes was dead.

She attempted to tamp down the crushing fear in her stomach, even as she vomited up the tea and toast.

It wasn't even seven when she reported Peggy missing.

17

A1

4pm. Tuesday, 7th November

The roads were busy, but he'd have liked them busier. He'd have preferred traffic to get lost in. Blaze after blaze of headlights travelling the other way, drivers keen to get home and out of the weather. London getting further and further away. Though still not far enough, fast enough, for North's liking.

"I talked to a Detective Chief Inspector Hardman. Huge. A heart attack waiting to happen," said Honor. "He seemed concerned. I liked him. At least he didn't laugh at me and tell me I was being ridiculous. He took it all down. The text she sent me. That she'd left work with no notice. The fact her purse was still at home with everything in it. And I told him about Ned.

"He wanted to know if there'd been any relationship breakdown, whether she might be escaping a negative situation, if she had mental health issues, any alcohol or drug dependency. I said no to all of it."

She wanted to trust the policeman. North felt the urge run through him. But she didn't trust Hardman. She didn't trust anyone but Peggy Boland.

"You know how many women go missing in the UK every year, North?"

Black stains covered her blue wool dress, tight against her figure. Her own dried arterial blood.

"Around 27,500 of them. Most are resolved within forty-eight hours. Ninety-nine per cent of cases are closed within a year. What if she's in the one per cent?"

He felt her sadness as she stood in the doorway of Newcastle City Centre Police Station where she'd met with Hardman. She'd closed her eyes. Willing herself to reach through the ether to Peggy. Willing Peggy to answer. Anyone could fake a resignation letter. Hardman admitted that. And time was ticking on.

"I was back in London by the time he talked to her – or someone pretending to be her. She said she was in Chile working. Miles from anywhere. A desert. Terrible line. She had rung him, but how would she know to do that? Said someone at the university got a message to her. Who? She apologised for the confusion. Implied I had no boundaries – that we'd had some catastrophic falling-out – which isn't true. Said she was sorry to hear about Ned but that he was a disturbed young man. Hardman was kind. He told me people never ceased to surprise him. That sometimes they simply walk out the door and start over – whatever heartbreak they leave behind. Told me to give it time.

"I didn't know what else to say, because if Peggy could ring a Newcastle policeman, why couldn't she ring me? It wasn't her – I know it.

"Who wants me dead, North?" Against the noise of the rain

and the engine, the back-and-forth screech of the windscreen wipers, her voice was small. "Isn't that where we start?" He kept silent. Choosing not to kill her was one thing. Defending her in extremis. Even keeping her alive. But betraying the organisation he had worked for over the last five years was something else, even if they were trying to kill him. The Board was powerful, secretive, and had been in existence for nearly five hundred years under one name or another. He'd been told its origins, its structure, and its modus operandi when he joined – secrecy was its eternal watchword. He couldn't and wouldn't betray Tarn like that.

The problem was Honor made him feel unsure. Threw out an energy which upset his coordinates. Locate the objective. Pursue the enemy up and until their surrender or conquest. She turned in her seat to watch his reaction to her question, and it came to him that she hadn't expected an answer. As a politician, she didn't expect to hear the truth, because she never told the truth.

The headlights of the oncoming traffic swept over her and away.

"Who are you working for, North?" She wasn't giving up. "Are you freelance?"

She was feeling for what he knew. Was he a mercenary? A criminal? Was this political? Was he political? An agent of the state? Licensed to kill? She was an interrogator with a Madonna's face.

North kept up with politics and current affairs out of interest and because, when he had to kill someone in the headlines, he liked to know who they were. He was a weapon of the Establishment, he knew that. Did that make him political? Or was his role purely practical? A means of human deletion, like pressing the key with the arrow which points left – editing what is already written and changing the story which is yet to come.

The silence between them filled up with her disappointment, which made it easy to hear the ringing of the dashboard phone.

When he first bought the Range Rover, he disabled the anti-theft device which would allow it to be tracked in the event of its being stolen. That would have been the first thing they thought to do. Then they'd have checked for a phone.

Green light and a harsh electronic buzzing filled the cabin. No one had the number, and the phone had never rung. But it was ringing now.

North cursed. They'd gone out through A&E where the ambulances stretcher in their passengers, moved straight through to the underground car park and were out of there within a minute and a half. But it wasn't fast enough.

He pressed the pick-up button.

"North, darling." Tarn's voice was distinct and clear as if he were in the car with them. "You've been a bad boy."

North glanced over his shoulder to check the back seat, half expecting to see Tarn, to smell cigar smoke. He thought of Bruno watching him in the mirror. The big man's hostility. North didn't know the nature of the relationship between Bruno and the judge, though he could guess. If Bruno ever got the chance, he would break every bone in North's body just to hear the snapping sound.

"Is she there?"

Honor shrank into the space between the passenger seat and the car door as North watched the road.

"The exquisite but needy Ms Jones? She needs her friend. She needs you. Take. Take. Take. Some women are like that. Don't you think?"

North wasn't worried about give and take. But if Tarn had the phone, they were tracking the car. He watched the rear-view mirror.

The black sedan was travelling three cars back, which meant two other cars were tucked in ahead. Fighting the wind, North swung out into the fast lane – a pause, and then the rearguard Mercedes S65 swung back out behind him. The driver let him get up to half a mile or so ahead on the straight road, before gaining on him again. Casual. Routine. Inconspicuous.

North moved back into the stream of traffic.

"Bring her in, darling one. Or, better yet, draw in somewhere dark and wrap your oh-so-capable hands around that pretty neck and squeeze."

Honor covered her throat as if to protect it from North's imminent attack. She'd asked him who wanted her dead. Here was her answer.

"It's not too late for you." Tarn sounded genuine.

But it was far too late. North wasn't beloved by the gods any more. He'd used up his lives. He was mortal and damned, and the gods would make him dead. Both of them – Honor and North together. He took a hand off the wheel, reaching over to reassure Honor and, instinctively, she slapped him away.

"She's using you, North." Tarn carried on. The prosecution making his argument to the court. "She doesn't trust you – how could she? You're a killer. You always were, even as a child."

There was an intake of breath from Honor.

"And don't believe that she's blameless in this." A note of impatience entered the judge's voice. "You can't trust her either. Give her up and come home to Papa."

There was silence on the other end of the phone as Tarn waited for North to speak, and it was alive and dangerous.

"You're not going to find her, North," he said, and there was regret in the soft voice. "You, above all men, should know better than to waste what time you have left."

And the line went dead.

North kept his eyes on the road but he could feel the weight of Honor's stare.

"That was him. The one who told you to kill me? He said we weren't going to find her. He knows where Peggy is. Who is he? Tell me."

He kept silent. Gripping the wheel. Ten to two.

Don't be distracted by a pretty face, Tarn said. Tarn had seen Honor's photograph, had held it in his hands before he turned it over to write her name on the back in green ink. Blown on the ink to dry it.

North couldn't tell Honor who Tarn was. Couldn't tell her about the Board. About the men he'd killed. She wouldn't understand. All he could do for her was to try and keep her alive and help her find Peggy. That had to be enough.

Later as the miles passed, her eyes fluttered, closed momentarily before she forced them open again. Had they doped her up in the hospital? Probably at least painkillers to keep the pain of the slashed wrist at bay. Or anti-anxiety medication.

"Sleep," he ordered. But she wouldn't.

Only when the winds set in around Yorkshire did she turn her back on him, draw up her knees and close her eyes. He switched on the radio for the weather update, turning down the dial so it didn't disturb her. Gale force 8 and building. That's what he needed.

What he didn't need was Tarn in his head. It was full enough.

A killer, Tarn said, *even as a child*.

Honor hadn't asked, and he hadn't offered any explanation. What could he say? That it was true? That he killed some no-mark who'd taken up with his mother? That six weeks after he was locked up his mother died of an overdose? That he wasn't there to save her? It was all too long ago, and too complicated.

A juggernaut overtook them, its load rocking as it passed. The forecaster had warned that drivers of high-sided vehicles and motorcycles risked being blown over. North held his breath, but the juggernaut made it, flashing its hazard lights in thanks as it slotted into the road ahead.

North never meant for anyone to die.

Not at first.

His mother was passed out on the sofa as the latest in a succession of her ape-like boyfriends ransacked the flat. It was the fact there was nothing worth stealing that did it, North thought afterwards. One hand clutching her grubby sweatshirt, her lover picked her up like she weighed nothing, all the better to pound her face. One punch after another. Like he was in the gym.

At thirteen, North was tall for his age, but he'd yet to fill out. He tried pulling Tony off his mother, but only after North broke a chair over the enormous back did Tony stop. Turning. *Come on then, you little fucker.* Grinning, teeth black in his head, he'd knocked North clear across the room. No, North didn't mean for anyone to die. Not at first. Not till he'd come to. Till he'd checked his mother was still breathing. Till he'd crawled into the kitchen to empty out the drawers and the cupboards. Till the hammer was in his hand and Tony staggered back downstairs. And afterwards, when it was over, no one spoke up for him. No teacher. No social worker. No one even seemed surprised.

He should tell Honor that he wasn't a man like the father who killed her mother. Not a monster. *Even as a child*. The way Tarn made it sound.

But she wasn't interested. She'd waved the unspoken words away. *I don't need to know. I don't want to know.*

He'd read the interview with her. *"Let's say I have a special interest in resilience. How children who've been the victims of domestic violence or witnessed that trauma close up are affected long term." "Is it something you have personal experience of?" "Unfortunately, that would be correct."*

They were the same. Victims. Survivors. Surely she would understand.

But she wouldn't go there. He let out a sigh. It was easier with her asleep. He wished he could do the same. Take refuge from reality. In the Army sleep was an escape from boredom or from fear. Close your eyes and will your mind under, press it down far enough till it stops struggling and oblivion comes, but he lost that skill when the bullet pierced his skull.

She stretched as she woke up, yawning, twisting around stiff wrists, turning her slender neck this way and that. It made him think of bed and sleep, of naked women in the early morning. Of squeezing her pretty neck till the breath went out of her, and going home.

"Where are we?" Confused.

She should be. More than an hour ago, he drove past the black and white road signs announcing Newcastle.

He glanced across. He was doing eighty miles per hour, yet her hand was on the car door handle as if she were considering leaping from the speeding 4x4 and out onto the dual carriageway.

"Don't panic."

"Don't make me."

"There was a photo of you and Peggy on your fridge."

She took a moment to catch up with what he was saying, to bring to mind the photograph, the day. The wind blowing their hair. Dune grasses in the background. The long walk over the sands with the wind pushing and shoving them onwards – pausing for a selfie, heads together. Hermitage Island off the north Northumberland coast.

"I checked with the Land Registry. Peggy owns something called Marlin Cottage. I have the coordinates. There's an outside chance she's holed up there. At the very least, she might have left something which tells us where she is."

He hadn't changed his speed after spotting the tail, taking the road fast but steady – fast enough for a night-time get away, steady enough for a man driving in extreme weather conditions who thought he travelled without an escort. It was time. Do or die. Without signalling, he swung right and took off down the narrow country road into the storm. Ahead of him, darkness. A roar of engine, the squeal of brakes and horns as the Mercedes cut across the A1 and set off down the narrow road in full pursuit. He checked the gun. If this didn't work there was nowhere else to go.

She saw it before he did. The road disappearing into the sea.

"You can't be serious," she said, her arms outstretched again, braced against his headrest and the window.

"Deadly."

Ahead of them Hermitage Island gleamed white and gold across the dark and choppy North Sea.

"It's only a mile," he said, attempting to sound more confident than he felt.

The lights of the Mercedes appeared at the top of the hill. The cars travelling ahead of him would take longer to make the turn.

"A mile across the sea," she was shouting. "We're in a car not a boat."

The wind blew fiercer again on the coast – the white-topped sea already across the causeway. Only the poles either side told him how far up it was – too far. He'd calculated it to the second but the wind was bringing the tide in sooner than he expected. The wooden refuge box stood on its stilts, water all around. The water at its deepest there. If he could get the car past the box, they might still make it to the other side. In his rear-view mirror, lights from the second car, then the third, showed at the top of the hill.

Crossing the causeway over to Hermitage Island on a night like tonight was madness – it was drowning weather. The sensible option would be for any pursuer to stop at the water's edge, to calculate they were heading for an island and to wait for the tide to go out and for the rain to stop before they came for them. They'd be like rats caught in the corner of a barn. As they passed the refuge box, a wave smashed against his window and Honor screamed. They weren't going to make it.

"Can you swim?" he asked her.

She swore – out loud this time as the car shifted, its front end swinging round, its tyres still on the causeway underneath the rapidly flowing water, its rear end sinking into the muddy seabed. He pushed against his door but the force of the sea kept it closed. He didn't believe in God – not for a long time, maybe never. Making a silent prayer to any god willing to listen, he pushed the button for the windows.

"Climb onto the roof," he said.

18

North Sea

8.10pm. Tuesday, 7th November

The rain was cold – the sea water colder – Honor's teeth chattering in her head before they even cleared the wash of the car. They could half swim, half wade to the refuge box – lie up till dawn and let the winds play themselves out until the tide turned. When it did, the watchers on the bank would come for them. As North calculated his options, the Range Rover drifted past, seawater rushing through the open windows, filling it, drowning and claiming it, the headlights shining as it sank beneath the black water. He'd loved that car.

Once in the box though, their pursuers knew just where to find them. They could sit it out in their own nice, dry cars and wait for dawn.

Honor made the same calculation. Kicking her feet, her arms in a clumsy crawl, she was heading away from the refuge box towards the island. If they made it to shore, they'd have a couple of hours before their pursuers managed to get hold of a boat. *If* they made it.

At the exact moment the water went over her head for the second time, he glimpsed the memory key floating on top of the waves, bobbing, accessible but out of reach. He thought about letting her drown – strands of Honor's hair drifting upwards as she sank. One last look at the memory key as it disappeared, and he dived for her under the crashing waves, his legs working ferociously. Dragging her to the surface, he swung her body behind so she lay on her back, her hair spread out in the water, and put his arm around her neck. Her pretty neck. She fought him, her hands pulling away his forearm.

"I can do it myself," she yelled, slapping him away and coughing up sea water.

In the Army, North saw men fight out of bravery, saw them die rather than be thought a coward, but this was the first time he watched as a woman refused to drown out of sheer bloody-mindedness. Most people don't know how they're going to die. North knew because the bullet in his brain would kill him. Death held no mystery, and for the first time in years, for the first time since an Afghan insurgent shot him, North realised the bullet might not have the chance to kill him, because Honor and the cosmic chaos she trailed were going to do the job first.

By the time they had crawled onto dry land, North was trembling as much as Honor. Spread-eagled on the beach, they lay with the stench of brine and rotting seaweed in their noses. For some reason he thought of evolution, of Adam and Eve gilled and fresh from the sea, and of starting over.

"You have to be the stupidest person I've ever met, and I work with idiots," Honor said, her face half covered in sand, her lips blue-black in the darkness. "Do you ever think about the consequences of your actions?"

North got to his feet, stumbled on a lichened rock, then steadied himself against the gusting wind and the horizontal rain. He checked the rucksack, attempting to keep its contents protected from the elements – but he might as well not have bothered. The money was so much as mulch. The pages of the passports running with ink, the thumbnail photographs either missing or cock-eyed. The two boxes of purple pills had been washed away. He checked his pocket – he had one final strip. The gun? Salt-water immersion wasn't ideal but the SIG would still fire – he was sure of it. He may well have been right, but the gun was gone too.

The missing gun proved nothing. It did not make Honor's case for her.

He spat once, the taste of salt in his mouth. On the upside they weren't dead yet, and they only needed to walk the length of the island through the storm to get to Peggy's cottage. And, bonus – he still wore his shoes. Things could be worse. It was all in your attitude.

Honor had lost her shoes in the water, her pale feet gleamed in the light from the rind of the moon. He started walking. Behind him, under the noise of the shifting shingle and the dull roar of the sea and the gale, she cursed him. Her language was terrible.

It took less than an hour to make it across the island to the cottage which Peggy bought a year before. It was in darkness, shuttered and locked up.

North considered the noise he would make jemmying open the door – who it might bring and the distance they lived – against the racket the wind was already making. It was a solid door, heavy oak with a cast iron lock. He needed a crowbar. At the very least, a piece of metal he could use as leverage, or a heavy stone to smash the lock. He was deciding they were safe enough in terms of the noise when, with her bare foot, Honor moved a conch on the doorstep to reveal a large black key.

"You'd probably prefer to break it down," she said, sliding the key into the lock and turning it in one swift movement. "Next time, eh, Slugger?"

She stood back, her face all-kinds-of-righteous, and North lifted the cast iron latch, the wind taking the door from him and almost pushing him bodily into the room.

19

Hermitage Island

9.10pm. Tuesday, 7th November

Inside the stone-built cottage the only glimmers of light came from the top and bottom of the wooden shutters. It was colder than it was outside, though at least there was no wind. They didn't have long. The cars couldn't cross the causeway for hours yet, but if they had any sense, one team was already heading back down the coast for a boat. No boat would put out in this weather, but as soon as the storm dropped, they'd come for them. He knew that. Nothing was more certain. But the roar of the shifting sea and the gusting wind was still going strong, and getting warm and dry was the priority before any search of the place, or Tarn wouldn't have to bother shooting them because they'd die of hypothermia first.

Honor's fists were clenched and buried in her oxters – teeth chattering as she sank down onto the single bed with its quilt of grey patchwork stars. She didn't seem to care that she was making it wet.

"She's not here." Her voice was hollow. It surprised him. Although there'd been a chance of finding Peggy here, he never believed it would be that easy. Honor must have known it was unlikely – even so, she sounded desolate. Uncowed by the sea, or the freezing walk across the island, the starkness of her friend's absence in the relative comfort of the cottage hit hard.

"And the memory stick with the list of other names?"

He shook his head.

"Lost?"

He didn't bother telling her if he hadn't driven into the sea they'd both be dead in a ditch by the side of the road.

She took a deep breath. "How long have we got?"

"No one can cross the causeway till the tide goes out, and it's too rough for a boat if you've any sense. I've none at all and you've less, so we'll get dry as quickly as we can, search the cottage and then go back out into the storm."

"How? Our car's in Norway by now."

"It's an island. There'll be boats."

He wanted to reassure her. They had one advantage: Tarn's men were following them, which meant they didn't know the exact whereabouts of Peggy's cottage. They would have to comb the island for them. Even so, from the moment the winds dropped, North figured they had an hour at most.

"I'll bring in firewood and light the stove. We've got time for that," he said. "You find us dry clothes."

The cottage stood in its own stony yard alongside a falling-down timbered outbuilding that he figured Peggy used as a wood store. North pushed his way through the wind, the oak door of the cottage banging good riddance behind him, back out into the elements and wrenched open the shed door, before throwing himself bodily inside and pulling it shut after him.

The good news was there was diesel in battered cans sitting on the plank floor and what looked like a broken-apart lobster pot. Did she catch her own lobsters when she was here? Or perhaps she let a local use the outhouse and moor up on her dock. He hoped so. He said it was an island and there would be a boat – in reality he had no idea. He pulled out a rusting metal bar from behind the cans. He'd have preferred a gun but he was prepared to improvise.

The outhouse was a wreck, but its roof was sound enough and the wood was dry, which was what mattered. From the tiny, cobwebbed window North watched the sky and prayed for the storm to be long and vicious. One row after another he pulled out the logs. Nothing between them. Nothing behind. With his foot he kicked over a can of diesel, watching it run under the door and across the yard, oily and slick under the rain. Having salvaged what he needed for the stove, he used the second can to damp down the tumbled wood from what was left of the log store. Nobody ever died from being over-prepared.

The hen only rose from the straw piled in the corner at the very last – a flurry of feathers and squawking that put the fear of God into him. But where there was a hen, it was worth looking for an egg. He found three.

Sodden and even more wretched, by the time he came back in, Honor had dragged a Second World War tin trunk out from under the bed and changed into an outsized gansey, its sleeves rolled up, and a pair of jeans tucked into fishermen's socks, which she'd turned over the raw edges of an outsized pair of rubber boots. Another woman would have looked ridiculous, Honor Jones was killing it. Careful not to stare, he placed the eggs in the cottage's only saucepan on the cottage's only shelf. He was hungry now he thought about it. Starving. The chicken was lucky he didn't wring its neck.

"They're Christie's – her dad." Across from him, Honor pointed at the Aran jumper and a threadbare pair of dark cords she'd laid out for him on the trunk lid. "He was a big bastard too so they should fit."

Big bastard. She'd said it fondly. She must have met Christie. Known him.

He turned over the words in his head as he pulled off his wet clothes, making sure to transfer the strip of purple pills. They were sealed. Honor was filling a kettle by the sink. Keeping busy so as not to see his nakedness, she unhooked the shutters and pushed them apart. North decided to believe she was warming to him.

The clothes weren't a bad fit. The sleeves a little short in the arm, but the cords buttoned, and they were at least dry.

"We smell of cedar," Honor said, wrinkling her nose, but it wasn't a complaint. Him and Her. Together. Both of them smelling of cedar.

There was a flint and dried moss, and skinny kindling in a wooden crate by the stove. The spark caught on the third attempt and the flame flickered as it decided whether to go out or burn. North blew on the tumbleweed of moss, willing it into life, till, against its better judgement, it caught and he could feed it twigs and kindling and the smallest logs he had.

With a fire going and the winds pushing against the walls, the cottage was simple but cosier than he'd first thought, with a back-and-forth rocking chair set by the hearth and a three-legged stool alongside. He surveyed the room. If you wanted to hide something of great value, where would you stash it?

In a cupboard? Under the bed? Under a floorboard? He'd already pulled apart the wood store. This was a one-room cottage with a stone floor and a front door to the yard and a narrow back door out to the lean-to netty and the beach. The search wasn't going to take long.

"What are we looking for?" asked Honor.

He shrugged. The art of looking was deciding what needed to be found.

The trunk was empty since they were wearing all of Peggy's spare clothing.

The cupboard under the butler sink was empty and the three drawers next to it held nothing but a couple of tea towels, a wooden spoon, a whisk, and a pair of ancient lobster crackers. A bottle of Glenmorangie whisky stood on the window sill with the solitary glass, along with half a dozen tins of soup and baked beans, a percolator and a tin of ground coffee, and that was it.

He pulled out a drawer in the battered kitchen table – one enamel plate, one bowl, fork, knife and spoon, and one mug.

"She doesn't bring anyone here," said Honor. "Even I've only been once when she bought it. When Christie died, he left her enough for this place. He'd been putting a bit by every week to leave her something. She cried when she was telling me. I tried to cheer her up by telling her that I had a runaway place too, because JP had just bought a mews in Edward Place, close by Harrods. So that we could play house without the relationship getting into the press. She said I was the only person she knew who'd have a holiday cottage in Knightsbridge with a billionaire." She looked downcast, perhaps at the thought of Peggy, or perhaps because JP wouldn't want to play house with her ever again.

It was hard to feel sympathy.

The cottage was basic but solid. The only thing out of place was the enormous telescope set up at the rear window, its barrel tilted upwards. North pushed open the shutter and sat on the stool, his eye to the eyepiece, a little further away, closer, and the night sky came into focus. A half moon, almost obscured by the dark scudding clouds of the storm, but shudderingly near. What it would be like to sit alone night after night by the stove watching the moon wax and wane, charting stars which died thousands of years ago? Did Peggy have a better perspective on her own mortality? Did she realise her insignificance? Accept it? Fight it? Did it overwhelm or comfort her?

He stood up from the stool. Wherever Peggy was, she wasn't on the moon, he knew that much. Whatever clues she had left to her disappearance, if indeed she had left any, were here on Earth. Hauling the mattress from the bed, he slid a knife into it again and again, feeling with the tip for something, anything, the same way as in another life he felt for an artery or an organ.

Honor watched.

"If I'd called the police," she said, "last night when you were outside my flat, what would have happened?"

Before the first blare of sirens, he would have faded into nothingness. As the blue light washed out the doorway where he stood through the night, the only thing it would have revealed was emptiness, broken tiles and cobwebbed corners. Then with the policemen's reassurances still hanging in the cold night air, and the red tail lights of the squad car moving off and away into the distance, he'd have faded right back into focus again. Press play and fast forward to her certain death.

He wouldn't lie to her. "I'd have killed you."

"How?"

Honor leaned against the rocking chair and it swayed with her weight, its runners making a small click against the stone floor as it went back, a louder click as it came forwards. Seeing through the feathers and the motes of wool between them to his hand around the grip, the blade, to the gaping sliced-apart mattress.

He would have used the knife he held. She didn't need his confession, because she understood.

Amid the ruination of the cottage, Honor spooned out scrambled eggs, yellow clumps falling from an aluminium pan onto the orange beans and cold corned beef. His in the bowl. Hers on the plate. She sipped the coffee with its shot of whisky, her elbows resting on the table, her hair tousled. Raising her arms, she re-knotted a red-spotted handkerchief around it, and darkness bloomed at the heart of a white bandage cuffing her wrist. This morning she'd almost died. Twice. And when he drove into the sea, he almost drowned her again. She was as hard to kill as he was.

"What did he mean? The voice in the car." Her attention snagged again on the ripped cotton cover of the mattress, the rusty springs. "That you should know better than to waste time?"

Tarn's words were designed to sow dissension and fear. The judge branded North a ruthless killer who lacked all conscience. Yet Honor had picked up on the throwaway remark about the time he had left.

Talking about it, acknowledging his wound, admitting his mortality, made him vulnerable. It was enough to live with it – he didn't need to talk about it. When he went to his Harley

Street appointments, he kept his eyes fixed ahead as if he were back in the Army, barely glancing at the neurologist. Barely answering the questions. Yes, he was fine. Yes, he had headaches. Yes, he had insomnia. He refused to talk about the voices or the pictures that came into his head. No, nothing bothered him. If he said he was fine often enough, one morning it might turn out to be true.

But she was waiting.

"Five years ago, an enemy sniper had a good day. It was a headshot."

Said out loud it was brutal. As if he'd slapped her. Should he tell her the bullet was still in there? Should he tell her without the purple pills he wasn't sure he could manage to stay sane – that his mind might fly apart into so many pieces? No, he wouldn't put that on her when she was relying on him to find Peggy and to keep her safe. She didn't need every last detail.

Her face was pale. Was she pale before? He hadn't noticed. Her eyes went to his face, searching it, up to his temple, along his skull to the white flare of hair covering over his bullet wound. Across the table, he felt her cool, slim fingers rake his scalp, looking for the ridge of a scar. If she looked long enough, she'd find it. Then again, didn't everyone carry scars? Didn't she?

"How did it happen?"

Honor was a civilian – he could tell her a story of bravery. That's what the citation said and there was a ribboned medal to prove it, its silk in pretty stripes. But it wasn't a story of bravery, it was a story of survival. They were on patrol – the day before they were due home. He was bringing up the rear when Jacko stepped on the first mine – the noise and dirt as it blew him apart, flinging him up in the air, tossing him through space, North's ears bleeding, dazed, men all around him that he'd fought with, eaten and slept alongside – men in pieces. The lifeless twenty-two-year-old Second Lieutenant, fresh out of Sandhurst. North taking over, calling it in, demanding air support, moving towards Jacko, desperate to reach him, watching for disturbed earth that hid other mines, copper wire snaking through the sand, certain that any moment another explosion would lift him up into the sky, towards the sun, only to fall down to the ground again – dead and broken. He thought he'd made it, that he was safe as they loaded Jacko onto the Merlin. But he wasn't. The sniper was in no hurry. Lined up North's helmet in his sights. Eased back the trigger. And fired.

If the air had stirred. If the sniper had only missed. If North had only moved. He'd be whole, or he'd be dead. But the sniper didn't miss and the Merlin took North too.

The bullet that passed through his helmet and his skull and the soft grey matter of his brain made him different from other men. He was going to die and he knew it. The fact was unavoidable and he lived with that knowledge. Faced it down. And lived anyway, as best he could. Most people denied the truth of how they would end and ran from death as fast and as far as they could. He didn't judge. If he could run, he'd run too. But it wasn't a war story to be bandied around a camp fire. "Have you heard the one about the soldier with the bullet in his head who didn't have the sense to lie down and die?"

"What does it matter? I got unlucky, then I got lucky again."

Rebuked, Honor sat back against the spindles of the rocking chair, and behind her the long hand of the clock jerked towards the half hour.

"Why aren't you dead?"

The question was pitiless. Honor's brows drew together as if she were trying to figure him out, and North's hand went to his jaw and he rubbed it hard. How often had he asked himself that question?

"The sniper was a craftsman. He cast his own bullets." North swallowed. If he started talking, there was a chance he wouldn't stop. "It's small and it didn't expand or break up, didn't ricochet. It stayed in the same hemisphere and didn't cross over. A one-in-a-million point of entry and pathway through the grey matter. The surgeons wrote a paper with a lot of long words – it said I was a 'scientific anomaly'. I figure it meant they'd no idea."

"Are you different?"

It took him a second to process that she wasn't asking about the migraines or insomnia, which she knew nothing about, or whether he retained full use of his limbs, or whether his memory was intact. She certainly wasn't checking on the state of his intuition, or indeed the extent of his delusions. She meant did the bullet make him a killer, because she was deciding if there were an excuse for what he did and the lives he had taken. There was even a term for it. He had come across it in his own research. If he were psychotic, the most telling symptom was deemed "lack of insight". Those suffering from this lack of insight had no awareness their behaviour was unusual. Like killing on the orders of another man.

He didn't want to go there.

There were no excuses, and he wasn't wasting anyone's time pretending. "I'm the same as I ever was."

Give or take his suspicion that the bullet might have triggered psychosis and tipped him into lunacy.

Across the table, Honor frowned.

She wanted an excuse to explain away his violence, but he

didn't believe in excuses. She didn't have to trust him or like him. He didn't need to hear what went on in her head because how she felt was written all over her face. She was pleased he wasn't justifying his violence because deep down she believed there was no excuse for what he did.

His head pounding. Nauseous – the smell of eggs turning his stomach. To Honor Jones he would always be the man who came to kill her. An executioner. Was she right? Is that who he was? All he was? An executioner?

Moreover, an executioner outside the rule of law? Which made him a murderer?

The hairs on the skin of his arms stood at attention, his spoon shrieked as it sawed through the yellow egg to scrape against the side of the bowl. He liked things clear cut – good and bad, friends and enemies, good men to die for and bad men to kill. There were worse philosophies to live by. If someone else had opened that envelope with that photograph in it. With her name. Or if she never lit that cigarette to wait for him – daring him to do his worst, it would all be over. Instead of being stranded in the wilderness, he would be home. If Honor Jones had put her own survival first instead of walking into a minefield for the sake of her friend. If she hadn't asked him that question: *Where's Peggy?*

She stopped chewing, pushing a mountain of egg with deliberation towards the turned-about fork, packing it on, piling it neatly, patting it down. He waited.

"I want to trust you, North, and I wish you weren't one of them." She put down the knife with a clatter, turned over the fork, eggs everywhere again, her voice louder. "But you are."

"...*Helicopter*..." He heard her unspoken alarm a split second before the ferocious clattering of the blades.

20

Through the thick, wavy glass of the window over the sink, the helicopter's brilliant spots swept the broken ground as it attempted to find a sure footing. It was almost down. North slammed and barred the shutters. Pushing Honor through a narrow wooden door in the far corner of the room, he grabbed for the rucksack as he shoved the table onto its side to slam it hard up against the front door – the tin crockery bouncing across the stone-paved floor, coffee everywhere. Even a minute's delay was worth having.

Ahead, Honor was already scrambling helter-skelter down the dunes, slipping and sliding over the slimy rocks. Outside it was still gusting and dark, the moonlight skinny and the trees bending and bucking in the wind. The rain had all but stopped. Even so, no commercial pilot in his right mind would agree to fly.

He caught up with her. Holding her back by her forearm, speaking directly into her ear, blonde hair over his mouth, the wind ripping away his words. "Find a boat for us if you can. If you can't, hide, and don't come out whatever happens."

She started to protest but he didn't have time to hear her out.

"If I'm not there in three minutes – leave. If there's no boat, keep to the rocks and work your way round the island till you get to a settlement. Then make as much noise as you can. Bang on doors. Shout blue murder. This lot will want to pull out before it's light and they won't want any fuss."

"Stay with me, North."

"Three minutes."

Head down, she turned away and he gave her a push to get her going.

The house itself blocked the view of the helicopter's crew. The chopper's engine shifted, amid the whoomph and clatter of the blades – a roar, and then a whine. Down. Two minutes at the most before its passengers leapt from its belly, hit the ground and headed for the cottage. Thirty seconds before they shot their way through the front door. Thirty-one seconds before they worked out their targets had gone out the back and they followed.

Keeping to the shadows cast by the dunes, North strained to hear voices. If he heard voices, he would know where they were. But there was only the wind, the EC130 motor and the noise of boots against the ground. Rocking, the helicopter was down, the pilot still in his seat, the massive blades slowing. North kept low. The blades stopped turning. Their attackers' focus was the cottage – a thin spiral of smoke coming out of its chimney, light behind the shutters like something from a fairy tale.

North counted five men including the pilot.

The first assailant was at the front door. He gestured to two of the men to go round the back, one each way.

North felt for the iron bar he'd left propped against the

woodshed door. Finding splinters, rusty nails, stretching his fingers, straining for the length of metal. His fingertips grazed it, felt the air shift as the bar started to fall – catching hold just before it hit the ground.

The first assailant was broad-shouldered and enormous in the dark. Something about the set of his slab-like head. Bruno. His boot was raised to kick in the door.

They'd left only the pilot behind with the helicopter. North backed up, circling the helicopter, coming up behind it in a swift, straight line. Praying Bruno's attention was fixed on the door. Praying that the pilot didn't decide to turn the engine back on for a swift getaway. As the sole of Bruno's boot landed against the door with a splintering crash, North thrust the metal bar up through the enclosed tail fan with his full strength, wrenching it till the bar caught. There was a shout from the glass cockpit as the pilot glimpsed him in the mirror. North came out from behind the tail. The pilot was out, his door swinging open, a gun already in his hand. North slammed his fist into the other man's jaw, spinning him round to catch his throat with his forearm, one hand over his mouth. The pilot's legs danced and North braced as he took the full weight of the struggling man in his arms. He felt the gun fall, heard it bounce into the darkness. There was a choking sound. The agonized terror and scramble of dying. The heart's frantic beat. A gurgling as North squeezed harder, the cartilage of the throat collapsing. Hope gone. The losing fight for air. Knowing. The last pump of blood, as all breath went out of the dying man.

Inside the cottage, the helicopter team were shouting. North couldn't make out the words. Half would follow out the back and, if they were well trained, the others would go out the front.

North dragged the corpse as far into the shadows as he could. Bruno would know the missing pilot was dead, but North didn't want him finding the body anywhere near the tail of the helicopter.

With the edge of the rocks just visible in the moonlight, he leapt for it, his feet hitting the hard sand, his body rolling as he tumbled over the rocks. He must have looked the wrong way because at first he didn't see her, then she whistled, long and low. She'd found the boat.

His feet pounding the sand, Honor was already untying the sodden, weed-shrouded rope from the mooring hammered into the concrete slip. She held the boat to the dock by the rusty metal stake. North scrambled aboard, his weight taking the boat one way and then the other, almost knocking Honor into the water, as he wrenched the cord to start the engine. It caught, then died.

North could barely make out Honor's voice over the crashing of the waves, but he understood the gesture of warning as she pointed towards the silhouette of a man who'd appeared at the ridge. Bruno's unmistakable Easter Island head. Then another. A third. All with guns.

He tried the engine again, nothing.

The first bullet hit the water – like a coin for making a wish. A sincere wish that they would both die.

He wrenched the cord, the angle different this time. Third time lucky. Fourth time dead. And the engine spluttered and caught. Bullets came thick and fast into the sea around them as he opened it up. The paintwork was cracked and battered but the engine sounded powerful enough.

The boat hit the waves with a thud, rising and then falling

back into the sea. He prayed he wasn't about to drive it straight into one of the rocks that littered the coastline hereabouts – rocks on which bigger boats than this foundered and were lost.

He turned his head to watch the men. It was dark but he made out Bruno grinning, thigh-deep in the surf, regardless of the cold and wet as his compatriots abandoned their shooting gallery, running for the dunes and the helicopter. Bruno lifted his hand, took aim and fired a make-believe gun at North. Once. Twice. He was in no hurry. North was his – sooner or later. In the meantime, Bruno was enjoying the chase – savouring the expectation of murder yet to come. *Peachy. Good enough to eat.* The boat was fast, but the helicopter was faster. North guessed it could reach one hundred and thirty knots compared to their ten. In an open sea, the boat had no chance of outrunning their attackers. North knew that, and he also knew he'd kill Honor himself before he let her fall into Bruno's hands. Quick and clean. She wouldn't know anything about it.

"Under that bench, there's something there." North had to shout to make himself heard. He looked back towards the island. Bruno was in darkness but North sensed he was moving away from the sea.

Honor leaned down, tugging, her grip slipping in the wet, holding onto the side with one hand to give her better purchase on whatever was beneath the bench.

There was the noise of ripping as the bundle came free of an unseen nail under the bench. It had caught in an ancient oilskin, ripping a chunk out of the sleeve. Honor took hold of the oilskin and pulled it away to reveal a black donkey jacket, which in turn lay over a canvas haversack. At no point did she look at him to see what he thought. North was irrelevant, he knew. Instead, she unbuckled the bag and upended the contents into her lap. It wasn't much. A heavy-duty torch. A map and a compass – the arrow swinging wildly with the motion of the boat. What did she think was going to be in there?

North reached for the map. It was the North Northumberland coastline – the rocks jagged and dangerous circled in red ink, a black cross drawn in the middle of the sea close to one of the islands.

Honor was trembling. Maybe from fear. Maybe from shock. Or maybe from disappointment. "Put it on," North instructed, pointing at the donkey jacket.

The wool cloth must have been cold because she shivered as she drew it over her shoulders, but it was at least dry. Not that she knew it but the jacket made her look younger, more carefree. North wondered if she was ever carefree. He thought not. There was £50 rolled-up in ten-pound notes – two rubber bands around the tube – in the pocket of the oilskin. He was beginning to warm to Peggy – she was a woman who thought ahead. He tucked the notes in his trouser pocket and was pulling the oilskin over the Aran jumper as Honor gasped.

The helicopter was trying to take off – the roar and whine of its straining engine carrying on the wind. North cursed whoever else could fly it. It rose and spun – its anti-torque system wrecked by the iron bar. Dipping then rising then spinning.

The helicopter disappeared from view, and a black plume of smoke rose from the shore, a billowing ball of flames from the aviation fuel; the fuel lighting up the diesel across the yard, the woodshed – then the boom hit them, the noise moving across the water like a wall. Honor watched the plume, the ball of flames, her pale face wet from the sea spray. "What did you do?" The wind whipping her voice off the boat and away to the grey and pink horizon. "Are they dead?"

North sincerely hoped their attackers were dead. He would light a candle to every saint whose name he could remember if Bruno died screaming in a blaze of fire.

But they were as far from safe as they could be.

According to the map, they were around twenty-five minutes from the nearest fishing village along the coast. In this weather it would take twice as long to get back to the mainland. He checked the compass, the coordinates, and headed for a bobbing orange floating buoy.

They needed a cover and if he were right, Peggy just provided the perfect one.

He cut the engine and the boat floated sideways on over to the buoy, the waves and wind pushing it hither and thither. "Keep an eye on the rocks – make sure we don't go too close," he told Honor as he leaned over the side of the boat into the freezing water, grabbing at the buoy and hauling up the saturated rope attached to it. With a sudden pop, the lobster pot broke from the water, black claws waving from one side and festooned with dark brown seaweed. Foaming water poured back into the sea as North steadied it on the side before heaving it into the boat. Plunging his hand into the roped and bound pot, he eased out a large lobster, its claws snapping closed as North wrapped them around with the rubber bands from the tenners. He threw the lobster in the large plastic box at the back of the boat and pushed his hands back in the other side of the pot for two large crabs.

He was about to throw the pot back in when Honor stopped him. "There's something in it," she said, her hand on his forearm.

North pushed his arm though the small gap where the lobsters crawled in, the nylon rope sleeve scratching against his skin. His fingertips touched something hard, wrapped in shredded green plastic, as if the lobster had tried to pick a fight with whatever was in there first.

They had got to it just in time he thought. Another day or two and the lobster would have won. His fingers found purchase. It was firm to the touch. Hard-edged. Perhaps some kind of box wrapped in heavy-duty plastic and tarp? More shreds fell away as he drew the package out of the pot. The refuse bags around it had been punctured and torn, but Honor took it from him before he could judge the damage. He waited. The natural thing was to open it; instead she sat with it on her lap, staring straight ahead. Her face was set. They were in Peggy's boat, using Peggy's map to find Peggy's treasure. A treasure Peggy had kept from Honor – a secret she didn't share. Honor needed time. He let her be.

He set the boat in motion again and gunned the engine.

Honor was right. Three. Two. One. Coming, ready or not. The children's game of hide the thimble played for adult stakes.

Peggy didn't hide herself, but she saw fit to hide something. In the sea, off an island, miles from home. It was dangerous or she wouldn't have hidden it. It was valuable or she wouldn't have kept it. She was supposed to recover it at some point, but she didn't. Did she keep it for insurance purposes? Or was it the reason she was in trouble? He glanced again at Honor but her face was turned to the sea. Her hair. The curve of her cheek. He couldn't read her.

He swept the boat around, its tail spinning out behind them, seething water slapping against its wooden frame, then dropped down, taking her between the islands to anchor. His instinct was to gun the boat, but it wasn't the right instinct. They had to slip back onto land like any fishing crew. Not hit land at full tilt and draw the wrong kind of attention.

They had to wait it out. And they weren't alone.

Regardless of the cutting winds and crashing waves all around, a colony of Atlantic grey seals lay fat and comfortable against the foaming water's edge. Small dark pups nuzzling their parents while braver souls flopped into the shifting, churning water. A sleek mottled seal emerged, close up and sudden against the boat, its liquid-brown eyes curious and trustful as it watched the strangers.

North looked at Honor, wanting to share the moment, but her gaze was already fixed on him.

"You don't care about anyone, do you, North? Not those men you killed. Not me." Honor's hands gripped the parcel as if she wanted to throw it back over the side and herself after it. She didn't look happy despite the fact the find proved her right. What did it tell her? That her friend kept secrets. Everyone kept secrets.

He stayed quiet. She did, after all, have a point. He didn't care about the men he just killed. He did, however, care what happened to Honor Jones.

The seal's head disappeared under the water, its shape a shadow, and then gone.

21

Northumberland

5:45am. Wednesday, 8th November

It was still dark as the boat came into the harbour at Seamouth. The storm dying away like it had never been. His hand gripping the tiller, North took it slow and steady, the diesel engine raucous in the chill of the early morning. He kept his eyes soft – there were figures on the quay, and at least one blaze of headlights. He threaded the nylon rope through the cleat at the stern before twitching the tiller to swing the boat round hard and reverse it stern-first into the quay, stepping around a hunched-over Honor, her shoulders around her ears, to drop the anchor from the bow, its splash reverberating across the churning water. Sometimes the worst course of action was to hide. The good thing about his position as he worked was the clear view it gave him of the watchers on the quayside. A police 4x4 parked against an ambulance, the police driver still at his wheel, the sergeant leaning against the bonnet, his chin tucked into the radio at his shoulder. North listened hard for the excitement, the bloodlust and scurry of predators sighting their prey, but there was only a tense waiting. He pulled on the anchor rope, the anchor catching in the muddy seabed, and the stern thumped against the harbour wall. Reaching up for a huge rusting ring set in the lichened brickwork, he hauled the boat close against the wall, tensioning first the stern line and then the anchor line. It wasn't a professional job, but from a distance it was good enough.

Honor stood up, the parcel still in her hands, and the boat rocked from side to side.

He reached out to steady her, but she batted him off.

"Let me go up, then hand me up the boxes," he said, his boots already on the first rungs of the ladder up onto the quayside. Climbing up, keeping his movement smooth. Something he did every day of his life. Come in from the sea. Climb up the ladder. Bring in the catch. If anyone wanted to take a potshot, they could shoot him first.

But there was nothing more than the screech of seagulls.

She didn't meet his eye, swinging up the plastic box he packed before they came into harbour, steadying herself in the rock and swing of the moving boat before hauling herself up the ladder, her hands one over the other, the parcel tucked in the pocket of the donkey jacket. He nudged her and they moved away from the side, standing together in the lee of a dry-docked boat, its immense hull high on its supports, paint peeling from the barnacled wood. In the shadows, North pulled the beanie lower over Honor's face and did up the buttons of her jacket. She didn't like his hands on her, but she suffered it. He stood back to admire his handiwork. Luckily, she was slight – from a distance she could be a boy. He rolled the sleeves of the oilskin up over the elbows of the Aran. He hadn't shaved. From a distance he could be a fisherman – if they made fishermen tall and wild and wary-looking.

He raised his hand in salutation to a boatman, who did as North hoped he would – raised his hand in salutation back. Look – they were regulars with friends on the quayside. They weren't strangers straggling in from the island like refugees from a fire fight.

Honor moved towards the police car, her eyes fixed on the burly sergeant – North's hand on her arm holding her back. "This has gone too far," she said. "We need to tell the police what's going on. I'm an MP – they'd have to listen." Honor was a woman who had been through enough.

He spoke slowly. "No one will believe you."

"I'll take that risk."

He blocked her, blocked the sight of her from the policemen. "Think about it. The police have to be involved for that body in your flat to disappear."

Part of him admired her innocence. The part that didn't mind dying. She shut her eyes as if the sight of him disturbed her. Opening them only as he pushed a lobster at her – its bound claws waving in fury, along with the last pot they'd pulled from the sea.

"Keep your head down," he instructed.

He didn't notice him at first, but he saw him now. Along from the police car was a black SUV – by it stood a lanky figure in a waxed brown riding coat that almost reached the floor. From a distance, the man appeared to have one eye, the other covered by old scarring, ridged and purple. And something about the way he stood as he looked out to sea made North think he had seen the man before.

Obscuring his own face, he heaved the box onto one shoulder as if it were heavy with their catch. Two more lobsters he'd lifted from other men's pots lay draped over the sides as if the box were brim-full. As if he'd worked a good night out there on the chopped-about charcoal-grey sea. Yes, he was a happy man: the money they'd fetch for him and the lad. He started whistling.

They were along the quayside as the lifeboat appeared in the gap between the harbour walls, the water slapping against the huge hull, its blue and orange colours loud in the misty dawn, the diesel engine even louder.

He heard the tutting and the groaning as they passed the florid-faced old captain sitting on a slatted bench under the harbour master's office, a stick propped against his splayed legs. The old man didn't even know he was making a noise, thought North.

"Is there a problem?" he asked. The old fisherman studied him – trawling his own memory for the younger man's name and his nets coming up empty. Not for the first time. Age was a terrible thing.

"Aye, bonny lad." Shaking his head, his rheumy eyes went back to the lifeboat, anxious not to miss the drama yet hating to watch it. "There was a car went across the causeway last night and the sea swept the driver away." He sighed again, noisily, too old not to take it personally when Death came calling. "The coastguards found the car in the early hours – the lifeboat's been out looking ever since, but the body's only just turned up."

Beside North, tucked into his shadow, Honor said nothing. Like the rest of the quayside, they turned to watch the lifeboat motor closer to the slipway. Doors to the ambulance opened the same instant as the sergeant abandoned his cigarette to rap against the window and alert his dozing colleague. They were on.

A sombre-faced coxswain stood on the deck, his crewmate hauling, exhausted, on the rope to bring the boat close in.

"Not pretty," he called up to the sergeant. "The rocks have made a mess long since."

Honor took a small gulp of breath. North found her hand and squeezed it and she shook him loose. They watched as five of the lifeboat men heaved the body bag up from the deck to shoulder-height, and into the reaching arms of the waiting policemen and paramedics.

"What if it's Peggy?" she whispered. Agonised.

From the way the police and paramedics struggled, the body was heavy, their knees bending simultaneously as they half lay, half dropped it on the ground.

"It's not Peggy," he said.

Surely it wasn't? Though he had to admit it would be a neat enough way to explain her death. Drowned crossing the causeway in a storm. And there wasn't enough luck in the world for it to be Bruno.

"Stay here," North instructed.

Honor let out a strangled yelp of protest but he ignored it. Best to see for himself.

In the blue morning light, he crossed the deserted road and onto the quay; out from cover, his skin prickled, his mouth tasting bitter as adrenalin pumped round his system. He broke step as the requiem from the onlookers gathered around the corpse washed over him. Remembered tears and a murmured chorus of "Shame" and "Waste" and "The sea, the sea". Forcing himself to carry on.

It was getting worse. The purple pills helped with the worst of the headaches. Their other advantage, which he barely admitted, even to himself, was that they smothered the worst of the voices and pictures that came into his head all unbidden. Twenty-four hours since the last pill, he was raw, scoured out and exposed to other people's pain. Or to his own.

He laid a hand on the shoulder of one of the fishermen, twisting a woolly hat round and round in huge, reddened hands – a helpless gesture of respect to the drowned or to the cold sea, North didn't know which. There were a dozen of them waiting – mostly fishermen or boatmen, a couple of divers – rubber suits pulled down around their substantial waists. The noise in his head – other men's sadness, their past losses and present fears, the coldness of their curiosity – was almost unbearable. Let it not be Peggy, he thought. For Honor's sake.

The sergeant tugged down the zipper of the bag, with his unspoken *Now then, sunshine* as gentle as if the body were that of a child.

Battered by the rocks, the face of the corpse was a pulped and crimson jelly. It was impossible to say whether death was from drowning or from injuries sustained before the body went into the water. And perhaps that was what he really wanted to know – whether it was Peggy, and whether she'd suffered. Whether she was beaten or tortured. Perhaps he wanted to know that so that he could exact vengeance. Vengeance is mine, saith the Lord. The Lord's and his. The sergeant gave another tug on the slider. Its teeth let go – the plastic canvas folding in on itself – and a torrent of pink water gushed out of the bag and onto the quayside. The mix of blood and salt water escaping onto the concrete and over the shoes and polished boots of the nearest men. A second, and the hand fell palm upwards, its little finger at a forty-five-degree angle, slapping the concrete – the sergeant scowling as his younger colleague leapt away, swearing in terror.

North stepped back, and the crowd of onlookers and emergency workers closed up the gap he left.

There was nothing to be done for the dead.

And it wasn't Peggy – Honor could relax.

But if he told her it was the young banker who lived upstairs from her, she would insist on the police. There was no mistake. A lifetime ago, North had noticed the broken finger when she'd touched the lad on the arm and walked away. The banker had been smitten. Staring after her. Perhaps he was on a day off, and came down, concerned at the to-ing and fro-ing in Honor's flat? Perhaps he disturbed them as they cleared away the corpse from her bathroom? Blood on the floor. In the bath. *What the Hell's going on? Where's Honor?* A credible witness.

Or perhaps they believed he knew where his neighbour went?

Honor would be distraught.

Judging by the lad's face, they beat him to death, making sure his teeth were in fragments, and then threw him from the helicopter some distance out at sea. They couldn't have his body found anywhere close to home. Bad luck for them that the corpse washed in. They'd have wrapped chains around his legs attached to a heavy weight, but at some point in the storm the chains unravelled and the body floated free from the muddy seabed.

North couldn't tell her.

This has gone too far. She'd tell the burly sergeant the same. It would be over for her and Peggy. The police would take her away in the back of their patrol car. She wouldn't last the day.

He shook his head to reassure Honor standing stock still by the stuccoed wall of the harbour master's office. But to any watcher, North was sad and sober at the sight of the destruction the unruly sea could wreak.

Taking his time, his head hanging, he walked back, nudging Honor into action, pulling her past the police while their attention was still fixed on the lifeboat. She was relieved, he thought. Relieved it wasn't Peggy. Relieved enough to walk past the police car.

"Who was it?" she whispered.

He shrugged. "No one important."

He risked another look at the tall figure in the riding coat – searching his brain. The one-eyed man was down by the body now – kneeling, inspecting the damage wreaked by the beating and the sea – the long face grim. Honor focused on the road ahead. Under the donkey jacket, her shoulders were hunched, her arms wrapped round the green-plastic-wrapped parcel again. And as they trudged up the harbour hill, even the lobsters stopped struggling.

It was raining hard by the time they reached the dual carriageway. The juggernaut slowed, its enormous wheels throwing up a sheet wall of filthy water and spray. North reached for the door handle and pulled it open. A fug of synthetic pine and real-man sweat blossomed from the cab. "How far are you going?" he asked.

22

Yorkshire

Ten years earlier

Peggy stood a little way from her father's grave, shaking hands with those mourners who weren't going on to the reception in the working men's club a few streets away. Her back was turned, but Honor knew she'd seen the gravediggers in the lee of the trees leaning on their spades, waiting for them to clear the graveside.

Honor hadn't gone to her own father's burial. Refused. JP was the only mourner, and she didn't even want to know where he was buried. Miles from her mother, she'd insisted. But there was a good turn out for Christie's passing. Honor walked to the lip of the grave and looked over. Sunflowers were scattered over the coffin. Peggy got up early and stripped her father's allotment and garden of every sunflower in them, and now their huge yellow-petalled faces lit up the dark down there.

One last goodbye. A final *thanks so much for coming*, and Peggy was there at her side. She slid her arm around Honor's waist and leaned in towards her, resting her head on Honor's. Lofty and Titch, Christie used to call them. Little and Large.

Honor had loved him and Peggy adored him. But they couldn't keep him. The size of a tree, over the last four months Christie had shrunk away to a bundle of twigs. Christie, who couldn't believe he'd fathered anyone as clever as his darling Peggy. *I did something right in another life*, he said in wonderment to Honor at Peggy's graduation, standing to applaud his glorious girl in his one good suit and his polished lace-up shoes. The same suit and polished shoes they buried him in.

It was quiet in the churchyard. The sound of birds. Distant traffic. Wind through the leaves of the yew tree.

"He'd put his arm around me on the back step and he'd point out the constellations. And the moon he'd save for last, and he'd say, 'That's where your mam is, Peggy lass. Looking down on us. Wave at Mam like a good girl.' It must have been so hard for him, but he never once complained."

Honor wiped away tears she hadn't realised she'd been crying with the back of her hand.

"What will I do, Honor? I'm an orphan," Peggy said, "and I've read the books. Terrible things happen to orphans."

Honor turned her friend away from the grave and slipped her arm through the crook of Peggy's elbow. She felt Peggy's resistance, the desire to stay rooted here among the dead, but she started moving anyway. Pulling her friend back into the world of the living.

"It's as well you've got me to look after you then," Honor said. "Lesson number one: write down the time you were born, which day of the week it was and your actual birthdate – somewhere you won't lose it in case you forget, or need your fortune telling. Lesson number two: never buy a cat – it will certainly eat you in your sleep or in the event of a fall. Lesson number three: never fall. It hurts. Lesson number four: drink – particularly gin, which is a consolation for orphans and is to be encouraged..."

And as the women walked together down the gravel path, the gravediggers stepped out from the shadows.

23

Newcastle

8.15am. Wednesday, 8th November

The Gallows Widow stood alone – her companions knocked to the ground years ago. A train passed by on the High Level Bridge alongside, and the pub shivered as if cold, while the painted sign with its crone clutching a noose creaked on its brackets.

The poster on the window advertised "Early-bird specials – all day." North didn't need to stop. They did however need to be off the streets to re-group.

"We need to eat," she agreed when he pointed to the poster, and North felt guilty suddenly at the blood she'd lost, and the fact he had barely considered it since. She wasn't him and she needed to rest up.

As he pushed open the swing door, someone somewhere pressed pause and all conversation stopped. An early morning pint glass held to a mouth. Warm beer unswallowed. Water that didn't drop from a tap. A rough-looking heavy and a washed-out girl in a jacket that hung to her knees. Nothing and no one. Play resumed.

A doxy with a face the colour of tomato soup broke off from flirting with an ancient postal worker to take their order for sandwiches and coffees.

"Do you have rooms?" he asked. An unusual request for so early in the morning. He kept the tone casual. If she did – fine. If she didn't, it was all the same to him.

The barmaid gave North a contemptuous stare. Honor a worse one. As far as she was concerned anyone who wanted to check into the pub's rooms had little money and no sense.

"£45 for a double. Shared bathroom along the corridor, but there's no one else staying if you're fussy that way."

"Clean sheets?"

"They used to be."

Two plates of bacon stotties clattered onto the counter in front of him and Honor opened her mouth. The early-bird specials. He shook his head. The tiniest of movements. The barmaid's back was to them as she poured coffee from a glass jug, its bottom burnt black from the hotplate, but North figured she was listening. They were strangers and strangers were always worth listening to.

North gestured at Honor to pick up the plates, as the barmaid rang in their cash – they were officially out of Peggy's £50 – waving her fat hand in the direction of a rickety round table to the rear of the room. She wasn't best pleased with the guests. She'd be the one changing the sheets.

★

It was warm in the bar and the bacon stottie and coffee was better than North had expected.

Honor slipped off the donkey jacket and hung it on the back of her chair. Quiet, her face was white like bone with violet smudges under her eyes as she pulled out the package. It was dry now. She placed it on the table between them, laying her hand over it, still in no apparent rush to open it. To see what it was her friend had hidden in the open seas. To think why Peggy would do such a thing.

"It feels wrong to be in Peggy's city when she's not here with me."

It didn't feel wrong to North – it felt exposed. Like they were doing what the Board would expect them to do. Looking for Peggy in her home town.

"Can you believe it was only yesterday that you tried to kill me?"

Yesterday, when she lived in a civilized world as an MP with prospects and powerful friends. Before her transformation into a mentally disturbed fugitive facing up to the prospect of imminent death with a one-time assassin her only ally. Her tone wasn't hostile, but even so North winced. She wasn't one to sugar-coat the situation.

She took her hand off the parcel to try and tuck an unruly strand of hair behind her ear – slamming her hand back down as she realised the vanity left the parcel undefended from him or from the curious scrutiny of the world. He didn't know which bothered her more.

"And now look at us," he offered, "sitting down to breakfast together."

She smiled, before remembering who and where she was. Her eyes went to the parcel again and he willed her to open it. To stop pretending that it wasn't all she was thinking about.

Proof of her friend's innocence, or proof of her guilt. And if Peggy were guilty, Honor needed to know. To accept the fact and to disown her. Maybe then he could broker a deal with Tarn. An amnesty for them both. He thought about Bruno. Bullets peppering the choppy sea. Tarn wasn't one for clemency, but he would have to try for Honor's sake.

A burst of laughter from an old woman knitting with her friend in the corner. The gentle scrape and click-clack of their needles hung with half-finished matinée coats. Maybe when you were that old, it came to a choice between laughing and crying. North told himself he was reconciled to an early death, but he wondered if Honor would get to be old – make that choice between laughing and crying. Because right this minute, her chances didn't look at all good.

"When I was fifteen," she spoke so quietly he barely registered the words, and he was forced to lean closer, "my father suffered a psychotic breakdown. That's what the TV was referring to. It was a big story at the time. My dad worked with JP, the business unwound, and Dad committed fraud on a massive scale. When JP found out, he brought in the police – that's the kind of man JP is. There's right and there's wrong. I admire that about him.

"My father was furious of course. Denied everything. Blamed JP. But that night, when he got back from the police station, he made us cocoa and laced it with my mother's sleeping tablets. While she and I slept, he nailed planks against the windows. He shifted all the wardrobes and chests to barricade the doors and stacked the chairs on top of the chests. That's what I came down to when I woke up in the early hours. Our very own prison. A tomb. And they were fighting – which they did sometimes. When my mother saw me, she started screaming at me to go back upstairs. I didn't want to but I was frightened. I thought my being there was making it worse, so that's what I did."

She paused in the telling, the screams ricocheting around her mind, but spoke through them.

"Days before, my mother locked up the shotgun cabinet and hid the key, but he smashed his way in. I knew what it was when I heard the bang. He loaded the gun and shot her in the face. Obliterated her. There was a minute of quiet while he reloaded, and then he came upstairs."

His tread as he climbed the staircase. The creak of the landing floorboards as he listened, then the hammering and shouting at her door. North's chest hammered in time with Honor's telling of it. The chest of drawers – her name picked out in sparkling mauve letters. But Honor was a quick study, and if a barricade could keep them in, it could keep her father out. The wardrobe tipped. Bent double as she drove the bed over the carpet and across the room to reinforce the chest. A teenage Honor curled up in the corner, hands over her ears, refusing to come out and play happy families. *"We need to be together...Do as I tell you...There's been an accident – your mother's hurt."* Frantic. Stabbing at the buttons of her phone. He'd wanted to kill her too, and when he realised the police were on their way he did the next best thing: he went back to lie down beside his wife's corpse and turned the gun on himself.

"I loved my father, but he was a violent man even before he did what he did. People knew – they tried to help. JP in particular, but my dad wasn't having any of it. After they died, after he murdered my mother I should say, I blamed myself. Ridiculous – but that's what happens. Survivor guilt – I've had therapy. You wouldn't believe how much therapy. I'd have gone away; that's to say I'd have finished myself if it weren't for Peggy at university. She was so dazzling and so kind. The only moral creature in our entire universe. I wouldn't be here if she hadn't looked after me. I owe her this, North – finding her. Whatever it costs, because I should have died a long time ago."

"*Extreme security risk.*" The order said.

The whole operation was a clean-up. The sort of clean-up required for an extreme security risk. Except it wasn't Honor who was the security risk. It was her friend and the loyalty Honor owed her.

Water dripped from the cuff of Honor's donkey jacket onto the red linoleum floor, giving the impression that something somewhere was bleeding.

"I wasted time because I was cross with her for disappearing." She made a face at her own ineptitude. "But I can't lose Peggy too. I've been frightened for the longest time, North, and now the worst thing's happened. Because the worst thing isn't dying – it's being left behind."

"*All my fault,*" he heard.

She moved her foot to sweep dry the small red pool under the dangling sleeve, and with it came back to the present.

Drawing the parcel to herself, she tore away the rotting green and black refuse sacks that the lobsters had done their worst with. North glanced around the room. A few florid-faced drinkers. A couple of baggy-eyed shift workers. The elderly and lonely in from the cold. No one was interested. For her next layer, Peggy had used black gaffer tape over heavier-duty refuse bags. The first few layers were sodden with salt water. The next few damp. The one under that dry, as was the waxed tarp it was wrapped in. More gaffer tape sealed the edges. It was a thorough job. The work of a scientist. With the last unravel of the tape, the contents slid out of the tarp and onto Honor's knees.

A black leather-bound book. Not a diary. A notebook. Laying it on the table between them, Honor opened it with one finger. Print-outs of graphs and pictures were glued to the pages of the book where they blazed in blues and oranges and bright gold. No numbers. No words. She turned the pages one by one.

"Do you know what we're looking at?"

She was silent. A second. Then another.

"Space? Noise? No idea. She always used to say 'Look for the unexpected' but I don't understand enough about her field to know what that is."

There was something they weren't seeing, he was sure of it. Why was he a target? Because Honor was a target and he didn't kill her. Why was Honor a target? Because Peggy disappeared and she made a fuss. According to Ned, Peggy wasn't the only one to disappear. But why was Peggy in particular a target? Because she knew something or was doing something the Board didn't like. What did Peggy know? She knew astronomy and physics. What did she do? She researched the noise the Earth makes. The jeopardy was somewhere in there.

"What was the name of the astronomer you talked to at Peggy's university?"

Honor thought for a moment, wrinkled her nose. "The one who took her office? Walt Bannerman. He's a first-class creep."

There was no choice. They needed an expert to decipher the notebook, and creepy Walt just volunteered.

"I'm going to show him the book."

She went to stand up, swaying on her feet at the sudden movement, and he tugged her back down into her seat – the chair scraping against the floor and the scowling barmaid looked over to see the cause of the disturbance.

"Me – not you. You're going to rest up." He kept his face relaxed and smiling. Nothing to see. "Nobody knows you're here, but they might be watching the university. I can get in and out of there easier alone. And you're exhausted, which makes you a liability."

He made the instruction sound brutal. No sympathy. Only the expediency of a professional speaking to an amateur. The line between her finely drawn eyebrows became deeper and longer, but she didn't argue.

One of the grannies snipped through her trailing wool with dressmaking scissors – the scything noise loud in an all-of-a-sudden silent pocket of time, white wool falling back to the skein lying next to her black orthopaedic shoes. And it came to him where he had seen the one-eyed man from the harbour – outside his Marylebone flat before he got the assignment, before his world turned inside out and upside down. North didn't think he was the Board, so who was he, and why was he following him? North did a rapid review of his recent jobs – the powerful men, the friends they had in high and low places. Had one of them come looking for revenge? Because the last thing he needed was another shadow chasing him. This one out of his past.

A shaft of sunlight hit the stained glass windows at the far end of the bar and spangles of red and blue and saffron yellow painted over Honor, leaving him in darkness. He lifted his hand, bringing it up to the sticky, varnished table where crimson covered it.

24

Newcastle

Seven years earlier

"Do you think you'll ever have children?" Honor lay stretched out on the carpet, Peggy on the sofa. Propping herself up on one elbow, she reached for the poker, before plunging it into the bed of coal, once, twice, three times.

Peggy turned her head to watch. "Yes, and you're going to kill that fire."

Honor attempted to stand the poker upright but it fell with a clatter onto the tiled hearth. She cursed and picked up the bottle of red wine, filling their glasses to the brim, before handing Peggy her glass.

"I don't want children. I've decided. Never. Ever."

"Why not?"

Honor made a face. "What if I had a boy and he looked like my dad? What if it stopped me loving him?"

"You'll change your mind."

Honor shook her head. She wasn't changing her mind.

"I'm probably too old already," Peggy said. "We're way

past our biological prime. Anyway, I might not be able to. My mother had seven miscarriages before me. Christie said they'd given up trying when I came along."

"Worry not, old lady. I'll carry the beastly sprog for you if you can't do it yourself."

Peggy looked surprised. Pleased. "That would be hard, though. Giving up a baby you've carried for nine months."

"No sweat, amigo. You'd do it for me."

"Bearing in mind what you just said, I want you to know I absolutely would."

Honor rolled onto her stomach to stare up at her friend. "What if I needed you to help me kill someone?"

Peggy laughed. "Do you have anyone in mind?"

"That's not the point," Honor said. "Let's say someone does something terrible to me and I decide to kill them, would you help?"

"How terrible?"

"Really bad. Rape. Buggery. Burns down my house. Pulls out my toenails. Throws battery acid in my face."

Peggy thought about it.

"What about the police?"

"He gets off. He has a great lawyer. A real bastard."

"Then yes."

"Would you help me bury the body?"

"Definitely. I don't want it lying around incriminating us."

"Is there anyone you'd like me to kill on your behalf?"

Peggy laughed out loud. "No, but thank you for the offer. I'll bear it in mind."

"If you want a baby any time soon, you need to get less picky about men by the way," Honor said.

"I could get a sperm donor. A Swedish rocket scientist who's an Olympic oarsman and is good to his mother."

"Chances are you'd get a donor who says he's a Swedish rocket scientist. There's a difference. And he probably is good to his mother, because he still lives in her back bedroom. Don't you want a man around to help with the baby at least?"

Peggy thought about it. "No." She sounded surprised at herself.

"What if you died?"

"That's easy. You'll look after her."

"The baby's a girl?"

"Yes."

"But I said I didn't want a baby."

"She's not any baby. She's my baby."

Honor grinned. "All right. Providing you know that I'll make a terrible mother."

Peggy grinned. "I wouldn't want you any other way."

25

Newcastle

A year ago

Peggy nailed it. If she said so herself. She was nervous as hell when they asked her to do the TED Talk. She had said no till she told Honor and Honor rang them back and said Peggy was congenitally deaf, had misheard and of course she'd love to speak. When and where?

She lay back against her pillow and pressed loudspeaker – Honor's voice filling the room.

"I like the part where you gesture with your hand. It's strong. I use it myself in the Chamber."

Peggy smiled at the thought of Honor chopping away in debate. They were watching it for the third time. Each of them in their separate beds, in their separate cities.

"Christie would be so proud."

"Do you think?"

Peggy didn't need to ask, but she wanted to hear Honor say it.

"The guys at the allotments would never have heard the end of it."

Jansky leapt for the bed, circling over and over till he decided it was safe to collapse. Peggy's fingers reached for him, and he rolled onto his back, spindly legs in the air, his narrow nose pointing at her, his pink tongue lolling and eyes pleading for more attention.

"You are a ridiculous dog," she said, as she tickled behind his soft ears, sliding her hand along his skinny ribs, ruffling then smoothing the fur. He whined in appreciation, his hind leg beating the air in quiet ecstasy.

She heard Honor's lips part, draw breath.

"Tell me you aren't smoking in bed," Peggy said.

There was a whoosh of air as Honor denied it. "It's my emphysema playing up."

"If you fall asleep with a fag in your hand, you will burn to death."

"If I fall asleep with a fag in my hand, he will be a lucky man. And also a little confused."

Peggy shoved the laptop off her knees as she leaned over the other side of the bed to reach for the off switch on the lamp. Immediately the room darkened, lit only by the golden glow of her own lamp, and the cool blue of the Mac screen as it powered down. There was a scratching noise from Jansky.

"And how is JP?" Peggy tried to keep the disapproval out of her voice, but she suspected Honor heard it anyway.

"Devoted."

"And more than twenty years too old for you."

"You like old things. Stars are very old. I heard that in a superb TED Talk."

"I like old things which are far, far away."

Honor giggled.

"I should go. JP is getting cross. His Viagra must be wearing off."

"That picture is now in my head for all time. I may puke."

"Kiss Jansky for me. Love you."

"Back at you."

Peggy reached for her own light, and there was darkness.

26

London

Peggy's lips were dry, her tongue thick and heavy in her mouth. She was getting used to the iron tang of blood, the white noise of pain like the sound of pulsars. She wondered if he'd come again to talk. He gave the impression he enjoyed their conversations, would miss them. Yesterday he ordered the thug she hated – the huge one with the wolf's teeth, who looked at her as if she were so much meat – to chain her where she could see the stars from the window. A small kindness. It was bitter cold in the cell tonight and the night sky dark and clear. Hugging her knees on the stone floor, she was home again. They were so far away. Billions of light years.

She missed her father. His arm around her when she was small, sitting on the backyard doorstep as he named the stars. *Wave at Mam, Peggy girl.* Missed her life. All of it. Honor's laughter. Her voice. Jansky. The sunshiney taste of grapefruit juice on a morning. Green tea. How it felt to decipher a pattern in the numbers, sense their beauty and order. The plaintive call of the curlew on the beach. The rock and motion of the boat as she fished. Friendship. Joy. The breathtaking smile of the daughter she'd never see. Leaving it all behind as she walked into the sky she knew so well, through the Milky Way, her hands trailing through the dark matter, energy running through her, absorbing her back into the cosmos. Solar flares and explosions. Noise everywhere. The thought – whether light years away anyone was listening?

And in the furthest corner of the bare room, a key turned in a lock with a soft, dull click and the door began to open.

27

Newcastle University

The physics department hummed with earnest young men and women in jumpers and spectacles, clutching folders and laptops to their chests. In another life this could have been him. If he'd been more locked on at school. If his mother hadn't been an addict, and if he hadn't killed a man when he himself was still a boy.

North kept his head down as he navigated the corridors. He'd filched his own folder and a mathematical textbook from the Blackwell's university bookshop he'd passed en route, stealing a plastic bag for good measure for added deniability. If he had more time, he'd have scouted out a beanie and scarf, but he didn't want to push his luck.

There was a smell of institutional cleaning fluids and damp in the hallway as he ran his finger down a list of tutors. A tiny, scowling Chinese girl, her hair in two stubby plaits, leaned against the noticeboard watching him, the heel of her gold Dr. Martens boot working away at a hole in the plastered wall. He hesitated at the absence where Peggy's name had once been. Moved down – Dr Walter Bannerman Level 3, Room 14.

"He's an idiot," she said.

Judging by the pile of plaster dust on the floor, the girl had been there some time.

"He knows more than I do."

She rifled through a file in her arms, ripped out an essay and thrust it at him. *Introduction to radio astronomy.* It was marked with an "F".

"Now you're even," she said, pulling herself away from the wall. She had the look of someone who'd been there long enough and knew it. "Ciao, moron-person."

28

Room 14 was three flights up and the door scarcely ajar when he reached it. The occupant, the dome of his bald head shining in the light cast by the Anglepoise, was bent over his desk, hammering away at a keyboard as if he hated it.

North pushed the door open wider – the movement of air enough to make Bannerman raise his head and frown: an unpleasant enough face made odder again by its lack of eyebrows and eyelashes.

"Did your mother not teach you to knock?" he said to the screen. "Come back later. I'm busy."

North's mother taught him how to roll skinny cigarettes, shoplift naggins of vodka without a coat, and how to fake an epileptic seizure if he were ever caught. Thinking about it, she never did teach him to knock.

Bannerman resumed his furious typing. The heat was intense – the office rank with body odour and stale caffeine. Cups in varying states of green and grey furred decay filled the windowsill above the industrial radiator turned up to

High – more lined up in front of the desk. Dr Bannerman didn't sleep well, North was guessing.

Ignoring the squawk of outrage, North sat down in the chair opposite the professor and drew out the book he'd rescued from the sea.

"Young man…"

"You spoke to a friend of mine – Honor Jones?"

Bannerman sat straighter in his chair, and tiny flakes of skin rose from his shoulders to fill the air around him, before falling and settling again onto the mustardy tweed. He pushed aside the computer screen to get a better view of North.

"The young lady looking for dear Peggy?" A wax-white tongue slid out of the hairless face to lick his cracked lips. "I hope they 'hooked up'," Bannerman leaned towards his visitor – an attempt to make him complicit.

"Hooked up" after all was an odd expression, thought North, made odder again by the breathy delivery. Sexual. Prurient. As if Bannerman hinted at something wet and intimate between the two women.

"They didn't."

"That's a shame. Peggy apparently had as little compunction letting down her friend as she did letting down her colleagues. Miss Jones was very concerned as I remember and God knows there's been a stream of oddities looking for Peggy since she left – some drooping Arab, her Chinese pet, not to mention that creature with the extraordinary hair."

North filled with Bannerman's resentment – envy writhing and squirming in the older academic's stomach as he watched Peggy walk the stage delivering her TED Talk. Loathing Peggy's brilliance, resenting her talent. Her looks. Her gender.

North pulled his T-shirt away from his chest where it had begun to stick to the skin. It was too warm in the office, the air dry and thick and coffee-tasting. Bannerman should turn down his radiator and open his windows to the world. It might improve his smell. "You didn't much like Peggy?"

Pursing his lips and making his already small mouth smaller yet, the professor rearranged his wall of disgusting cups so their handles pointed outwards at the same angle.

"I've been in academia a long time, young man. I'm not a populist – I'm a scientist. A purist. The Peggys come and go. One lucky piece of research. The right publication. Some dumbed-down science show on television because they can talk faster than they can think, and suddenly they're Einstein."

North said nothing. Bannerman didn't need him to. His face was alive with malice. "The research money gets channelled to them and they still witter on that it's not enough. Their maw is ever open wanting more money. Bigger telescopes. More of them. Better facilities. Commercial partners. Fame. I hope she's happier in Chile."

"She didn't go to Chile."

Bannerman waved his hand. "What does it matter? Perhaps it was New Mexico with the VLA. That's to say the Very Large Array." His tone was supercilious as he pointed to the wall, making it clear he didn't expect his visitor to understand. Next to his bookcase was a large black and white photograph of twenty-seven huge dishes pointing up to the sky. "I've done work out there myself. A few years ago admittedly, but at the time it was well received. I made something of an impression."

North didn't believe Peggy was in New Mexico any more than she was in Chile. He was beginning to think Bannerman didn't believe it either.

"Wherever she is, I'll say this. When a colleague leaves the field, particularly a colleague of Dr Boland's standing, those of us left behind – the dutiful, the poor bloody infantry – are required to step into the breach."

He waved a hand at the computer and the stack of papers on his desk, which North guessed were meant for marking. North didn't envy the professor's students – particularly his female students. He couldn't see him as a generous marker. And he had no great hopes Bannerman would be willing or indeed able to translate whatever was in the black book.

But he had to try. Moving aside the mouldering coffee cups, North laid the notebook on the desk and opened it on the first page.

Bannerman's eyes narrowed as he drew the book towards him. He flicked from page to page to page. "How do you have this?" For the first time Bannerman sounded engaged. Curious.

"Peggy left it for Honor."

Did she? Or did she leave it so she herself could retrieve it? Peggy must have known she was in danger if she hid the book, and Peggy knew her friend. Honor was an obsessive – relentless. Which meant she must have known Honor would come looking for her. Which meant she must have known the chances were that Honor would find it.

"Do you know what it is?" North said.

Bannerman chewed at his dry lips like he wanted to hold back the words. "It's hard to tell without any of the numbers attached, but they're pictorial representations of noise coming from the Earth, while these pages further on are preliminary calculation work. Nothing complicated or special. Nothing my third year students couldn't come up with." His disappointment appeared genuine, as if he'd expected more of Peggy.

"Her main work was noise cancelling?"

The professor nodded, his eyes still on the book, his hand over it, dragging it closer. "I'll keep it for you and try to get a better idea. Perhaps if I spoke to her PhD students? Or even the Chinese misfit? "

Did he see a chance to profit from Peggy's work? To claim it? To build on it? Did he see himself on the stage, in the spotlights, holding forth to the world? A million views. A million likes.

North stood. It was too hot in here and too close. And the man in front of him too full of bile and wanting.

"Chinese misfit?"

The little girl in plaits and glittering boots kicking down walls.

Bannerman had his top drawer open – the book was poised halfway over it.

Disappointed or not, North didn't need the bullet to tell him that Bannerman wanted that book.

"Absurd. The girl's only fourteen – she's still at school. One of Peggy's lost causes. She keeps hanging around hoping Peggy will come back. I've told security not to let her in but I do believe they're frightened of her." He relaxed – he thought the book was his – and celebrated. A wheezing noise came out of him. What passed for laughter. "She needs to crawl back to her takeaway, egg-fry some rice, and stay there."

What would drive a respectable academic to buy duct tape and tarpaulin and leave her work in the sea? What did she think might happen? Did she think Walt Bannerman might get hold of it? Bannerman was an academic rival. Envious and unpleasant.

But did Peggy suspect he was more than that? Worse than that?

North reached across the desk and scooped up the notebook as Bannerman wailed, flakes of skin falling to the desk as he tried and failed to snatch it back. "I wouldn't put you to the trouble."

29

As the door closed behind the rudest man Dr Walt Bannerman ever met, he reached for the phone. He'd memorised the number. He was good with numbers. Excellent. But he'd never had the recognition he deserved. Never been lucky. But with more money invested in his research, he had complete and entire confidence he would win prizes, and that the name of Bannerman would be one to reckon with. He'd shown such early promise and it would all be his again.

"He was here."

It was all he needed to say.

That his visitor was an animal. Abrupt. Ignorant. That despite himself he had been frightened if only by the man's size, by the lurking violence in the deep-set eyes.

But he played it beautifully.

The money would arrive via an international respected scientific grants trust. The first indication of glory yet to come. The Vice Chancellor would be astonished.

Bannerman put down his hands and rubbed them together palm against palm, a blizzard of white swirling around him, the new skin rubbed raw and red as he opened them up like the book he'd wanted to keep tiny pinpricks of blood rising everywhere. It was a shame the thug hadn't handed over the notebook, but it might yet come his way, though it really didn't seem to be anything he hadn't seen already. Peggy. He'd always known she would flame out.

Yes, the glorious future that would be his was surely worth a small betrayal and a little work on the side. Sacrifices were always necessary in the name of scientific progress, and frankly he never did like Peggy Boland.

30

Newcastle University

9.59am. Wednesday, 8th November

Outside Bannerman's study, North brushed himself down. He couldn't see any of the professor's skin flakes on him but he didn't want to take any chances. Honor was right – the good professor was stomach-turning. The less they had to deal with Bannerman, the happier he'd be.

He checked with the departmental secretary about the Chinese student. Mrs Craggs was almost as unhelpful with him as with Honor, but then Honor didn't possess North's slow smile. He used it on the secretary like a Pathfinder missile to take out her defences. It didn't yield much but it did yield the information that Peggy was helping a particularly bright teenager.

"Not a nice child. At all." He pictured the girl's scowl. Her scorn. *Walt Bannerman is an idiot.* The intense brooding waiting. Was she waiting for Peggy? Hoping she would walk back in?

"Kids," he'd said, not having any idea what it meant, but

noticing the picture of three ferret-faced children on her desk.

Mrs Craggs softened, simpered, nodded, and he took it to mean *What can you do?* and *You do your best* and *It's never enough* and *I wish I'd never had them.*

The Chinese girl didn't come into the department the normal way. She wasn't a pupil at a school with established links or where students did outreach. So how had Peggy come across her?

He felt his own temper rise. She'd been right in front of him. She'd spoken to him and he'd let her walk away.

"*Ciao, moron, person.*" The kid called that right. Honor would not be happy.

31

Wiping his face with the corner of his arm, North stopped by the wooden-slatted bin. Fast-food wrappers and plastic bags of dog faeces running with water were piled up against the base. It was pouring with rain. If he ever bought that boat, he was mooring it somewhere sunny and never getting wet again unless you count the tropical sea.

College days were over and he wouldn't miss them. Roll on spring break. Tossing the empty folder and textbook, he turned, then stopped. Slumped on a wooden bench close by, a tramp watched with interest.

North reached back into the bin to lift out the textbook, weighing it momentarily in his hand. He wasn't a moron-person like the kid said. He could use a book – even a book like this one. It might come in useful. The supermarket trolley loaded with plastic bags was parked up alongside the bench. North smiled in apology. The guy could salvage the file, but he was hanging on to *Advanced Mathematics* a while longer. He dropped it back into its plastic bag, folded it over and over, and carried on walking.

32

It didn't take him long to get back to the Gallows Widow.

It would have taken even less time but he doubled back on himself several times in case he was being followed.

His feet tacky on the Widow's lurid carpet, he rapped once on the peeling painted-wood door of Room 7, and Honor hauled it open so violently the handle slipped from her grasp to bounce against the wall. Her eyes were red and swollen as she glared at him, her anger slamming into him so hard he had difficulty lifting one foot and then the other to follow her in. He breathed deeply, holding himself still as he resisted the rage blowing through his brain, knocking down and trampling over his own consciousness, taking over each and every cell in his body.

Accommodation was on the first floor of the pub at the back with a slanting view of the arcing Tyne Bridge, the silvering river it crossed, and the steady falling rain. She was standing in front of the window, the newspaper shaking in her hand. Her mouth moved, but he couldn't hear her, focusing his attention instead on the shifting River Tyne pockmarked by the reflected lights of the city spread out behind her.

It came to him all in a rush, her words emerging from the white noise of anger. The missing banker. Hugh Carrington, twenty-five. The back of her hand smacked the newsprint like she wanted to punish it. *Look*, her voice was raised. Look at Hugh's mother, distraught, held upright only by the fifty-something man next to her. Silver hair. Lean. Distinguished. Trying to be brave, a press conference asking Hugh to get in touch. Quotes from his colleagues who'd reported his absence from work. The man child she'd flirted with, given hope to.

Killed. The sea-drowned corpse North abandoned on the hard, cold concrete of Seamouth harbour. *No one important.*

He had already done his reckoning on the quayside. Honor trailed four dead bodies in her wake: Ned who tried to tell her a secret, the unfortunate Japanese tourist who broke Ned's fall from grace, the nameless killer in her London bathroom, and Hugh who moved too close to the wrong woman.

Hugh's death wasn't her fault. She had to know that.

North took the paper from her and tossed it onto the blowsy chintz duvet covering the bed. The trust between them, fragile at best, lay in ashes and ruination. If he didn't rebuild it, their alliance was over.

Ask me again.

Ask me who wants you dead.

Who'd killed the young banker just as his life was starting? And North would tell her, because she had the right to know.

But Honor didn't ask.

Instead, she slapped his face.

The pain was sharp. Sudden. Stinging. Delivered with all the pent-up force of a woman who had wanted to wound him since the moment she first saw him.

"That was Hugh's body on the causeway. The one you said was 'No one important'."

It wasn't a question. It was an accusation and she made to hit him again, but this time he caught her hand by the bandaged wrist. Which must have hurt, but she didn't cry out – glaring at him as if she expected no better, and he dropped the wrist like it burnt him to touch her.

He should have told her at the time. Explained the Board had to be in a rush. That they'd collected Hugh in the clean-up. It would be too much of a coincidence to leave his body in London. The body of an MP's neighbour. An MP slated to die any minute. Who knows how they planned to manage it once Honor was dead. Perhaps they'd have pointed the finger at the missing banker? Implied he was obsessed enough to kill her and disappear afterwards.

North knew he should have told her, but he was trying to protect her. Surely she would understand. They had needed to move. Slide away from the police and the one-eyed man. It was a mistake. He was sorry.

"You leave bodies everywhere you go, North. Did you think he didn't matter?" She was crying. The first time he had seen her tears. "That I didn't need to know because he was – what? Collateral damage? What did you call him? Yes, I remember – 'No one'. He wasn't collateral damage – he was somebody. He was somebody else's son, and you people are animals."

She picked up her jacket and shoved her arms into the sleeves, forcing her way past him. He blocked her exit and she went still. Dangerous. "I'm not that nice a person, North. Not like Peggy. I look after myself first, last, and always, but I'm not giving up, do you understand that? Whatever this was between you and me though – this is over. Things are getting worse all the time, and you're part of that."

The pictures came and he wished they wouldn't. Ned falling through the sky, legs and arms flailing. Her own struggle for breath which wasn't there in the bloody bathwater – the rippling face of her attacker looming over her. Waves coming at them as he drove them into the North Sea. Bullets spitting around them in the darkness. Terror. And knowing exactly who North was – right from the start. The sound of geese and his own face cold and brutal and terrifying. Refusing to forget, or forgive. "Give me back Peggy's book."

He hesitated. Weighing up his options. Honor was making a mistake. Reacting emotionally to the deaths and the chaos. He understood, but he couldn't help her with that, because he didn't have the words. He could help her find Peggy though. Because they finally had a chance. Peggy collected protégées.

Ned was dead.

But there was a Chinese teenage nightmare out there who was very much alive and mad as bejesus.

He was going to find her, and when he did he needed Peggy's notebook.

"Give me back Peggy's book, or I'll take it back." Honor's voice was eerily calm. He passed over the package and she shoved it into the pocket of the donkey jacket. "Bannerman was no help, was he?"

"There's a Chinese girl Peggy was teaching."

Honor waved her hand in dismissal. "I know all about her. I'm not dragging innocent children into this mess."

He opened his mouth to explain, but Honor showed no sign she was listening. She had got what she came for – Peggy's secret. The thimble. And she was leaving. Because she saw North for what he was. Trouble. She couldn't trust him. Never had. Never would. And why should she? He couldn't trust himself.

209

His hand reached for her but she crackled with her own force-field of scorn and he didn't dare touch her. He didn't want her to go. He'd been alone for a lifetime and never felt it. But he felt it now and she was still in the room.

"He's a liability and a sociopath."

Her voice? Or did his mind tell him exactly what he needed to know? Either way, Honor regarded him as a reckless criminal, and she had a point. Thought he was a bad'un, and maybe she was right about that too.

"I'm going back to London and doing this through the proper channels."

"There are no proper channels. They'll kill you." Feeble. He knew as he said it, and whatever the truth, it wouldn't stop her.

"I won't give them that chance. I'll make the authorities listen to me. Things have changed because I have Peggy's book, and she's missing. They can't pull their Chile stunt twice. That dead boy on the quayside was my neighbour. What is that? A coincidence? I'm an MP for God's sake and JP is a powerful man. The balance of probability has shifted, and it's on my side. Something is rotten, and I don't need you, or whatever it is you think you can do for me, any more."

She hadn't forgotten that, in the car as they drove through the night, Tarn called him a killer, but he wasn't that today. He was more than that and less than that and different from who he'd been. Because of her.

It must have been in his eyes, because there was a nano-shift in her attitude. The shadow of a whisper of the start of what might have been a softening. Pity. She pitied him. He caught it and tried exerting his own gravitational pull to reassure her and draw her closer, but she didn't feel it, or resisted it. He was too much the stranger and she was too far away and moving further with every second.

"Let go, North." It was a Dear John. "For me, this is personal. It's not that way for you. I'm ringing JP. He knows all sorts of legal types – we'll get the police involved at the highest level, and I can't do that with you around. How do I explain who you are?" She put the question with the patience of a teacher to a slow and struggling child.

"Disappear. Catch that plane you're always talking about. And try not to kill anyone ever again. Okay?"

He took a step back. Putting distance between them. Peggy was everything to her, and nothing to him. Letting JP Armitage use his money and influence to make things better made all sorts of sense. Honor did right to get away. She was smart – no pushover. Without him, she could work within the Establishment to find her missing friend. Maybe JP Armitage would indeed keep her safe. Lock her in an ivory tower and set his New Army to guard her while he turned the world inside out to find Peggy. The tycoon couldn't do a worse job than North himself had done.

North would catch a plane and buy a boat. He tried to hold onto that logic. To the thought of warm seas and the warmer bodies of strangers. To the logic of letting her go.

She slammed the door as she left and the walls shivered.

Discretion was critical. Tarn said that from the start. It was bad enough when he didn't kill her. It got worse when he killed the next guy along. It got beyond worse when he drove into the sea, brought down a helicopter with a handy iron bar and wiped out a small army. Escape. Freedom. They weren't what he wanted now. They weren't luxuries he had earned. They were what he needed to stay alive himself.

From the window he watched and waited to see when she emerged. The rain had stopped.

She made him unemployable. Worse. Turned him from an asset into an extreme security risk. Status: critical. Termination: essential, and written in green ink.

If anyone could keep her safe, JP Armitage could, but the only person who could keep Michael North safe was Michael North. And the bullet in his brain meant he couldn't even trust himself. For five years, he stayed on the margins as time ran through his hands. Believing that, if he tried to hold onto it, leaving would be all the harder. Death was nothing. He told himself that every time he killed a bad man. It was a judgment, a verdict. How all life had to end. His own included.

The door was obscured by the pub sign with its noose, so he didn't see her face. Only the blonde head and her back as she walked away. She didn't look back.

The room was bleak. A place for travelling salesmen and shabby affairs by insurance clerks. Only the Edwardian wardrobe of shining walnut and dark oak lifted it into something grander. In its silvering oval mirror, he watched himself close the door behind him. He didn't need to be here.

No one would blame him for running.

The walls along the landing corridor had been painted over so often it was impossible to make out the pattern of the embossed wallpaper, but he ran his fingertips over it anyway trying to make sense of it.

He should get far away and do it fast. Dig down to a place of silence and darkness and hide himself as best he could all the days he had left to him. Buy a calendar. Strike through the days he lived. Monday to Sunday. Each one a victory over dying and over Lucien Tarn.

The stairs down from the bedrooms to the ground floor were steep, the mahogany rail sticky with spray polish and the sweat of other people's hands.

The problem was he didn't live on the edge of things any more. Honor dropped him plumb-centre of the battlefield where those who loved life fought in hand-to-hand combat for what was theirs. He wanted to live. She made him want that. Showed him there was value in it. And he was fighting for whatever life he had left. Fighting for Honor, whether she wanted him to or not. And he was finding Peggy who fixed things, or he was dying in the attempt.

The downstairs bar was almost empty. No elderly early-bird knitters. Lunchtime drinkers not yet at their posts. Behind the counter, the barmaid was opening and closing the till, lifting the drawer out to look under it. Her head craned to the back as she called through some question to an unseen colleague.

North stepped around the to and fro of a dirty mop head as a hunched-over cleaning woman marked time. The slops making things worse not better, bringing up a heady scent of last night's booze and vomit from the black and white chequered floor or the mop or both. Honor must have gone this way. Down the stairs and through the public bar over the wet floor. The char following her over to the door, slow, methodical, erasing the footprints even as she walked, making it impossible to follow.

Straight out of hospital, refusing more rehabilitation, rejecting Tarn's offers of help, he took a doorman's job in an East End club. An unspoken death wish. Take on the biggest and the ugliest and the most vicious brawlers in the place and hope that one of them would hit him so hard it would all be over. He'd hated it, not because of the loud-mouthed drunks and the Big-I-Ams, not because of the aggro and the regular knockabouts, but because of the cheap dinner suit he had to wear. In the evening, as he slid his arms into the sleeves of the jacket with its polyester lapels and sewed-in hanky snippet, shame filled him up to the brim. Out of his uniform, out of the Army and back in the gutter where he'd been born.

The only good thing about working the door – the permission to do violence. That and the access it gave him to women. Women who would bring him over drinks he wasn't supposed to drink and stand by him, their long legs painted an unnatural brown, giggling as the Every-Night-Is-Ladies'-Night trebles took hold, tossing their shiny, fake hair and licking their shiny, sweet lips. They were toxic and the thought made them irresistible – his foot-to-the-floor route to oblivion.

Something about the smell of the pub took him back there.

He stepped out into the fresh air. Walking over to the edge of the quayside, he tossed the final strip of purple pills into the moving river. He'd used them to dull whatever was going on in his brain long enough. Leaning against the railings, he pulled out the black book. A textbook on advanced mathematics, first and second year, the same shape and heft of Peggy's notebook, wrapped in a bookstore plastic bag, shoved deep down into Honor's pocket. He'd made the switch. He wasn't proud of himself and Honor would be furious, but he was doing it for her own good. This wasn't a civilised world and every second counted. Honor would waste time travelling back to London. Persuading JP to credit her incredible story. North didn't have that luxury because he had a plane to catch. Destination: Freedom.

Just as soon as he found out the whereabouts of a scowling Chinese waif in blinged-up bovver boots.

33

Newcastle

11.00am. Wednesday, 8th November

Chinatown was fifteen minutes' distance from the riverside up through the city's shopping streets. He'd checked out the route when he thought he and Honor would be going there together. As he walked, North pulled out the F-grade essay.

"Radio astronomy is a branch of observational astronomy that grew out of technology developments in the 20th century. It enables scientists to detect electromagnetic radiation from cosmic sources at centimetre or millimetre wavelengths – wavelengths that are much longer than those of visible light to which our eyes are sensitive."

He began to wish his brain – with or without its bullet – were bigger.

Flipping open the black notebook, he stopped walking long enough to set Peggy's flaring pictures and the rising and falling pop and fizz of her graphs against the essay. "Preliminary calculation work," Bannerman said, dismissing the notebook. He didn't appear to be lying – even so, North didn't trust him. Bannerman was a rival academic with his own agenda, which made him the wrong choice as interpreter. They needed a disinterested expert as a proper translator. All he had to do was find her.

He stared again at the essay. Why hadn't she written her name on it? Isn't that what students did? He looked again at the F. Scrawled. Messy.

What if it weren't an F?

What if it were a Chinese symbol?

34

Chinatown, Newcastle

11.15am. Wednesday, 8th November

He started at one end of the street – down from the Chinese archway with its scowling guardian lions. Yin and Yang. Male and Female. Both of them covered in the graffiti and excrement that passed for political comment. There was increasing anti-Chinese feeling in the country since the latest price hikes by the Chinese corporations who had taken over the utilities. These days people didn't need much of an excuse to dislike a neighbour or a foreigner.

Staff at the Golden Wonder all-you-can-eat buffet, £7.95 a head, hadn't opened up yet, though behind the glass he caught glimpses of white-jacketed cooks moving through the dark restaurant – all of them ignoring the stranger knocking at their window.

The thirty-something manager in Jade Gardens did at least take the paper and examine the character before shrugging. *Divn't have a clue, mate.*

Not till the eleventh restaurant, the Royal China, did the

young lad in a bow tie abandon his table-laying to translate the character for him.

"Yu," he said. The lad took out his own phone and did a search. "Good job you aren't looking for her in China, there's more than seven million of them over there."

He shouted through to the kitchen and a bespectacled woman, her black hair in a French pleat, came out. North smiled but the French-pleat woman didn't smile back. He guessed she blamed him for the abandoned knives and forks and the unpolished wine glasses.

"Auntie, this guy is looking for a family called Yu with a fourteen-year-old girl studying at the uni. He thinks they run a takeaway."

35

Newcastle University

1.30pm. Wednesday, 8th November

Mrs Craggs loathed the way she got older and uglier, while students remained young and beautiful. No one liked her and she knew it. The only one of the academic staff who made time for her was Walt Bannerman. Ten years ago, she wanted to marry him. Five years ago, sleep with him. There was an embarrassing fumble after one departmental drinks do that neither of them acknowledged afterwards. But Mrs Craggs was glad it happened because it released the sexual tension between them. These days she was happy enough to pop her head round the door to offer him a butterscotch and spend a few minutes gutting whoever was attracting her ire. Like that flibbertigibbet Dr Peggy Boland, for instance.

Balling her damp man-size handkerchief and tucking it into her cardigan sleeve, she gathered up the few envelopes belonging to Bannerman. Everyone else had pigeonholes, but Mrs Craggs was happy to hand-deliver Walt's. That's what she called him – "Walt".

Everyone else was Dr This or Professor That. But Professor Walter Bannerman would always and forever be her Walt.

Her new shoes rubbed her heels. She wondered if he would notice them. Tan leather loafers with tassels. She wasn't convinced about the tassels. They seemed rather racy outside of the shoe shop, but when she was trying them on, they had made her less unhappy. She hoped that Walt would be kind. He could be a little abrupt.

His door was closed. It often was. Especially over lunch. He didn't like students any more than she did. He was a brilliant man, and it was entirely wrong of the university to expect him to teach when his skills would have been better employed in research. She knocked twice in rapid succession. The knock of a tasselled woman. Her knock – different from all the other knocks in the world. One Walt would recognise. She didn't wait for him to say come in. A woman who had "surrendered" herself to a man had certain rights.

Bannerman was smiling as Mrs Craggs pushed open the door – at least that was her first thought, her heart lifting, till she realised it wasn't so much a smile as a bleeding line scored across his throat, blood soaking the shirt, making it look as if the dead man wore a bib ready for a dinner he was never going to eat. When she opened her mouth and screamed, her piercing voice echoed down the staircase, bouncing off the green-painted walls, and something in her brain registered the smell of mouldering coffee mixed with Walt's blood.

36

Newcastle

The Oriental Dragon was a dingy hole, its metal shutters daubed in obscenities and spray-paint tags squeezed between a boarded-up bookies and a burnt-out laundrette in the worst part of the worst part of town. During his years in the Army, North must have eaten in grimmer joints – he just couldn't think of any.

As he pulled out the astronomy essay, the tiny takeaway owner unlocked the mesh grill between her and any customers, lifted the melamine counter and waved him through as if she were in a hurry. Her lack of surprise meant she'd been warned by the Royal China, but North expected that.

The little woman didn't look at him, because that way she didn't see him. Instead, she bolted the grill again, flapping her plump hand at North as if he were a fly she wanted to kill. At the very least, she wanted him out of sight before paying customers came round.

He pushed his way through the red, white and blue plastic ribbons into the smell and pop of cooking grease.

Standing over a hob, an even smaller white-haired version of the front-of-house fly-killer threw handfuls of chicken feet into an enormous metal wok of sizzling oil, flames hissing and flaring. The smell of rice vinegar and pepper. With a gnarled and bony finger she pointed upwards, her eyes on the dancing chicken feet and not on the bad ghost bringing bad luck she didn't need. The thought crossed his mind that he was wasting his time, as through the steam, Granny made a pushing gesture with her hand, towards the white-painted plywood door behind him. He bowed his head in thanks, but she turned back to the wok. The bad ghost – someone else's problem now.

Behind the door, the narrow staircase reeked of damp and incense. Condensation from the cooking ran down the walls, but it was at least cooler than the kitchen – as if every window upstairs were open to the elements. He hadn't quite reached the top of the stairs when the razor-sharp steel throwing star whistled past the tip of his nose to embed itself in the moist wall. The fact the star wasn't quivering in the parietal bone of his skull had less to do with skill and more to do with the moving air along the landing. North took the final few steps onto the landing, the palms of his hands damp. He wanted to think from the wall.

"I didn't say you could come up." The voice was mulish.

The girl had thrown the star from a sitting position at her desk in her study. She was still in her golden boots, her hair braided into two tight plaits either side of her round face, watchful eyes hidden behind heavy square black frames. She sported a "Hello World" T-shirt and a ferocious scowl. At the university, although she was slight and short, he'd presumed she was a student; here at home, it was obvious she was still a child. She stood up from the desk to move towards him, her hand reaching for the door, ready to slam it shut.

"You were right about Bannerman," he spoke quickly, because the girl didn't seem the patient kind. "He's an idiot."

"I'm always right." She lifted her small chin, daring him to argue the case, the door closing fast and hard on the blue and green blaze of computer screens behind her. North rammed his boot in its way and she glared down at it as if considering the best way to sever his foot from his body.

"You were waiting for Peggy today, weren't you?"

"Peggy who? I'm compiling, bozo." The kid wasn't winning any congeniality contests any time soon.

"Let me help."

"You're too stupid to help me, old man."

He was beginning to feel a degree of sympathy for Mrs Anne Craggs. The kid was an immovable object powered by a neutron bomb.

"Then how about you help me?" He smiled – to show her how it was done, as one of the cooks from downstairs opened the door and shrieked up the stairs. The girl shrieked in return, making him jump. A torrent of outraged Cantonese, and North figured her mother had asked her if she was all right with the bad ghost and the girl had told her to go back to Granny and the chicken feet. In so many words.

He glimpsed what might have passed for a softening, perhaps at the mention of Peggy or perhaps because he'd helped irritate her mother. She snorted, moving back to her desk, and he followed.

It didn't qualify as a bedroom. Maybe once upon a time silver butterflies and sparkling fairies flew across a strawberry-pink duvet and an adorable girl-child tacked posters of fluffy kittens to lilac-painted walls. These days it didn't even have a bed and the only poster had five throwing stars embedded in it, one for each member of the boy band she appeared to hate. What it did have though was computer power. Banks of monitors and servers, some of them ancient, two of them Macs, lined the room, each monitor compiling code at a rate of knots, open text boxes in each, one discussing the latest reality TV show, the others tech-speak North couldn't begin to understand. From what he could gather from the message boxes, her hacker name was Miho.

North ceased to exist for her. Her interest in him extinguished itself as she went back to her typing, her fingers blurring over three separate keyboards, lines of numbers and symbols across the screen moving faster than he thought possible.

"Miho?"

She sighed at the fact he was still there – talking, breathing. Tapping her watch, holding it in front of her like a shield, before she brought it back to read the time. Except it wasn't the time.

"Michael North. Blah blah. Boring. Chalfont Securities. Suit-man. Bad tie. No further images. No social media footprint. No believe you."

She had facial recognition software installed on the smartwatch. One she had to have boosted. Impressive. One picture of him existed on the net, matching him to his cover.

"And do I call you Miho?"

"Fangfang."

He kept his face straight. "Like bang bang? Bang bang. Pop pop. You're dead – I'm not?"

"You good at bang bang, pop pop, huh big guy?" she snorted.

"What does Fangfang mean?"

"It means 'Chinese mother does daughter no favours'."

Fangfang swivelled her chair to face another screen – this one a battered laptop with a multi-level sword-fighting game on it; she made her move, lopping off a troll's head with an axe, arterial blood gushing everywhere, then took a mouthful of Diet Coke, pushing the glasses back up off her button nose onto her head, dismissing him again. He was willing to bet the Coke was warm from the heat of the machine. A smell of hot metal and fried prawns in the room – the buzz and hum of the monitors inside his head.

"How do you know Peggy?"

Fang shrugged, but behind the teenage disdain North sensed that Peggy mattered. Or had done before she'd turned her back on her protégé. He heard Fang swallow the Coke and start chewing gum – the sound wet and sticky against her teeth.

"School." She abandoned her pretence at pigeon English and slid straight into thorough-bred Geordie. "Say I'm 'disruptive'. It is so not true. I do not disrupt – I contribute." There was a note of outrage.

Class after class. Exasperated, red-faced teachers as she took control of their whiteboards on her smartphone. Her headteacher shouting, his arms windmilling after she crashed the school's server. North had been there himself. Disrespecting staff, overturning desks, slamming his way out of class. The other kids' wariness. North knew nothing about children but he knew that Fang was different and difference was a capital crime at fourteen.

School persuaded Peggy to take her on. Doubtless they'd used terms like genius and gifted, rather than "disruptive" and "pain in the arse".

"Dr B. said they didn't know what they were missing. I'm a 'prodigy'." Fangfang placed theatrical emphasis on the word "prodigy". Peggy's word. Peggy who had taken damaged, faithless Honor under her wing and healed her. A woman who always knew the right words to make things better.

"And?"

She shrugged again. "I did some work for her. Crunching data. Trying to make sense of it. She always said 'Look for the unexpected'. And she promised to talk to Mam and Granny Po about getting me over to MIT early. She was okay."

The word "okay" sounded odd in her mouth as if it were the first and possibly last time she'd admit to such a thing.

"I don't care she went away – it was lame anyhow. I like computers not space shite." She cared enough to stake out the university department day after day, waiting for Peggy to walk back in. She was let down, gutted. The power house brain that of an adult; the devastation that of an abandoned child.

"Peggy didn't walk out on you, Fangfang." The girl returned to her coding – showing him just how much the prodigy didn't care. "She's disappeared and I'm trying to find her."

A more casual observer than North might have thought Fang stopped listening when she blew an enormous blue bubble then popped it, fragile skin exploding over her nose and lips. But North knew as her pink tongue worked the skin back into her open mouth, she was taking in every word. She just hadn't decided how to feel about it yet.

He pulled out the black book and laid it flat on the desk, opening it at a random page, turning to another.

"Tell me what it says."

"Moron-person, I don't give it away," she said, rubbing her index and middle finger together against her thumb.

A teenage mercenary. He wished again for the bundles of red notes that had filled the rucksack that now lay at the bottom of the North Sea.

"I'm good for it."

Fang's fingers drummed on the desk. She wanted money, but she wanted to show him what she could do. The kid had thrown the star as a warning. It was a showy gesture meant to impress.

He left it a beat.

"I thought you'd want to help me find Peggy, but maybe it's too hard for you to understand, kiddo? No harm. No foul. Go back to your dragons." He reached over her to take back the book but she swivelled in her chair so he couldn't quite reach it. Her reactions were faster than Bannerman's.

"She didn't go away like they said? To Chile or some place full of saddos?"

"She didn't go anywhere she wanted to go."

From her mouth Fang extracted a piece of pale blue gum and stuck it behind her ear and under a plait. She licked her finger and thumb with some daintiness, before wiping them this way and that on her T-shirt and took hold of the book, pausing at each page, turning one or two of the pages upside down, reading some right-to-left and some left-to-right. She was too young. She didn't want to admit she didn't know, he'd decided. He would go back to Bannerman and threaten to kill him to help concentrate his mind. In his experience, people got a lot more helpful with the barrel of a gun pressed against their temple.

Pulling the keyboard towards her, Fang turned her head to pick up the paintbrush tip of her plait and slide it between her teeth, sucking as her stubby fingers stroked the keys all in a rush. North couldn't keep up as the girl pushed through the pure mathematics and complex calculations. Explosions of white light and electric impulses surged through her, fizzing and popping. There was a shift as her fingers paused over the keyboard and she spat out the plait. Irritation. A sense of being lifted, held over the void and a rushing, terrifying dislocation as something in her hurled out the distraction that was him. Was it real? Did it happen? Or had his analogue brain blown a digital fuse in its attempt to keep up with what he could see happening on Fang's screens?

He shook his head from side to side. The surging energy and excitement had felt real. The speeding numbers he could never begin to calculate. Did the girl sense some intrusion? Typing again, gum gone from behind her ear, Fang popped another blue bubble then gave a magnificent burp smelling of synthetic raspberries. He couldn't tell. He wasn't going back there. If it was a delusion, he could do without it. If it happened and he staged a home invasion on Fangfang's brain, next time she might throw him clear out of his own mind, let alone hers, and straight into an abyss from which there were no return. He could decide if he were mad later. Right this second it was easier to watch the screen.

Fangfang was in some sort of cloud, not one he'd ever seen before, picking her way through. When she got knocked back, she tried again. Different numbers. Different letters. Spooling out the yarn to navigate her way through the maze. JocelynBellBurnell235641. Suddenly she was there. Inside Peggy's work, and he was staring at the same pictures and graphs as those in the book. Only this time there were numbers and calculations attached. And more of them. Lots more. The kid was a thing of wonder.

"Jocelyn Bell Burnell discovered radio pulsars. Men got the Nobel Prize – she didn't. Peggy had a sick poster of her.

235641 – 23 hours 56 minutes and 41 seconds, the length of a sidereal day."

North looked blank. It wasn't hard. Fangfang rolled her eyes.

"That's the time taken for the Earth to rotate once on its axis in relation to the stars. It's nearly four minutes shorter than the solar day. We had this joke about what time I turned up for sessions – sidereal time or real time."

She made no effort not to look smug.

"A friend said all her stuff was locked up. Behind some weird password."

Fangfang shrugged as if some weird password was nothing to her. "This isn't regular stuff on the university server. She said she didn't trust old man Bannerman not to steal it. This is her private vault in the deep web. No one knows it exists 'cept me and Peggy."

Bannerman, thought North. Bitter. Covetous. Reaching for the book. Fury when denied. How far would he go?

"This is where we stored the work. I number-crunched some of it, because I saw connections her PhD students didn't. That's what she said. She locked me out when it was done, but I knew the old password – NGC1952. That's her favourite nebula."

"Do you understand what's here Fangfang?"

"Not all. There's masses of data." It was a major concession on Fang's behalf and she didn't want to admit it. "All I know is she came up with some algorithm you could write into a smart chip. This must be it. It suppressed the radio interference from any device it went into. If the smart chip was in enough devices, she said it would be easier to pick up the signals from space. The sweet thing was that the algorithm made the device more energy-efficient. Which made it cheaper to run. Everyone would want it, she said – energy companies, utilities, manufacturers, communication companies, people deciding which phone to buy. She was ultra-excited – said she knew someone. But she didn't want to sell it – she was giving it away to get it out there."

Peggy left Honor a clue. Play hunt the thimble. She was relying on Honor to find Fangfang, but she hadn't wanted to leave her work out in the open in case it fell into the wrong hands. Like Walt Bannerman. Did she think Bannerman would want to sell it rather than give it away?

Everyone would want it. How many devices were there out in the world? One billion?

Ten billion? Fifty billion within five years? All with the same chip. All connected.

North swung Fang round in her chair. His heart pounded in his chest, frightened suddenly for Peggy, for the teenage girl who sat in front of him, for himself.

"Who did she know, Fang?"

"Some guy she called the Pyjama Man. She said he was a creep but it was his kind of thing."

Pyjama Man? PJ Man.

PJ or JP?

JP Armitage?

JP who was riding to Honor's rescue. JP and Peggy knew each other. Had done for years. And JP had commercial interests in communications like he had commercial interests in everything else – including the New Army. Peggy wanted the world to be a quieter place so she could hear the noise from the stars. JP could make that happen. But why hadn't JP mentioned that he was working with Peggy when Honor was worried? He said he had his own people looking for her and North had taken that as a lover's gesture to reassure

Honor. But maybe he was looking for Peggy because she had something he needed? Something which was worth another fortune. Or maybe he knew exactly where she was?

The geek girl shrugged. A teenager again. Adrift in an adult world. "But then she shut me out. Said for us to focus on getting me into MIT and that all this was too much of a distraction. Said I could come study with her after MIT." Her lower lip came out at the memory of it. The sulking child. She'd been furious. He saw the tantrum she'd thrown as Peggy watched. Calm. Waiting for the temper to subside.

Did Peggy push the child away when she realised it was getting dangerous? That there were those who would corrupt her pure science into something that could wreak damage?

Someone like JP?

Honor. The thought of her went up like a distress signal. She was going back to London, straight into the arms of JP Armitage, and North had no way to warn her.

37

Newcastle

2.35pm. Wednesday, 8th November

Fangfang hacked the flight manifest but there was no trace of Honor. The Board had to be watching the train station. Watching the buses. Watching the roads in case she tried to thumb another ride. Hire companies. Fangfang crashed the mainframe to pull up the CCTV at the train station. Spooled backwards. He missed her the first time. Had moved on to service stations. Went back.

On the concourse of the central station, a hunched-over figure in ugly shoes and a shapeless anorak pulled along a huge tartan case. The woman stopped to have a word with the guard. Asking the platform number? Shuffled through the ticket barrier and onto the platform, head down as she waited on the bench, as if she were dozing or daydreaming.

Waiting as the train pulled in. Gathering herself. Smoothing down the A-line skirt. Lifting the suitcase first – climbing on board.

The train. Cash. No names. What had she done? Found a charity shop? Bought a case? An old handbag? Changed her walk. Greased down and tied back her hair. Streaked too much face powder and grey eyeshadow over her face. Playing at looking older just like she did when she was sixteen. Honor was adaptable. He'd give her that.

The London train took three hours and she had left two hours ago on the 12.30 service. There was no way he could make it in time, even if he stole a car. Honor, who thought JP Armitage was her best ally and hope.

The blue light didn't register though it was on. He was walking away from the Oriental Dragon back into the city, still considering which car to steal and how fast to drive it down to London, when the police car swerved up onto the pavement in front of him.

38

London

From a fast-food café along the Strand, Honor perched on a stool in the window, sipping tea and watching the doors of Coutts for an hour before she made her move. As far as she could see, she was the only watcher. She knew the risks, but she was being careful and she was out of money. The charity shop and the single ticket to London took every penny she'd stolen from the pub till. She felt bad as she slid behind the bar and rang in No Sale, stuffing the brown notes into her pockets. But not bad enough to walk away without the money. As soon as she had some cash of her own, she'd send it back with interest and a note of apology.

She was fast becoming a criminal. It was all North's fault – he was a terrible influence.

At least she paid the old dear in Cancer Research for the brown plastic handbag and the tartan case, as well as the ugliest pair of shoes she could find. She hadn't paid for the skirt or anorak, just stuffed them into the case along with the notebook. When the little old lady found the donkey jacket hanging without a price tag, Honor thought she'd understand. In an alley round the back of the shops, she'd rolled up the legs of her jeans and stepped into the skirt, pulled on the anorak and the shoes, discarding the rubber boots in a wheelie bin. In a public convenience she'd plastered down her hair with water, and used the testers in Superdrug to do their worst. When she admired her handiwork in the mirrors – plain, dumpy and twenty years older – even she was astonished at the transformation. After that, it was all in the walk and the attitude. Rounding her shoulders. Pigeon-toed. Trodden down. Her name was Monica Jean, she decided; she liked cats and read the *Daily Express* from cover to cover. She wasn't worth looking at twice.

In the train toilet, she rolled down the jeans and washed off Monica Jean's face. The Crimplene skirt, anorak and the been-around handbag went back in the tartan case, which went back on the rack above someone else's seat. When she disembarked at King's Cross, only the notebook dangled from her fingers in its plastic bag. A student coming home to visit family, she decided. Casual. Happy to be back in The Smoke.

This moment though was risky. Three months ago JP set up an account in her name and insisted on putting fifty grand in. She had gone berserk with him, but he'd ignored her protests. *Spend it or give it away to charity, I don't care. We're going to be married and what's mine is yours.* She never touched a penny. Swore she never would. She'd pay JP every penny back when this was over. Did the Board know about the account? And were they watching the bank?

She took a breath, pushed back her shoulders, head down, crossing the road on the diagonal as if heading for Trafalgar Square before veering sharply right and into the doorway.

It was all pin striped efficiency in Coutts, and afternoon tea in exquisitely thin porcelain cups. She wanted £10,000 "walking around money" – JP insisted. "Pre-wedding expenses." At the mention of the tycoon's name, the obsequious account manager couldn't sign over the money fast enough.

And later, walking up the Strand close to the buildings, not trusting herself yet to claim the middle of the pavement, convincing herself that North was a grown-up. He could look after himself. It wasn't as if he were her friend. He was a stranger with a late-blooming conscience. She had one friend in the world.

Peggy.

Thinking of Peggy. Wanting her like a drug. Not thinking of North. He was someone from a bad dream and she'd woken up.

She planned it all out. Bring JP into line and get him to leverage his contacts in the judiciary and police. Go public and make as much noise in the media as humanly possible. JP had the best PR in the business so it wouldn't be hard. The faked suicide attempt was a smokescreen for these animals to operate behind. It would fall to dust if enough light were shone on it and she would deny it till she was believed. Poor dead Hugh was proof of conspiracy if anyone needed it. His corpse was undeniable. He was a city banker – what was his body doing hundreds of miles away in the sea?

Honor glanced into a shop window. The reflection of the busy street behind her, tourists and office workers passing this way and that, black cabs and red buses. She'd done it. Slipped back into London city without anyone realising. How long did she have in the open? Not long without protection.

Her eyes moved from the hustle and bustle behind to her own face, to the usually perfectly blow-dried hair hanging limp and greasy. Her face might be clean but the strain of thirty-six hours was showing. The manager at Coutts was too well trained to pass comment, but she caught the widening of his eyes at the state she was in. Another rich eccentric – is that what he thought? She paused, looking past the glass at the cloth dummy in the tailored French navy suit and the raspberry-pink silk shirt. Court shoes. A rip-off Birkin bag just big enough for the notebook.

Convention dictated that she needed to look the part. She'd operated on that principle her entire life. Look like a grown-up. Look like a talented lawyer. Look like an MP going places. Look like a whole person unscathed by her shipwreck of a childhood. In her experience people took you at your own estimation. She was back and she was about to look like trouble for whoever and whatever was going on. They had no idea who they were dealing with.

The Savoy Hotel was used to wealthy people who didn't follow rules. Honor Jones may not have carried luggage, but she did have shopping bags and, most important of all, Honor Jones had a great many bundles of cash. It took seven minutes before she also had the keys to Room 107.

39

Savoy Hotel, London

5.50pm. Wednesday, 8th November

From her room, she dialled 9 for an outside line and called JP's private number.

He was furious. She let him eff and blind for a while then put the phone down on him.

Perched on the side of the bed, she unscrewed the lid from the bottle of mineral water and poured its sparkling contents into a tumbler. Welsh. Her favourite.

The second time she rang, he had himself in check. "Honor. Please. I've been frantic."

She could hear him waving off his PA, shouting to *shut the damn door.*

"Where have you been? What were you thinking checking out of hospital like that? And who the hell was this 'brother' who picked you up?"

As he rattled out questions and commands, she sipped the water, gazing out of the window at the golden lights strung along the South Bank, and the memory of Ned plummeting from Westminster Bridge slammed its way into her head.

JP was still talking. Barely pausing for breath in his relief. She let him – enjoying the sound of his voice. The familiarity of the flat Yorkshire vowels.

She needed JP. Needed his arms around her. Needed to weep into his chest and feel safe – that it would be all right. More than that. She needed what he could do for her. But the last time they were together she was at a disadvantage – half drowned, with her wrist slashed and lying helpless in a hospital bed. He'd seen the bloody bandage, her pallor and desperation, and he'd shut down in his own horror at the prospect of losing her. He'd barely listened, and what he did hear he didn't credit. This time had to be different. She had no intention of meeting him on his territory – not in the city office, not his place in Chelsea, and not the mews. Westminster was impossible. And she wasn't going back to the flat where she'd almost died. Somewhere public then because she wanted to talk without interruption. That's why she'd checked into the Savoy after all.

He drew breath.

"JP, I will buy you a drink. Not least because, after the last couple of days, I need one.

I'll see you at the American Bar in the Savoy Hotel at seven. Don't be late." He didn't argue.

40

Newcastle

6.15pm. Wednesday, 8th November

The overwhelming noise in the interview room in Newcastle City Centre Police Station was the buzz of the ancient digital recorder, but outside the room came the banging of far-away doors, the occasional drunken yell, and a raucous chorusing of the Blaydon Races.

That and the ticking. Louder and louder in North's ears.

41

Savoy Hotel, London

7pm. Wednesday, 8th November

The cubes of ice clinked, one against the other, all but drowned in the Tanqueray gin and artisan tonic, which JP ordered with ice, no lemon, for both of them. Honor opened her mouth to ask for whisky – Glenmorangie – then closed it again.

For a brief second she thought of sitting with North in the bar of the Gallows Widow.

His face as he listened to her. Absorbed. Open. The shape of his mouth. She wondered if he'd left the country yet. She'd been hard on him. But it was better this way. Cleaner. For the first time since she opened the paper and saw Ned's death, she allowed herself to relax. She was bone-tired, but she was back in the real world. Her world of laws and due process and power. She was finding Peggy this way, not on some mad quest with a psychopathic sidekick, and JP was going to help her do it.

He held out his heavy-bottomed glass. The drink clear and honest like water. He was relieved, she thought. More than relieved – ecstatic she was sitting in front of him, in a smart suit and a silk shirt. Sane and together. She panicked him with her disappearing act. Of course he believed she tried to kill herself, and who could blame him? Devastated, he presumed she went away to try again. There was guilt on her side then. She'd been cruel to leave like that. To have so little faith in the man she was to marry. She should have given him another chance to hear her out and to believe her.

The sight of him made Honor want to weep. She was wrong to keep him at a distance. She should have married him when he asked – certainly the third time he asked. Hadn't he looked out for her since her childhood – been a better father than her own father, been a better lover than a man half his age? Everything he possessed he built himself – coming from nothing to have everything. He wasn't perfect – he had political convictions which verged on the extreme, but she could moderate the worst of them.

"Drink," he said. "You look like you need it. I bloody know I do."

They sat in the far corner away from the pianist – the notes flying round and over them. *What'll I do when you are far away*, she hummed along. Frank Sinatra. Or Bob Dylan. She preferred Bob Dylan – JP would be a Sinatra man.

"Honor…" JP was calling her back. "Tell me all of it " he said, and she forced herself to ignore the flicker of irritation she felt at the order.

She took it fast but JP Armitage kept up, and she didn't have to repeat herself or explain any of it. He knew some of it already – Peggy's disappearance and her meeting with geeky Ned. His death. His eyes widened as she took him through the run in the park. North. Her attacker in the bathroom. North again.

The pianist stopped wondering what he would do and admitted he was a fool for love.

JP sat up straighter in his chair at her mention of North's role in her departure from the hospital, but she pretended not to notice. The drive into the sea. The helicopter. North wasn't a criminal. She didn't know what he was, but she didn't care. There was Ned, and Peggy, and now that poor young banker's body pulled from the sea. A simple DNA test would prove who it was.

JP had to believe her. Did he?

"Honor, what you're telling me is incredible." He stared into his drink. He hadn't even touched it – ice melting, bubbles almost gone. It was murky, she noticed, its surface oily from the gin.

She reached out to him as he raised his head. And she could see that he believed all of it. Every word. Relief washed through her. He'd never looked so angry, so in charge, and she rejoiced that he was older, wealthier and more powerful than other men. That he knew what was to be done, because she needed him, and need was the best kind of love of all, wasn't it?

"You've been to Hell and back."

As he slid his huge, square hand over hers, she smiled at the touch of a man who thought about the consequences of his actions. Who knew right from wrong.

"Show me the notebook. Are there names in it?"

She picked up her new handbag, unzipped it, pulling out the plastic bag with the notebook in it. Except it wasn't Peggy's notebook, it was *Advanced Mathematics* by Thomas J. Jackson. A black, shiny cover, white font. How had she not noticed the difference? Because North had bought a book as close in size to Peggy's notebook as he was able. The same shape and weight to make the switch that much easier. Bastard North.

"He took it."

Her brain did a rapid calculation as to the effect this would have on her credibility. Would JP take it as further proof of the insanity she was denying?

"He's a criminal – of course he took it."

But there was something else. Nagging at her.

"He'll sell it or he'll use it to bargain with." JP shrugged. "Don't worry. We'll get it back."

Armitage slid his hand over hers again, warm and dry, keeping her safe. An itch in her brain.

She hadn't mentioned the notebook in her story, so how did JP know she should have it?

"Do you trust me, Honor?"

Did she?

Could she?

Ned's voice. *Trust no one.* But he didn't mean the man she was going to marry. He meant North, who stole the most important thing she had: Peggy's notebook. She was exhausted. It was an easy enough mistake to get confused about what she had and hadn't said. She must have mentioned it when she told him about escaping from the island.

She'd always known that a man could look like a husband and father and turn into a violent predator. But a man could look like a husband and father and be just that. A defender. A protector. A partner. JP's face was so familiar to her. When this was over, she'd marry him. A huge white wedding in Westminster Abbey with two thousand guests and vintage lace and satin and a diamond tiara. He'd like that. And maybe she would have a baby with him. Do that for him.

Do you trust me?

If she weren't willing to answer that question with an affirmative, she couldn't marry him, and she wanted to marry him. A spring wedding with boughs of deep-pink cherry blossom in the Abbey – she'd carry a sprig in a hand tied bouquet. Her mother always loved cherry blossom.

There was a sharp pain in the back of her hand, as if a dozen wasps had stung her all at once. She made to pull away, but JP kept hold as if he were never letting go of her again. Happiness drained from his face. His expression darkened. Intent. Tormented. His brow furrowed. He didn't understand. "I need to explain better," she thought, but her mouth refused to work. Swaying in her seat as JP swam in and out of focus. Fighting it. She had to stay awake for Peggy. Her world tipped, the piano music discordant, crazy sharps and flats, and JP lifted her from the seat, waving away the waiter.

"It's all good," she heard. "One too many." Her head against his broad chest, his heartbeat, his powerful arm around her, the muscles, his broad hand at her waist, as the buzzing, tinkling room dipped and spun. Too warm. A walk. Desperate for fresh air – he realised without her speaking the words. He took her key card, half carrying her out of the bar, across the Art Deco foyer, but not towards the front door. She wanted the door and the green-coated porters with their stove-pipe hats. The outside and the black cab. North. But it was JP holding her up. Not North. Holding her tight to him. Here comes the bride. For richer, for poorer. In sickness and in health into the elevator. Watching him. Blurring. His face distorted in the shining brass plate of the elevator. Not who he should be.

And before she knew it, before she could speak, she was out again into the spinning, topsy-turvy world with its marshmallow floor and its numbered bedrooms with their spying eyes. The endless corridor, her hand reaching out – grabbing hold – but the wall slipped from her grasp. Resisting again at her doorway. Like an over-tired child who didn't want to go to bed. Like a hopeless drunk wanting to stay at the party. Overcome. Feeling her weakness.

Pushed into her room where she staggered, half turned, her eyes closing, feeling herself falling through space, spread-eagled, onto the bed.

42

Newcastle

Detective Chief Inspector Slim Hardman's hands rested on the steel desk – the wedding band cutting into the pink flesh. The fat man had an open attitude, a triple-chinned smile that said "Try me – I'll understand, my friend."

They'd taken North's clothes for forensic testing. The white paper suit was cheap and noisy against his legs, his feet sweating in the tight white plimsolls. Under the desk, he rubbed at the ink from his fingertips.

Much good would the fingerprints do them – there was no sign of him on any criminal, or indeed military, database. Michael North worked as a hedge-fund manager for Chalfont Securities. There was a head and shoulders shot of him on the corporate website. He was very well qualified. After all, he had an MBA from Harvard and there were Harvard academics willing to attest to his qualifications. He was pretty sure a Harvard man wouldn't slit the throat of anyone but a Yale man.

And, bizarrely, he was innocent. Bannerman was dead but Michael North hadn't killed him. North was working it out in his head. Bannerman had to have been involved. When North showed him Peggy's notebook, he'd barely been able to control himself. Then again, if he were working with the Board, if he were useful to them, surely he'd still be alive?

North's mind turned to the man at the quayside. The figure in the riding coat. Standing waiting for the lifeboat to bring in the body of the young banker. Hunkered down. His face grim.

"I already told you, Inspector, I'm an old friend of Peggy Boland. I went to Peggy's office – as I said I've known her for years and I've been to her office before."

He had never been to her office, but try proving it.

"Bannerman was working there. He said she'd left but he didn't have a contact number for her, so I asked the secretary if she knew where Peggy's young student lived."

When you tell a lie, you stick as close to the truth as you can. Snivelling, Mrs Craggs described the stranger who came looking for Peggy's Chinese prodigy that morning. Tall. Very tall. Broad. Muscled. Close-cropped hair. Hard face. Good-looking if you liked that kind of thing. Which she didn't. But mean – despite the smile. Dangerous, if you asked her.

And in the chaos of her filing, despite her snot and gulping misery, she found Fangfang's address – the Oriental Dragon in the worst part of town.

Hardman sent two patrol cars into the city's West End – prompted by the ear-to-ear slash across the corpse's throat rather than Mrs Craggs' instincts. They picked North up a quarter of a mile from the takeaway.

"I've never met Professor Bannerman before today, Inspector." North's tone was that of a law-abiding citizen shocked by the distasteful business of violent death. "He wasn't helpful and I may have pointed out that fact, but when I left his office he was alive."

"You're a witness then – like a Jehovah's Witness?" Hardman smoothed his tie over his belly, enjoying his own joke. "Because I'm more of an atheist. Of course in court I'll always swear on a Bible because juries like that, but really, lad, between you and me I simply believe in the truth, the whole truth and you know the rest."

They patted him down before they put him in the patrol car and found no weapon. The only thing he was carrying was the notebook. Hardman hadn't yet mentioned the fact there was no ID, wallet or money.

"But you spent fifteen minutes with Walt Bannerman, we're told by Mrs Craggs."

The neon strip lighting behind its cage began to hum in sympathy with the buzz of the recorder.

"He gave me a notebook Peggy left behind. He said he found it in a drawer when he took over her office." North spoke with deliberation, as if doing his best to be of help to the police. He was lying but Bannerman was dead, which made it hard to call him on it, and Peggy did leave the book behind – only in the sea rather than in her office drawer.

Hardman pushed over the book, which was now in a plastic bag. "I can't make head nor tail. What is it?"

North made the smallest shrugging motion. He was a fund manager not a physicist. He took it as a favour to his good friend Peggy, to pass on as soon as they met up. It can't have been that important or she'd have taken it with her.

"You left Dr Bannerman's office at ten, then you went to have a chat with Mrs Craggs.

The professor's body was discovered at 1.30pm. You've told us you were in Chinatown, which checks out, but we can't say for certain what time you went to Chinatown. I suspect we have at least forty-five minutes to one hour which you can't account for."

North raised his eyebrows and lowered the corners of his mouth as if to say he understood Hardman's problem but he shouldn't let it worry him.

"Forget it, Jake. It's Chinatown." North smiled, but instead of returning the smile, the policeman noticed a grease spot on his tie – his immense fingers lifting the silk for inspection, dropping it down again, and there was a sudden smell of steak and kidney pie, the splintering of glaze and puff pastry. As they'd walked into the interview room, a passing sergeant had asked Hardman *"How's Mary?"* Something in the tone of the sergeant's voice. Sadness. Affection. Hardman's wife made the steak pie from scratch, and she wasn't well.

Breast cancer.

And Hardman worried about her on her own. Because he loved her.

He was the faithful type. The till-death-do-you-part kind.

North wondered how the policeman would react if his "person of interest" enquired about the state of his wife's health. He was guessing not well. Especially if North had it right. He sighed. Not knowing the extent of your own sanity was exhausting.

Hardman's blackcurrant eyes were on him. Cool. Appraising North's size. The bulk. How he sat. Taking all of him in. "Were you ever in the Forces?"

He couldn't admit it, so he denied it, and Hardman let out a small hmmm noise.

"I've normally a good instinct for it. Ex-Forces men – they carry themselves a particular way."

North kept his face polite, listening. His chat to the police an "experience" to recount over metropolitan dinner tables.

"The thing is I've a dead body. Which is bad enough." The policeman shook his head from side to side in sorrow, and, seconds later, his jowls followed. "But the dead body is that of an astronomer."

North focused on being a good citizen caught up in events and willing to go wherever the policeman was taking him.

"And as it happens, would you credit it, I also have a missing astronomer – that's to say your would-be dinner date Dr Peggy Boland. Now that is, what we call in the policing business, 'odd'."

Hardman beamed as if he'd told a joke at the golf club bar, and North smiled back as if he too played golf, as if he knew the rules of civilised behaviour and engagement.

"I say 'missing', but there's confusion over that. Dr Peggy Boland was 'reported missing' by her friend. An MP no less. A real looker by the by. You'll know her too, I imagine?"

"We've met." North gave him that, keeping his voice steady, though the mention of Honor, even indirectly, sent electricity surging through every part of him. Was she in London yet? Was she safe?

"But that very day, Dr Boland rings me and denies she's missing. Explains she's working in some desert. Atrocious line. It quite cheered me up though – the fact I could tell her friend to stop worrying – because she was distraught was the MP. Understandably. The strangest thing though, Mr North. My colleagues pulled in a no-mark a couple of days since. Small-time, petty drugs dealer by the name of Jimmy the Sniff and he starts burbling to my colleagues about a missing woman. How, if we overlook his little problem, he'll help us out with information. He's the chatty type. But, they explain, we don't have a missing woman, so Chatty Cathy shuts his mouth pronto."

Jimmy the Sniff?

The policeman's voice was a confiding, sentimental baritone. North beat down the sudden urge to please the DCI, to win his approval and to be deemed honest. He could tell him about his medals – the Army, the bullet, and plead for help. Hardman would like him then, see him as a decent man in a bad fix.

"I'm not one for coincidences. I'm asking you does Dr Peggy Boland need finding all over again?"

There was silence between the interrogator and witness, as the second hand set off from one moment before landing on the next.

He was tempted.

But if he said yes and told the truth, it couldn't be the whole truth and nothing but the truth. The best scenario involved the police keeping him for hours with their questions.

He was tempted.

But he didn't have time to waste when there was a man out there called Jimmy the Sniff desperate to tell what he knew about a woman no one knew was missing.

Sometimes a lie was the only way to go. He couldn't tell Hardman about the Board, which meant he couldn't tell him anything. Honor was right. How did he explain himself in the civilised world?

Hardman waited.

"I've no idea, Inspector. As I say, I'd a few days so I stopped off en route to Edinburgh to take her out to dinner."

He gave Hardman a smile one man gives another when he says dinner and means more.

The detective reached out his arm and turned off the tape recorder – white noise replaced by sudden silence, even the light above them quietening. Hardman sat back in his chair, although his enormous belly still pushed against the table.

"If you need my help in something, Michael, this is the time to tell me."

Hardman struck him as an honest man. Thoughtful. Sharp.

He was tempted.

He said nothing.

And across from him, the DCI's face hardened. The arm going out. The recorder going back on. Noise starting up again.

A picture of Bannerman. His throat cut. Blood.

Behind the jokes, the avuncular smile, Hardman was a cold-to-the-touch lawman who wanted the guilty put away in a dank cell with its own facilities and for more years than there were numbers.

"Are you right-handed, Mr North, or left?"

"Right."

"When we get your clothes tested, will there be blood splatter indicating you came back to the department and you stood behind Dr Walt Bannerman and cut his throat? What do you think, Mr North?"

North hadn't cut Bannerman's throat. But it wasn't beyond the Board to make it look like he had. He kept quiet. Even a good citizen might start thinking about a lawyer when asked a question like that.

Hardman leaned forward, crushing his enormous belly against the metal desk. His voice was cold. The favourite uncle routine over. That was for witnesses. North was sliding headlong into suspect territory.

"Fortunately, we have a witness who noticed a man leaving the department with blood on his right shoe. Unfortunately, the witness cannot recall the exact time of the suspect's departure. You'll be formally arrested and read your rights before the ID parade."

There was a knock on the door as a skinny constable leaned his head into the room and the fat man stood up. Hardman adjusted his trousers over the immensity of his stomach, his steely gaze still on North, before crossing to the door.

It was ajar but North couldn't make out any words. He turned Bannerman's murder over in his head. Bannerman was slimy and duplicitous. He'd hated Peggy and he wanted her notebook, but why would anyone kill him? North's innocence was beside the point. If the Board killed Bannerman, Tarn might well decide North made for a convenient patsy. And if the police charged him with the murder and locked him up, chances were before any court case a guilty conscience would prompt him to throw himself down a twisting cast iron staircase, or hang himself with his own bed sheet because his cellmate had a deviated septum and snored at night. All very unfortunate – especially for Michael North.

The door opened wide again, and the fat man beckoned – his pudgy forefinger rolling up and down. Show time.

North glanced at the clock – it was a minute before eight. The police could hold him for ninety-six hours if they got the go-ahead from a magistrate. The long hand moved to make it eight with a loud click. He wondered whether Honor would survive without him. He thought not.

43

Newcastle

9.30pm. Wednesday, 8th November

He stood at number 4 in the line-up. Hardman hadn't rushed it, and the police hadn't worked too hard to find anyone who looked like him. A swaying, puce-faced drunk they must have pulled from their cells stood on one side, a skinny, resentful Asian pizza-delivery guy on the other, along with three meatheads who looked like they used the same barber – the biggest with a tattoo of a tarantula climbing up one side of his thick, razored neck, a Gothic "Bite me" on the other. North was the tallest by at least four inches.

A voice from a loudspeaker above the window instructed them to turn to the left and then to the right. North planted his eyes forward, legs foursquare at each turn. Sweating innocence. As if he were on parade, boots shined for inspection. As if he were a decent public citizen doing the police a particular favour by coming in for a line up. As if he were innocent, which should have made it easy. But didn't.

"Step forward, number 4," the voice instructed. He took a step forward and stared into the glass.

If Hardman got an ID, it was over. Locked up he would be dead within days, and Honor wouldn't make it that long.

"Step forward, number 6."

Spider-man stepped forward. It looked like he had done it a million times before. Like he would again. That sometimes he would be nervous and sometimes he wouldn't. That sometimes he would look into the glass and hope whoever watched from behind it didn't recognise him. Today though he didn't much care.

"Okay, number 6, step back. Number 4, step forward please."

North took a step – lifting his foot, setting it down, lifting the other, setting it down. His reflection stared back at him. He could do with a hot shower and what passed these days for a decent night's sleep. He thought about a narrow bed in a police cell smelling of piss. Even that had its attractions right this moment if there weren't the real prospect that he'd close his eyes and never get to open them again.

Time stopped.

Behind him the minds of the men opened up – curious, incurious, raging and bleak, the taste of stale booze and cigarettes, curry and something dark and unholy from Spider-man. The tears of a wife. He shut them out – he was either on the edge of complete insanity, or his brain was dialling up his intuition past the point of bearable.

Focus.

Who stood behind the mirror?

A witness saw a tall man leave minutes before the discovery of a bloody corpse.

A jolt of recognition. As if he were in there with them,

North saw it all play out in the dark room behind the glass. Hardman's best uncle routine, the inspector careful to reassure, the witness blooming under his kindly smile, his support and praise for her citizenship. Take her time. No rush.

"Step back into the line, number 4, please."

Although North could not distinguish figures behind the plate glass, he sensed movement. A noise like a door slamming. They would let the witness leave before allowing the line-up out from the room.

Their own door opened and the skeletal PC appeared. "All right, lads. Usual deal. The desk sergeant will see you right." North started to follow Spider-man. "Not you, sonny," the constable said, a hand on North's shoulder.

As North signed the custody record for his watch, the inspector leaned in close, Hardman's breath warm and smoky on North's ear. "Sudoku teaches you patience, Mr North, and I'm a patient man."

North fastened the strap of his watch around his wrist, his elbow leaning on the duty sergeant's desk. Picked up the notebook. Slid it into the pocket of the oilskin as Hardman looked on.

"Here's a puzzle for you, Sergeant."

His colleague stood to mock attention, readying himself to play the inspector's straight man.

"Normally, when we put forensics in, as you know, it takes three weeks – sometimes more. They like to take it slow in the labs."

The sergeant tutted loudly.

"Sometimes, I have to go along and shout at them. Sometimes, I send the wife – she doesn't like things taking too long, which can be a relief for a man my age. But North here – his results came back very quick. No evidence against him whatsoever. No witness ID. No comeback on the prints despite the fact he admits himself he was in the office. No DNA at the scene. No blood on his clothes or his shoes or that nice watch or his book. And the Chief Constable himself rang for a chat, suggesting Mr North should get back to his life. Funny that – because he's a busy man the Chief Constable, what with all the silver buttons he has to polish and arses he has to lick."

A frisson of shock from the sergeant, his eyes flicking left to right checking for eavesdroppers. Hardman carried on regardless.

The witness didn't ID him from the line-up.

Hardman had to let him go, and he wasn't happy. North was more worried about the Board. His name was in the system and it wouldn't take the Board long to discover it if they hadn't already. The longer Hardman talked, the more chance there was of finding another body on his streets all too soon – this one belonging to one Michael North.

"So here he is, going home in his own shoes and his clothes with his own watch and that intriguing little book, when by rights those things belong here, and I don't like that one jot because I like things done the old-fashioned way. I'm a simple man, and this makes me 'uncomfortable', which is very close to making me 'cross'. And he really wouldn't like to see me 'cross' would he, Sergeant?"

The duty sergeant's response was understood.

"I don't know what or who you are, Mr North," said Hardman, switching his focus back. "And I'm not sure I want to. Despite your name, you don't belong here. Take my advice: be on the next train out. London…" Hardman jerked his thumb away from him "…is that way."

44

Newcastle

11.07pm. Wednesday, 8th November

Her thumb and forefinger in her mouth, the redhead whistled – low and piercing.

North was across the road, but even fifty yards distant, he could make out a body that promised the world. Grinning, the freckled girl stood up from the low brick wall opposite the station and, with the sudden movement, her hair tumbled from its bird's nest, bang-on ginger curls escaping like they were keen to be up and partying. She raised three fingers before slapping them against her bicep, then with her two index fingers drew a circle in front of her. Three words. The whole thing. A beautiful stranger wanted to play charades. She raised her eyebrows.

He nodded. He'd play. It wasn't like he had anything better to do.

The girl rubbed the end of her freckled nose with her fingers as if she had a cold. He stared at her. Blank.

She made a face that said *What are you? Stupid?* and

rubbed the end of her nose harder, widening her eyes this time and shaking her head as if the hit had just kicked in. As if she were rubbing off white powder.

Jimmy the Sniff – the drug dealer Hardman mentioned. She knew Jimmy.

Game over, she winked, and started walking away, her long legs scissoring in baby blue paint-on jeans. Why were women always walking away from him these days? The Detective Chief Inspector's words came back to him: *"Be on the next train out"*. It was excellent advice, and he watched her go.

Except that North wasn't ready to leave town yet.

He stepped out into the road, back onto the pavement, her side of the street now.

Following. Admiring the view. He had felt dead inside for the longest time – since he got shot? Since his mother died? Since he was born? He'd had no sleep for days, he was starving and Honor had abandoned him, but one thing he didn't feel was dead inside.

The Board wanted Honor dead because she was making a fuss about her friend's disappearance. If she were dead already, there was nothing he could do. If she weren't, her best chance of survival – and for that matter his best chance of survival – was knowledge, because it was the only leverage they had. And Jimmy the Sniff seemed as good a place to start as any.

The kitten heels of the ankle boots tip-tapped along the pavement ahead of him. The redhead walking like she was in a hurry, like she had some place she wanted to be, swaying and unsteady as if it had been a long day and she wanted done with it. She turned left, then right towards the river, glancing at him once, the suspicion of a dimpled smile before she ducked into a doorway and disappeared. North hesitated.

He still had time to catch the train Hardman told him to be on. Clear town before the Board sent a clean-up man in. Time to forget he ever met Honor. He peered down the narrow stairway, lined with black and white headshots of old Hollywood movie stars, and which led down into a basement. He thought about what Jimmy might know, the denim sway of the girl ahead as she rounded the corner. Honor's sea-green eyes. He wondered if the redhead would let him use her phone to call Honor's parliamentary office. Maybe Honor was okay? Maybe she would ring in? Maybe she'd even go back to the Commons? He could explain why he kept Peggy's book. There were all sorts of reasons to follow.

There must have been a sign at the door, though he hadn't noticed it. But perhaps not – some of these clubs liked to pretend they were decent, the sort of bar a businessman might find himself in to "unwind". Nothing sleazy – nice girls, respectable.

It took a while for his eye to adjust to the gloom. Flickering candles on each table, tiny pin prick stars across the ceiling. On an empty stage there was a pole and a girl who seemed to like it, while the banquettes around the walls were a crushed midnight-blue velvet – the nap worn at the edge from sweaty hands of sweaty men getting sweatier as the girls did their dances. At first glance he'd thought the club empty aside from the dancer – his redhead vanished into dry ice and the bass beat of Eminem. Then the other women came into focus. A muscled blonde behind the bar, the sides of her head shaven and dyed like pink and purple leopard skin, and two scantily clad lovelies perched on stools admiring the contortions of the pole dancer. No one looked surprised to see him.

The pole dancer watched as she dangled upside down, her arms holding the bar – biceps bulging, her hair lost in the billowing smoke, her right leg wrapped around like a python, the left pointing to the stars, her best assets fighting gravity, glittering green and gold in their all-in-one bodysuit. He thought of the Lambton Worm, some story dragged out of his childhood of a woman turned into a dragon who wrapped itself around a well three times – devouring sheep and cattle and babies. The pole dancer shifted her grip and her leg unwound itself out from the bar, the left moving down and away till they formed a wide-open V like the maw of a snake ready to swallow its next meal. In the mirrors around the club, smaller python women did the same thing over and over again.

He wondered if he'd miscalled it. If the redhead hadn't done the come-hither. If his instincts were off and what she had been doing was walking away as quickly as she could when she saw him come out of the police station. But there'd been the charade, the dimpled smile, the sashay – his admiration. The way she'd seemed to sway all the harder the closer she got to her destination.

"I'm looking for a friend," he said. "A guy called Jimmy the Sniff?" Close up the barmaid's face came in two halves, the right side dragging down, her mouth twisted out of kilter, the left plain ugly. A stroke? Bell's palsy?

She took her time pouring a hefty vodka shot into the glass of coke sat in front of each girl, the bottle held low then high then low again, the sleeves of her plaid shirt rolled tight to her shoulders, her biceps heavily muscled and forearms tattooed and meaty, the hands large and workmanlike, red and purple, as if she had problems with her circulation, though the nails themselves were long and oval, covered with tiny green crystals – like the nails of another woman.

"You don't look the friendly type," she said when she'd done, her lower jaw that of a bad-tempered bulldog.

"Don't mind Stella. I'll be your friend, pet." A skinny arm draped itself over his shoulder as one of the two watchers took hold of the brass bar clamped to the oak counter and swung her stool closer, bringing with her the smell of coconuts and warm oiled flesh. The other girl's breasts pushed against him as she too closed in. "You can never have too many friends, hinny," her breath caramel-sweet and fizzy. They worked as a team. If they were planning to pick his pockets, they'd be sadly disappointed.

The leopard-skin blonde frowned at the girls, the lop-sided mouth a jagged scar, transforming the already strange face into a ruin. Stella didn't like him, yet in the smoky mirror behind the optics as she stowed away the vodka, she'd authorised the come-on. North saw it – the slightest of nods as they looked to her for their cue.

Picking up a bottle of champagne from a metal bucket of melting ice, water trailing from it across the polished bar, she emptied it carelessly into a grubby coupe as one of his new gal-pals slid her bony hand into his lap and started burrowing.

He removed the hand.

"Like your boss said – I'm not the friendly type, much as I appreciate the thought."

Bubbles scurried and popped in the glass in front of him. It was inviting but he had no money. He pushed it away.

"You're our best-looking customer today, babe." The barfly to his left giggled. "Anyway, the first drink's free to members. And everyone's a member."

Cheap champagne wasn't his go-to, but it had been a long, hard bitch of a day. He drank it – tipping the shallow glass back in one swallow, the taste sharp and bitter and gritty.

See how you like that, he caught, and the barmaid pulled out another bottle, gripping it by its long neck as if she might pour it or swing it against his head – she didn't much care which.

Did we do good, Stella? Did we? The girls' voices were cawing rooks strung out along a telegraph line in the fog. Tired – he hadn't understood how tired he was till this minute. He flinched at the pop of the cork, his hand going for a gun that wasn't there, and from a long way off he heard the two women laugh, pushing up against him, their small hands patting and pressing up and down his body as if they were searching him, rather than caressing him, caressing him rather than searching him. The champagne ran from the new bottle, deep gold in the lights that bounced from the overhead spots. He reached out – his hand huge suddenly. Unwieldy. The glass tipped as he picked it up, champagne spilling across the polished oak. The barmaid's hand over his, another at the elbow, as he raised the dregs to his lips and tipped it, powder on his teeth, and he swayed, crumpled, and fell.

45

Newcastle

12.13am. Thursday, 9th November

His lolling head jerked upright on his spine and, as he came to, he vomited once violently and efficiently, green bile rising into his throat, unstoppable. He spat – his head thunderous, as if the bullet were ricocheting around his skull, bouncing from wall to wall and destroying everything in there.

Awake.

The redhead. A body like that always spelled trouble. She was waiting for him.

Someone instructed her to bring him here. What was he thinking?

His forehead was freezing: a bag of ice pressing against his temple; he shrugged it off, regretting his haste as the earthquake in his brain brought down buildings.

A scrape of a chair along the floor and the spotlights blazed, smashing against his retinas like fists wearing knuckledusters.

"Would it help if I said I'm from TripAdvisor?" North coughed and spat again. The Mickey Finn left a taste like chewing green and rotting meat.

The pole dancer had disappeared, along with the two barflies. The leopard-skin blonde still had on the plaid shirt but now she sported a tan-leather shoulder holster, and a Glock 17. Its weight unloaded was 25.06 ounces. Its weight loaded: 32.12 ounces. The gun, like the woman, looked to be on the heavy side.

The good news was the Board hadn't caught up with him yet. The bad news – he moved on his chair and Stella's steel-toe boot came out and under it, tipping it to smash him, first against the pole and then against the floor. He willed the bullet in his brain to move and kill him where he lay – if only to take away the pain.

His mind filled with a storm of Stella's invective as he gazed up at her, her eyes baggy and cold, white-blonde hair with its leopard-skin pink and purple trim shorn like a marine.

Extraordinary hair. An alarm was ringing at the back of his skull that he couldn't switch off.

"The only reason you aren't dead yet is that our Jess has a kind heart."

For a second he wondered who she was talking about, then realised it was the redhead standing behind her. Jess winked at him.

"Does she take after her father?" he said. Stella heaved the chair back up till it rested foursquare-bang on its legs – North suspected for the simple pleasure of smashing him against the floor again when the mood took her. He braced, because she didn't seem a patient woman.

"I didn't kill Bannerman if that's what you're thinking."

Jess was the witness behind the glass. Reliable. Authentic. The only problem: she was a born liar, sent by her mother to get him out of police custody and into their own.

"That's a shame – Bannerman was a twat. But I'm more interested in what you've got to do with Peggy Boland. A little bird tells me you're trying to find her."

A little bird called Fangfang Yu – North would put money on it. Teenagers had no loyalty, especially when you hadn't paid for it yet.

"It's like I told Fang." He spoke in the even-tempered voice of a zoo-keeper locked in a cage with a slavering beast that hadn't been fed for a while. "Peggy's mixed up in something she doesn't want to be. And I'm trying to help."

Stella snarled, and Jess laid a hand on the pumped-up arm. The girl's nails matched those of her mother. She must have painted them for her. He wondered at the tricks genetics play – the adorable hour glass beauty he'd followed through the streets, and this pierced bruiser of a harridan.

"And where does my nephew fit into this? The nephew we bury next week."

Nephew? He didn't need any bullet in his brain to sense the woman's fury. She was raging. Extraordinary hair. Walt Bannerman mentioned a woman with extraordinary hair came looking for Peggy. Instead, she must have found Fangfang. And after the teenage geek smashed her way into Peggy's vault on behalf of a stranger, she called her only other ally.

Her nephew was Ned Fellowes.

And Stella knew Ned didn't fly off any bridge. Didn't credit such a thing. Moreover, if she thought North had anything to do with the lad being thrown to his death, she gave every indication she would take him apart, pack his body parts into a barrel and roll it down the cobbles and into the Tyne.

"There's something about you that smells wrong, North."

She knew his name, but did she know he used to work for the same people who killed her nephew? That if he had been told to kill Ned Fellowes instead of Honor Jones, he would – without hesitation – have seized him around the knees and tipped him over the edge of the parapet of Westminster Bridge, walked away, and never thought of him again?

Under her scrutiny, North did his best to smell of clean sheets and sunny days, before the woman with leopard-skin hair shot holes through him to make him smell of blood and shit and dying. He decided to take as a good thing the fact she drew up a chair, swung it round and sat down opposite him, her forearms resting on the back of it, the gun dangling in her grip.

"I admit Ned was odd," Stella said, "even as a kid."

"A weirdo." Jess added.

"But our weirdo."

Jess's hand rested on her mother's shoulder. A Victorian portrait: Beauty and the Beast, and North decided if Jess's smile was the last thing a man saw before he died, that man would die happy.

Resting the barrel of the gun on her forearm, Stella closed one eye to align the rear and front sights, and sat back to take all-the-better aim at his crotch. "Last Friday, my sister rings, and I can't make out what she's saying at first." Her eye opened and she came forward again as if she were enjoying the craic too much to break it up with the small matter of killing him. "Your auntie's the hysterical type, isn't she, Jess?"

Although Stella's question was addressed to her daughter, she wasn't looking at her.

"She tells us that Ned's dead," said Jess.

"Which, by the by, completely fucks my rota," said Stella.

"She tells us he killed himself."

"In London, of all places," said Stella.

"The thing is – he's not the suicidal type, is he, Mam?"

"More the stick-around, right pain-in-the-arse type. I'm upset, aren't I, Jess?"

"You trashed the place, Mam."

The knuckles of the hand which held the gun were red raw and purple with bruising. "I get to wondering about this astronomer he was obsessed with, so I decide to talk to her. Maybe she upset him, I'm thinking. But I can't talk to her, because no one knows how to get hold of her. Instead, I meet little Fangfang and we discover a mutual interest in Dr Peggy Boland. That was yesterday. Today, you turn up round Fangfang's, and guess what? There's a murder at the university all over the news, and a one-eyed, vicious-looking length of piss is round the streets asking has anybody seen Michael North because there's money in it for anyone who has. You're in demand."

The hair on North's neck stood to attention. The one-eyed man from outside his London flat and from Seamouth harbour. Here.

"I'm not one to make assumptions. But I'm thinking I should do Fang and Jess and me a favour and make you go away." With the hand that wasn't holding the gun, Stella clenched her fist as if holding tight to something magical, then let it go – whatever she'd held, flying to the four corners of the world. "I don't want me or my girl ending up dead, because I didn't take precautions. Because it strikes me that asking about Peggy Boland isn't good for anybody's health right now."

"Mam, we don't know he hurt our Ned. Maybe he did jump."

Jess started to cry, she wiped a tear away with sparkling fingers, her head bowed, and Stella's face clouded with concern. Jess sobbed louder. The girl walked across to the chair and sat in his lap, pressing her body against him, laying her freckled face against his chest, bright red curls everywhere as if she were overwhelmed with the need for comfort and a place to rest. Honey-made woman, the firm swell of her breasts against him. As a human shield she took some beating, and at any other moment North might have enjoyed it.

She was a girl used to getting her own way. He hoped she insisted on it, while Stella had the look of a woman who wanted to redecorate the club once she shot him, then shoot him again for getting blood all over its walls in the first place.

Jess hiccupped, sniffed then puckered, her eyes closed – like a small child waiting for a kiss goodnight. Her mother was going to kill him. Of course, if her mother weren't going to kill him, and then he kissed the girl – the mother might just kill him anyway. Jess's violet eyes opened and she grinned up at him, revealing a fetching gap between her two front teeth, then dutifully puckered again. Strawberry lips. He took the chance.

A nervous tic started up in Stella's right cheek. Holding her own in club land was one thing. Managing her daughter something else again. She gestured the girl up and away from North's lap, sliding the Glock back into the holster as she stepped onto the stage, before leaning down to pull a narrow knife out of her boot.

"You've nothing to fear from me, Stella."

"Because I have a knife and you don't?"

"You could help me."

"Why should I?"

The blade balanced horizontally on her index finger, tipping down then rising up, down then up, like the scales of justice.

Why should she help? It was a reasonable question.

"Because you're a compassionate woman."

"If only that were true."

"Because Ned didn't jump. You're right – his death is linked to Peggy's disappearance, and I'll find out how for you."

"Resurrections don't come round till Judgement Day."

"Then, because I can pay you."

It was a reasonable answer.

As she sliced through the nylon ropes holding North's wrists, Stella sighed. "I'm going to regret this in all sorts of ways."

They fixed on a ten-grand helper's fee. Information and equipment. Paid as and when North next had access to money. He would pay her and Fangfang, and consider it cheap at the price. The only reason he didn't have his bank wire it through as a matter of urgency was in case the Board were across the account.

Stella already knew what Jimmy the Sniff was saying round town, because she already knew Jimmy the Sniff. Stella knew a lot of the wrong kind of people, probably because she was one herself. But anyone willing to fry eggs and a plate-sized sirloin and fix him a pot of coffee was okay with him.

Back on a seat at the bar, he sucked the last of the salt and meat juices from his teeth as she watched him in the mirror.

Her voice was low and musical in his head. She'd reached out for the small-time drug dealer but there was no sign of him on the street.

"Where will I find him?"

She thrust out her jaw and scratched at her cheek with her absurd nails. She climbed down from the bar stool and went back behind the counter. On her mother's orders, Jess had disappeared upstairs to bed an hour before – the girl drooping with fatigue but desperate not to miss out on the excitement. She'd geared up to fight it, but her mother's face told her this time she wouldn't win. Closing the door, she'd blown him a kiss and he imagined it beating its velvety wings like a lipstick butterfly to land, poppy-red and incriminating, on his cheek.

"When he's not dealing or breaking into cars, he hangs out with another scraggy-arsed no-mark in a dump off the Scotswood Road." Stella found a pen and wrote the address on his hand, on the flesh between his thumb and forefinger – a strangely intimate gesture. "He's not at his own place, I've had one of the girls go see."

Reaching for the cognac through its brother bottles, she uncorked it, keeping the cork between her teeth to pour a slug into each of their coffee cups, then spooned in brown sugar. Alcohol fumes wreathed around them, seductive and dangerous, as she spat out the cork.

"In my experience, respectable types like this Peggy tart," she said, pouring cream over the spoon and into the cup, white covering over the black like a smile covers sin, "have secrets they'll go a long way to keep. Does your Peggy want to be found?" Another good question, and he hadn't asked it.

One wrong decision and a person's whole life unravelled. He sipped the scalding coffee through the spreading cream, raising his eyebrows as the cognac and brown sugar hit his blood stream, the smell alone honing an edge on him, leaving him sharp and dangerous to know.

"What's she to you, after all?" Stella slotted the bottle back in its place behind the cheap stuff the punters drank. He was getting used to the strange face with its different profiles – grim one side, ruined the other. He didn't even have a favourite. They both had their own particular appeal. "Leave it be. She seems to have brought you nothing but trouble."

"I made a promise." North offered up the explanation as if it were the first time he had heard it, the first time he even thought such a thing, but it was the truth. He made a promise to himself. Holding the cut-apart flesh of Honor's wrists together as the blood pulsed out of her, he'd known she'd die for her cause – whatever crusade it was that she had embarked upon. He saw that, and saw too that he was going to have to help her because it was the only way to keep either of them alive.

"I only ever made one promise," Stella said, "and that was the day Jess was born when I promised her she wouldn't grow up hungry like me."

She said "hungry" but North heard more than that. North heard the fear and the pain of a child clutching a toy leopard, its ears chewed away to nothingness, hiding under scratchy woollen blankets, terrified to fall asleep because of who or what might wake her. North knew the feeling.

46

Newcastle

2.45am. Thursday, 9th November

The two halves of the cannibal car were held together by an even seam of rust, scarred soldering and spit. Parked up on breeze blocks in the cement front garden, the Ford Mondeo had a silver front end and a battered blue rear end. It was the work of a lock-up optimist, because only an optimist would have thought the welded scrap could make it past ten miles per hour without the two parts breaking apart in sparking, shrieking shame.

He stepped around it, and over the bags of powdery cement which made him think of bodies buried under concrete, and between the discarded spin drier and pitted fridge that stood in for garden ornaments. The fridge door swung wide as he edged past it, letting out a smell of putrification and a cloud of mould. He tried not to breathe.

From the outside, the house was everywhere you wouldn't want to live, and North suspected it was worse on the inside. But good or bad in there, he couldn't see which, because the curtains were drawn and cardboard fixed to the inside of the windows with brown packaging tape. He knocked, and when no one answered, knocked louder – this time with his boot and the full weight of his body behind it.

With the splintering sound of rotten wood, the door gave.

The stench of cat urine hit him first, and hanging onto its tail a stagnant, faecal sweetness. The garden was bad, but the stink of the house worse. Breathing through his mouth, North stepped into the rancid darkness. Floral wallpaper peeled from the damp walls of a narrow corridor lined with boxes. North hit the light switch, which flickered, sparked blue and died. He shoved one of the larger boxes against the front door to keep it open as much for air as light, and ran the car key along the join to lift its flaps. He started back as the deflated latex face of a sex doll stared up at him, her red mouth open in delight. He closed the box back up again. Hadn't internet porn killed off latex dollies? He'd once known a sergeant who hid a sex doll called Gloria up a chimney, only to light a fire and set the house ablaze. His wife of ten days blacked his eye and left him that night. Rumour had it that the sergeant was more upset at the loss of Gloria than his wife.

But that was years ago.

There was a clatter from the rear. Cautiously, he moved through the gloom of the hallway towards the kitchen. Underfoot was soft and hazy, like walking over damp rags on top of rotting wood on top of a graveyard. There was no door.

By the sink in front of the kitchen window, a scraggy tabby licked herself, as if she wanted the fur to come off in fleshy strips, rubbish and mouldering food piled on every surface – pizza boxes mixing with Saturn-ringed saucepans of shrivelled beans, corrugated silver containers of half-eaten curry on top of engorged bin bags which, on smell alone, were full of dead goats.

If the cat hadn't moved as North reached out to stroke her, he wouldn't have seen the reflection of the arm bearing the hypodermic scything towards his neck.

Jimmy the Sniff had been an addict for as long as he could remember. He wasn't big and he wasn't strong, but he was scared and a man scared for his life is a formidable opponent as North well knew. He grabbed the arm as the needle touched North's skin, hurling Jimmy away and into the sink – filthy pots and pans cascading to the ground, and with an unholy screech the cat leapt for safety. Only it wasn't safety, it was onto Jimmy the Sniff's face who in turn shrieked like a banshee. North stood back from the fray as man and cat fought – man for freedom, cat for purchase, scattering piled up pots and leaning towers of plates.

As Jimmy threw the cat against the wall, he scrabbled for a knife on the zinc counter – the hypodermic crushed underfoot on the shard-strewn, greasy floor.

"I'll cut you up," he snarled.

North hit him.

It didn't take long for the dealer to come round – twelve minutes. It would have taken longer but North helped by holding his head down the toilet and flushing it repeatedly. The cat watched. She looked like she approved. Jimmy spluttered and retched as he came round, then retched some more as he saw what he was looking into.

"Divn't kill me!" He fought to free himself from North's grasp, his hands everywhere and nowhere, as North tried and failed to flush the toilet again. "Please, mate. I wouldn't have cut you." The dealer slumped to one side, wiping his face with a grubby sleeve, his shoulders heaving, his ribs as skinny as a picked-over chicken carcass. "I canna stand the sight of blood. It makes me come over reet queasy."

North leaned against the wall. The rankness of the house was on him. Poverty smells different in its particulars but childhood memories of neglect and squalor were beginning to churn in his gut. He suffocated them.

"What do you know, Jimmy?"

The dealer began to shake, rocking himself back and forth, his grubby fingers to his mouth. North's hand slapped itself against the pigeon chest, took hold of the dealer's hoodie and hauled him to his feet, then upwards.

"You're a hard bastard, you. If it got that bloke at the uni killed, it's ganna get me killed – and it's ganna get you killed too." North couldn't fault the dealer's logic. "I can't be dead – I've tickets to the match this week."

North shook him anyway – Jimmy's head snapping back and forth like a puppet's. "I canna remember anything – it's the stuff y'kna. It drills holes in your head." The addict dangled in North's grasp, his birdlike claws over North's hands, the touch dry and insubstantial, his feet fighting for purchase on the slimy floor. "Ah'm telling you the God's honest truth, man."

Jimmy, he reckoned, wouldn't recognise God's honest truth if the angel of the Lord came down from heaven and announced it in his front room to a trumpet fanfare.

What did Hardman say?

That Jimmy swore he'd seen a woman snatched up from the street. He attempted to tune in to the addict. What had he seen?

It was dark and Jimmy was hunkered by the side of a car, a lock-pick in his hand together with a halved tennis ball. He had a leather bag by him on the ground. He was breaking into cars. A quiet residential street.

North half dragged, half carried Jimmy the Sniff out into the corridor. The dealer clawed at the boxes, but North kept him moving out of the house and over the threshold, into the wasteland of a garden, alongside the gaping fridge and the wreckage that passed for a car. Jimmy covered his eyes as if the streetlight were a sharp and hurtful thing and North kept one hand on him as he opened the door to the 4x4 Stella had lent him. He shovelled him in.

"There." The bony finger trembled as Jimmy pointed at the house on the corner. He needed a bump – North felt the dealer's urgent need in the pump of his own blood, in the quickened rise and fall of his breath. Any profits Jimmy made as a dealer weren't going into a pension plan, but were reinvested straight back into the business. North thought about the purple pills he'd taken for the pain in his head, and the Harley Street doctor who wrote prescriptions for a patient he believed to be all but dead, a doctor who smelled of cologne and money. Not all dealers were as honest as Jimmy the Sniff.

The Edwardian villas overlooked the Town Moor, grassland stretching out to the Great North Road beyond, a tinny buzz and a snaking trail of traffic. In the early hours, the suburban street was quiet, a deep mulch of brown and blackening leaves on the ground. A nice street with a nice aspect. Quiet. Number 21 at the end of the terrace was shabbier than its neighbours – the home of a single professional preoccupied with her academic work rather than the state of the front garden. Honor said Peggy had a refugee family living with her, but the house was shuttered and silent.

"I don't know who they were." Jimmy's voice had a wheedling tone to it as he pushed a plaited silk friendship bracelet round and round his wrist. The sort of thing a child would make. Did Jimmy have a child somewhere? A little girl who called him Daddy? He'd adopted a cravenly apologetic mien for not being able to give North everything he wanted. Having decided North wasn't going to kill him, he'd become anxious to please instead. North almost preferred him with a syringe in his hand.

"I was out for a walk…" Into which North read *I was out breaking into cars…*

"What time?"

"About now." Jimmy the Sniff was rubbing his dry hands together hard enough to spark up tinder. At three in the morning, clubbers and students were tucked into each other's beds, bodies awash with cheap drink, hard drugs and easy sex. At three, the night shift was not yet awake and up and at 'em. Three – when souls depart the old and the tired of life to slide out of hospital windows left open by the wise and superstitious medic alike. A time to choose if there is harm to be done. A time North himself used in a different life.

"I felt really bad for her y'kna, but I was out of it."

When Jimmy the Sniff started talking, he didn't stop. North could almost taste the other man's curiosity, his fear. His heart almost stopping as the car's headlights shone on him, then swept around. Pausing, reversing, wheels turning as the driver swung into the space. A late return. Parking up. Jimmy relaxed then. Stick to the darkness and the night would be his again soon enough. Waiting, as the driver pressed the button. A blip. Locking the car. A woman. Tall. Big boobs. Probably the boobs were the reason he didn't see the men. At least four of them. The van with blacked-out windows. The ambulance that drew up parallel to the car – no siren, no blue lights. The woman drooping. Hooded. Half carried into the ambulance. No light in the interior. Low voices. Smooth motors. No extraneous noise. Over and done with. The ambulance gone. Van. Woman. Car. All as if they had never been. Jimmy spooked at the coming and going, heart pounding, not wanting to know, not wanting to be there or to be seen, moving onto a different street.

Still, if he could help now, he would. And he wouldn't normally ask, but times were hard for the small businessman. North ignored him.

Had Peggy been taken ill in the night as she worked late at her desk? Had she called from the car as she drove for an ambulance to meet her at home? Unlikely. North turned it over. Paramedics needed light to work by and this was an operation carried out in darkness and silence. Their patient hooded. But no one questions the comings and goings of an ambulance in the middle of the night.

Shame she didn't make it into her house.

Or perhaps it was a lucky escape for the family she had opened her home to. He gestured Jimmy out of the car and into the street.

"Ever broken into a house, Jimmy?" He could do it himself better but he had no intention of letting Jimmy the Sniff out of his sight till he was sure there was nothing else to know. "I always enjoy seeing a professional at work."

47

Newcastle

3.40am. Thursday, 9th November

Like Honor's before it, Peggy's garden gate creaked as they opened it. North cursed. It was the middle of the night and he didn't want to take the risk of a neighbour reporting a break-in. He pushed Jimmy past Peggy's front door with its two terracotta pots of spindly lavender and along the path by the scrap of unmown grass to a back door.

He didn't see it at first – figured it for a shadow in the lee of the wall.

The outstretched body of a greyhound lay on its side in the grass. Asleep? What did Honor say the dog was called? Jansky – the name came to him.

The dog didn't move. Not asleep. Dead.

Jimmy knelt by Jansky's corpse. With grubby fingers, he attempted to loosen the thin plastic cord wrapped around and around the throat. A washing line, North guessed. Jimmy raised the bony head and half a dozen white maggots crawled out of the dog's eye, and the dealer hurled himself away, landing on his bottom and hands, scrabbling away like a crab.

North hauled him to his feet – the dealer shuddering in his arms. "That's not on," he said. "That's sick, like."

He'd never have pinned Jimmy for the sensitive type, but appearances – they could deceive.

They knocked first. Quietly – in case. But there was no response. North never thought there would be. The Board wasn't one for loose ends. For all that Jimmy wasn't much of a dealer, he was a talented enough burglar. The dead dog forgotten, he grinned at North as the lock clicked, pleased with himself – his mouth black and gummy. North pushed him back from the door.

Jimmy the Sniff's home was a rancid, crawling, stinking pit of dirt and disease, but this was worse because this was a dead house. No sweet-faced children. No grateful refugee parents. No great surprise that the house was echoing and empty. North opened a cupboard door in the kitchen. No food. A drawer. Nothing. Bleached clean. Even the unmoving air tainted and chemical.

North went from the kitchen through to a small sitting room on the right and a larger living room on the left. If there had been sofas and bookshelves and a television, they were long gone, and the windows to each room shuttered.

He moved up the staircase to the bathroom and the bedrooms – the master bedroom, a study and a guestroom. Nothing. No toy, no small sock, no sign of life. No sign there had ever been life. An antiseptic smell. Every surface wiped, every carpet lifted. Not a home – an empty house.

Honor said the refugee family were staying in the house till Peggy returned. Two children. A pregnant woman and her husband with no jobs to go to, with barely any English and no place to live.

Either the family decided to move on because they sensed trouble and wanted no part of it.

Or they were persuaded to go.

Persuaded by large men who were wiping away signs Peggy ever existed. Like the fact she'd left behind a home. And an ugly dog.

Jimmy the Sniff pounded up the stairs. "North, mate." The dealer had decided they were friends now they had broken into a house together. "I've just remembered. That ambulance, like – it was an Army one, and there's someone…"

Which was the exact moment the world exploded around them, lifting Jimmy into the air and blowing him across the room as a crater opened up in the bedroom floor. For a second North fought for understanding. He was in Afghanistan. There was a bomb and they were under attack. Then he came back. He was home and surrounded by flames. Somebody, somewhere groaned. Him. He was groaning. Lying on his front, wreckage and plaster across his body. He moved, his head screamed and he moved anyway. The heat filled him – the marrow boiling in his bones. His hand touched his stomach, a large piece of wood stuck out from it like a pin in a voodoo doll. Gritting his teeth, he pulled out the wood, before clamping his hand to the wound, which spurted warm and red. The blood all the brighter for the flames.

Jimmy was sprawled beneath the window, his face pulped. North groped his way towards the limbs like sticks, finding a faint flutter of heartbeat under the cage of ribs. *They killed*

Bannerman, they'll kill me, they'll kill you too. The dealer was right. Or at least they tried and might yet succeed.

Flames lit up the stairs. Whatever was used to clean down the house was acting as an accelerant. A tongue of fire crawled across the walls and the ceiling, then another and another – feeling over the house, claiming the rooms before they filled up the space with searing heat. North slammed shut the door then went back to the windows, wrenching open the shutters with his free hand, the wintering cherry tree was up against the sash window.

Had Peggy seen it blossom? He wrenched open the window. It was stiff on its runners. He heaved it the last few feet. The branch was slim. He had to hope it would hold his weight if he used it for a matter of seconds to reach the broader trunk. The problem was Jimmy the Sniff.

At his feet the dealer lay crumpled and bleeding, his eye sockets sunken, a narrow line of blood trickling from his mouth. He'd watched and done nothing when Peggy was snatched. He was toothless trash who sold misery in baggies. He'd be missed by clients till they found another dealer and a nameless cat, and North wasn't too sure about the cat. He might or he might not have a child, and wore a friendship bracelet because, despite the odds, somewhere somebody loved him. He was nothing and everything, and North wasn't leaving him to die. Ignoring the pain that shot through his abdominal muscles, cursing, he dragged Jimmy into a sitting position, took hold, and threw him – sack-like – over his shoulder.

Crouching on the narrow sill, swaying with the weight of Jimmy, North swung his feet over onto the narrow branch. The heat was at his back. They didn't have long. Jimmy's head and arms dangled into space – the tattered braided silk falling from the bony wrist into the dark. With one hand holding the sash open, North reached with the other for the trunk of the tree. Stretching. The flames were through the door and there was a splintering of glass from the front of the house as the devouring heat claimed the bow windows. Half standing. Standing – he transferred his weight to the branch as his fingertips reached for the trunk, their tips touching against the bark. There was a ripping noise as the oilskin caught on the frame, jerking him back. Jimmy groaned, lifted his head, and North's equilibrium shifted. They weren't going to make it. There was a crack as the branch splintered under him and he grabbed with both arms for the branch above, but it wasn't there. Beneath his feet, the branch gave way, there was air and there was falling. He and Jimmy together.

48

Suffolk

3.55am. Thursday, 9th November

The screaming had been going on for some time before she managed to open her eyes. The high-pitched, agonised shriek corkscrewing its way through Honor's ear drum and into the soft matter of her brain to fill it with someone else's pain and wanting, but still she hadn't managed to persuade her eyes to open.

She fought them. Lids thick and heavy, intent on keeping her in darkness. The taste iron and bitter, leaving her mouth parched and her tongue swollen. Water. She needed water or she was going to die. The wanting dragged her into consciousness, forcing open her eyes. Water. It was all she needed. If she could taste water, the pain would stop and there would be silence and peace.

Her vision blurred then came back. A beaker of water sat by her bed next to a jug. Ice in the thick plastic jug. Condensation running down its corrugations. She attempted to move her arm to reach for the glass, but it lay useless and disconnected by her side. What was happening to her? Honor willed herself to focus on the glass. She inched her way across the bed, forcing movement into her unwilling limbs – her legs, her arms. Her hand was stiff and clumsy as it moved towards the beaker – reaching for it, knocking it. The beaker sliding, falling, water spilling across the mahogany bedside cabinet, cascading down the drawer, the cupboard door and onto the thickly carpeted floor.

The clatter was enough to bring the nurse.

A plump, shiny-faced woman, the nurse's greying hair was slashed into a vicious bob, each wing clipped into its rightful place with a rainbow-coloured barrette.

Tutting, she picked the beaker from the floor and filled it again, moving it just out of Honor's reach. Honor let out a small groan as the nurse swept dry the cabinet, mopping the thick carpet with a towel she took from a sink in the corner of the room.

Water would have revived her. It turned out anger did the exact same thing. Honor fought to remember. She was in Newcastle.

It came back to her in a rush.

With North.

Looking for something.

Someone.

Peggy.

North was a bad man.

She felt fear at the memory of him. The knife. His eyes. His smile.

But he was helping her find Peggy.

Anger.

No it wasn't North she was angry with.

It wasn't Peggy.

She was angry with JP Armitage. JP. Who betrayed her into darkness, and screaming. He'd said one of his companies owned some place in Suffolk. *More like a spa than a clinic. The best people. Superlative care. Everyone goes there.*

The nurse spread the towel on the floor, her white shoes stamping on it, crushing the water out from the carpet – "Rowantree Psychiatric Clinic" woven into the hem. Only when she was satisfied did she pick up the towel and lay it, soaked and filthy, on the bedside cabinet beside the beaker. She gave a martyred sigh as she held Honor's head away from the pillow and raised the drink to her lips. The transparent smell of cold water. Honor kept her mouth closed.

JP wanted her out of the way, and it hurt. Worse yet, he had to be involved in whatever "this" was. She was going to pull him limb from limb.

She heaved herself onto her elbow, taking the cup herself, her left hand with its tiny puncture wounds trembling. *Suit yourself.* The nurse turned away – making for the door, as Honor swallowed the sweet water. She was on her own. How it used to be.

49

Newcastle

3.55am. Thursday, 9th November

That he was still alive came as a shock. Lying on his back on the hard ground, unable to move, pain everywhere, the house towered above him, flaming from every window.

Smoke belching and billowing from Edwardian brickwork. It wasn't empty any more, but filled with darkness and Hell's flames inside and out.

He lost her. She was there and then she was gone. He tried to feel happy about it, retain that satisfaction with himself and his place in the world. Drawing himself in. Praying Honor was still alive. Then he saw her – walking towards him. Unsmiling and lit up by the flames. Relief. Guilt. Knowing that she didn't want to be there – that she would rather be somewhere else, anywhere else but with him.

Deep within him something shifted, and he felt it like another explosion, like blast waves in the aftermath of a bomb, moving away from his core and through him. Like vibrations from immense silver bells pealing out across the countryside. Like there were music in the universe and he could suddenly feel it because he was part of it – feel it in the soul he didn't think he possessed.

There. In front of him.

Her face.

"North. North." Calling him. Needing him. Shaking him. "North."

Shouting. Loudly. His head breaking apart with it.

He opened his eyes.

It wasn't her. The sensation of loss all over again.

Desolation.

Stella drove with one hand, shaking him with the other. He sat slumped in the front passenger seat, his forehead pressed against the cold window. Every bone in his body hurt. He moved his feet – he might as well know if he'd smashed his spine to dust in the fall. He turned his head as the blue light swept the interior of the car and the first then the second of the fire engines went by.

Jimmy?

Stella's hand, which had been on him, went back to the wheel.

Hardcore, he heard. *Poor bastard.*

"You were taking too long. The car's got a tracker, and I wanted to check you were okay." She made a tight right. Her half-and-half face set like a death mask. "Jimmy's dead. You don't mess around – I'll give you that."

She thought he set the house ablaze. Her first instinct was that he killed Jimmy the Sniff for knowing too much or not knowing enough. He opened his mouth to explain that the Board had found him. Something was wrong. His stomach felt fleshy and raw, a pain at the core of him. His hand wet. His head hurt – daylight flooding him with pain. Jimmy the Sniff's *"North, mate..."* his last thought.

50

Newcastle

7.20am. Thursday, 9th November

North stirred, blinking his heavy eyes as names and numbers swam in and out of his vision. *Beer delivery Thursday. No lager.* Noughts and crosses. Strings of credit card numbers with names against them. *Katya can't do Fridays.* Hangman with a dangling stick figure, its face blank under the half-finished word *"DANG_R"*. Drawings of pendulous breasts, flowering vulvas and immense penises. More drawings of copulating couples in intricate poses. Jess's name over and over like a graffiti tag.

Across the room the green-shaded lamp lit Stella as she worked at the desk, her hunched shadow huge and monstrous as North struggled to bring the room into focus. She put down the phone and turned to scrawl something, and the chalk shrieked, hurting his ears, insinuating itself into his brain. He closed his eyes then opened them again.

His name was North, he reminded himself, and he had a job to do. He raised his head from the scoop of the pillow and a grenade went off inside him, throwing him back into the dark. Hours passed. He didn't know how many, but when he opened his eyes again, the first thing he saw was his watch – the green figures in the gloom; it was past noon, and Stella was gone. He hadn't dreamed it – the breasts and the hanging man were still there, chalked up on a wall which had been painted with blackboard paint. Cardboard boxes lined the other three walls. Gin, whisky, cigarettes. North fought the urge to open a box, then a bottle, then another bottle and blot it all out like he did five years ago when he left the Army and tried to drown the voices in his head. Peggy's notebook? He lifted his head again. There was no notebook anywhere close. It had burned along with Peggy's house and Jimmy the Sniff.

The truckle bed was lumpy and narrow but it beat the cold hard ground he hit a few hours before. As did the sight of Jess in red leather trousers and a hot-pink halter-neck in the doorway.

"Mam says you attract trouble like dead meat attracts flies." The girl sauntered towards him, the scent of popcorn and temptation coming with her. The red curls were loose now, artful and dishevelled, like she'd lifted them off the nape of her neck to shake them before she made her entrance.

"You say that like it's a bad thing." North eased himself up in bed, which rocked precariously, revealing his nakedness. Naked that is aside from a bandage wrapped tight around his stomach, and he thought of Honor's bandaged wrist, wondered if it were healing. He covered himself over with the sheet and blanket.

"Stella brought me back to the club?"

"She says you promised her money and she doesn't want you dying before you hand it over. But I think she likes you."

Perched on the edge of the bed, her warmth against the length of his thigh, North did his best to ignore the sensation.

"Mam doesn't usually like men."

"She must have liked your father."

"Nah. She shagged a bull or a swan or the Holy Ghost. Her story changes depending on the drink and the moon. When I was younger, I decided she liked a man once but changed her mind after, and ate him like a fat, hairy spider."

She moved a fraction closer – dimpling as she pressed the back of her hand to his forehead as if to check his temperature. Her fingers were cool. "We should get married before she gobbles you up. We'd make beautiful babies. A girl and a boy, one for you and one for me."

He removed her other hand from beneath the tangle of sheet and blanket at the exact moment Stella appeared in the office doorway, bringing with her a smell of smoke and burning.

"Out," she barked, and Jess eased herself up from the bed, her legs impossibly long.

"Cheryl for the girl," she said, glancing over her shoulder. "And Sting for the boy. Or Bonnie for the girl and Clyde for the boy. Or…" Her voice wailed in protest as Stella shut the door on her.

North heaved his legs over the edge of the bed, his skull filling with blood. Pain screaming out through his eyeballs as he swung himself around, all the while attempting to ignore his shrieking bones. He allowed his fingertips to graze the bandage.

Thought of the New Army ambulance which drove Peggy away into the unknown.

Peggy's notebook.

The rending noise of the jacket.

Falling.

"It didn't go that deep. It's clean and I put a stitch in it." Stella tossed a bundle of clothes laid over a bent elmwood chair towards him. "It won't be that kills you. And I'm adding the costs of the new outfit to your bill by the way."

"What will it be then?" North eased himself into a long-sleeved black jumper as she pulled at a chain and the dusty roller blind snapped open – streetlights glaring in through the narrow, grimy window.

"Me – if you mess around with Jess."

Gingerly he pushed his legs into the jeans, pulling them up his legs and over his hips. "I don't chase tornados."

"But do you set light to houses?" Stella's arms were folded across her considerable chest. "Do you kill no-marks?"

North shook his head. "Not my style."

She was staring at him. Hard.

"If you didn't burn down that house and kill Jimmy, that means someone else did. Whoever you're up against, Michael North, isn't messing. Ned had no street-smarts. People like you and me though, we know how to get through. And this isn't the way."

North thought about everything he'd done to survive. The Army. The Board. The sins and crimes. Enemies he killed before they killed him. Those he killed because he was told to kill them. He didn't know what Stella did, but he was guessing – bad things. It was in the eyes. Always. Right at the back.

She had him all worked out too. At least who he used to be, but he wasn't that man any more.

Honor was in London in the arms of the man he had failed to warn her against. If she weren't cold and dead already. Her chutzpah on the park bench as she smoked the cigarette and waited for him. Stretched out in the bath, scrabbling at the hands of an assailant who wasn't distracted by her beauty, someone who hadn't seen her as anything but a job to be done. A line to be drawn. The memory stick they risked her life for that he lost in the deep blue sea. Peggy's notebook in ashes.

"Give it up, North. This isn't your fight and it only ends one way."

He smiled at Stella. Not the courteous smile he spent on strangers. Not with the easy charm he used on easy women. But the smile of one pal to another. Stella came looking for him when she didn't have to. Not for ten grand. She rescued him when she could have left him to lie on the ground and die there. There were no silk-ribboned medals in it for her. But you didn't leave a friend, wounded and bleeding out in the field, whatever the cost to yourself. You went the distance. Risked everything. Regretted nothing.

"Can you get Fang over here?"

51

Fang arrived with a Yoda backpack, and North had a moment's conscience. However fast she coded, as Honor said, she was only a child – her nails bitten to the quick. Would she understand what he needed? Because he wasn't sure he did.

"Cute name," said Jess, and the younger girl scowled. But Jess was made of stern stuff. "What does it mean?"

"It mean..." Fangfang's pigeon Chinese ticked like a home-made bomb, North decided, "...moron-people who need big favour from smart people best not ask stupid question."

As she pulled out her MacBook Air, she snapped her fingers in the direction of Jess. "Diet Coke. Ice. Crushed. Lime slice."

She drew her chair into Stella's desk, her eyes already focusing on the screen, and Jess's mouth opened in protest, but her mother gestured for discretion.

Extracting a bottle from one of the boxes stacked around the walls, Stella poured out a lemonade. She set it down in front of Fang with a bright smile, before using her open palm to slap the top of the shining head. "On the house," she said.

Jess smirked as a glaring Fang rubbed her head. North figured she got hit round the head more than most.

She pointed at the wall scrawled over with names and numbers and obscene art. "Old school, huh?" she said and snickered. "Chalk? I didn't know they still made it."

Stella looked as if she were contemplating slapping Fangfang harder this time.

"Fangfang," North said in warning. He needed them all on the same side. "Jimmy the Sniff said the New Army took Peggy away."

Fang's eyes shrank down to black points at the mention of Peggy.

"But he's dead and we have no proof."

"Jimmy the Sniff was a liar and an addict, remember?" Stella said from the shadows where she'd retreated to a bentwood chair, her arms folded.

But the New Army was also the plaything of JP Armitage, who was Peggy's financial backer.

Plus, the New Army could accommodate, feed, guard and keep as many people as they wanted under lock and key. And the Board had to put the missing somewhere. They had to put Peggy somewhere. It was worth a shot.

Fangfang's fingers hit the keyboard all in a rush. North glimpsed code, then a spinning globe, a blue ball bouncing from one city to the next – Newcastle to the Azores, onwards to Bogota, up to Sacramento, out to Christchurch and into the heart of the Ukraine. The girl sat back in her chair, the tips of her gold sparkling feet pushing against the floor this way and that, while she played Candy Crush on a mobile phone he hadn't even seen appear. When the ball stopped bouncing, an IP address emerged on screen – North had to guess it was nowhere near the basement bar in Newcastle.

Fang pulled up her Tor browser, decoupling the searches from those curious enough to come looking for her, as North's hand went to his jaw. The rasp of stubble as she brought up map after map. Laying one over the other. Coming together to form the UK. Dots appearing across the country. Dozens of them. All of them New Army bases.

Stella was behind him.

"The Good Lord giveth and the Good Lord taketh away," she said. She sounded cheerier than she had all morning.

Fang stared at the screen, flicking between the dots, the camps and headquarters, miles from each other.

"There's more than a hundred," said Fang, and for the first time she didn't sound happy with her efforts. He put a hand on her shoulder.

"Now we narrow it down, kiddo," said North.

But they couldn't.

52

Five hours later

Stella was still with them, stretched out on the truckle bed, her arms crossed behind her head and her eyes closed, but Jess had been dispatched to bottle up and get ready for opening.

Fang accessed the camps' running costs. North didn't want to know how. They saw no change from one month to the next. No "special provision".

She accessed their power and water consumption and the three of them crawled over the figures. Some were high, some were tiny, dependent on the size and purpose of the camp and the number of troops they supported, but there was no discernible shift in the figures in the last month. The only surprise was the size of the Army. When North left, he calculated it stood around 80,000 troops. The New Army was currently closer to 300,000. Enough to go to war.

North's fingers gripped the desk as he stared at the chalked wall. The suspicion of a headache was beginning to creep up behind his eyes. No purple pills, he reminded himself. He willed it away. What was he doing? He was up against the Board. He of all people knew what that meant.

They were nowhere.

"We start over," he said.

Stella groaned, swearing under her breath, as he walked towards the chalk wall.

The pain in his skull came again – Bruno's face, flames – as he picked up the chalk stump from the filing cabinet, using a grubby J-cloth to wipe away Jess's pictures. The girl had both a filthy and creative mind, he decided. Peggy Boland, he wrote. Honor Jones. Ned Fellowes. Jimmy the Sniff. Dates. Times. The names of the missing that he could remember. Bunty Moss. He drew arrows between JP and Honor, between JP and Peggy, between JP and the New Army, Peggy and the New Army. Fang broke out a game of Fruit Ninja, cutting and slashing all comers.

He lifted the cloth again to create more space, and a cloud of chalk dust rose from the rag.

"Don't!"

North turned at the distress in Jess's voice.

Her face was white under the freckles as she dumped a tray loaded with drinks down on top of a box, the door open behind her. "Ned said leave it up there."

Leave the wall?

"I know we have to wipe it soon, and start over, but not yet. Not today."

North turned back to the wall. He'd already scrubbed off a good half of the obscene cartoons and graffiti. Stella had copied down a credit card number of a regular, but she'd been indifferent otherwise.

Why would Ned tell Jess to leave it?

"Ned was a barman," said North. "He worked here?"

"He made the best White Russian I ever tasted." Stella sat forward, her forearm resting on her bulging thigh. A tattoo of a hooded cobra ready to strike coiled around her arm.

Breasts. A hanging man. Copulating couples. Letters. What had he wiped away? And what was still left?

North moved his head one way and then the other, letting his eyes sweep over the wall. Nothing made sense. He tilted his head to stare at the column of tiny numbers, some of them with dots between them, written from top to bottom in the furthest corner. With a scrap of chalk, he copied them down in a horizontal line from left to right, putting the dots between them, breaking the numbers up into four distinct groups. He stood back from the wall.

"This is an IP address. IP – Internet Protocol. It's how computers communicate." Behind him, he sensed Fang break off from her game. "Ned said the missing had their electronic communications shut down the same way. Accessed with the same password. Maybe the same operator on the same machine handled it all? This one." He pointed at the numbers. "I think this is the IP address for the machine that shut down everyone's electronic communications – including Peggy's."

Fang was already typing – so fast he barely had time to absorb where she was. A registry. A search box. Entering the IP number. Spooling through a form – UKTelecoms. A list of what looked to be communications companies. She pinged between the companies – apparently comparing numbers of subscribers and reviews – before plumping on U&MeMobile. Mid-sized. Poor reviews.

"What's she doing?" Jess whispered in his ear.

"I'm guessing she's trying to get a geographical fix on the computer."

"Can you do that?"

"Absolutely not, but I don't think anyone told her."

A low hum of office calls unspooled from Fang's laptop – a background of tapping phones calling, a gentle hum of conversation as she moved from an audio-sharing file on to a company website, sliding up and down a list of staff and their responsibilities.

Fang caught the paintbrush tip of a black plait between her blue-wired teeth, and reached for her mobile. She tapped her glass, and Jess reached over to the tray to hand her a bottle of Diet Coke complete with a striped straw topped with a pink parasol which was speared through a green cocktail cherry. Fang raised her middle finger in silent thanks.

"This is Jenny from the Met Police Liaison." Fang swung her body away from the distraction of Jess to squint into the mid-distance. "Who do I have the pleasure of speaking to today?"

Fangfang's voice was velvet. No Geordie accent. Middle-class. Middle-England. Optimistic and upbeat. The kind of voice anyone would want to keep listening to. Fang pressed mute, ate the cherry, stuck the parasol in her hair, put her mouth to the straw and blew a tornado of bubbles into the coke as she opened up LinkedIn and half a dozen social media sites.

She pressed unmute, and the bubbles died back to pop and drown in the caramel-coloured froth.

"Well, Jean-Genie." The voice again. Thirty-something. A quiet authority. Charming. "Could you please put me through to Law Enforcement Liaison? Remind me who it is again?"

Her small fingers danced over the keyboard and the face and details emerged of Caroline Lane. Caroline had been in the job at U&MeMobile three years. A shaggy haircut. Dark roots. Divorced. A pug dog. A fan of Wine O'Clock.

"Hey, Caroline. Jenny here from Met Police Liaison. We've got a problem, and there's going to be a real stink when it gets out."

Silence.

"Let's just say one of our senior officers is for the broth pot. Between you and me, he'll go down for this. I can't go into detail, but we're talking grave misuse of the IP request process. Grave."

Silence.

"Yep – unbelievable. No authorisation. I shouldn't even be telling you this, Caroline, but he's tracking his ex-wife's every move. Cameras in the house. The phone. He's all over her laptop. I need you to fax me through all the requests which have come in this week – all of them – so our guys can figure out which of them aren't in the system."

Silence.

"No, not the usual number. We can't risk it getting back to him. Again strictly between you and me, he's got 'friends' everywhere. Funny handshake brigade.

"I knew you'd understand. We take this kind of thing very seriously, Caroline. Internal affairs says this has to be by the book. Okay the fax is…" she read out a fax number on a page North hadn't even seen her pull up. "You're a sweetheart. I'll let you know how it goes. His poor ex, I tell you. I feel so sorry for her."

North opened his mouth, but Fang held up her palm to silence him. Artist at work. It took forty-five seconds before the faxes came through. Fangfang rifled them – one after the other till she found what she was looking for. Something from the child exploitation team. She copied across the document.

Changed the IP number at the top of the Met Police request to the IP address that Peggy's password change came from.

New screens.

New internet service provider. UKTelecoms. Stella was standing next to him.

"I could make a serious amount of money with this kid," she said. "Only there's nothing to spend it on in prison except for Pot Noodles, and I'm watching my figure."

Fang hissed at Stella like her granny had hissed at North the day before. This was getting serious.

The voice again. "Jenny here from Met Police Liaison. Can you put me through to Law Enforcement Liaison? Remind me who it is again? Yep that's right. Actually would you put me through to his secretary please?"

There was a pause.

"Yes I hope so. This is Jenny from Met Police Liaison. Would you be good enough to put me through to Bob? That's right, Met Police Liaison. Tell him it's urgent. Thank you so much."

There was a pause as his secretary told him the Met was on the line.

"Hey, Bob." The voice shifted down. Still charming. Carrying a promise for bald, chubby Bob Larson, married, a six-year-old girl and a baby on the way. At UKTelecoms for seven years. Photographs of a beaming Bob in a dinner jacket.

"Nice to talk to you again, Bob. We met at that thing last year – I'm sure you don't remember."

"Yep. That one. I got a lot from it. A great bunch." Fang stuck two fingers in her throat and made as if to vomit over the desk.

She shifted into third gear. Niceties over. More authority. "I've a request for an IP subscriber identification here and I hate to put this on you, but it's way past urgent." She gave a laugh. Self-deprecating, but used to her own way.

North was standing behind the fourteen-year-old geek. He could see the chewing gum behind her ear peeping out from under the plait. The parasol in the blue-black hair. But he was hypnotised. Was she Fangfang? Was she Jenny? She sounded like she was Jenny. She also sounded like she'd done this kind of thing way too often before.

"I can't wait that long, Bob. This guy's filth. You don't want to know what he's doing to these kids and we've almost got him. Give us a location and he's ours."

"He'll move on, Bob. That's what he does, and these kids'll never be the same. I'm looking at a photo here and the girl is six if that. You don't want to see the expression on her face. We want him off the streets."

"You are a shiny star. I'm sending in a memo to the Chief Constable saying so. I'm faxing the request as we speak. Sure, I'll hold."

Fangfang allowed herself a glance in his direction, her hand over the mouthpiece. "God's truth. You frighten me," North said, and Fang's black eyes went back to the screen, grinning at her reflection, at her own cleverness, bright blue braces making it ghastly in the green glow cast by the screen.

There was a beep and Fangfang clicked to open the fax Bob had sent. "Thanks, Bob." For the first time, she sounded like herself.

National Defence Force: Otterton Training Camp. Proud possessor of a computer which had changed the passwords of thirty-three missing, people including Peggy Boland. Bob had done Jenny from Met Police Liaison proud.

Fang typed the details into Google Earth to pull up a 3D satellite picture of the New Army camp. She spun the image, tilted it, magnified it, then put her finger smack bang over it before she looked up at North.

"You still here, moron-person?" she said. "Go get Peggy. Or shall I do that too?"

53

Suffolk

3pm. Thursday, 9th November

The group therapy session in the overheated lounge wasn't
going any better than her one on one with the psychotherapist
earlier. Honor ran her fingers over her chopped-about head.
It felt matted and uneven, her scalp raw in places. According
to the incident report, she hacked off her own hair in the
hotel bathroom with a steak knife, and blonde silky hanks of
hair falling into a blinding white sink came back into focus,
bleeding from what used to be her memory. A slim dark-
bearded addict opposite, his upper body shaking, spared her a
spasm of a smile as she sank lower in the uncomfortable chair.

"This is a safe space, Honor." When the counsellor grew
excited or agitated, she wriggled her fingers and there was
a clacketty-clash of metal scraping against metal from the
silver and turquoise rings on each of them. "You're protected
within our supportive community." She flung out her arms
as if she were a mother and the motley group of eight blank-
eyed, twitching patients her most beloved children, and her

rings smashed one against each other. "This is a sacred place of absolute trust."

Honor folded her arms across her body and stretched out her legs. She crossed them at the ankles. No surrender. The silver-haired counsellor sighed with apparent disappointment, excluding Honor by skewing her droopy body towards an easier mark – the bearded man and his coke addiction.

What was the point of speaking? Even Honor thought Honor sounded like a lunatic. Like a paranoid narcissist with suicidal tendencies. Like her father, in fact. Someone who trusted no one. She rubbed her upper arm where blue bruises bloomed under the skin. Certainly not the nurse with the apple cheeks who pinched her under the pretext of helping her dress. Not the avuncular psychotherapist this morning who with his fingers steepled, the tips pressing against each other, "brought her up to speed" with the "psychotic incident" at the Savoy. "Screaming, nudity, faecal matter and food spread over the bedroom walls, violence to staff," he read from the admission forms in a kindly voice, and Honor was paralysed with shame. It came as no surprise when he refused her requests for access to a telephone. "Let's concentrate on you for the time being."

Trust? She had no intention of trusting this beringed dabbler in broken souls prodding her through the bars with a specially sharpened truth stick.

Dougie, the Glaswegian sex addict with a cocaine problem, who drank himself to sleep every night before breakfasting on a bowl of uppers, drew breath. He had "shared" enough to have the counsellor bug-eyed with good will as she wound up the session and congratulated "everyone" – a sorrowful glance at Honor – on their excellent work. Same time tomorrow, people.

The talker's goatee suited him; he patted her hand as he left the session. "Stick with it, darlin'," he said. "I should know – it's my fourth time in here."

The lounge door closed behind the last of the group – an over-eating compulsive hoarder – and Honor was left in silence, but for the ticking of the ancient radiator. The kindness of the stranger's touch sank through her flesh and bones to lie upon her soul. In the magnolia emptiness, she took out the thought that "they" were right. That she was breaking apart into pieces. That despite her best efforts to control herself and her surroundings, she had inherited her father's murderous insanity. That it was better for everyone if she were in here. The tiny pin pricks on the back of her hand were gone – had they ever been there? She drew her fingers over the crimson line along her wrist, plucked at her tufted hair again. She looked like a convict. A lunatic. Was she self-harming?

Obsessing? Neurotic? Delusional? Honor shivered. Had she sailed over the edge of the world? A place she vowed never to go. And was she still falling? According to the psychiatrist, she checked herself out of Tommy's hospital and straight into the Savoy on Tuesday and went to ground, brocade curtains drawn, refusing housekeeping and food – hotel staff growing increasingly worried for her welfare.

She hadn't been on her own though, she'd explained to the consultant. There was a witness to everything. North.

The consultant listened. His hand covering his mouth when he wasn't scribbling notes.

Had she considered that North represented a delusion of her manic imagination? The dangerous, damaging protector with the power of life and death. Who looked at her like he wanted to save her, like he wanted her to save him.

"*It's telling,*" the psychiatrist said, "*that you invented this guardian angel, as it were, with a bullet in his head. Your own mind acknowledging the fiction, that a figure like this is a powerful, persuasive construct of your damaged psyche, a representation of your mental crisis – a crisis repressed since the trauma of childhood.*"

Her head was thick and muzzy from whatever they pumped into her at the Savoy to subdue her; pins and needles crawling across her skull and down her neck. She rubbed her fingers over her forehead, rubbing away the confusion. Peggy left and it triggered madness. Maybe she left because of her? Because she was a lunatic? Because she thought Honor was a danger to both of them. Worse yet, perhaps Peggy didn't even exist? Holding onto the idea of Peggy's arms around her. The excitement in her face whenever she talked about space, about galaxies and supernova and everything there was still to know. Peggy at least was real. She had to be.

On the seventies glass coffee table at the heart of the circle of empty chairs, the vanilla-scented candle flame spluttered as it fought to stay alight in the puddle of wax. A week ago Honor believed she survived her childhood. Triumphed. She had a career and status. She was making a name for herself as a serious political player. She had a wealthy, skilful lover ready to marry her whenever she said the word; it was true she had no great talent for friendship, but she had a best friend to love and a future. She didn't have that any more – she didn't have anyone or anything. With a sigh the twisted wick with its bud of flame bent over into the molten wax, lay down and died.

54

9.25pm. Thursday, 9th November

Pushing against the metal bar of the fire door, Dougie hardly seemed able to get it open, till it gave with a bang and he looked back at Honor with a smirk. The advantage of having been in the clinic before, he'd boasted, was that he knew which day was lime jelly, which orderly could be bribed to bring in cigarettes, and exactly where was safe to smoke them. She should stick with him.

The fresh air was cold on her face. Aside from the morning run she'd never been one for the outdoors, but the windows of the overheated clinic barely opened wide enough to slide a palm of a hand through. Honor took a deep breath. She'd fought against the medication but they were insisting; Nurse Apple-Cheeks pushing tiny pills through her sealed lips, smashing them against her teeth and holding her jaws closed till she swallowed. When she got out, she wanted that nurse defrocked – her watch snipped from her apron and her uniform burnt from her body with a blowtorch. When she got out. If she got out.

Truth to tell, she didn't know the way, because whatever

the pills were they left her foggy with a ringing headache like an iron band round her temples. Recovery – was it even a possibility when the disease was in the blood? One final gift from Daddy dearest. She'd never permit herself to have children, she knew that much. At least she could stop the bloodline. She was right when she told Peggy that years ago. Peggy. She shook away the thought. She'd think about Peggy later when she wasn't so exhausted. She wrapped her arms around herself to stop from shivering. Put her head back. Drizzling, the freezing spats of water jerked her into wakefulness like so many volts.

Where was Peggy?

When she opened her eyes, Dougie was watching. A cigarette drooping between his lips, he stood on the edge of the flat tarmacadam roof, leaning against the crenellated wall. He held out the olive-green packet and she walked across to take one. Temptation.

The death wish.

The skull and crossbones. She hesitated.

"I gave up."

Gave up when she met a construct of her imagination in the park.

"Good for you, hen." He tucked the packet back into his trouser pocket.

The crenellation dipped where she stood, a thin iron bar bridging the gap, offering a view of the terrace lit up by solar torches, the urns speckled with the last of the blood-red geraniums, the wintry gardens with their evergreen trees, yellow gravel avenue leading to the closed wrought-iron gate and the spread-out patchwork pastureland and dark woods beyond.

The scratch of his stubble on her bare neck startled her. A sex addict – of course, he was going to try his luck. She laughed, polite, not wanting to offend. Raising her hand to ward off the kiss and as she turned she almost tipped, reaching her hands out to either side of the wall to keep herself steady, the safety bar pressing against the back of her thighs. Dougie pressed the length of his body against hers and she moved to shove him off, but he kept hold of her arms, stronger suddenly, bending her, tipping her backwards against the bar, his legs tight against her, the only thing keeping her from falling. Out of her peripheral vision, she caught sight of the roofline against the night sky, the Queen Anne facade, the flat windows of the second floor. No one could see her. No one would hear her scream so there seemed no point in it.

Close up, his eyes were bloodshot – amused by her fear.

"It's a shame we don't have the time to get to know each other better, Honor," he said. "After all, we're the only sane people in here."

The Glaswegian accent had gone. Instead the voice was upper class, patrician. He was cold and controlled, and no part of him shook.

A dawning realisation came on her. Dougie wasn't a sex addict or a drug fiend. He had lured her to the roof with one intention. And it wasn't to smoke a cigarette.

He was a killer sent by the Board.

Unbalanced, held out into nothingness by a man intent on nothing less than her death, Honor revived. She wasn't mad. Misguided, patronising, controlling JP tried to keep her safe and make her better, but the Board found her anyway. Dougie – or whoever he was – had waited for his moment, until it was just them, and until her death could be explained away. She was supposed to kill herself – like Ned. A most convenient suicide.

She gripped the lapels of his corduroy jacket. Men who kill women. Anger flared in the darkest, most primitive part of her at the prospect of dying at the hands of a violent man. Dying the way her mother died. Except she wasn't her mother. Weeping. Pleading. Screaming at Honor to hide and not to come out. Extinguished. Taking tighter hold. If he pushed her off, he was coming with her.

"I understand your young friend Ned Fellowes died recently." Dougie was enjoying his power. She could see it in him. The compulsion to control. "Let me extend my sympathies."

The fire door, whipped open by the wind to smash against the wall, brought him round with a start. Honor raised her knee, pulled it up hard and the man she knew as Dougie doubled over, clutching himself, releasing her as he grunted in pain. She moved away from the edge of the roof. She thought afterwards that she didn't have to do it. That she could have run, hauled the fire door closed behind her as her mother would have wanted, taken the stairs two at a time, found a public space. Even at that moment, some part of her knew that. Knew it and decided against it. *Let me extend my sympathies.* Dougie killed Ned. She took a step back and turned her shoulder towards him before she ran at him. Too late, he realised what she intended – realised only as his thigh hit the rusting iron bar and he tipped and fell, down, down to the paving below, to the stone urns with the last flowers of the winter.

She leaned over the parapet; the dead man's arms and legs spread-eagled like a swastika, soil and flowers and black blood spreading across the paving and down into the smooth, green grass.

Satisfied at the stillness, with her two hands over the thin cotton shirt, she ripped it as a man might rip a woman's dress in violent frenzy. The rending of cloth audible even over the sound of a woman screaming.

55

Northumberland

The signs hammered to the wooden fence posts spelled it out. All lands within the marked boundaries were property of the National Defence Force (Inc.). New Army exercises were taking place and live artillery firing ongoing. Red flag. Danger. Access Strictly Prohibited. Prosecution or Death guaranteed in the event of any and all trespass. North tapped the Glock Stella had given him for luck. He wouldn't need a lawyer.

The woodland beyond the signs was scrubby and hard to walk through, but it had the advantage of discretion. Out on the Northumberland moorland, he'd be exposed. Even in the dark among the trees, with his face and hands muddied, he felt like a marked and hunted animal. This was the Army. The New Army admittedly. But still the Army. They had infra-red, night-vision equipment and a great deal of brand new weaponry which they liked to use. And that's if his instinct about the disappeared people was right. There was a chance he had it wrong, and he was about to get himself shot or blown up for no good reason. Which would, he decided, be annoying.

Scanning the ground between the trees in front of him for stray incendiary devices or mortar shells, he trod with caution. There was still the best part of four miles to cross over rough terrain before he reached the barracks. His belly throbbed. Stella had done a good job, but despite the neat stitching, the yomp had opened up the wound. He gritted his teeth, aware of the lips of the wound gaping, blood wet against his top. Pain was a state of mind. It wasn't going to kill him. He glanced down at the compass he "salvaged" alongside binoculars, from an Army surplus store when he left the bar, the tip of the needle oscillating on the pivot, and checked the Ordnance Survey map. It felt strange, as if the years were rolling backwards and he were a soldier again. This time though he was on his own and, if any other soldiers spotted him, they would undoubtedly shoot him.

Clouds covered what was left of the moon. Without it the sky was dark – unspoiled by pollution from houses and roads and cars and people. He liked it that way. There were those who closed their curtains against the darkness and huddled together round the hearth to tell stories and to keep safe. But that was never him. As he stepped out from the woods, a bat on leathery wings swept towards and past him, and he caught his breath, reaching up to ward it off, but it disappeared back into the night as quickly as it came. He stood still. Was he making too much noise? So much noise that they would hear him across the miles and come for him? Enough that they would find him? A barn owl shrieked across the distance and the wind moved through the copse of scrubby pine behind him. A birdwatcher. He had binoculars. He could tell them he was a birdwatcher.

But they wouldn't believe him.

According to his watch, it was another two hours before first light. He forced himself to take a step. Another. Crushing and snapping the stalks of grass. Plunging into and out of the mud. He had to believe there was enough noise to cover him, providing they didn't have eyes on the ground. He had seen no cameras, no drones. The New Army's protection lay in isolation, wire fencing, large wooden noticeboards with maps and skulls and crossbones and warnings of death and disaster for the foolish and rambling. *"I didn't figure you for a rambler, Michael North,"* Honor said to him from her hospital bed. No, he wasn't a fool and he wasn't a rambler. Yet here he was.

It took less than two hours. It took one hour and fifty-four minutes, which was as well because dawn came early. He spread himself flat behind a rising clump of grassland and to the left of yellow-blooming gorse, both legs wide to keep his profile close to the ground and the Glock within easy reaching distance. The position wouldn't provide much cover if anyone looked hard enough, but he trusted they wouldn't. He trusted that the guards at the barracks were concentrating on keeping people in, rather than keeping people out.

The guardhouse stood back from the twenty-foot steel and mesh gate. Judging by the churn back and forth, the camp operated in a state of high alert. He counted four men in the guardhouse itself with eight more patrolling the perimeter fencing, which was topped with barbed wire coils. North had no eyeline to the rear gate, though he knew there was one, and he guessed there'd be the same number of guards there. From Fang's research he also knew that the steep-roofed huts of the barracks could accommodate up to four hundred troops on field training exercises. He kept his sights focused on the three huts to the left. Close by, the perimeter fencing ran in parallel lines – a few yards of broken earth between the neighbouring wires. Anyone on the inside wanting to make it to the outside would have to break through the first mesh fence then cross the no man's land before negotiating a second set of fencing with its own concrete posts and barbed wire topping. The enclosure would be the perfect place to hold prisoners.

It took another twenty minutes to distinguish between the patrolling soldiers by their walk, by the chink of the largest who carried loose change in his pocket, the low chat between them as they scanned the horizon with glazed-over eyes. It wouldn't be long before the day shift came on – even from a distance he could sense the fatigue, the longing to be off their feet, hungry for a hot meal and a warm bed.

The ear habituates itself to the rhythm of the countryside, the movement of the grass, the roll of the wind. Across the moorland, the occasional bleat of scattered sheep waking to another dawn, a curlew here then gone again. But the child's voice cut through it all – wailing as if he were awakened too early and somewhere he didn't want to be. A soldier glanced across and grimaced at the noise.

The binoculars were heavy, the optics adjustable to each eye – Royal Navy issue from the Second World War, ancient but effective. Behind the diamond mesh, a tide of people spilled out of huts, their slow progress towards the cookhouse, steam pouring out of a tall tin chimney. Seven o'clock breakfast. Soldiers stood to one side, at ease, with weapons cradled in their arms. They weren't worried about being rushed, or overpowered. The hungry people they guarded were civilians – more women than men, along with a smattering of children.

The pounding of North's heart felt as if it came up from the core of the Earth. The crying boy with the shock of dark hair held his pregnant mother's hand, a toy lamb clutched in the other, his feet scuffing the ground, dragging at her. As if the child sensed him, he turned towards the moorlands beyond the wire, at the wide pale blue and soft pink sky, the washed-out gold of the rising sun, and pointed as if in warning.

The sound was unmistakeable. Behind North a gun cocked. Then another. The thick grip of the Glock so close, but not close enough. He laid down the binoculars, raised his hands slowly, wrapped them around the back of his head, interlacing cold, stiff fingers. There was an etiquette at times of surrender. He hoped it included not shooting him. He moved sideways a fraction, enough to give him a chance of the Glock. But his captors were ahead of him. A wrenching, blinding pain as a boot drove itself into the fork between his legs, up the stem of him and into every neuron in his body as the Glock was kicked away. The boot that came in for his ribs seconds later was a welcome diversion.

56

Northumberland

7.05am. Friday, 10th November

The corporal who dismantled the Glock, flinging the magazine, slide and frame in all directions, was five foot nothing. The private bigger, but not big enough. North felt their temptation – the rat-faced corporal out of sadism, the dead-eyed private out of boredom – to beat him into bloody unconsciousness. But between the blows came the creeping awareness that if they did, they'd either have to risk splitting up or carry him bodily to their Land Rover.

He hadn't heard them approach, which meant they'd parked it at a distance. He willed himself to look huge and heavy.

With a final punishing kick – the sole of the army boot hard against North's sacral bone – the corporal sent North sprawling, his jaw slamming off the ground, making his head ring. He vowed vengeance.

The nasty boys stood at a distance, their rifles pointed at him. North swayed as he got to his feet, raising his arms in surrender, widening his eyes to bring his two captors into focus. Two, plus guns, against one. He liked the odds.

The corporal grinned – there was a black gap where his two front teeth should be, which was a shame, North thought, because it meant he couldn't punch them out for him later.

"See anything you fancy?" The binoculars swung from a strap over the corporal's shoulder.

North spat blood and phlegm from between swollen lips.

"No, but you must get that a lot."

There was a time delay before the squaddie sniggered, but temper blazed, immediate and dangerous, in the smaller man's eyes.

There was something askew about the soldiers. Nothing a civilian would have noticed.

But North was no civilian.

Aborting his inferior's laugh, the NCO used his palm to chop through the air. The Land Rover lay in that direction, north-west of the stake-out position. They must have left it by the copse, half a mile away. Nowhere it would have been seen.

If it hadn't been for the two men pointing guns at his back, North would have enjoyed the early-morning walk. He had stiffened on the ground. With movement, his bruised muscles shrieked at every step, but at least the kinks and knots were unravelling. The day after all was fine, and the game was on.

The uniforms were too new. Serge. Standard issue, but stiff, the pressed creases ever so slightly out of sync with where the creases should be.

The haircuts were short but not short enough. The boots they'd kicked him with, dull. And the private had a tiny scrap of tissue pressed against a shaving cut that had decapitated one of his crimson boils. Sloppy. Careless. Classic New Army. Even if the corporal were a regular, he'd been recently promoted.

North stumbled, then groaned, putting his raw-knuckled hands to his belly as if there might be internal bleeding – or an injury to an organ painful enough to mean he didn't pose a live threat – and the teenage squaddie jabbed him in the ribs with the business end of his rifle.

They won't like it... he heard from behind him.

As the bloodlust from the beating dropped away, the corporal was working out exactly what North would have seen through the binoculars. The women? The children? It was the break in concentration North was waiting for.

He staggered, then lurched to one side, as if his foot caught in a tussock and the beating knocked all sense and balance out of him. The corporal caught him under the arms, the gun to one side between them. In thanks, North reared up and backwards, smashing the back of his skull into the smaller man's nose. A roar of outrage and pain as North swung round, taking fistfuls of uniform and the skin under it, to fling the bleeding corporal bodily into the younger man's arms. North closed in, seizing hold of the gun barrel and wrenching it from the corporal's hands before slamming it into his face – once, twice, three times. Behind him, the squaddie panicked – squealing, unable to free his own gun from under the NCO's body. North swung the rifle wide to slam the butt hard into the corporal's temple, who folded down onto his knees and flat onto his face, exposing the acnefied teenager to the air and North, and freeing his rifle. Eyes wild, he lifted it to point the barrel at North.

"So much as think about firing that gun at me, and I'll kill you with it, sonny," he said.

The private began to shake. Hand-to-hand combat was a professional skill a well-trained soldier could acquire. The instinct to kill has to be born in him.

"Not like *Call of Duty* is it?" North said. "Put down the rifle."

They were more evenly matched than the lad knew. He had his finger on the trigger. North had been using the other rifle as a club. His hands weren't where they should be. But subduing the enemy was more than a matter of mechanics, sometimes it came down to animal instinct. North raised himself to his full height and leaned in towards the private. He scowled with all the anger and ill temper he could muster – the beating he'd taken making him seem monstrous. The private's spirit broke and North gestured for him to throw the rifle to the ground.

"I'm going to ask you a question – the most important question you've ever been asked." A dark patch bloomed in the lad's crotch and North lowered his eyes to the stain travelling down the right leg, then raised them again. The private blushed. "Did you call in the fact you'd seen me?"

"Corporal Mac wouldn't. He said we'd bring you in. That way there'd be a bonus in it."

God bless privatised soldiers.

"I'm going to ask you another question."

The soldier looked confused as if he could cope with one but not two. That two were higher than he could count.

"How do you feel about getting naked with me?"

57

North made sure he went in the side entrance rather than the rear gate the Land Rover had left from. If the nasty boy lied to him about the time they were expected back, if he'd given him the wrong docket, North was lost. The mobile was in his right hand, partly obscuring his face, and he kept the left on the wheel. The ammonia smell of the lad's urine filled his nose. He slowed to a crawl but didn't stop, using his knees to keep the steering straight, raising his hand as if in thanks, as if he were in a hurry. In uniform. Driving a barracks vehicle complete with permit. If he could get them to wave him through, he might just make it.

The guard on duty was having none of it. The barrier stayed down. North dropped the mobile on the seat next to him and it slid into the dip of the corrugated seat. Two rifles lay between the seat and the door. He estimated it would take him five seconds to pull one up from the gap, turn it and fire into the guard's face. He estimated it would take the guard four – three if he were good. By his reckoning there were another three men in the hut and at least four within calling distance of the gate.

"You're late." The guard's nose zig-zagged across his face, giving his voice a mushy nasal tone. A second guard came out and slowly started his circuit of the Land Rover as if he'd never seen one before. North fought back the urge to have done and shoot them both. "Docket?"

"Traffic," North said with a grin, handing him the patrol form with the vehicle's licence plate. A biting wind had blown up out of nowhere, coming over the deserted scrubland to fling itself against the wire and into the camp. From a distance, bleating started up as if the flock had caught sight of a wolf, while through the window of the guardhouse, a pale moon-face regarded him. Then another, this one long and thin. The shorn hair on the back of North's neck rose. His fingers itched for the rifle, for its stock and its trigger. Was he going to have a firefight before he made it through the gate?

The guard smiled against his better judgement, tucking the docket into his top pocket and buttoning the flap, and North grinned in return. He had patrolled enough god-forsaken spots himself. Boredom and winter could make miseries of the best of men, and he doubted very much whether the crook-nosed Welshman qualified as the best of men in the first place.

"Anything out there?" The guard gestured towards the great outdoors, rocking back and forth on his feet. North got the impression he was a city boy, Cardiff probably, and that the desolate moorland worried him. He leaned his elbow on the door frame of the car, happy to talk, to pass the time of day: to hell with where he should be, to hell with orders.

Anything out there? Not unless you were to count the two soldiers tied back-to-back in the copse, the corporal still unconscious, the snivelling private wrapped in a tarpaulin from the boot of the Land Rover. He didn't want the lad to freeze to death.

The guard moved the weight of his body from one foot to the other, flicking his eye to the passenger seat, back to the unfamiliar driver.

"And it's worse now the toss-bags have cut the morning patrol back to a one-man op." North made it sound casual, resentful, a matter of Them and Us. "Mac's not happy."

"No one told me." The guard scowled as if it were North's responsibility.

He shrugged. A half-smile of sympathy. They were privates. They were in this together.

He turned the key in the ignition. "I'll be sure to get the CO to copy you in." Sure he would like to talk more, but there were things to be done. He revved the engine ever so slightly.

The guard sighed, stepped back, nodding his head. "Do that." He gestured for his colleagues in the guardhouse to raise the barrier, watching as the Land Rover slid through.

58

He drove as if he knew where he was heading. He was in. Best not to think too hard about whether he'd ever get out again.

Tanks under tarps lined the roadside, interspersed with armoured vehicles and multi-wheeled low-loaders. Privatisation pumped significant capital into the New Army's hardware – hardware that looked as if it might be on the move any day. Back from the road, nasty boys marched in formation, eyes forward, combat boots crunching on gravel. The squaddies were new too. He could tell by the hesitation in the rhythm of every third or fourth recruit. Was it Left or Right? Which was Left? Which Right? The exasperated drill sergeant risked a swift look at the vehicle and its driver, concerned in case an officer were judging the performance. Only a private. He relaxed enough to shout a string of obscenities at the recruits as they wheeled left away from the road, and North breathed again.

Ahead, a double-storey building stood, bigger than the rest, its shallow concrete steps leading to double doors. HQ. Other Land Rovers were parked in front of it alongside a dozen or so civilian cars. The barracks were jumping. He drove into a space between a black Mercedes and a silver Porsche. Army pay had to be on the up.

No sign of the civilians. If they'd gone for breakfast, they would have finished by now and they'd be back in the huts. Honor Jones and her friend Peggy might both be dead, and this might be for nothing. He might be about to spend what time he had left behind bars in an Army brig, or very dead himself. Honor had green and gold eyes. He tried to remember them. He tried not to remember that most of the time she looked like she despised everything about him.

"Do you ever think of the consequences of your actions?" she'd shouted after he drove into the sea. Yes, he did. It just didn't look that way when you were drowning.

He slung one of the two rifles over his arm, tucking the other under the passenger seat. He didn't want anyone glancing into the vehicle and wondering why there was a rifle and no soldier. He slammed the door and started walking. He hadn't had to walk like a soldier for five years. There was a knack. Don't overthink it. Instead, trust your own body to know where to go. A bit like fighting. Hup, two, three, four. About turn. Pick it up. He found himself walking in time to the distant marching of the parade ground. Faster. Best plan: get in and get out before anyone knew he was here. Because once they did it was getting grievous, and fast.

From his vantage point out on the moorland, he'd made out the mesh wire wall running between normal barrack life and a no man's land, alongside another mesh wire wall separating the no man's land from the holding camp of civilians. He hadn't however picked out the gate. He waited with apparent patience while a soldier, red-nosed and bleak with the bitter cold, hauled it open. The nasty boy didn't look at him, only waved him through then banged the gate closed behind him, leaving North caught in the churned-up open ground between the two fences.

Exposed.

A rat in a trap.

His skin prickled as, inch by inch, the second gate into the enclosure opened.

Same rat. Bigger trap.

A low buzzing this side of the wire. Engineers had brought in generators to flood the inner fence with electricity. North tightened the grip on the rifle. Hup, two, three, four.

The holding pen seemed bigger once he was through the gates, with three long, low huts and a brick building out of which poured the greasy fumes of frying oil. The civilians had their own canteen – which made sense. Eating together maintained the division, the Other-ness. There were soldiers and there were prisoners – guilty by the very fact they were here.

The door to the first hut stood ajar. The smell hit him first. The sweat of bodies too closely confined. The harsh institutional antiseptic of bulk-bought cleaning products. A sweet underlying note of over worked Army latrines, which no chemical could kill. Then the colours – only greys and washed-out blacks. In a crumpled shirt and a knitted tie, Bible clasped to his chest, an old man lay under the covers of the cast-iron bed nearest the door. Ranged around a large Formica table towards the back of the hut, thirty or more women sat alongside two dozen or more children. Ned had severely underestimated the numbers of the disappeared.

There was no sign of Peggy at the table.

No one had heard him come in. The old man's breathing rasped in and out like sea over shingle, like something hurting.

Ned's voice. High-pitched and irritating. The old man's eyelids were thin and veined over sunken eyes and his lips tinged with blue; even so, North sensed his wakefulness. Ned's list of the disappeared. Arcing wipers against the wet glass. Blazing headlights. The face in front of him was crisscrossed with a thousand lines and older than the thumbnail photograph North last saw in the car. Honor's warmth next to him. Who was he? North struggled to recall the name – Anthony Walsh, veteran union leader.

"What is it you want, lad?" Walsh's voice was alert and hostile as the eyes opened.

"Peggy Boland." North kept his voice low and hoped the old man wasn't deaf.

He glanced towards the door. That's where they'd come from. Because some point soon, and it wouldn't take long, the corporal and private would be missed. The parked Land Rover would confuse the situation. It implied they were back from patrol – unless anyone checked with his new best friend at the gate. If they did that, North had a problem sooner rather than later. But however it played out, the clock was on him. Not least because he needed to leave before the next patrol discovered the last patrol, an alarm went off and an anxious-to-please recruit who couldn't yet march in step shot him. Leaving would be the sensible thing to do – how to stay alive, because there are some things better left unseen, and there are some things which cannot be unseen. And men, women and children snatched up from their homes and imprisoned behind an electric fence on remote moorland guarded by New Army soldiers was one of them.

Walsh attempted to sit up in bed, his breathing harsh and broken as if there were a storm blowing up over the sea.

"You're too late." Abandoning the attempt, he sank back against the pillows with a rasping sigh as he reached out to lay the Bible on the wooden chair next to him. Argument filled North's head, Walsh young again and angry, speaking to a crowd, urging them on, outdoors, cold rain falling on the upturned faces and the NUM banners.

He picked up a tiny brass bell lying on the blanket that covered him. "Brace yourself, lad. We'll have to bring in management."

The tinkling bell.

A doorbell.

A young soldier ringing, then knocking on Walsh's door, the furtive glance over his shoulder, the warmth of the old man's greeting. Walsh knew the soldier, had done since he was a child, the lad's shorn head bent, steam rising from the mug of sugared tea he held. A New Army recruit known to Walsh – a family friend? A neighbour's son? He'd told his dad about the prisoners – that it didn't seem right. There were women and kids. His dad had said to talk to Tony, see what the old man thought.

And what had the old man done? Rung the Ministry of Defence? Enough to draw attention to himself, and end up here. If North had it right, he didn't want to think what happened to the young whistleblower. If he were lucky, the reluctant nasty boy was in a military prison or "peace-keeping" somewhere hot and dangerous a world away. If he weren't, he was buried close by in a shallow grave out on the English moorland.

There were times North hoped he was delusional, because otherwise his country was a darker place than he'd ever thought possible.

At the back of the room, a dark-eyed woman sat surrounded

by children bent over jigsaws. Her arm was wrapped around
a boy pressed up against her, clutching a toy lamb – the boy
who cried on his way to breakfast. She turned at the sound
of the bell, her belly huge, and from across the hut, North felt
the pregnant woman's disturbance, her raw fear at the sight
of the uniform, sensed the steady heartbeat of the child inside
her. Behind the backs of the children, she pulled at the arm of
the older woman along from her.

The white-haired woman was tall when she stood. In her
sixties, he guessed. She put a hand on the head of the young
girl next to her. Carry on. It was coming together perfectly.
Bunty Moss, captain of ladies' golf at her Surrey club. Her
clipped bob emphasised the exhaustion in the long face and
the coldness of the grey eyes as she walked towards them.
One slow step. Then another. Refusing to be rushed by the
sight of the enemy.

Walsh reached for her as she neared the bed and she took
his hand, gentle but firm, as you'd hold onto a child about to
cross a road. Warmth. Camaraderie. Respect. North felt it go
through him – tried to hold onto it, take part of it for himself,
but couldn't.

"This young chap's asking for Peggy."

North glanced towards the other women and children to
check. The men must be in a different hut. Presumably, Walsh
was in here because he was ill and the women were looking
after him.

"Who are you?" Bunty's voice was well-bred. Home
Counties. Imperious.

"A friend. Is she in another hut? I've come to get her out."

Bunty Moss took a moment to decide whether to trust him
or not. What was there to lose?

A decision.

"She was here at the start when there were only a few of us. A day, that's all."

North cursed. He'd missed her.

"Do you know where they took her?"

Bunty Moss frowned. "I only wish I did. She punched two of them. Put one out cold. Told them she'd see them all in Hell. I believe they wanted her to do something for them, but I doubt very much that she'll do it."

They didn't want her to name a star after Judge Lucien Tarn – that much was for sure.

"Young man. Can you help us? We've children here. Babies. You can see Sonja is eight months gone. She needs urgent medical attention." Bunty watched his face. "Can you get us out of this place?"

They were penned in, locked behind mesh fencing and barbed wire, surrounded by bleak and empty moorland – unless you counted the sheep, the red grouse and the skylarks. Moreover, they were guarded by soldiers who fought for money not for King and Country and certainly not for each other.

"One of you," he said. He'd have brought Peggy out. He could at least attempt to take out Bunty Moss. Sonja was an impossibility – the risk too huge. He could feel Bunty's wanting. The temptation as she closed her eyes imagining home, her husband's arms around her.

But when she opened her eyes again, she said: "It's all of us or none of us."

The grip on the old man's hand tightened, her knuckles white, and North sensed the balance shift as the old man consoled the woman.

"This is a scandal." The old man waved at the wooden hut, the lines of beds. "These are decent people, and they've been interned like enemy aliens – children among them. We're not at war."

North had the impression the old man made this speech in his head a thousand times a day. Walsh balled his fist as he hit the mattress, then grimaced with the pain of it. "I'm too old for all this." He was grief-stricken, not for himself, but for the battle he wasn't strong enough to fight. "You though – you're young." He looked at him appraisingly and North wondered if he could see the deaths he was responsible for, the darkness in him. He hoped not.

No court of law judged the people North killed over the last five years guilty. Only the Board. Did that mean those men were innocent? He didn't think so – he saw their guilt over and over again. Their corruption and crimes. He read it in their files, he heard and felt their guilt course through him, and he saw damnation in their eyes over and over, before the last breath left their bodies. It was a ruthless justice, but it was justice of sorts. Wasn't it?

"You can't get us out but tell everybody. Not all my friends are in the grave yet..."

"Ring my husband at least." Bunty reached out to touch his arm. "Let him know I'm alright. He'll be frantic. And tell him he is on no account to pay them a penny or do whatever it is these despicable people want."

North nodded. He could do that.

"His name is James Moss. Get him at work. He's Chief Executive of Heathrow. Call there. Talk to Pam his PA. Tell her you're my brother and she'll put you straight through. My brother died last year so James will know to take the call."

Heathrow. A stranglehold on a way in and out of the country. Everything ratcheted into place.

Respectable people.

KILLING STATE

"Emily and Gemma Dolan?"

Mrs Moss looked surprised he knew names. She nodded towards the table. At the far end sat two freckled girls braiding each other's waist-length hair, each girl the mirror image of the other. They were being advised by a frizzy-haired thirty-something woman in a tired suit.

"The twins' mother is the Deputy Director General of the BBC. The young woman next to them is Jasmine Ramesh, her husband is head of British Telecom's cyber security system. These are professionals for the most part, not the families of oligarchs."

He pointed a finger at the pregnant woman.

"As I said – Sonja. Surname – Al-Farwaz." Bunty briefed North as if she were making introductions at a cocktail party. A name. An interesting fact or two. "She has two children with her and her husband, Rahim, is in the other hut. She's a refugee. Barely has any English. Her family certainly can't ransom her."

Sonja – Peggy's refugee whom Honor had persuaded to stay in Peggy's house. She should have followed her instinct, and left before the nasty boys came back. But the refugees were there because they had to be tidied away. Not like Bunty Moss or these others.

Was it really possible? Was Tarn so ambitious? Because, outside, the New Army was preparing to move. Tanks and armoured vehicles were chained and ready on low-loaders. A great many of them. Doubtless it was the same at every barracks across the UK. They had thousands of newly recruited soldiers and the latest hard core weaponry, and they also had something very old-fashioned: hostages. And not just any hostages. They had hostages that would give them access to the utilities and infrastructure of an entire

337

country. Husbands and wives, sons and daughters, mothers and fathers. Beloved and precious. Not only to their families but to the ruthless, secretive organisation that had watched over a country for more than four hundred years. The New Army had everything in place for a coup. And the New Army was a tool of the Board. Tarn had told him its history when he recruited him. Sir Francis Walsingham, Elizabeth I's spymaster set up the Board to protect the sovereign and the sovereign nation. North didn't think Walsingham would have approved. He didn't approve either.

But he did have a plan.

His plan was to stop it.

All he had to do was get out of a heavily guarded prison barracks in the heart of an Army camp in the middle of nowhere.

59

When the alarms went off, he wasn't surprised. They'd found the corporal and private out on the moorland, or they'd found the Land Rover parked up and checked the paperwork. It was irrelevant which.

As the first soldier hurtled through the doorway, Bunty pointed at the far end of the hut away from the women and children.

"Back there," she screeched. "He has a gun." She was a woman used to issuing orders, her voice loud and authoritative over the screaming children. Which is why the soldier was watching her and not the shadow by the door who knocked him to the ground with one ferocious punch.

"This animal attacked us." She pointed at the unconscious man, as three more soldiers dashed through the doorway, almost knocking each other out of the way in their rush.

"Search the hut for weapons." North issued the order like he was born to it as he strode out. "Don't harm the prisoners. Bar the doors and don't let anyone else in here."

In the main camp, nasty boys poured from buildings, transforming their own base into a battlefield full of armed and dangerous men in pursuit of an unknown enemy. Adrenalin. Weaponry. Inexperienced soldiery. The perfect conditions to get shot.

And he was still locked behind an electric fence.

Could he blag his way out like he blagged his way in? Not for one second. The camp was on lockdown.

He summoned the soldier who let him pass through into the hostages' enclosure. The nasty boy came close to the gate and North gestured for him to release the lock on his side. He needed out, urgently if not sooner.

From a safe distance, the guard called out: "Orders says when the klaxon goes off nobody's getting out of there. We need the prisoners secure."

North nodded. Of course, the prisoners needed to be secure.

"Yep. But you need this – quick, man." He held out Walsh's Bible, careful to keep the gilt edges in hand so the soldier couldn't see what it was. The Bible was stolen, but he didn't think Walsh would mind. "It's how they're communicating with the outside. You need to take it to the CO. Right now, before the next transmission."

The boy swore, opened the first gate, stepped into no man's land, then hesitated, glancing behind him.

"Hurry, soldier," said North, "or we're all buggered. You and me most of all." He pointed towards the shed as if he feared a surge of rioting prisoners.

The boy drew close to the fence, to North's outstretched hand, and North shot him once through the kneecap. As he dropped to the ground, North reached through and hooked the key.

Shock was the only thing stopping up a scream, but it was coming. One second. Two. North stepped over the writhing figure whose bloody hands clutched at the shattered kneecap. It was a hard lesson, but he was still alive to learn from it. Who did he think he was guarding? What crimes did he think dying men and little children committed? The guard opened his mouth to scream in agony, and inside his teeth were rotten. North couldn't have him shouting for help. He balled his fist and put him out cold. Best pain relief he knew.

The recruits were trigger-happy and North's wasn't the only shot fired. He moved at a fair trot, but not running. The pace of a man under orders from command. Heading for somewhere he was supposed to be.

Pulling open the door of the eight-wheeler, he hauled out the driver by his arm and leg. A yell of protest before the man's bald head smashed down against the pavement. North heaved himself up and into the cab, throwing the rifle onto the passenger seat, locking the doors, and turning the key in the ignition all in the same movement.

There was a shout and the rapid report of gunfire as the driver's crumpled body was spotted. North crunched through the gears to throw the juggernaut into reverse and straight through the row of cars behind, the crunch of metal against metal, the shattering of glass and shouts of angry men. North swung the huge wheel and crunched his way back up the gears as he accelerated away – a Mini with a Union Jack on its roof caught in his back bumper dragging behind him. North grinned. It was what he'd hoped. Some clever soul had souped up the engine to cope with the iron screens protecting the windscreen and front of the cab. His boot against the metal pedal against the floor, the engine roared and he ducked as a bullet came through the window ploughing straight into the back of the vinyl seat.

A Land Rover took off behind him, then another, but they couldn't get past as he swung the huge wheel first one way and then another, the Mini shaking loose, tipping and rolling as one of the 4x4s smashed into its front end.

The barrier was down. The mesh gates closed. The sentries had their General Purpose Machine Guns ready and, he was guessing, fixed for sustained fire. A glimpse of the Welsh guard's face. *I'll be sure to get the CO to copy you in.* The bullet spray came hard and fast into the windscreen, the glass splintering, cobwebs breaking out across the entire screen as the lorry smashed through the barrier and into the mesh of the gates. The impact shuddered through his foot, his leg bones and up into his spine, and for a nanosecond North wondered how it would be to die at the wheel, before the gates gave with a shriek of metal, and he was through and onto the open moorland.

60

Four Land Rovers bounced and roared through the gates after him. He counted them through his rear-view and wing mirror as he calculated the odds. There were more of them and they outgunned him. Then again, the truck was a difficult target. Built to withstand assault. Too huge and heavy to side-swipe him from the access road and onto the rough ground. Most important of all – they had to take him when he was still within New Army territory. If he made it back to the public highway, they could hardly start a firefight against one of their own.

The driver of the first vehicle must have made the same calculation. A roar of engine and it disappeared from his mirrors – bullets embedding themselves in the driver's door, pinging off the iron mesh against the window. North swung the wheel and the force of the collision travelled up through the steering column and down his spine this time. If the bullet didn't move after this ride, it wasn't ever moving. The Land Rover bounced off the road, its front near-side crushed

– smoke billowing from underneath the bonnet. One down: four to go.

The other two were on him. Pulling in front in tandem, flooring it. Ahead, they drove as if they were yoked. Together they veered right and left, then turned towards each other, passed and without hesitation floored it again as they headed straight for him. It was a suicide mission. The collision might well wreck the lorry, but it would certainly kill the drivers of the two Land Rovers. They expected him to turn the wheel, take the lorry onto the moorland where its speed would be cut in half. North breathed out. Steady. He had no future. He was counting on the fact his pursuers did. Wives. Girlfriends. Kids. He could see their faces. White and terrified as they pulled their wheels to avoid the truck, bouncing off the road. The vehicle on the left slamming into a low stone wall, driving through it; the vehicle on the right not so lucky, catching the lorry's bull bar, rising into the air, spinning, turning over and over before smashing into the ground, rolling again and again, metal everywhere, the bodies of its passengers flying through the air. Sometimes the future didn't last all that long.

One left.

The road ahead was straight. He rammed Walsh's Bible onto the accelerator, levering it backwards till it caught beneath the steering column. He jerked out the trailing seat belt and knotted it into a loop before sliding his arm through. It caught on his elbow. He seized the rifle and swung open the door, the trunk of his body immediately hanging out into thin air. He put his eye to the sight of the stock, aiming at the Land Rover, and pulled the trigger. Missed. The truck hit a pothole and North felt his body rise and jerk, his arm wrenching. Fired again. Missed again. Bullets coming at him as a nasty boy pumped his machine gun. North let go his breath. Fired.

Immediately, the hole opened up in the windscreen of the 4x4 behind him as the driver collapsed over the wheel, the vehicle moving faster, veering off the lip of the road into oblivion. North swung back in, the door swinging after him. He checked the mirror. The Land Rover was gone – North didn't care where.

He spotted the ancient Saab parked up by a footpath leading out onto the moors. He slowed. Maps were scattered over the passenger seat. Hikers. North said a silent prayer for a sunny day. If the weather held and their walk went well, it would be hours before the car was missed.

Half a mile further on and he slewed off the B road, careering along the rough grass – the top of the lorry grazing the underside of the bridge, before it ground to a halt. He broke off branches of a bush to lean them against the tailgate. He was out of New Army territory, but they'd already have more troops looking. The bridge wasn't much of a hiding place, but it was better than he deserved going into the camp without a plan to get out again.

Maybe Honor did have a point about risky behaviour.

Clambering up the bank, he jogged back to the car, keeping to the scrub, jumping at every bleat and note of birdsong, but the road stayed clear.

As he smashed the window and wrenched away at the plastic moulding to expose the ignition wires, North thought of Jimmy the Sniff. He brought the wires together and twisted the copper strands. The car thief had been right about the New Army taking Peggy. The sound of him hammering up the staircase. "*North, mate...there's someone...*". Jimmy saw something. And instead of slipping out the door and beating a retreat, instead of keeping himself safe as he did when they came for Peggy, this time Jimmy tried to warn him. The ignition caught.

North made the first call at York railway station, using the payphone on the concourse.

The personal assistant to the Chief Executive of Heathrow Airport put him straight through to James Moss, just as Bunty said she would. She didn't ask questions after he told her he was Bunty's brother.

"These people are going to want you to do something for them, Moss. Stop flights out? Stop flights in? I know it sounds insane..."

Moss was a man of few words.

"They warned me that you'd call, Mr North. My wife's a formidable woman whom I love very much, which is why I'm sorry I can't help you. I'm sure you understand my dilemma. I doubt my wife will, but I'm prepared to take that risk."

And he hung up.

61

2.30pm. Friday, 10th November

York railway station short-term parking provided a silver Audi which smelled of coconut air freshener and drove like a bitch, but it got him to London within three hours.

Surely Honor knew not to return to the Commons, and she wouldn't go back home where she'd almost died in a bath of her own blood.

He drove by her garden flat twice to make sure, but the house was quiet. Curtains drawn downstairs, and he imagined the rooms still and silent. A bunch of pizza takeaway flyers stuffed into the letterbox – dead leaves scraping and scurrying over the path in the wind. His eyes went to the blank upstairs windows. North wondered if the parents had recovered the battered corpse of the young banker. If they even knew he was dead and lying in a steel drawer in a far-away mortuary. Hugh, he reminded himself. He was called Hugh and he was someone important.

62

London

3.10pm. Friday, 10th November

There were no drivers sitting in stationary cars. No shadows behind windows. The Knightsbridge mews felt empty, otherwise he would have kept driving.

He pulled over, parked the Audi a little way down on the main street and sat awhile.

She'd left in search of JP Armitage who might well have handed her over to the Board or locked her up behind the walls of his Chelsea mansion. After everything he'd witnessed in the camp, North had to hope Honor had more sense than to rely on the tycoon who was up to his neck in whatever this was. The only place left to try was her "playhouse".

"*We all need sanctuary,*" she'd said, as the storm raged around Hermitage Island – when she thought there was such a thing. Sanctuary, where you rapped the knocker at the church and the priest kept you safe and prayed for your atonement. Except Honor never struck him as someone willing to atone.

He walked back up, his pace slow and casual, towards the side street with its white-painted dolls' house. The rifle he'd taken from the corporal on the moors wrapped in a rug he'd found in the boot of the car.

JP Armitage didn't stint himself or his intended. Two round bay trees guarded the front door, curly railings and blue curtains pulled over the ground-floor windows. For all North knew, she was dead already. Without JP to protect her 24/7, staying in London was a supremely dangerous thing for her to do.

The chances were if there was anyone home, it was a New Army goon. North shook the rug from the rifle, raising the weapon as the front door opened.

The bread knife fell from Honor's hand and clattered to the red and white tiled floor as he lowered the gun. Her desperate reconnaissance slid over him, behind him and out on to the cobbled street, searching for Peggy. Only when she absorbed her absence, only when she was prepared to admit it to herself, did she turn on her heel. North followed her through, shutting the door behind him, turning the deadlock, sliding the bolts across. He wasn't trusting the bay trees to keep out any invaders and the fact he hadn't seen anyone watching meant nothing.

In the tiny kitchen, a half-eaten plate of tagliatelle was on the table, an upright fork plunged into its heart. She sat down in her seat and pushed the plate towards him. She looked different – pale, dark circles under her eyes, and her hair was wrong. Short and spiked, it exposed the lines and planes of her face, giving her beauty nowhere to hide itself. She blushed as she appeared to remember her hair, touching her scalp, pushing the congealing plate further over, as much a diversion as an offer of hospitality.

He sat down across from her.

"This isn't a good place for you to hide out."

"It's worse than you think." She didn't expand. "But I needed somewhere you could find me. I hoped you'd remember about this place."

The last time he saw her she was blazing at his betrayal. That he'd kept Hugh's death from her. That he was mired in violence and blood. But she sought refuge somewhere she hoped he would find her. Risking herself again, but this time because she needed him.

"You didn't go to JP for help?"

As he drove down, North ran over in his head how to explain his conviction that JP was involved in Peggy's disappearance. Honor wasn't going to take it well.

"I did."

She spoke with due consideration, while he forked the strands of lukewarm and rubbery tagliatelle into his mouth. Ravenous all of a sudden. "Orchids and an asylum for the brittle-minded. JP's old-fashioned that way."

There was no oversized diamond on her finger any more, he noticed, and in his head the movie played backwards – unscrewing the ring, hurling it from a great height out into a garden, hacking at her hair in the mirror, the feel of JP's traitorous arms around her as he walked her to the lift. Orchids of the palest green with crimson throats on the white cotton sheets of the hospital bed.

When she did see JP again, thought North, she was going to nail him to a door and leave him there. Remembering the fortitude of Bunty Moss and the old union boss dying in a strange bed without even his Bible to comfort him, North would hold JP upright while she did the hammering.

He assessed the sleek kitchen – its only window looked out onto yellow brick across an alley. He didn't like it – they weren't in their own secret foxhole – dug in, hunkered down and heavily armed. They weren't even on neutral ground, anticipating reinforcements. They were trapped in hostile territory with bullets flying. He wanted them out of here.

"Officially – a crazy man attacked me while I was there, then, thoroughly ashamed of his actions, jumped from the roof."

Something was wrong. The tone of her voice? The fixed regard. A difficult memory, but it was more than that.

"I demanded a lawyer, told the clinic I'd sue them senseless – oh and by the way they have a psychotic nurse – so they let me go to avoid the scandal of a raped celebrity. The suicide…" she didn't hesitate at the word. But the crazy man wasn't crazy. He didn't jump. She pushed him. He saw it play out – her attacker's fall lasting forever, the sprawled marionette body on the ground, black blood, "…was bad enough. Terrible for business among a certain class of lunatic. Excellent, however, for me."

Was he reading her right?

Did she kill a man in cold blood?

Or, did she kill to save her own life?

Had he infected her with his own violence? Or was it there all the time in her own DNA?

She stopped talking, as if she'd had enough of the half-truths.

"Unofficially – he was one of your colleagues. He killed Ned – he virtually said as much."

North winced. She would never forget what he'd been. But if he found Peggy for her, she might forgive him.

"Does JP know you're here?"

"He must know I'm not at the clinic. He might guess I'm here, but he hasn't come looking. Probably because I will have his balls."

"JP's involved in Peggy's disappearance," he said, and Honor looked as if he'd slapped her.

"That's not true." She sounded stricken. "He's a control freak of the first order and an overprotective bastard, but he's not involved. He would never do that to me. He has people looking for her in Chile. He told me."

"Peggy was working on a smart chip to cancel out noise and he was going to distribute it. He's doing it already."

She shook her head. "Impossible." Did it again. "They don't even like each other." Peggy thought he was a creep, and JP resented anyone Honor loved more than him.

Peggy was a rational creature and JP a logical choice. JP was a successful businessman and Peggy was an unworldly genius.

It wasn't up to North to persuade her of the truth. It was up to her to accept it.

The acknowledgement of the deception passed over her face. "Why didn't they tell me?" Her voice was sorrowful.

North could think of any number of reasons why JP wouldn't tell her. That he intended to rip Peggy off and charge for technology which she wanted to be free to all comers? That he intended to buy Peggy's good opinion? Perhaps Peggy was embarrassed that she needed him after everything she'd said? Or perhaps she had every intention of telling Honor till she figured out something was amiss. Peggy Boland was a scientist. She would have wanted evidence she was right in any suspicions about JP before going to Honor.

He told her about the camp. The hostages – Sonja. The

imminent coup. That in some way Peggy's work played into it.

"We go public," she said when he stopped talking. "It's our only chance."

"Have you stopped being mad?"

"North – three hundred and fifty miles away there's a camp full of innocent people who say I'm sane. We can't leave them there. Sonja is going to have a baby. That old man is on his deathbed – you said so yourself. There are children."

When he broke into the camp, he changed the game. Bunty Moss knew that if no one else did. Hostages were a valuable commodity but they could be stored elsewhere. North didn't stick around to watch the re-location; he didn't need to watch lorries roll in to know there wasn't a shadow of civilian life in that camp any more. No suggestion of illegal internment. Only marching soldiers waiting for the order to move out.

Honor worked it out for herself in the silence between them. "I told Sonja to stay – that she'd be safe."

"You weren't to know."

She still wasn't thinking about her own survival. So he had to do it for her.

The mews was barely a home and it certainly wasn't a permanent refuge. Nor was it a fortress and that's what she needed. She wasn't safe. Couldn't be, till he took apart whatever was going on. "Whatever JP's involvement, you can't stay here, but I know someone who can get you away and look after you till I finish this."

One way or another.

"An Army buddy?" She wrapped her arms around herself though it was warm in the tiny house. Too warm – the kitchen window locked against intruders, late winter sun breaking through, backlighting her, lending her a glow. Radiant like an early saint, like a virgin martyr stuccoed onto the plaster of a Saxon church wall.

He shook his head – partly in answer, partly so he didn't have to keep looking and not touch her.

Not an Army buddy. Someone who could handle themselves. Smuggle her out of the country. Someone who didn't mind getting their hands dirty. Someone like Stella. He'd called her as he pulled out from the camp. A couple of hours to roust out decent passports in London – she knew someone who knew someone. Of course she did. Before a hop-skip-and-jump to Amsterdam and flights onwards to Florida.

"Holidaymakers. We'll get lost in the crowds – Jess always wanted to go to Disney World." She'd be with them as soon as she could.

He was changing the arrangement. Honor had a burner they could use to text Stella from the car and they would meet en route to the airport. He didn't want to wait another minute in the mews.

Honor looked around her – desolate he thought. Not at leaving the Wendy house, but at the idea of running away after all. Despite her best efforts. *I'm not getting on any plane,* she'd announced in hospital.

"You're still alive, Honor. You haven't won, but you haven't lost. Let me find Peggy and stop whatever it is they're trying to do. If it doesn't work…" If he died in the attempt, he meant. "Use your contacts in America. In Europe. Tell them what's going on. Create an almighty stink."

The fighter in her still struggled against what he was saying. To cut loose. Quit. Run as far and as fast as she could.

"I didn't know if you'd come," she said. "You had a chance to leave it all behind. I told you to go."

It was a lie but he didn't judge her. She'd known even as she walked away that he would never let it go. He couldn't, because it turned out there was more than one kind of freedom.

North reached across the kitchen table for her hand. It was small in his and he brought it to his lips, unfolding her fingers to expose her soft palm then folding them back over. It wasn't a diamond ring. It was a kiss. A salute. A consolation, and a goodbye. They both allowed him that.

63

He didn't hear them coming.

64

Their attackers smashed their way through the front and back doors simultaneously, the front windows seconds later. North reached for the rifle, but it was already too late. A mountain knocked it out of his hands, balling his fist as he came, a glint of metal from the knuckledusters taking North under the chin, sending him into the air and across the room. Pain smashed its way across his jaw into each and every tooth, up through his neck, into every hair on his head, and down through his vertebrae to take over his nerve endings.

The mountain-man still coming for him, through the open door into the lounge North watched as she fought them, all flailing arms and legs. Bruno appeared from nowhere. The only one not wearing a balaclava as if he wanted North to see his face. He swung his massive fist, and Honor's head cracked back on its spine, then forward, her knees folding as she collapsed to the floor. Roaring Bruno's name, North staggered to his feet, two assailants blocking his path, sledgehammer fists pummelling his stomach intent on bringing him down. Dark figures dragging her to her feet, holding her while Bruno pulled a black hood over the slumped blonde head, her elbows and wrists already tied at the back. North's consciousness in shreds, a thunderous ringing in his ears, he felt rather than saw Honor ripped from the room. A final triumphant smirk from Bruno.

White-hot anger. Upright, reeling, his vision still blurred, North broke from his attackers, aiming for the corner of the room where he imagined his rifle to lie alongside the broken lamp, but he was too slow. Weight slammed into him, crushing all air from his lungs as he and mountain-man hit the floor together – North breaking the assailant's fall, glass shards from the bulb crunching under him, cutting through his khaki shirt. He swung his fists wildly, desperate for purchase, for a blow to land and crush bone; instead the attacker found North's throat, the fragile larynx between the stranger's fingers as they squeezed what was left of the air from his body. North fought for breath, darkness crowding him – the threat of oblivion. Temptation. He thought of Hugh, beaten to death, and scrabbled at his own throat, finding his attacker's little fingers, bending them backwards as far as they would go. A churning double snap – enough to break not just bone, but the grip. As his opponent pulled himself upright and away from North, North brought up his legs, his boot in the other man's face, smashing his nose, a cheekbone, mule-kicking him away.

The small kitchen was made smaller by the table. On the one hand, its size made escape impossible. On the other, his four attackers struggled to operate as an effective team. North had to hope the mule-kick had taken the mountain-man out of play, which left three. The biggest, whom North judged to be the leader, had no intention of letting their victim get upright. With the enthusiasm of a professional who resented the fact North wasn't dead yet, he pulled back his booted foot to drive it into North's ribs. As the giant's boot came in for his head, with both hands North caught hold of the heel and toe, wrenching it one hundred and eighty degrees outwards – his knee dislocated, the assailant screeched in pain then went silent as North wrenched it back the other way, using the man's own considerable bulk and his frail balance to tip him up and over, the man's head slamming against the door of the larder with a bone-shuddering crunch. With a pack animal roar and their way clear, the two others leapt at North, pounding him, bringing him down to his knees. He seized hold of the testicles of the nearest, twisting and wrenching savagely. The guy screamed, and North used his free hand to find his throat and use him as a battering ram, bringing himself upright through the other assailant.

A click from the doorway.

Winter light from behind threw Stella into darkness, the right side of her face slipping from the bones.

"Change of plan, lads." She shot the mountain-man, his arms wrapped around himself in the corner, his crippled hands tucked out of harm's way in his armpits.

"I have to admit, I'm really…" She swung the gun towards the second man, his eyes wide, and pulled the trigger.

"…Looking…" The giant cowered against the wall, but there was no place to hide.

"…Forward…" The last man stood still, resigned to his fate, to the red blossom opening up over his heart.

"… To Disney World."

North let himself breathe again, sucking in a mix of gunpowder, blood spray and citrus cologne.

Long enough to remember Honor.

"They have her away already, North. She's gone."

He reached down to pull the balaclavas off the nearest bodies. Buzz-cuts, broken noses, hard, been-around faces which told him nothing.

The Glock 43 lay just under the giant's body. Its short barrel jutting from beneath the hip bone. The giant must have had it in his pocket. North pushed his foot under to clear the gun from the corpse and bent to pick it up.

He didn't make it.

"The first thing I'm going to do is find an orange tree and pick myself an orange." Stella's gun pointed at him. He stood – slowly – as Stella took a step towards him. "Do you think when I cut it open that it'll be warm inside, North? That it'll taste of sunshine?"

"I've never liked oranges."

Stella's snakeskin jacket lent her skin the green tinge of rotting vegetation. "You should have let it go, North, but you'd have to be born over."

"You told them where we were." It wasn't a question. It was a statement.

"You were never going to find that Peggy tart. They were never going to let that happen." There was a note of regret in Stella's voice. He'd have thought there was pity, but he didn't think Stella ran that way. She never promised him her friendship. Never said *Trust me*, though he did. Never said she was his ally – only behaved like one.

Desolation.

Stella fronted up Bannerman, and the good professor informed the Board there was a grieving family asking awkward questions. Fortunately, Stella's grief for Ned could be assuaged by money.

"When did they get to you?"

He was trying to work out when the betrayals started.

"You walked out the door looking for Jimmy the Sniff, and Bruno walked in looking for you. I told you Michael North was all kinds of popular."

Poor dead Jimmy the Sniff. Jimmy saw her. Called out *"North, mate...there's someone..."* in warning. Stella cleaned the house for Tarn by burning it down. Disposed of the only witness to Peggy's abduction. But North was never supposed to die in that fire – only druggie, no-mark Jimmy the Sniff. If North hadn't tried to climb to safety, Stella would have doubtless rescued him herself. Broken into the house. Dragged him to safety and left Jimmy to burn, snapped his neck to make sure of it. Made herself that bit more indispensable. They wanted him watched.

"Before you went into the camp, they thought they had her. Honor – isn't it? She was holed up in some fancy asylum, but she gave them the slip."

The Board needed North to lead them to Honor.

He'd been naïve. Complacent. Trusting.

The implications of Stella's betrayal – not just Newcastle, but that Tarn knew he was at the camp all along. That hurt. Bunty's faith, and Walsh. The conviction he could help when he was only ever bait. The Board let him break into the camp, and leave again. The nasty boys who died as they chased him over the moors were casualties of war. Tarn let him go because he calculated that North was only ever going to carry everything he knew straight back to Honor. And what did North do as he made his way back to London? What was his first thought? To call Stella, and tell her where he was heading. A place no one knew existed except JP and Honor and Michael North. His first thought was to reach out to his friend and ask for help.

"And Ned?"

"You weren't straight with me, North. Bruno told me all of it. You're one of them."

"Not anymore."

"None of us walks away free and clear from the past."

Even through his boots, he had the illusion his feet felt warm, wet from the blood spreading around each of the bodies. No surprise. He stood in the blood of other men, and had done for years.

"The Board killed Ned – not me, Stella."

"What does it matter?"

"He left a message. Said to tell his mum he loved her."

"I'll pass it on."

"Said to tell Jess."

"Jess doesn't need telling."

"But why go to all this trouble when all they want is Honor dead?"

"Someone's stepping out of line, and the good news is they've decided she's leverage. At least for the moment. She's a looker I grant you, but there's no happy-ever-afters there for you. I know the type."

"And these guys?" They tried to kill him. But they were on her side.

"Bruno told them to beat you to death and to take their time doing it," Stella shrugged. "Even so, I'd have my money on you because you're one hard bastard. Don't get me wrong – I like that about you. But I also like to sleep at night, and I've you pegged as a man who bears a grudge. My way's better for both of us. Quicker for you. Safer for me."

The distant roar of a far-off jet on its way into or out of Heathrow. Stella smiled without showing her teeth. The only reason Stella ever smiled was the thought of Jess.

"Do you know what this is, Stella? These people are planning a coup. This is real."

"Not to me. All I know is I've a plane to catch before they shut down the airports."

As she raised her hand North lifted his foot and stamped hard on the belly of the dead man nearest him. The noise that came from his throat was ghastly. North didn't think he was alive – just that the last of the air trapped in his chest had forced its way out. But if he had been alive, he wasn't once Stella had shot the corpse again once, twice, three times.

The distraction wasn't much. A matter of seconds. But it was all he had. North threw himself through the air into the living room and onto the floor, rolling as he grabbed for the Glock 43, using the sofa for cover. As Stella appeared, still firing, he lifted his own gun. The bullets ripped through the snakeskin jacket before they ploughed through the flesh and muscle and into her stomach. Staggering, she clutched her belly, then dropped to her knees.

Her face was ghastly. As if the blood had other places to go.

Slumping back hard against the wall, her legs splayed, her hands pushed into the wound, blood pulsing, squeezing itself between her fingers, their tips still sparkling green.

North stood over her, the gun in his hand. He had a code. He didn't kill women. Except he just did.

A picture of Jess in the concourse of an airport filled his head. Stiletto heels. A mock-croc vanity case at her feet. Huge fake Louis Vuitton handbag. Glossy mags: *Vogue* and *Tatler*, *OK*. Passports in new names – both in hot-pink leather covers.

Tickets to Florida for her and her mother. Were the pictures real? He didn't know. Either way, Stella wasn't coming back. She had sold up the bar and liquidated her interests. Survival was everything. Start again. Where oranges grew in front yards and Jess wouldn't go hungry.

He felt Stella's urgency for Jess to do as she'd been told – climb on a plane to Nowhere even if her mother didn't show. Especially if her mother didn't show.

"You still owe me ten grand, North." The voice was husky with pain, with the effort of staying alive. "Shake my hand and we'll call it quits."

Stella reached for him. The brush of her sleeve against the reptile body of the jacket. A fleshy suck and pull; her right hand vivid and gory, as her life's blood gushed from the gaping wound. Regardless, she kept the hand out, trembling with the effort. A stomach wound is a messy way to die. Men died screaming, but Stella wasn't the screaming kind. He moved the gun away from her with his foot, pulling across the chair to sit astride it as Stella's hand fell back to her lap.

"Did Jess know what you came to do?"

Jess. The only person Stella loved more than Stella. More than money. Stella bit into her lower lip, shook her head. More blood. "She's better than us. You know that."

"They'll kill her anyway. She's been too close to all this. And you won't be there to keep her safe."

The pain of his prediction – its self-evident truth – would have killed a weaker woman outright. Instead, Jess's mother made to stand up, and behind her hand pale pink guts pushed and squirmed their way from behind the prison of her fingers, into the light.

"I'll call her." He made it sound like a reasonable thing to do. Obvious. "She's at the airport, isn't she? I'll tell her to leave. Go to art college. Marry a dentist and have American children with perfect teeth. Cheryl and Sting."

He dipped into the snakeskin jacket pocket for the iPhone. "One six zero five." She told him her password, her teeth bared, incisors too long, and he pushed the numbers, found Jess. Her daughter's smile wide and a little wicked – the picture taken on a summer's day.

North hesitated, his finger over the green call button, as if something had crossed his mind, as if clarification was needed. Stella rested her head against the wall, struggling to keep her eyes focused on him.

"Where have they taken Honor?"

It wasn't the inevitability of death, nor was it the wrenching pain that pushed the solitary tear out from Stella's bloodshot eye, down the ravaged face to drop off her jaw into nothingness. It was the fact she didn't know. That she couldn't make the trade and that Jess was going to die. "Please, North…" For the sake of her only child, she offered the only thing she had. The notebook she was holding out was drenched in her gore. Stella had taken it as he lay unconscious and fire destroyed Peggy's house. An insurance policy against the Board.

A bubble of blood broke from the corner of her mouth. Another and another, a honeycomb of blood. The book fell, and Stella's eyes rolled into her head as North took hold of her. He rattled her back and forth, between Life and Death, but Stella had gone. On the ground, next to her mother's body, an anxious tiny voice. "Mam. Mam?"

He picked up the phone. His hands dripping with Stella's blood. "Run for that plane, Jess," North said. "Call the boy Ned – name the girl after your mother. She'd have liked that." He didn't wait for her reply.

65

Banqueting Hall, Westminster, London

7.40pm. Friday, 10th November

North picked up one of the silver trays of champagne flutes from the kitchen counter and pushed his way through the swing door at the same time as a young waiter burst back into the kitchen. "It's carnage," he said, pushing his floppy blond hair out of his eyes and dropping the empty tray onto the counter with a clatter.

"Isn't it always," North said.

The reception crackled with the self-conscious energy of international power and personal ambition pulled tight together in the same room – its only release a frenetic hum of conversation and chink of crystal.

North kept up links with every official catering company operating in London. His security clearance and impeccable silver service credentials proved useful more times than he could count. This evening at the reception of the G8 heads of state, he replaced a twenty-five-year-old Australian actor-cum-waiter who rang in sick. "Sick" and £5,000 wealthier than when North met up with him an hour before. Everyone was happy – the Australian happy to help "the Metropolitan Police" with their man in the kitchen, the catering company with their ever-reliable first reserve who had rung in so opportunely, and most of all, North himself.

Above the guests in evening suits and designer gowns, above the brass chandeliers with their curling arms and electric candles, the Rubens ceiling glowed, the Divine Right of Kings ignored by one and all in favour of frantic politicking, discreet influence-trading and outrageous gossip. The bas-relief columns along the walls were uplit in red, white and blue as North, wearing the politest of smiles, ignored the reaching hands as he dipped and swerved, his head reeling from the expensive scents and the polyglot babble, in search of his target.

Lucien Tarn didn't so much as glance at the waiter in the white tuxedo as he took hold of the long-stemmed glass of Veuve Clicquot. North had come up to the group from behind and found his way blocked by the throng. An arm reached out. Another. Trapping him. A discussion among the powerful about money, a discussion among rich people about power. Tarn nodding as the grey-bearded man next to him held forth on government debt spiralling out of control. The smell of cigar smoke. The journey in the Bentley.

Affable laughter at some joke, and North stepped backwards and away. The elite didn't see those that served because they didn't need to. Glasses filled. Glasses refilled. He was invisible. North let the crowds fold around and carry him away.

Tarn was here. In the same room. It wasn't the original plan. Should he take him instead? Catch him and finish this? But Tarn was already on the move, steadily, through the crowds. Weaving and travelling further away. At the doorway he turned, his razor-sharp focus slicing through the churning moving throng and his eyes locked with North's, the slightest smile. He knew. Had known as his darling boy stood sentry serving him while considering his death. Untouchable. Untouched. Predator not prey. North cursed as the door closed behind the judge, and the nearest party goer looked at him askance before forgetting he existed. There'd be another day for Tarn. They both knew it. He looked around the crowds. But it wasn't happening twice.

Ripples spread outwards from the US President. From around each head of state surrounded by security, political minders, hangers-on, their own ministers, other countries' ministers, their own diplomats, other countries' diplomats, the ambitious, curious, and star-hungry. For a deal-maker, for a money-maker, for a politician, it was the hot ticket in town, the only place to be – which made it all the more surprising that JP Armitage was leaving.

Under his tan, JP Armitage was sweaty with the heat coming off the crowd. Tucking the paisley silk handkerchief into his top pocket of his dinner jacket, he was moving away from his companions, the famous smile switching off like lights going out over a city. North kept him in sight as he steered his way through the crowds, clapping old friends on the back, shaking hands with new ones, pumping up-down, up-down, index finger pointing to the select – "I see you" – kissing cheeks as he passed, but stopping for no one. For a second, North asked himself whether Armitage too had clocked him, but the eyes had slid over him – another lackey, insignificant, nothing to be gained from shaking his hand or acknowledging his existence.

North let the thirsty grab for his glasses, the last a mature, full-hipped blonde in a black silk cocktail dress who winked at him, blowing a glossy, scarlet kiss. "Thanks, hon – I'm sweatin' bullets here," she said as she took the flute before turning back to the elegant, dark-eyed woman next to her. "Would you like a sparkling water, honey?" For a split second the huge dark eyes met those of North and it was electric. Desperation. Terror. Need. North hesitated. But with the door already closing on Armitage, there wasn't the time to wonder why. Instead, North lowered the silver tray, keeping it tight against his side before sliding it behind maroon velvet drapery as the waiter became one more guest at the party.

Out of the huge oak doors, the hubbub of global citizenry dropped away to only the leather soles of handmade shoes, slapping against the shallow steps. Armitage had already started down the stone staircase, towards security and the exit.

"Mr Armitage." Anyone listening would have put North's accent somewhere in the cultured streets of Georgetown, Washington, via Harvard and an expensive, affluent childhood in the mid-West.

Armitage turned. His brows were gathered. This was an impatient man. A power to be reckoned with – call him back at your peril.

North smiled with smooth East Coast insincerity. He raised his voice – allowing it to travel to the police guarding the exit. "Mr Armitage, the President very much hoped for a word. He's a big fan of your New Army. He thinks it's great – so great."

If Armitage had been feathered, the assumed courtesy would have swelled him to twice the size. Even so, the tycoon frowned, appearing strangely dismayed by the invitation, his handmade, patent dress shoes still pointing away from North and towards the door.

"It will only take a few minutes. The President insists – you understand." The perfect political aide stood back, holding out his arm. The leader of the Western world waited.

For Armitage to refuse would have been remarkable. With a heavy sigh, he made to go back through to the banqueting hall, but North shook his head, a charming smile. "A private word." He emphasised "private" – privilege indeed. North guided Armitage back up the stairs towards another door, this one with its own keypad and through which he could only hope would be a private function room, an office – he would settle for a broom cupboard. Armitage checked his Rolex as North keyed in the numbers which he'd watched the harassed banqueting manager punch in earlier and pushed open the door. To the left was a narrow stairwell. Straight ahead, a closed door. North held his breath – hoped luck was with him. He turned the handle. It was unlocked.

Deferential – the suave courtesies of a political lackey in the presence of a superior, North stood back to allow Armitage entry, and as he passed through, Armitage checked his Rolex again. Seven fifty-one. North already knew what it said. He followed Armitage, almost stepping on his heels – the heady smoke and pepper of expensive malt – pulling the door closed behind them, turning the old-fashioned brass key in the lock.

Armitage scowled as he took in the emptiness. The old-fashioned desk with its captain's chair – the ancient computer next to a grimy phone. He was a busy man. He had to be somewhere else. Could not wait. Another time. Pass on his apologies to the President. Tomorrow he had all the time in the world if the President could free up five minutes then.

He stopped talking as North drew Stella's gun.

"Where are you in such a hurry to be, Armitage?" In North's experience, given the choice between a gun and a watch, men watched the gun. But Armitage stared at the Rolex again, apparently hypnotised by it. Seven fifty-three. The tycoon's gaze flickered to the door. He took a deep breath – steadying his nerves. Stopped himself from checking the time yet again though North felt the urge in him – felt the magnitude of each and every second as it passed. As if Armitage were ageing in front of him.

"Who are you?"

"Does it matter?"

The door handle rattled as someone on the outside attempted to turn it, and Armitage opened his mouth to call out. North raised the gun, sighting it so the bullet would go down the tycoon's throat. Armitage closed his mouth and the rattling stopped. He was sweating again, beads of perspiration running down his temples – the smell of him spiced and expensive. It crossed North's mind that, although the tycoon was steady enough and there was no slur to his speech, Armitage was thoroughly, stinkingly drunk.

"Whoever you are, we need to get out of here."

North perched himself on the green leather-topped desk, one knee bent resting on the polished seat, his foot on the floor.

"If we don't, we're going to die," said Armitage.

Men exaggerated in the face of death. *"I'll give you anything,"* when they had nothing. They lied. *"I didn't do it,"* when they did. Said *"I can explain,"* when they couldn't. But North believed Armitage. Time was running out for him.

"Then talk fast, and be on your way."

For years, the bullet had made North doubt himself. Words, pictures, the worst kind of emotions came to him unbidden.

He had enough bad memories of his own, enough violent urges, and too many things he should forget. But the urgent, ruinous call in Armitage's eyes made him curious, made him want to go beyond, to step over the threshold into the darkness at the very core of the man with him. But if he went walkabout in that wasteland of misery, North didn't know if he'd ever find his way back.

Armitage blinked.

With a sensation of pulling away from the brink of a chasm, North came back to himself just as the old-fashioned metal keyboard smashed against his hand. There was a moment of blinding pain as the gun dropped to the floor only to skitter under the desk. Armitage seized hold of the captain's chair, using it to keep North away as he made for the door. Armitage wasn't a coward, but he wasn't a man whose job it was to kill other men either.

North gripped the curved back of the chair and seat to force it upwards, overbalancing Armitage, making him stagger – knocking the tycoon sideways and into the wall, as he brought the chair down against the other man's head and shoulders. If the wall hadn't taken the brunt of the blow, Armitage would have died then and there. Instead North took hold of him and dragged him across to the wall on the other side of the room, slamming him against it, then flipping him, pressing his face to the plasterwork. Before Armitage could gather himself North pulled back both arms, ripping the phone wires from the ancient phone to coil them around and around his wrists, knotting them as he wound the other end around the old Victorian radiator. Armitage's voice was shrill as he attempted to wrench himself away from the radiator. Instead, the wire tightened itself and the tether pulled him brutally short. He made for the door again, almost dislocating his shoulders – his hands already crimson as the blood vessels constricted.

"Honor Jones?" North smacked the other man's face once with the palm of his hand, and once with the back. He needed him focused and sober. "Where is she?"

The struggle stopped. The tycoon leaned back against the wall as if he needed its support, and laughed. A hollow, cold noise. "I don't know."

"Is she alive?" The touch of Honor's skin, her lips against his. He didn't know whether the sensations were from his own desire or Armitage's memories.

A piece fell into place somewhere. "You're the one she talked about at the Savoy. North." Armitage took in the brutality. The gun. His youth. "Then you're one of these people – or you were. 'The Board'. You're one of their killers, except you couldn't do it, could you? Were you as flattered as I was when you were recruited? That's what they count on, you know."

As Armitage talked North thought of the elegant, dark-eyed woman at the reception, crackling with desperate sorrow. The memory of her nagging at him.

"We were at a party like this one when Tarn said 'Do the right thing.' Invest in defence, in the New Army. Help us stand against Russia and China. It was patriotic, and privatisation brings its own efficiencies. The country's all but bankrupt. Men like me – we keep it together. Everything I'm doing is for the right reasons. The fact it's been profitable has been a bonus, that's all. Tarn persuaded me to manage the money for them, launder it, act as banker. Who knows where my investments start and theirs end? Not even me anymore. But whatever it used to be, the Board today is made up of fanatics, North – you must know that. They think democracy is over, that the market only gets us so far, that the country is dying without the leadership it needs."

North had seen her before. He knew he had. The fearful almond eyes turning, assessing, dismissing him. Turning away.

"As for this? They've assured me it's necessary. I've chosen to believe them, because they have Honor and I have no choice."

"Someone's stepping out of line," Stella said before she died. JP Armitage had stopped being a believer, if he ever was. Had stopped thinking about the money he could make, and started thinking about everything he had to lose. They took Honor to keep him loyal.

Hesitation on Armitage's side. "You've only known her days. I've known her since she was a child."

Honor's face younger. Smoother. Rounder. Sprawling sun-tanned limbs by the pool.

And there was guilt in there. A narrow black line running through Armitage and buried deep. Covered over. Betrayal and money and figures on a page. Honor's father didn't commit fraud. Armitage wanted him out of the way – coveting what the other man had.

His firm. His model wife. His teenage daughter. Nothing he deserved. The daughter and the mother would be better off in his care, Armitage assured himself. Happier. Looked after. How was he to know his friend was so close to the edge of sanity?

North's brain felt as if it were flooding with blood. Was he constructing his own narrative for Armitage or was the tycoon's sin darker than North had even imagined?

"I loved her mother, North, and I've seen Honor grow into a remarkable woman." Armitage's face contorted and North realised it was with regret – an emotion so strange to the tycoon that the muscles of his face weren't sure what to do, where to go. How many years had he spent justifying his role in the tragedy, the destruction and unravelling of the perfect girl by "being there" for her? An old friend of the family who smashed that family apart and put the picture back together with the jagged pieces of a guilt-racked survivor who thought she had to save the world or die trying.

"I tried to keep her out of it till this was over. Somewhere safe. She's important to me – you have no idea how important."

The tycoon had Honor committed to hide her from the Board. From his own people. Armitage was the reason Honor was "off the books", the reason North wasn't sent the usual briefing. JP didn't care what happened to Peggy once he had the smart chip. But Honor was different. The Board didn't want the tycoon knowing they were going to kill the woman he wanted to marry. When he found out, he threatened to bring down the temple.

"Tell me where she is, Armitage."

That was it – the dark-eyed woman at the reception next door was at the camp, sitting at the table surrounded by children. And she was pregnant. Peggy's refugee whose name was Sonja. The same Sonja standing in the reception with a curled fist pressed into her ribs, her knuckles white. The beating heart of the child inside her.

Armitage shook his head, impatient with his captor. "They want Honor close by so I don't 'disappoint'. I'm not letting them down, North. Everything's ready to go. Anyone who might get in our way has a personal stake in our success – their children, their husbands and wives. I'm no different. Peggy's smart chips are already out there. We started manufacture months ago and they're going into everything. This country first but it'll be global fast enough, especially because we aren't charging anyone for the technology. We're embedding the chips in their weapons systems. Communications. Utilities. In time, we'll control all of it. Peggy did something magnificent. She's making the world a quieter place. And more energy-efficient."

"And what else?" Armitage looked sick.

"We tweaked it. Bannerman put in a backdoor. Information is power and we'll have all the information we need, and if information isn't enough, we'll take control, dismantling GPS, disabling entire industries, oil, nuclear, defence systems, turning them on and off to suit."

"Peggy found out?"

Armitage's eyes went to the door again and North felt the panic building in the other man, infecting him. His own panic running alongside that of Armitage, matching it pace for urgent pace. Trying to make sense of it.

The Board wanted Honor dead because she was looking for Peggy. And now she was more use alive to bring JP in line.

A hammering against the door. Perhaps it was the noise of their fight or perhaps security had decided the door had been shut for too long? That the President was in the banqueting hall and not in a private meeting with a British industrialist?

"Did Peggy find out?"

"She was always too damned clever for her own good."

North stood over him. They were of a similar size. Neither had to look down. They breathed in time with each other. Honor's mouth. Dust on the black silk lapel of Armitage's jacket. The chimes of Big Ben striking eight o'clock hanging small on the cold, wintry air.

"Look after her." Armitage's whisper was barely loud enough to be heard. Afterwards, North thought that perhaps he hadn't heard him say it at all.

Perhaps North only joined the dots as the room blew apart. Glass and dust took the place of air. The noise came later. The end-of-all-things – an enormous bang travelling through the marrow of him as if the explosion started and finished in his bones. Bricks and stone and metalwork started to fall – a few at first then all at once, travelling towards him faster than thought. Armitage lost – darkness so black it was as if the light of the world had been extinguished. A black hole. Dark matter. Peggy lost. Honor lost. North fought for oxygen as the air was sucked out of the room, almost sucking out his innards with it. He tried to persuade his body to sip its breaths. Wasn't that what you were supposed to do? Wasn't that the training in another existence? But desperate for oxygen that wasn't there, his body wasn't listening. Lifting, shifting, as if gravity had been suspended – the world upside down and roundabout; with his eyes rimed with grit and ash he could see nothing as he flew, turning, spinning, slamming, the door, the thick stone wall gone, the twisting staircase, the wall into the banqueting hall disappeared. Trying to remember what he had been supposed to see, what should have been, finding nothing. Jacko. Where was his unit? The young Second Lieutenant dead again. And where the party had been, the throngs of statesmen, the great and good, the unborn child, everything covered in white ash, tattered flesh and blood. No Jacko then. Relief. But no anybody.

There should have been somebody.

North must have lost consciousness for a while. He didn't know how long. Minutes not hours, and when he came round, he spat blood and dust from his mouth, coughing as he brought up he didn't want to know what – a high-pitched squealing the only thing to cling to. The rest of the world muffled, dead. There must have been screaming, but he couldn't hear it. As his vision came and went and came again, he attempted to get to his feet but they slipped on the stone, a sensation of softness under him. He patted himself down. Reeling. Was he there? All of him? No limbs missing, blood in his hair again? He reached for a door – missed it, stumbling, on his knees, sharp pain pushing though the cloth, into flesh. He stood up again, extracted an inch-long nail and threw it to the floor – or where there should have been a floor. Beside him the floor had fallen away, the sides broken beams, yawning open ready to swallow him down. Limping, he kept to the walls, what there were of them – hoped what was left wouldn't decide their time was done and take him with them.

"Armitage…" He knew himself to be calling but he couldn't hear the words. He called again, coughing with the exertion of it. Perhaps Armitage could hear even if North couldn't?

Armitage knew about the bomb. Had been trying to leave. And he stopped him. Killing him. Killing his only hope of finding her. And the only reason the Board had to keep her alive.

Flames were catching, creeping up the walls, crawling across the end of the hall.

Time to leave. He took off his shredded jacket to press it against his nose and mouth, the cloth sticky and wet. Briefly wondered about the bullet in his brain. This much he knew about bombs, the impact of the blast waves on the brain could kill you without leaving a mark. What damage could they do if they already had a bullet in there to work with? Fire caught somewhere. Electrics. Burning wood and roasting meat mixed with the cordite and what he was guessing was PETN – pentaerythritol tetranitrate. A major ingredient of Semtex, from the same family as nitroglycerine. Colourless crystals capable of detonation by electrical impulse. The explosive of choice for terrorists everywhere – including it seemed dear old London Town.

He stepped back as his foot caught, pressed against something under it. Crushed under a collapsed beam, his body half hanging over the gaping hole into the arched vault below and beyond, JP Armitage, billionaire industrialist, traitorous lover, with an estimated personal fortune bigger than the GDP of some countries. Dead and gone. No mark on his face, only a thin layer of white powder covering the mane of hair and the heavy features like a Georgian dandy. They were keeping Honor alive to keep Armitage in line. The building shifted, the slightest tilt as history gathered itself. Plaster dust fell, ancient timber struts snapped, and Armitage still tethered to the cast iron radiator slipped inch by inch away. North grabbed for him. Cloth. The tail of the silk-lined dinner jacket sliding through his hand. A dry slither, Armitage's body picking up speed all of a sudden, down, hands tied, a swallow dive into what North could only guess was Hell.

Amid the billowing dust and gathering smoke of the banqueting hall, there was movement on the floor, a rolling and unfurling, arms reaching as if the guests had been dead and were rising again because the trumpet had sounded and Judgement Day come upon them. To his knowledge there had been eight heads of state in this room, together with some of their key ministers. He wondered how many of them were dead.

The young waiter lay crumpled over the debris – an ever-expanding pool of crimson seeping out from beneath him. *"It's carnage out there,"* he'd said, excited to be part of it. North sank to his knees. A tinkling sound as he lifted the handsome head onto his lap – the body covered with sparkling fragments of glass reflecting the flames. A Pieta, the thought came to North from some religious tract of his mother's, a marble Madonna and Christ cut down from the cross, but a floppy-haired Christ not yet dead and smelling of aftershave, and dust and blood.

"It's all right," he tried to say, but he still couldn't hear himself. The boy opened his mouth and North thought he groaned, the groan turning into a cough that convulsed the broken body and then a guttural rattle – his panicking eyes fixing on North. "You're going to be fine." He laid a hand over the curly hair. He'd comforted soldiers before. Waited with them as they bled out.

Something in the brown eyes shifted as the boy recognised him from the kitchen, and his hand found North's and squeezed. North smiled. For the sake of the boy, as if he were glad he had this chance to talk together. As if this were their lucky day.

He wanted to move him, but North had seen death in the field before and it was coming on fast. But the boy didn't have to know that. All he needed to know was that he wasn't alone, because no one on this earth should face death alone and sooner than he should. North knew that for a fact now if he had never known it before. A noise came up from the young waiter, North felt the sensation. The boy's urgent need for his mother's touch. But there was no mother, no time – blood leaking from the corner of his mouth.

Stillness. In the sudden space where there should have been a heartbeat, the eyes glazed. North moved his palm down over the face. Pennies, he thought, though he didn't know from where. There should be pennies to weigh down the eyelids. One final price to pay for being alive, alongside the loss and the suffering. He swept the narrow chest of glass – tidying him, making him presentable for the next life, regardless that the glass was making his fingers bleed. He laid the boy back on the ground, gently does it, so as not to wake him, and stood.

His ears ringing, in the silent movie of billowing dust, a figure was waving him over. Man or woman, he wasn't sure. It took time for him to recognise the curvaceous blonde who had taken his last flute of champagne, the American in the black silk dress who winked at him. Her mouth moved, the gloss stuck over with ash like tiny grey feathers, but he couldn't hear her. Then the voices came:

I can't feel my legs.

Mom.

Oh my God.

Dead – he has to be dead.

An agonised weeping babble from a mixture of nationalities – some he recognised, some he didn't. German. Danish. Japanese. A dark-suited man with blood running down his grey face laboured regardless in the corner, moving pieces of rubble, throwing them right and left, determined to get to what lay under it, knowing already there was no point. North gazed around the ruined hall, the scraps of what he took to be flesh, the limbless and the crushed, one or two of the more able-bodied bent over the injured, the dying. He couldn't understand the barrage of voices that rushed into his head, there were too many speaking too many languages and the panic too intense – he fought to block them out before they swept away all reason. He was glad he couldn't understand most of the words, but the screaming? The screaming didn't need a translator. It filled his mind with the white noise of anguish.

Fire caught the dry timbers of the hall as he left it. He carried the blonde in his arms, keeping tight hold against the slippery wet cloth. She'd said "Thanks, hon" again, though he didn't think she recognised him, smiled as he'd lifted her – though she had to be in agony. White smoke billowed from the building, turning blue as it caught the flashing blue lights of the emergency services parked across Whitehall. A yellow-jacketed paramedic came to lift the woman out of his arms, but he could tell from the weight of her head against his chest, from the stillness, that she was dead, and he didn't want to let her go. She'd said "Thanks, hon," and smiled at her luck in getting the last champagne. She'd have wanted him to hold her – not some stranger. Someone threw a silver foil blanket over him, and he felt a steadying hand on his forearm. The paramedic blocking him was speaking, but he couldn't hear him. He watched the mouth move up and down, the sympathetic eyes. He wanted North to let her go. So he did.

66

London

They dressed his knee in A&E, pumped antibiotics into him, counted three broken ribs, checked him for concussion, and for wounds that had drenched him in gore but the blood wasn't his. If the junior doctor weren't so overwhelmed by the casualties and the trauma stacking up in triage, she might have asked about the ridged scar through his hair. But she didn't. There were lives to save, limbs to save. No time for conversation. Instead, the walking wounded sat with sweet tea in the waiting room and along the corridors of the hospital. Someone made a joke that they had to be the best-dressed patients the hospital had ever seen, but no one laughed. A TV played out in the corner: estimates had it at more than forty-eight dead and more than two hundred and fifty wounded. Unconfirmed reports claimed the Prime Minister and her Italian counterpart were dead. They could confirm the German Chancellor was seriously wounded and five other UK ministers were believed to be dead, including the Chancellor of the Exchequer and the Home Secretary. President Trump was unharmed and already on Air Force One heading home. He'd tweeted his outrage. No one had yet claimed responsibility. The bomb, however, was believed to be the work of an ISIL splinter group operating out of Libya. Complaints were already coming in about the response of the emergency services.

At the news of the Prime Minister's death, a young girl began to sob and an elderly man who had earlier described himself in a clipped tone as "Foreign Office" rubbed her back, round and round, patting it every now and then as if she were a babe in arms. Two policemen in bullet proof vests wandered the corridors, catching the injured, harvesting names and addresses, asking them what they had seen, where they had been standing when the bomb went off. If they had consulted their pocket notebook, they would have remembered the big guy who had wrecked his knee was Jack Keegan, a waiter with Blue Arrow Catering, and no, he hadn't seen anyone suspicious. He'd been by the door, his tray empty about to head back in for refills when the bomb went off. Thank God eh? Or he might be dead too. Of course they could have his address and mobile – whatever they needed. All he could tell them was it was just the usual function with more security. His friend died, another waiter, and he'd carried some nice American lady out – she was dead too. He'd gone quiet then, which hadn't been an act. They'd liked that though. The sergeant patting him on his upper arm. Telling him "It's all right, son." And North thought about the Army and how much he missed it.

Occasionally a relative or friend, North wasn't sure which, stumbled among them searching, raising people's heads, looking for husbands or colleagues – their fear of loss, of discovery, almost unbearable to him. They would plead with a nurse, she'd shake her head and they'd leave again, no wiser and no sorrier, but that much closer to the inevitable fact of death.

The injured sat on – in no hurry to leave. Even though they had been treated, glassy-eyed, their heads bandaged and wounds stitched, they found another plastic seat and went back to waiting. North had seen it before – the consolation of a stranger who'd shared the same experience worth more at that moment than the warm arms of a wife who hadn't been there – could not imagine the horror, the realisation that what you had been through had changed you.

A groan from the assembled patients, a chorus of "Nos". He looked back at the TV. Two white-coated doctors and a handful of pale, exhausted nurses had emerged from curtains and cubicles and tiny rooms. North couldn't understand the pictures, couldn't process what he was seeing. Overcome, a young nurse collapsed weeping against a colleague's chest. The ticker tape spelled it out – bomb attacks in seven venues in London. Aside from the banqueting hall, three other suicide bombers wrapped around with plastic explosives, the devices triggered by a pressure switch, one in The Dorchester, the others in the Westgate mall and Whiteleys shopping centre, one suitcase bomb on a timer at Victoria station, along with two car bombs of pressure cookers loaded with nails and pieces of metal outside Buckingham Palace and Chelsea Barracks triggered remotely.

A pressure switch. Sonja's sorrowful, panicked eyes. Her hand had been wrapped around a pressure switch. Let go the switch – on purpose or accidentally – and boom.

Anarchy came to town.

"These people need locking up." The middle-aged city slicker, one eye padded with gauze, had been furiously stabbing at his mobile phone since he sat down. Mobile communications were down across London and the South East, the news report had already announced, and servers were working to resume normal service as soon as they could. But it didn't stop him. As if he might get lucky and his text make it through. As if the rules didn't apply to him.

A murmur of assent from the assembled crowd. "They should throw away the key." The elderly diplomat who had been patting the young girl's back stopped long enough to agree.

Then there she was. On the TV screen. Honor Jones – in a silver quilted jacket. Blood covered the pale skirt and there was a mauve bruise against her cheekbone, which somehow made her eyes even greener. Her short hair was tousled as if she had run her hands through it, but even so it framed her face perfectly. She spoke directly to the camera against a backdrop of flames and burning shops. A nurse behind the desk turned up the volume.

Underneath the picture a tag line "Hero MP saves hundreds in shopping mall bomb disaster". The picture cut away to grainy mobile phone footage, the shot dipping and falling – Honor mustering screaming shoppers. Her voice calm as she pointed to the exit. The power had gone and the only light was from the phone, but Honor's face remained clear of worry or fear.

"I've got you...Nobody panic. Hold hands. Keep together and keep moving, everyone."

There was something odd somewhere. The banker next to North who had stopped trying to text started again, but he cursed and someone hissed at him to be quiet. That was it.

The mobile network was down, but somehow this footage got through. And what were the chances that amid the communications chaos, the pictures to emerge were of Honor Jones MP?

Maybe the call was a lucky one – routed through a Wi-Fi network? North considered the chances as the news cut back to Honor. She hunkered down, wrapping a foil blanket around the young girl weeping next to her. She stood up as a reporter asked a question – her face gleaming and perfect and suffering in the lights of the gathered cameras. Honor was smart. She knew something was off from the start. She must realise the Board was behind the bomb. This was her chance to denounce the conspiracy. To end centuries of manipulation and murder.

There was motion at the margins. A hum and a shuffling and the screen filled with people of all ages and colours and states of injury crowding into the space around Honor. Their need to be close to their saviour. Their need to listen. She pulled the little girl into her so they weren't separated, her left hand resting on the child's shoulder, and the child smiled broadly into the camera. Someone handed Honor a baby smudged with ash. "This is a truly terrible night. But I want to say this. We will not be defeated by acts of cowardice and terrorism. We pull together and we do whatever it takes, and mark my words..." She handed the baby off to a by-stander and pointed a finger directly into the camera "... those responsible for tonight's events should not sleep easy. Because I, Honor Jones – No. We, the people, serve notice this night – we're coming to get you. This country has fought wars against the odds before. Liberal values have their place, serve their purpose. But strength and security serve a purpose too. Keeping our citizens safe. Safer than our political system has kept them tonight. This nation is a great and sovereign nation. We will fight to our last breath to keep it that way. Britain Forever."

She was Boudicca. She was Joan of Arc and Elizabeth I at Tilbury. It was perfect.

Inspirational.

A masterpiece of beauty, patriotism, courage, rhetoric.

It was a leadership bid in a country which had just lost its leaders.

A ragged, gathering cheer went up in the waiting room, picked up along the corridor as pain and shock were replaced by a heady, unholy joy, by a rush of devotion and righteous anger as a wounded country fell in love with Honor Jones MP. Only one person wasn't cheering – Michael North. He wasn't one for coincidence. She worked it out. The camp full of innocents. The targeted bombing of the political elite. The coup was on. JP Armitage was dead and Honor Jones was without a protector. They'd snatched her up. And as far as she knew, North too was dead – his corpse rotting in her Knightsbridge Wendy house. Stella never said she was his friend and Honor never told him she cared. No man ever kept her safe. Her murderous father. Her traitorous lover. North who came to kill her and who failed to save her over and over. Her best friend had disappeared, and her mother's last words were to barricade herself in and stay alive at all costs. Unless she made herself useful, the Board had every reason to kill her. She was a comet trailing destruction. She'd pushed one man to his death from a rooftop. In calculating the odds this time, she had switched to the winning side. A sensible decision; the work of an ordered mind in a chaotic world. Persuasively, with skill and charm, she doubtless talked the gun out of Tarn's hand. She had done it before. *I understand. You've a job to do. But tell me one thing...*

Why then did it feel like a betrayal?

The leather jacket hung off the back of the chair in the café, its dark brown sleeves puddled on the floor – its owner leaning in over the tiny zinc-topped table to talk to his companion, one arm around her. North shrugged himself into the leather jacket as he walked away from their table. He needed it more – on the streets of the capital his own shredded white dinner jacket was too obvious, bound to attract attention, curiosity – sympathy he didn't need. His shirt was worse but he zipped the jacket up, checked the pockets – only coppers, flipped open the expensive Italian leather wallet he had lifted from the mobile phone addict in the waiting room. £90 and half a dozen credit cards – two of them platinum. As he turned his back on the crowded bright lights of the hospital, he kept the cash, discarding the wallet and cards on a brick wall. Somebody's lucky night.

67

London

4.15am. Saturday, 11th November

His head pounding, his knee throbbing, it was still dark when he got to the Percy Hotel in the backstreets of Camden. He limped up the stone stairs, holding onto the metalwork separating this seedy dive from the next seedy dive, from the next seedy dive – No Vacancy flashing orange in the gloom. The sallow-faced concierge barely looked up from the early morning copy of *The Sun*. An observer might even have said that the concierge made a point of not looking up as he slid a key across the pock-marked melamine counter. North wondered when he fixed up the room rental whether he was throwing away his money. But for three years, every six months, he spent at least four hours working his way across London, losing anyone who might be tailing him, losing his own shadow, to pay an exorbitant rent in hard cash and harder drugs. The hotel owner didn't ask questions – he'd forgotten how, and the night-desk concierge simply didn't see him. He needed the job and didn't need the trouble. North was after all the perfect tenant. Regular. Paid his bills on time. So quiet you hardly knew he was there.

He checked the door to Room 13b before he went in. The arrangement involved absolute privacy. No housekeeping, no curious look-arounds, and no favours to working girls with low expectations and ready money who needed an hour in the dry, but the hair seal attached to the frame remained unbroken.

North pushed open the door and clicked on the light, taking care to close the door after himself and lock it. He put his eye to the spyhole but there was no one there – the fisheye lens distorting the striped bile-green wallpaper of the corridor into bulging prison bars. The room didn't bear close scrutiny, but there was a plastic boxed shower in the corner reeking of damp, a dusty hotplate, and an ancient armchair – a spring poking through the seat covered by a tapestry cushion. It would do. He crossed over the threadbare carpet of sickly, swirling orange and brown, to push aside the yellowing nets at the window. Underneath, the rail tracks ran hither and thither. A goods train passed by, the walls of the hotel vibrating as the engine gathered speed, and behind him the mirrored door of the plywood wardrobe creaked open and then closed again. He figured it did that a lot.

North crushed the heavy-duty opiates he'd swiped from the trolley as the nurse dressed his leg, and washed them down with a glass of lukewarm water tangy with rust; the tap screaming at him as he turned it, a brown stain chasing the hairline crack through the sink. Flowers in another sink. Ceramic shards. He refused to think about her. Refused to look at himself in the mirror – what was there to see? Only a fool.

The Board didn't only seize family connected to key players working within their strategic targets. They mixed in the hostile and disposable. They'd strapped Sonja and God knows who else up with explosives and blown apart society. The coup was under way and they were already winning. He was too late.

And Honor, who believed there was good in him, was lost.

North threw himself down on the single bed – almost passing out with the pain from his ribs, the springs shrieking in protest, the raspberry-pink candlewick coverlet damp under him. Tarn bought Honor. The only question was – what with? Surely not money, she had plenty and would have had more with JP. The promise of safety? If you become a monster yourself, what's to fear from the monsters under the bed? Or with power? The country was leaderless – the Prime Minister and her most senior government ministers were black and white memories, but every television channel pumped out Honor Jones in fabulous technicolour with her blood-soaked mandate for change. A heroic celebrity telling the nation she would lead it through the valley of the shadow of death to glory, glory, hallelujah days of milk and honey. It was beautiful. She was beautiful.

But they hadn't bought her with the prospect of power, she wasn't the type. She was an MP because she was a believer who wanted to save people from themselves, and from each other, which meant Tarn bought and sold her for that most dangerous of commodities – love. For the promise of Peggy's return if she behaved. A promised return she probably didn't even believe in her heart of hearts was possible any more. North understood the temptation. Not to be alone. Honor decided if she couldn't beat the system, she would salvage what there was to salvage, and North couldn't fault her logic.

But she should have tried. She was wrong and she had been wrong too about the fact there was good in him. There was no goodness in the world and certainly no goodness in him. There never was. There never would be.

Trembling with pain, finally, he slept. Two hours. He woke to carnage but it was only in his head. Another hour. JP Armitage's hand gripping his own – slipping from his grasp. Falling. Another hour. The bomb's impact or the rumbling trains startling him into sweating, terrified wakefulness. Honor Jones – he should have her name tattooed on his body as a warning to himself and others never to believe. Trust was dead. First Stella and last Honor. He turned onto his side, groaning, pushing his face into the foam pillow that smelled of long-ago strangers, his broken ribs, the laser claws of migraine gripping him, ripping into his flesh that would grow over and over again, devouring it all. The flash and white-hot burn of red and orange clashing light scouring his eyeballs, making them bleed.

The opiates gone. No purple pills. No one and nothing to get him through the pain and wakefulness.

68

Once he thought he heard something. Sensed a body pressed against the door, another man's breathing the other side of a thin wall. His eyes opened, watching the door handle, waiting for it to turn, but there was no adrenalin surge. His muscles stayed heavy, his body torpid in the hollow of the damp bed. He wasn't ready to move. Didn't care. Life or death. It was all the same to him.

The floorboard creaked. Once. Stillness again. Silence. North imagined the bulky shadow, the crepe-soled shoes. He closed his eyes against the light and the sight of the door opening, the barrel of a gun, till he knew somewhere in the most instinctive part of himself that the shadow had gone. Whore? Punter? Chambermaid? Killer? Whoever had been there listening for him wasn't any more, and he was alone again. How it should be.

69

London

6.35am. Monday, 13th November

Hunger finally drove him from the room. Light-headed, limping, his leg still stiff, and drawing shallow breaths courtesy of the broken ribs, he passed through an empty reception out onto the streets. It was sheeting with rain and too early for the hurly-burly of commuters, but even so it was too busy for his taste. Nervous and dry-mouthed, he slunk along the crowded pavements. He wondered about the bullet – whether it had moved with the force of the pressure waves, how long he had until it killed him, thought about the fact no one would mourn him when it did. He caught a glimpse of a smashed-up face moving alongside, the temple raised and purple with bruising, the lips pulped and swollen, his heart pounding; he then realised it was his own reflection trapped in the plate glass of a down-at-heel café.

Frankie's Diner was as good a destination as any. Once upon a time Frankie nailed photographs of the Coliseum and the Trevi Fountain above the red plastic vinyl banquettes.

These days the photos were foxed, foam guts spilled from the ripped plastic, and the only atmosphere came from a heady mix of rancid chip fat and the stale bodies of the clientele. A tramp sat hunched in the corner, his filthy, shaking hands with their blackened ridged nails hugging a mug of tea, two skinny white slices of bread and spread on a plate in front of him. The vagrant didn't want the bread – he wanted a cheap bottle of spirits that would kill him before his time. North knew the feeling.

North sat with a clear view of the door, the back of his head against the cold wall, the window to his left – condensation over the glass, black mould running the length of the sill. He kept his head down as he ordered, his voice rusty with disuse, his elbow on the table, a hand obscuring his battered face, but the greasy-haired waitress didn't notice or didn't care about the damage. He couldn't decide which.

The tea was stewed but the all-day breakfast of eggs and sausages, bacon and beans was piping hot. North ordered another tea when he'd done and the waitress graced him with contempt and a steady pour of brown gunge, slopping over the top and filling the chipped saucer, before she clattered away with the dirty plate.

The bell over the door tinkled – fresh, cold air, the smell of rain and the hum of building traffic, there, and then gone again, as the door swung shut. Shaking out a black umbrella, furling it before he hung it on one of three button pegs, a lanky man in a long coat approached the counter. *A mug of tea and apple pie à la mode, Frankie*, he instructed the elderly owner at the till, his back to the tables. *Shocking morning out there.*

North rubbed at his temples. The fatty protein-heavy meal was reviving him and he wasn't convinced that was a good thing. If he revived, he'd start to feel and he was getting used to the emptiness inside – it was safer that way. He could live with being nothing. Feeling nothing. Having nothing, though now he considered the matter of the opiate stash, he wanted more. He was in the process of running through how to access purple pills when company slid over the vinyl bench and into the seat opposite him.

North calculated it would take him seven seconds to reach the door – twelve if he hit the one-eyed man first, longer if the one-eyed man had a gun.

The question was, did he have a gun?

His companion leaned back against the bench, revealing the silencer.

The answer, then, was yes.

The one-eyed man thanked the waitress as she neared the table, and the girl slowed her approach at the sight of the jagged purple scar that ran through the dark, empty socket and down the cheek. Gawking, she placed the mug and pie down on the melamine with due reverence, and clacking on her white plastic heels backed away from the table, step by step, her mouth open all the while.

"Some women rather like it," the one-eyed man said, apparently to North, as he picked up the fork, polishing the tines on the paper napkin he had pulled from under the plate.

"You're good, Mr North. I've only ever chased one man longer than I've chased you. Which is impressive." The one-eyed man forked a piece of pie into his mouth, the gelatinous apple almost falling to the plate from the thickly sugared crust.

"And what happened when you found him?"

The one-eyed man chewed and North forced himself to look into the solitary eye rather than be drawn into the black socket.

"He took out my eye, and I killed him." The accent was Belfast. "But I like to think we both enjoyed the course."

North's ribs were healing but they would slow him. The waitress cleared his dirty plate when she topped up his tea and he wished she hadn't. The cheap knife had been blunt but it would have been better than nothing. The table was screwed into the linoleum floor – too many late-night drunks. Perhaps he could wrest the man's fork from his grasp and stab him through the other eye? But somehow he doubted it.

North wished he'd eaten a better meal if it were to be his last one. At the very least, he should have ordered dessert and died with sugar on his lips.

"Rest easy, Mr North, I'm not going to shoot you." The one-eyed man brought his right hand up, showing him the palm, and laid it on the table – he was a southpaw, the left still held the gun in his lap. "I'm here to offer you an opportunity."

"You killed Bannerman." It was neither a question nor an accusation. It wasn't North and it wasn't the Board. It was why Hardman asked if he was right handed or left.

An almost imperceptible nod from his companion.

"Why?"

"The greatest question of all. I took you for a warrior rather than a philosopher, North."

The astronomer's smooth crimson smile, the sheet of blood down the shirt front. An execution. Professional. Clean. A kind of justice.

His companion used the paper napkin to catch non-existent crumbs at the corner of his thin-lipped mouth, then unfolded it with a small flourish to spread it neatly over the remains of his plate like a linen sheet over the dead, before using his index finger to push the shrouded remains to one side. The table between the two men was clear and empty of distraction.

"Let's say he wasn't on my team. Peggy, however, is one of mine. I'm responsible for her."

Honor's friend was supposed to be an unworldly academic. Not someone working in the darkness alongside one-eyed men who talked so easily of slitting throats over apple pie à la mode.

"Bannerman's death will buy Peggy a little more time. He allowed them to use him. Welcomed it and profited from it. If she's still alive, his death might keep her that way a while longer."

"And is she still alive?"

"I'm an optimist, as is Peggy. An optimist ready to serve her country. Two years ago we approached her and explained our problem with Armitage – that he was immoral, disreputable, and a member of the Board. We asked her to reach out as a way to get to Tarn. The science was already there for her noise cancelling, the energy-efficient smart chip that would save governments and companies millions of pounds. China's been working on something similar for decades, but Peggy beat them to it. We knew the access it provided would be catnip to the Board – that they wouldn't be able to resist harnessing it for their own nefarious ends – and so it proved. She wanted to destroy it, write its own destruction into the program, but it had to be credible. We couldn't take the risk because it was the best chance we've had in a generation to bring down Tarn. We thought we could pull her out before it unwound, but the Board moved too fast for us."

The Board used Peggy like they used North. The one-eyed man used her like he doubtless wanted to use him.

"In return she asked us to keep Honor Jones safe. We moved one of our best men in to keep her close."

The banker who wasn't a banker. The banker with the broken finger who stared after her, watching her walk away. Hugh, who was set to guard her and who ended up dead and drowned in the North Sea. The man opposite him, crouched and vengeful over the body of his operative.

"We've known about you for a long time, Mr North. Watched you – kept count. We were ready to kill you that morning when you followed Honor Jones into the park, but then you didn't do as you'd been told, did you?"

North closed his eyes. The park. The smell of wet foliage. Dampness on his face. Geese rising into the air. Was he in someone's sights even then? Hugh's? Even as his hand grasped the knife. As he heard her speak. Heard her question. *Where's Peggy?*

"To our astonishment, you even went so far as to try and save her. And we saw something bright begin to shine in the darkness that is Michael North."

Peggy didn't tell Honor what she was doing because it was safer that way. She was unravelling Armitage, a man she never liked, not for reasons of patriotism, but to protect Honor from him. Or, for reasons of patriotism, and to protect Honor Jones from him? Her reasons had ceased to matter.

Where's Peggy? Honor asked, a lifetime ago, and he sensed the need in her, the love and loyalty. Did Peggy feel the same way? The compulsion to drag her friend out from the vortex that was JP Armitage. A need which the man sitting in front of him exploited for his own ends.

"The bombings were always going to happen. Tarn wants his toy soldiers on the street. These recent deaths were just the start if he has any say in it."

"And the camp?"

"The press know all about the camp – there's a D-notice banning all mention. They're not happy but they can't write about it because they understand internment is necessary – that 'enemies of the state' don't goose-step across borders all dressed up in pretty uniforms any more."

North was in no doubt Tarn used a handful of their more disposable hostages to pump-prime the bombs. Anthony Walsh would die of natural causes if he wasn't dead already. His remains discovered by a dog-walker months from now. Others would never talk of what happened for fear of the consequences, which would be explained in vivid detail. When their family members cooperated with the conspiracy, they became guilty men and women themselves. They were trapped in Tarn's web.

"Do you have a name?"

"Edmund Hone."

Was it a real name? North doubted it. "And who is Edmund Hone?"

"I'm sure you ask yourself the same question every dawn. 'Who is Michael North?' Is he a loyal soldier? Or a psychopathic killer? Hero or villain?"

"You're not police."

Because police don't slit throats.

"Are you MI5?"

"Lately, my colleagues have taken to calling themselves the Friends of Cyclops. I can't think why – I don't have any friends."

Hone allowed himself a tight, cold smile, transforming his scarred face into a thing of nightmares. "Nature must have its balance, Mr North. Good, bad. Black, white. Positive, negative. The Board and Us. Let's settle on the idea that we're a branch of MI5. Select and working under my direction. Deniable and kept apart for just this moment. *Quis custodiet ipsos custodes?* We 'guard the guardians', Mr North. Whereas the Board is secretive, we are accountable. The Board has its rituals and history, we have civil service pensions. The Board, and Lucien Tarn in particular, believe they know what is best for this country: we have no agenda other than the security of this democratic state. Its genuine security. Its genuine democracy. The Board is effecting a coup and 'we' are going to stop it."

North kept silent. Tarn had his own Army, the technology and enough hostages to control the country's infrastructure. Tarn was responsible for all of it – the bomb blasts. Dead. Injured. The disappearance of a scientist, and the corruption of Honor Jones MP.

"The Board has always had its own role to play, and we were neutral regarding their activities, including your own. But Lucien Tarn is a wildcard and we have ceased to be a neutral party. Which is where you come in, Mr North. Because what he is doing has nothing to do with the greater good and everything to do with power. You are awake to that fact. Lucien Tarn believes he answers to no one. But he is wrong, because he answers to me and to you, Mr North."

North forgot the other man's gun till he tried to rise from the chair.

"We gave you time to recover physically. But you have committed crimes, North – this is the moment to make reparation."

North regarded the cavern where the other man's eye had been, the purple-ridged scar left by a man long since dead.

"We understand you're upset about Honor Jones."

North's fists clenched.

"She's a lucky woman. If JP Armitage had made it, Tarn would have killed her. Armitage was, above all, an adaptable creature; he would've coped. His death – which I imagine you to be responsible for – gave her a chance in the same way I've tried to give Peggy a chance. They had to improvise – they need a communicator, a plausible rallying point in these dangerous times, and Honor Jones fitted the bill. Don't take it to heart. You were trying to keep her alive, weren't you? Mission accomplished. She's on the verge of great things. Don't begrudge her Willy Wonka's golden ticket."

North filtered the information, tasting the irony in it. The Board meant JP Armitage to fill the vacuum when they took out the country's political leadership. Charismatic, tough talking, straight dealing, traitorous to a fault JP Armitage. Instead they had the charismatic, persuasive Honor Jones.

"The suicide bid?"

"They've changed the story. The media got it wrong – it wasn't suicide. It was a miscarriage. They were about to be married when she lost JP Armitage's baby, and now, worse yet, she's lost Armitage as well. Tragic eh? Pulls at your heartstrings, doesn't it? And it makes it all the harder to challenge her when she demands change.

"This won't do, Mr North. Your inertia. Make no mistake democracy is dying out there. Tarn has his people everywhere. The Army is already his. Key figures in the police are his. The secret service." He paused as if to acknowledge the seriousness of what he was saying. "The government is passing an Executive Order to arrest whomsoever they please – the camp you were so concerned with is legal. Among the detainees are enough Britons home from fighting holy wars in messy places to make sure nobody cares about who else is there or when they arrived. Internment after all has a great and glorious tradition – the Boers, World War One, World War Two, Ireland. And the bombings were just the start. Tarn has something bigger in mind. The strongest of governments. A militarised society at war with liberal values. When Trump's America stepped away from its defence commitments in Europe, the US gave up all influence here along with its military bases. We chose to walk away from the European Union and all that goes with it. This, right here, is our new world order. In any event, no foreign power will speak for us because they will all too soon be preoccupied with the consequences of Dr Boland's smart chip. Tarn is imposing a regime of his own choosing, and one from which there is no going back."

"But why now?"

"Because they have an army. Because there is fear on the street. Because Trump got elected. Because it was always going to be sometime, and most of all because Tarn is an angry old man who is tired of waiting."

North shrugged, feigning indifference. He was done with it all, with fighting an enemy bigger than him.

"This is a revolution, Mr North. You've been that man's creature for a long time. I despise who you are and what you represent. But I need you, and you have no choice. Did I mention that? I say this with a degree of reluctance, because we have no time for dialectics. We'll kill Honor Jones. We will find and kill everyone you ever met – a massacre of the innocents. Sweet and luscious Jess. The gifted Fangfang Yu – which would be a shame because GCHQ would love her. Your old Army buddies. Their pretty wives and adorable children. You can go to their funerals. Each of them – one by one, young and old. Until you agree to do what we want."

"Don't threaten me."

"I don't make threats. I haven't the time. This is the end of days, Mr North."

Honor Jones made him believe he was better than a killing machine. To rejoin the fight now would put them on opposite sides. Would make her his enemy. It would take them right back to the start. Him on one side. Her on the other.

"You can get close enough to take off the monster's head. Tarn chairs the Board. He values you. He'll welcome you back – the prodigal son."

"I doubt that."

"Maybe not. But you're uniquely placed – you can get close enough to one man and that may be enough."

This time he was expected to kill not Honor, but Tarn. Who began it all and who intended to change the world into something that suited him better. Tarn ordered the deaths of his adversaries, interned the innocent, and set a bomb in the heart of government. He used North till North wouldn't be used, and then threw him away like he had only ever been nothing. Because Tarn wanted society remade in his own image and that could only ever be a darker, greedier, more violent place.

The picture of a ketch. The name Liberty painted on her side came to mind. Gentle waves against the clean lines of her hull. A soft breeze as he cast a line into the azure sea – an ice-cold beer at his bare feet, warm against the polished deck. A tug on the hook bending the rod.

It would never happen. He would never fish off the stern of a boat as it sailed warm and foreign seas.

He let it go.

North didn't have a choice.

Tarn was guilty. And killing people was what North did.

Hone pushed across a folded piece of paper. "A more salubrious address. Its former occupant wasn't on my team either. An elderly Serb – she too is keen to make reparations for her sins. It's a place where you can arm yourself, and you'll need help. Prepare yourself, Mr North, for battle is upon you. You're one of the good guys now."

70

London

7.45am. Monday, 13th November

The Mayfair address just off Oxford Street was an affluent one. Expensive cars purred along the streets, expensive women dangling designer handbags shimmied past him, their steps slowing, their predator-eyes holding his just a moment too long, the scent of jasmine and civet in his nose as their footsteps receded, tapping their way to West End offices. He thought of Jess alone in Disney World with her glorious body and her gap-toothed smile.

Thousands of miles away from him, and still not safe enough.

A brass plaque to the right of the Edwardian villa's door sported six vertically stacked buttons alongside six empty name slots. He buzzed the third one down as Hone instructed, and heard a dull click as the studded door released its electronic lock. The hum of traffic fell away to nothingness as the door closed behind him.

Outside was respectable; inside shabby, the mahogany hall table dusty and sporting a brown-leaved aspidistra, the smell of mildew everywhere. Still, next to the dump at King's Cross, it was a palace. Ignoring the ramshackle lift, he took the stairs three at a time, his foot slippy against the worn-away runner. Third floor. There was a squeal of delight as he pushed open the door to the apartment and the fourteen-year-old geek hurled herself at him.

Fangfang's hair was loose and messy. She looked older than he remembered. Is that what happened with children – turn your back and they grew on you?

But a fourteen-year-old is a child, with or without the plaits. And who brings a child to a war?

A one-eyed man with no compunction. North had a sudden urge to wrap his hands around Hone's throat and squeeze till the other eye popped from its socket.

"Get your stuff and clear out, Fangfang. Go back home."

The geek girl's smile switched to Off. She glowered, her brows pulled down low over cold black eyes, the turquoise blue mesh of the braces just visible behind her bared lips. It wasn't the reaction she'd wanted or been expecting. She was stricken, but he wasn't caving. Did she think this was some sort of adventure – a game she played on her computers with warriors and dragons and imaginary weapons that appeared with a twinkle? Did she think that he needed her help to get through a magic gateway to a different level? Because this was no adventure – it was the real world and real people were dying in it everywhere he looked. And one of them wasn't going to be Fangfang Yu.

He pushed her away, but she clutched his hand, dragging him from the narrow hallway into the bow-fronted front room. Lit by a grimy chandelier hanging low and festooned with spiders' webs, its dim light barely touched the shadows. Fangfang pointed at the bank of screens stacked up in the gloom in front of the shuttered windows.

"I'm going in through the London University computing system to get the processing power I need." She gabbled acronyms and numbers and systems at him. He guessed it meant she had it all worked out.

"You need to go home, Fangfang," he repeated, keeping his voice slow but firm. The voice of authority. "Back to Newcastle."

"Moron-person." She stood on tiptoe and flicked his forehead with her thumb and middle finger. It hurt. Apparently she wasn't listening. "After I help you…" She spoke to him as if he were an idiot, "I get £50,000 in bitcoins and three passports in different names that are completely legit…" She balled up her fists and rested them on her non-existent hips. "You are so not taking that away from me."

He surrendered. He couldn't control a fourteen-year-old girl. What chance did he have of defeating the Board?

Fangfang hadn't met Hone till that morning. She went to sleep in Newcastle and woke up in the London apartment with a thick head and an urge to vomit – her MacBook on the sofa next to her. He would put money on ketamine. Her mother and grandmother weren't happy at her disappearance, but she'd reassured them in the phone call she was allowed. "Working for the government. Hush hush. All good." North wondered if they were relieved their troublesome genius-child was making trouble somewhere other than upstairs. Disposable phones, pizzas, burgers, cheese, crackers, chocolate, gum and a dozen cans of Diet Coke appeared, and Hone said he'd a daughter her age and who knew how far a girl with her skill set could go these days? It was a woman's world. North didn't believe a word of it. Even if it were true, even if his pink-cheeked daughter was the apple of his one eye, and he kept pencils in a mug inscribed with "World's Best Dad", Hone would kill Fang without breaking his step.

"Is he the devil?" she asked, pulling herself into the bank of computers, and North didn't know how serious she was being. He hedged his bets.

"I don't know yet."

The Friends of Cyclops? A distant arm of MI5 wanting yet more distance from the operation. One thing was certain – Hone's first concern was not keeping Fangfang or North alive.

"My guess too, they've installed their own spyware and everything we do," she waggled her small, stubby fingers at the bank of computers, "they're across. But..." she leaned into him to whisper into his ear, "I could disable it? Block the outbound traffic – intercept it and play a pre-recorded feed to them?" She sat back in the seat, waiting for his agreement.

Being across everything they were across worked both ways. It meant Hone assumed he and his "friends" knew everything North knew. It would instil confidence, and the sense they were in control. But there were all sorts of ways to control a situation.

North shook his head. "They'll enjoy watching you work, Fang. Dazzle them."

She understood when he laid it out for her. Armitage was dead. He'd handled and grown the wealth of the Board as he'd handled and grown his own. The Board then had to be in disarray as they picked their own way through the morass of figures and hidden accounts to pull back their money from the financial gaming tables across the world. Doubtless the Board was already filling JP's directorships, steering his companies, transferring funds, winding up businesses, shutting down accounts, and deleting hard drives. North and Fangfang were in a race, because housekeeping was under way, and every minute that passed made what they were going to do harder.

"What happened to Stella?" she asked as she typed. Her voice was unconcerned, but the answer mattered.

"Nothing good," he said.

"And the stupid one?"

"Disney World."

Fang snorted. "Peggy's not coming back, is she?" She'd saved the most important for last. The teacher who taught her she was special.

He didn't know what to say, because he didn't know the truth of it.

"But this is going to hurt them, isn't it – the ones who took her?"

"That's the idea. Maximum damage. No mercy shown."

The black eyes lifted, resting on his face for a moment as she reached for the nearest can of Diet Coke – the rip of the ring-pull, the explosion of air loud in the room and caramel froth spilled from it. She took a noisy swig, holding the Coke in her mouth as she settled at the keyboard, swallowing as the first fingertip hit the first key. It was like home. And she was doing it right.

North stopped existing for her. He smiled. Admiring her skill, her focus. He wondered what his life might have been like if his talent were hacking systems rather than killing people.

Fang was settled. Meanwhile, his ribs still hurt from the bomb blast and he needed coffee. Badly. Somewhere in this liniment and decay-smelling apartment there had to be a kitchen. Yellowing sheets covered a sofa, the sagging belly of its webbing spilling out its sawdust guts over the ancient parquet floor. He lifted a corner of another sheet as he passed, revealing a dusty velour armchair, its seat cushion dished as if its owner had recently stepped away. From the impressions in the carpet, the chair usually stood in front of the ancient three-bar electric heater, which itself blocked a magnificent marble and peacock-tiled fireplace. The former resident apparently regarded the open fire as a luxury she couldn't afford.

The kitchen might have been installed in the thirties but it was better than North expected. At least it had running water, and the oven, though old, was clean enough, three battered aluminium pans nesting one in the other on the hob, their lids balanced precariously across the smallest. Best of all there was a battered yellow plastic kettle. Was instant coffee too much to hope for? He tugged open the overhead cupboard, the wood sticking, snarling against the carcass. Three rusty tins of jellied chicken, three basic range beans, two tins of branded soup which he was convinced they didn't make any more and one small jar of grey coffee, a thin layer of white fur across it. He swallowed down his disgust as he scraped away the fur with a tin spoon. Maybe the coffee at the bottom would be okay? As imminent risks to his life went – it was down there.

It was the sudden thought of some remnant twist of fresh coffee that made him pull open the fridge door.

The old lady's tiny body toppled to the floor with a thud, her sheepskin-slippered feet catching on the shelf, the woollen stockings long since set in frozen manacles around her skinny ankles, the frosted corpse of a Siamese cat clutched between her bony fingers. North leapt back, his body smashing against the cooker, rattling the aluminium pans, knocking the lids to the floor. He reached out to stop the pans following after. He didn't want Fang in here.

He listened hard. His own racing heartbeat. The sound of her tapping, the occasional curse as she found her way through the corporate firewalls blocked.

Exhaled.

The old lady's body lay on its side against the linoleum. Her sparse grey hair rimed with ice, the grey eyes staring out of a yellow and purple face. An elderly Serb, the one-eyed man had said. Keen to make reparations for her sins past. She owned the apartment. She probably owned the whole house. No husband. No children. No nosy neighbours. North couldn't see a wound – the crimson bruise against the temple, the mark of a strangler's grip, not even the neat entrance of a bullet. He hoped there was one. That whoever had killed her didn't bundle her into the fridge, throw the cat in after, and leave her to die. He looked at the fingernails. They were black-tipped, the nails broken. The nails of a prisoner who had tried in vain to open a cell door, the nails of the dead and buried who woke in the coffin to scrabble against the lid and scream in the lonesome dark.

North breathed out once and in again. Hone needed discretion for this operation. You didn't get more discreet than dead. He didn't know when she was killed, but North had no doubt her corpse was left there as a reminder that it was safer to be on Hone's team because bad things happened to those who weren't. It wasn't subtle. Stepping away from the body he eased open the grubby sash window, leaning his hands on the sill, the fire escape zig-zagging down the side of the building, the noise of sirens and traffic and London filling the room. What had the old woman done? He'd probably never know. He glanced back at the twisted fingers – he doubted she was any sort of innocent. He had to hope she wasn't.

Hone threatened everyone North loved. There weren't many. But there were some. He attached no value to his own life – but he attached it to theirs, to Fang and to Jess, to the men and women he'd fought alongside. As he sat across from Hone in the North London greasy spoon, he believed the threats. If there were the slightest doubt then, there wasn't any more. "You're one of the good guys now." He didn't think so. "Play fair by us," Hone instructed, "and we'll play fair by you." The old lady served a purpose – provided a safe space and a reminder. Fang and North were serving a purpose too. He hoped they wouldn't end up the same way – with a prayer for the dying.

Leaving the window open, he moved back to the corpse. Gently, North went down on one knee to pick the old lady up in his arms. Whoever she'd been, whatever her crimes, her bones were fragile and her flesh clammy and cold, the cat's front leg snapping as he pushed the two bodies back into the fridge, and closed the door on his dead landlady, his back against it.

Fang watched as he emerged from the kitchen, a steaming mug of the de-furred coffee in his hand. She had plaited her hair again into two stubby black ropes, and the machines around her hummed and buzzed as if they were talking to her. Had she heard the crash of the lids after all? He sipped the coffee as he walked – trying for casual, she was a kid, she didn't need to know – and his gorge rose at the bitter taste of something old and dead and gone.

Fang's attention switched back to the screens. She waved in the general direction of the chair she wanted him to draw closer to one of the terminals. Code covered the screen, a horizontal bar at its heart, a red cursor flashing in the corner. Numbers counting down in the bottom right-hand corner. Thirty-two seconds, thirty-one.

"Did you ever kill anyone, North?" Her round black eyes behind their *Joe 90* spectacles were fixed on the numbers rather than his face.

Was she scared of him? He was a stranger to her, and he was a killer. Fear was an understandable response.

"I was a soldier, Fangfang."

She was certainly scared – he could read it in her now she was close. A fluttering. Shallow breaths and pale, cold skin. And she was right to be scared. He was dangerous to know.

"When you weren't a soldier?"

Twenty-two seconds.

Was it his imagination or had the numbers got bigger on the screen? What would happen when the countdown reached zero? She was supposed to be breaking and entering JP Armitage's personal files. Why then was Fangfang sat on her hands – her legs swinging, her feet not touching the floor? If the Board realised what was happening they would wipe everything away and start again. Fang had to know that. Was she prepared to let the Board know the hack was under way?

Besides which, he couldn't tell her how many people he had killed. There were too many. But he wouldn't lie to her and claim to be an innocent.

The changing numbers were reflected and reversed in her glasses as she waited. Something was wrong. Because if she weren't cooperating, Fang wouldn't rely on the Board to discover and block the hack. Teenage pride would never let that happen. If she had decided not to cooperate after all, she'd sabotage it herself – wipe everything away that they needed to break apart the Board. Destroy the only hope they had of beating the enemy.

She'd plant her own cyber bomb. Wait for the detonation, the fireball, the mushroom cloud to go up. That's what the numbers were, he realised. A countdown. Fang was showing him what she was capable of.

This was an interrogation, because she was still deciding.

It was a question of trust.

Could she trust him? Because she needed answers and honesty.

Did he ever kill anyone?

Soon after Tarn recruited him, out of the Army, out of rehab, hanging from a leather strap on a crowded tube, when he wasn't sure yet whether he could kill in cold blood, he'd watched another passenger tucked behind the partitioning glass – fifties, his coat laid neatly over his lap, respectable and dull.

There was nothing about him that drew the eye, yet North couldn't look away. The physical sensation of imminent danger, as the commuter filled in the last few clues of a crossword, the *Telegraph* folded perfectly across and along. His busy eyes on the empty boxes, on the clues, avoiding the elderly, pregnant women, any mother with a child. Only allowing himself one lingering glance towards a blazered girl, standing down the carriage from him, her head bent over her phone. He was used to being unseen, North thought. Relied on his insignificance. When he'd looked away from the girl, North thought that he'd misjudged him.

The traveller put away the pen, and allowed his hand to slide beneath his coat.

Excitement. Mounting tension. Almost unbearable glee. The tube train rattling along the line. Carriage lights. Black tunnel walls. North could scarcely credit what he thought the commuter was feeling set against the impassive face. Was it the schoolgirl? Surely not?

Then he'd seen that the man's unblinking gaze was transfixed by the child's reflection. And North understood the traveller's urge to do unspeakable violence. The bloodlust. The urgent need for everything he'd promised himself. The sweet flesh. Last breath. Dying light.

As the tube train drew into the station, the girl looked up from the phone and stood by the doors. They opened and she stepped out onto the platform as the commuter stood, tucked the crossword under his arm, his mac over his forearm, and followed.

The escalator. The ticket barrier. The exit. North kept back. Was he right or wrong? Would the man turn for home? Take a different route from the girl? She turned left, and so did he.

Outside, away from the blaze of the tube station's lights, it was dark – winter. The girl's headphones were on.

"A man was going to hurt a girl – not much older than you – maybe not that night, but soon, so I stopped him."

Or did North kill an innocent commuter with a roving eye? He never knew, but he trusted his intuition because the alternative was to gamble with the girl's life.

Thirteen seconds.

The puzzler was wearing his coat as he turned left again past the big houses – the girl's kilted figure ahead of him, matching his pace to hers. He'd done it before, thought North. Would do it again. Waiting for the perfect moment. When the road tightened, North walked up behind him, put his arm around his throat and slid a knife between his ribs. "Seven down," he whispered into the man's ear,

"Azrael." The commuter never made a sound. The girl ahead kept walking.

Fang turned. "You don't know that he'd have hurt her."

Fang was used to a virtual world where computers provided the answers. In the real world you had to make your own mind up. Am I in love? Is there a God? Do I kill this man? There was no program for some things.

"Call it an instinct."

And who knows, maybe that night he murdered an innocent man who took the wrong route home? North lived in the chaos of never knowing, because he had no choice.

Seven seconds.

They even killed the cat. He heard Fang's voice as loudly as if she'd spoken the words into his ear. Did Fang know what was in the fridge? Not what, he reminded himself – who.

"Would you do it again? To protect a girl you don't really know?" They were strangers. He was a *moron-person* next to her.

But he was older. Bigger. Stronger. Altogether more dangerous.

And the child in front of him needed protection. Needed to know he was there for her.

That they were in this together. To find Peggy, or to punish those who'd hurt her.

Four seconds.

With a blaze of light the screen filled with numbers and symbols, bathing her round face in a white light. And he saw it. Saw her open the fridge door. Before he arrived.

Because her name was Fangfang and she opened doors.

She wasn't staying for bitcoins and passports. She was staying because of her mother and grandmother. Because she had no choice in the matter. She was terrified of the one-eyed man, what he'd done, what he would do, and she was right to be. But his name was Michael North and she didn't have to be scared of him. They were on the same side. Their own.

Would you do it again to protect a girl you didn't really know? Three. Two.

"In a heartbeat," he told her – his reward the briefest of blue-wired grins as she pressed the cursor and stopped her program detonating the only chance they had of taking apart the Board.

Zero.

He must have slept, JP's dusty face filling his mind – the tycoon's power and energy extinguished, his body tumbling into darkness and dust. When he came to, he was slumped in the armchair, his eyes gritty and sore, Fangfang asleep at the desk across from him, her head resting on her crossed arms behind a wall of Diet Coke cans she had built between her and the door. He nudged the oversized office chair to one side, careful not to disturb the sleeping girl.

Deals, mergers, brokerage, philanthropic giving – Fang had found it all. Incomprehensible emails to financial chief officers and agents across the world to buy and sell, to shut down, break up, build up, and expand. Tentacles reaching over continents amassing fortune after fortune. Obscene wealth pulling everything towards it – eating up the universe. The odd philanthropic exception like the biomedical centre for academic studies he funded in Cambridge. Trying to assuage his guilt, thought North.

"These are JP Armitage's personal files stored on the second home network he set up to access the office." Fangfang's voice was sludgy as she knuckled the eyeballs behind her spectacles till they squeaked. "Latest security, top-level encryption. Props to me."

Her own skill appeared to hearten her and she sat up straighter in the chair. "They've erased him out of existence at home and in his office – locking him out as user, changing passwords, deleting files, but this was still out there – different user, different passwords, access to the whole caboodle and set up to override everything."

"He had another way in?"

She nodded. "A backdoor he used a lot and that's gone. They'd have expected that. This one though, it's more of a tiny attic window; he only used it once – I'm guessing to check he could, and he never used it again. I almost missed it myself." Fangfang sounded resentful.

JP Armitage kept the way in as insurance. The good thing for North was that he was there to cash the policy even if Armitage wasn't.

Fang stared at the computer screens, drawn back into the rows of figures and companies. "And all this?" Her bitten-down forefinger pointed at the pound signs, the dollars, the rows of endless noughts. "What do we do now we've found it?"

"Eat," said North reaching down a discarded box, its bottom greasy. He flipped open the lid and picked up a slice of cold, oily pizza before handing it to her. "Then we make it disappear. But there's one more thing before we do that."

He placed the notebook on the desk between them. Stella's speckled blood was dry now but the cover had rolled back on itself and the edges of the pages were curled up and edged in brown.

"What did Peggy always tell you to do?"

Her little jaws were busy and her lips greasy. She chewed noisily as she remembered. "Look for the unexpected," she said.

North took hold of a corner of an early printout and peeled it back. The page underneath was covered in tiny black symbols. Coding.

Fang sat forward. She was all woken up.

He made more ancient coffee to go with the pizza. He didn't open the fridge, and this time Fangfang demanded one. Her cup sat under a blank monitor, steam condensing over the screen. He didn't approve; he'd have stopped her drinking it, but he didn't believe he could stop Fang doing anything.

The pictures were grainy and in black and white. Nine suited men and two women sat around in a horseshoe of polished desks.

The figure of the woman in the black suit was unmistakable – Honor Jones, her head on one side listening, smack-bang in the heart of the establishment, and the heart of the conspiracy.

"She's pretty." For a second the child sounded envious of the woman before she blew an enormous bright blue bubble and popped it. To one side, the blank computer screen had been rubbed clean and dry as if by a sleeve.

Fangfang's tongue was still bringing in the remains of the bubble gum from the corner of her mouth. Bored. Finding Honor hadn't been a stretch compared to picking her way through Armitage's financial empire.

"She's not hiding. She's in the Intelligence and Security Committee meeting in the House of Commons. Private session."

With a blare of static, the voice came through – the warm, authoritative and persuasive tones of Honor Jones.

"We've been too scrupulous. The security agencies couldn't predict the attacks because we castrated them. Let them off the leash. Together with the New Army on the streets, they're our only real protection. People deserve to feel safe. We have to give them that."

The committee didn't like it – not all of them anyway – he could tell from the unhappy faces and the murmurings of dissent, but she carried on regardless, waving her hand to dismiss whatever they were saying as if it were so much smoke.

"I need to talk to her, Fangfang."

"Bad idea, moron person."

"They turned her round. She needs to face in the right direction, and I need to get their attention, Fang. Do it. St James's Park. The Bridge of Spies."

The girl snorted. "You old people have zero imagination."

Fangfang pulled down a screen of green numbers and attacked the code. On the screen, Honor stopped talking to reach for her iPhone, sitting still as she read the message. North's eyes flicked back to Fangfang's green screen. "St James's Park. The bridge. Meet me." Honor barely moved. Another committee member took over from her – it was the time for drastic measures, he agreed, his double chin quivering with excitement. They were coming round. North stopped listening. The only noise the thudding beat of his heart loud in his ears. She wasn't leaving the committee room. She had no intention of meeting him on the bridge or anywhere. She had no intention of ever seeing him again. Bleakness filled him up, overwhelming him. Fangfang chewed her lip. She tapped at the screen again, pressing Send before North realised what she was doing.

"Nxoxo" Fang dry-retched, her shoulders hunching as she tapped out the hugs and kisses.

Honor must have heard the ping of the message as it came in but she left the phone where it lay. One. Two. Three seconds. Didn't she care? Then she reached for it, her hand sliding it across the desk and into her bag in one smooth move. She stood up from the table. Her back to the camera, North couldn't see her mouth moving, her voice if she spoke at all was soft and low, but judging by the perturbation of her fellow committee members as she walked out of the door she hadn't explained her departure at all.

Fangfang looked up at him. "My granny always says 'One misstep can cause a thousand-year disaster'." He put his hand on the teenager's narrow shoulder, the fragile collarbone, and she let it rest there for a second before she shrugged him off. "Mind – Granny Po's a right buzzkill."

71

London

10.05am. Monday, 13th November

The air was cold and damp on his face as he let himself out of the building, pulling the heavy door behind him with a thud. Fang needed another five minutes to set up the playback of the session recording her working, then would use the kitchen's fire exit to leave the building.

They were watching – not just virtually, but eyes-on. He left his regard soft, casual as he swept the street. It was too busy a thoroughfare to sit any watchers in a car – they'd be too obvious, the neighbourhood too monied and vigilant. It was a neighbouring apartment or one close by. An apartment like the one opposite. Probably with its own corpse. Behind the heavy nets of the bow window on the second floor, a dim golden light was just visible. A shape moved as he did. The watcher waking up to the fact that North was out and on the move. As the front door pulled open, North turned. They heard him tell Fangfang he was going out. They had spotted him and they knew where he was

424

heading. All they had to do now was follow him down the rabbit hole.

Did the one-eyed man pose a risk now they had found the money?

He wanted North to take apart the Board and tracing the money was only one part of that. Money though had a way of concentrating minds. North wasn't one for chances – the chance they would stop wanting blood and start wanting the money more.

He had to break the Board before the Board broke him. Him and Honor and the entire country. The one-eyed man and his cronies weren't going to help. They were going to use him to get to the Board and, when his usefulness was done, they would tidy him away along with Fangfang. He glanced at his watch. It was all in the timing.

North took a cab for the first few streets, but when it ground to a halt round Green Park, he got out and ran. He wasn't sorry – remembering to breathe through the pain from his ribs, the movement of his legs, his feet pounding against the pavements. The steady stride gave him something to do – other than dwell on the woman he was going to meet. Maybe he'd be late? Half of him hoping she would have changed her mind, reached the bridge and, when he wasn't there, turned away. It was because he was thinking of Honor that he ran straight into the protest spilling across the Mall.

Barriers lined the broad avenue. The police were attempting to funnel the crowd along the Mall rather than letting them spill into the parkland and across to Downing Street and Whitehall. Blocking his way to Honor.

Ahead of him and either side young and old stood, arms aloft, smartphones and wristwatches to the sky filming the nano-drones which were filming the crowd of ad hoc civil rights groups, anarchists, socialists and liberals – all of them apparently unhappy at the security clampdown. The drones buzzed and swooped and hovered as the crowds jeered – the more reckless throwing up stones which missed the machines but fell back amid screams and shouts. Placards were everywhere. *Not in my Name. New Army – Old Story! Democracy matters! If Nasty-boys are the Answer. What the Hell is the Question?* Numbers grew by the minute – protestors bumping against North, closing off his exit. The initial good humour and enthusiasm for the cause sharpening minute by minute into a more dangerous mood – more reckless. North fought off other people's fear, their urge to do violence as a bearded man hurled a bottle out from the crowd and into the ranks of the police, glass and urine shattering over their polished boots. The mood shifted again. Another bottle came and another. Protesters at the front of the crowd yelling abuse at the police, others yelling at the bottle-throwers safe behind them.

North fought his way to the side of the road where the police line was thinner, elbowing protesters out of the way. His only chance of making it to Honor was through the barricade. Next to him a young boy in a scuffed-up biker's jacket was looking around him wildly.

"The coppers won't let anyone out," he said to North – a note of rising panic. The lad spoke into the visor of the policeman in front of him. "I'm not in this, mate. Let me through will you please? I'm late for my shift – I'll get fired."

The policeman laid a large hand on the boy's chest and

pushed him away, the boy almost falling, almost bringing down North.

An unseen command and the riot police moved into the crowd, pushing them back with their shields, spreading out in a V, two of them grabbing the bearded bottle-thrower, his arms behind him, lifting him off his feet to carry him back out of the crowd behind their own lines, their ranks closing up again before the protesters further away knew what happened.

A cheer went up. When the massed ranks of riot police had closed up again, they'd fallen back – a footstep, no more, but the crowd felt the realignment. An easy victory to those who hadn't witnessed the take-up – except it wasn't.

A scuffle next to him as the teenage boy grabbed at North, using him as an anchor against the pull of a policeman attempting to drag him from the crowds.

"Hey." North put his arm on the policeman's. He had to shout to make his voice heard, swatting off a drone as it buzzed them to film the arrest. "He's done nothing. Don't take him."

The policeman's gauntleted arm swept away North's. His face vicious behind the visor.

"Piss off," the policeman grunted as he took better hold of the kid.

North wasn't sure what the sound was at first – the pounding. The roar of diesel. Heavy machinery. Motor vehicles. Lorries. So many that he didn't immediately distinguish the other sound – the rhythmic tramp of soldiers on the move, of boots against a road, the sound of an army on the move. The New Army. They were reinforcing the police with soldiers. Out on the streets exactly where Tarn wanted them. It was happening.

North had his own fight. But he was trapped in this one. Balling his fist he took the policeman in the solar plexus – holding him upright before punching him again, followed by a knock-out punch to his right temple. The copper's eyes closed. North didn't want him falling, drawing attention to himself. He gestured to the teenager to support the policeman on the other side – yelling as they approached the police ranks to let them through. At the sight of their colleague, ranks parted. "Some bastard back there," yelled North, gesturing with his head into the crowd, making a silent apology to the protesters and the police went back in.

He put a hand on the teenager's shoulder and pushed him through the lines, past the armoured weaponry. "Keep moving," he muttered to the lad.

Only when they made it to a quiet side street did he let go of the boy.

"Thanks, mate," the teenager was pale. He remembered to hold out his hand, the gesture of a civilised man rather than a scared child, and North shook it. "It's like that Honor woman says – at least we can rely on each other, eh?"

North slowed as he reached the entrance to the park, the bank of oaks and elms occluding his view of the bridge; his breath ragged, shallow, his heartbeats fast. Honor was there, waiting. He watched her. As he'd watched her before when all he had to do was kill her. Before it got complicated. Across the dark-grey water, the reflection of trees and clouds, her head turned towards the orange-beaked pelicans, their ungainly walk over the sloping, fouled concrete bank, their elegant ride through the flat, clear water.

She saw his reflection before she saw him – didn't look round, her hands gripping the iron rail, the knuckles white.

"Pelicans are a symbol of the Resurrection. Did you know that, North? Of Christ. The Pelican in her Piety shows the mother pelican piercing her flesh and letting the chicks drink her blood. Some stories have it the pelican actually kills the babes then revives them with her blood."

"Sounds like an excellent reason not to be a pelican."

The noise of the protest carrying on the wind – the shouts, the blare of loudspeakers. "I've a soft spot for flamingos," he said. "They change colour depending on how much blue-green algae they eat."

"And here I was thinking you'd prefer the phoenix rising from the ashes. I should have guessed."

"Too showy. More your style. So tell me – what happened to the old Honor Jones? The woman who never gave up?"

She pulled out a packet of cigarettes and made to light one. The flame flickered then caught. Inhaling. Exhaling. Smoke curling between them. Ignored him.

"You nearly killed me in a park like this. You'd have saved us both a lot of trouble."

"I like trouble."

What did Jess's mum say? *"You attract trouble like dead meat attracts flies."* *"You say that, like it's a bad thing,"* he'd told her. As if it weren't.

Finally, she turned to look at him. Her eyes as cold and deep as the sea.

"You killed JP." It wasn't a question. He killed the man she was about to marry. He would have killed Armitage without hesitation if he had to. Snapped his spine. Squeezed that thick neck without compunction. But all he did was stop

Armitage leaving the banqueting hall. Did that put the death on his shoulders? He didn't think so. He felt no guilt, no responsibility. He didn't strap explosive around a pregnant woman.

North moved his left hand up to Honor's collar to brush off a dead leaf carried there in the wind. "In Newcastle when I was arrested, I met a policeman – DCI 'Slim' Hardman. You met him too. Now, Hardman's an honest man, decent, and I wanted him to think well of me. I didn't feel that way about your JP Armitage."

He couldn't tell if she was listening. "JP and my father were friends, you know that. When I was with JP, it reminded me of the happy times in my childhood. Without him, there's only how it ended." She gave up on the cigarette, tossing it over the railing and into the rippling water. "Tarn told me JP died with his hands tied together, and that you died with him." She watched as it sank. "I wore black."

"For me? Or for him?"

"You were both dead – does it matter?"

He willed her to look at him again, so that he could read her better, and as if she knew, she looked up, winter sunlight across the left side of her face softening it, the other side shadowy and cold. And he thought of Stella – her treachery, her friendship, and he grieved for both of them.

The last time he saw Honor she was hunted and struggling between the hands of her captors. Today she was the heroic poster girl of change. What did the Board plan for her? To stand for the party leadership? To win? To lead the country for real exactly where Tarn wanted it to go? He could reach out and touch her but they'd never been further apart and it came to him that Stella was right. Honor was never meant for him. She'd never been anything but a stranger.

"Tarn promised me they'll let Peggy go as soon as everything calms down." Tarn, who always promised what you most wanted. A father. A family. A friend.

"Is she alive?"

Honor closed her eyes as if there were things she didn't want to see. "Peggy has to be alive, North, or all this has been for nothing."

"Has he proved she's alive to you?"

A winter's storm of grief broke in Honor – harsh and cruel and noisy as a cold wind moved across the white-iced buildings, the trees, and the two of them shivered and broke apart in the water. She turned her face to the grey sky. "They say it might rain. It'll move the protests off the streets."

"Honor..."

"I can talk to Tarn for you, North. Explain. You only did what you thought was best."

"I'm sure he'd appreciate the irony in that."

"You need a longer game. I can help you."

"I never learned the rules, Honor. All I know is when they knock on the door and ask you to play – when you get that call – you have to pick a side."

She was a collaborator. She was worse than a collaborator – she was a fool to believe Tarn's promises, and the urge to hurt her crashed against him. To wound her, anger her. To reach her and wake her and restore her to who she really was.

"What do you want from me, North?" She looked at him, and it was like the first time. Stripped bare and desperate. "I messed everything up. It's too late."

He knew what she did before rough hands reached him and the nape of his neck understood the metal of the gun pressed into it, before the needle sank into his neck and there was violent sudden darkness. She opened up a hunger in North he fought against his entire life. She did exactly as he wanted. Exactly as he never wanted. Made him love her.

72

One of them knocked her to the ground – the hand pushing against her chest keeping her away from North. She landed badly, her head slamming against the metal railings. She attempted to stand, nauseous suddenly, calling after North, her vision blurred with tears as they hustled him away, their arms around him, the toes of his boots scraping along the path.

From somewhere a cyclist and an elderly lady were holding her upright. Passers-by.

Strangers. But no one who could help.

She touched the back of her head and her fingertips came away bloody.

North was a fool – they were both fools. She was under surveillance at all times. She thought she'd given them the slip in the Commons. And they had to be monitoring her calls.

He had to know that, so why did he come?

The desolate, desperate thought came to her that North was dragged away thinking she betrayed him. Betrayed him twice over. Betrayed herself too. And Peggy. Because there was no way Peggy would have wanted Honor to do what she was doing and compromise her very soul. To stop fighting, because she was frightened of something that had already happened.

Peggy was dead.

She knew it.

Had known it from the start. That the worst had happened. That she'd been left behind again.

She had to stop herself groaning out loud.

And surely North knew that even though she wouldn't ever have given him up, they would be watching and waiting for him. Any which way, he was as ever a reckless fool of the first order and she was too, for wanting to see him just one more time to explain herself, and to try and save him. When all she'd done was make his situation worse.

Cold, shaking, she thrust her hands into the pockets of her mackintosh and her fingers found the mobile phone. She hadn't felt it but she knew he'd dropped it there with his left hand as his right brushed against the collar of her coat. Distraction. Sleight of hand. *What happened to the old Honor Jones? The one who never gave up?*

She almost dropped the phone as it started ringing. Pushing away the concerned strangers. Brutal. Faces falling. Sympathy rejected. Turning away from them.

When they knock on your door, when you get the call to come play, you have to pick a side. Was that what he said before they dragged him away?

She pressed the green phone icon to answer the call, lifting it to her ear with a hand she had to stop from trembling.

"Yes, this is Honor Jones. Who is this?"

73

London

11.45am. Monday, 13th November

The reek of stale sweat was the first thing he was aware of. Then came the pounding in his skull and the knowledge there was only pain where his arms used to be. North blinked, searing light, darkness pocked by rainbow spangles, and back to white-blazing light – the small movements shifting the skin, nerves shrieking with the effort as the world swayed around him. He willed himself back into consciousness, back into the pain, hauling himself, hand-over-hand, up from the darkness. Who was he?

His name was North.

And there was a woman. What was her name?

Honor…it slid from him… Honor Jones. He held onto the idea of her, the need for her once he'd named her.

Before the darkness was Honor. Before Honor was darkness.

As the room ratcheted back into focus, it took him a moment to understand he was dangling in thin air, chained to a steel butcher's hook screwed into an oak beam in the roof of a subterranean gym. The boxing bag which usually hung there – discarded on the varnished pine floor like the trunk of a dismembered corpse.

No sign of Honor any more, nor the bridge, nor the strange birds crossing the rippling water. Instead there were shadows, spotlights above, buried in the ceiling, throwing down narrow tunnels of light which didn't reach the corners of the room. North's eyes fought to make sense of the space. Another body hung across from him, and a broiling pit of fear opened up at his core. He was strong and he knew the price. But Honor was a civilian and they would kill her as soon as she stopped being of use to them – break her into pieces for sport. He shook his head and the other body did the same. He took a short breath. It wasn't her. It was him. Two of him hung in the mirrored room. The real North and the reflection. They wouldn't die together after all; he was alone and the tiniest and worst part of him knew regret before he extinguished it.

There was a small cough as Bruno stepped out from the darkness, a grey figure either side of him. North watched him through the mirror. His companions were shorter and wider than Bruno – identical twins, their muscled arms crossed, their chests swollen, moving as Bruno moved, their knobbled heads shaved like those of their boss, full of paranoia and rage, he could see it in them, see that they were pumped up on steroids and the urge to hurt. He knew the type. Paid well for services rendered but they weren't in it for the money, they were in it for the permission it gave them to damage, to inflict hurt and death.

Now he thought about it, his cheeks stung – he had the distinct impression someone had been slapping them hard to wake him, and he guessed that someone was Bruno.

He looked away from the mirror and back to reality. The big man grinned at him – his pointed teeth long and yellow. The compulsion in Bruno to cause pain, the cleaving of flesh and the grinding of bones, smashed itself into North's brain. The satisfaction that North would soon be dead at his hands. At the picture of his own gasping, empurpled face, the breath dying in him. North swallowed hard. There were only three of them, he reminded himself he'd had worse odds.

"Where am I?"

Bruno regarded him, his head tilted to one side as if he were enjoying the view. "Home, so you need to mind your manners."

Judge Lucien Tarn lived in Fitzrovia, close to the British Museum. Much as Bruno loathed him, he didn't have the authority to hang him from the rafters. But North was no longer Tarn's favourite son. He was Tarn's enemy and North knew how Tarn treated enemies – he dispatched them to Hell.

"Yours was religious wasn't she, North? My mother was the superstitious sort."

Bruno's tone was conversational – cheery, even. "I'm a bit that way myself – superstitious." Bruno's huge hand lay against North's chest, the fingers spread wide. The movement of a striking snake, the heel of the hand crunching into North's solar plexus and North swung like a pendulum, beating down the sudden ferocious nausea, the back-and-forth movement agonising down the length of his tethered arms. One lucky punch from Bruno, the bullet would shift and he'd be dead. Would he feel it? Or would the world screech to a sudden stop?

"Horoscopes though, they're for pussies. But, would you believe, today the horoscopes, they caught my eye. Taurus. A day of revelations and joy."

With a stubby forefinger Bruno pointed, fussy as the swaying slowed. "Tyler," he instructed and one of the bulging shadows moved towards the hanging man, balling his oversized fist as he went. "And what do you know?" Bruno regained his good mood. "Here you are. Revelations and joy. I may have to change my morning routine. Nice cup of tea. Shit a brick. Read Madame Zara."

North built his abdominals into his very own Berlin Wall, but Tyler's right fist came in close and hard and fast as a wrecking ball, and he willed himself not to groan when it hit.

"Kyle." Bruno gestured at the other man, and Tyler took a reluctant step away. Kyle went for North's face as if he'd been kept waiting, and in the waiting, had taken a vicious dislike to it. With a crack, North's jaw swung wide, hung round awhile, then came back home. He breathed out then sucked in air again just to prove he could as Tyler moved back in for a right hammer blow and a left hook into either side of his rib cage. North swung wildly on his hook, and his eyes snagged and kept hold of Tyler's before his hanging body brushed against the length of the other man's. Tyler liked it up close and personal.

"I'm willing to bet your horoscope made for gloomy reading though, North. I bet it warned you not to step on any cracks in any pavements or you might just fall down them and disappear."

The two heavies sniggered at Bruno's joke, their bulging eyes sliding up to him for acknowledgment, their foreheads gleaming, the leather holster tight under Kyle's arm already dark with sweat.

North shook his head, his neck creaking between his up stretched arms. Pretty soon, he'd have lost all use of them.

"It said three was my lucky number."

Against the mirror was a Mac 10, its stock extended. He felt its pull, the coldness of the metal.

Bruno raised a thick eyebrow. "Is that so? Do you hear that, lads?" And he moved back in, punching North once, twice, three times, hard and fast in his kidneys.

"And are you feeling lucky, North?" Bruno said. "Because that's what your mates called you isn't it? 'Lucky'. Maybe you were once – but not now. You see, if the judge loves you, I loves you. The shame for you is, the judge has gone off you something terrible. Which makes me remember that you're an arrogant maggot. After everything he did for you. All you had to do was what you were told. Kill the woman. It's not hard for a craftsman like yourself."

A line of blood trickled from the corner of North's mouth, made a swerve into the deep cleft of his chin, and splattered onto the varnished floor where his feet should be.

"Even worse, this time you've stolen our money." Bruno's pale blue eyes followed the blood down with cold interest. "And surprise, fucking surprise." The monolithic face loomed up at North, the yellowing-whites, crazy-paved with broken capillaries, the scent of lime cologne making North dry-retch. "We want it back, gobshite."

North spat a glob of blood and phlegm onto the big man's patent leather shoe. "Ask nicely then."

Bruno waved back Tyler and Kyle and looked down at his left shoe, wiping it on the back of his trouser leg, flexing his right hand all the while. Not till he had glossed the leather to his satisfaction did he speak again.

"Please…" He punched North hard in his gut, North's knees instinctively coming up to protect himself – just not far enough or fast enough.

"Can..." With each word came another hammer blow, and anger bloomed inside North, unfolding itself slowly, standing, stretching, suffocating the pain and fear.

"They...Have...Their...Money...Back...You...Son of a Bitch."

The thing about pain was that it stopped. Accept it. Step into it. Breathe through it. Use it as nuclear fuel, because it's not the pain that kills you. A mistake for amateurs. North let his head fall onto his chest as if the blows were getting to him. What the professional does is focus on payback. Focus on Judgement Day, death and destruction.

"There's something not right about you, North. I told him." He meant Tarn, "But he wouldn't have it. Not his golden boy."

A techno-chirrup and the rhythm of the beating hiccupped and shifted as Bruno checked his phone. He gave an ugly grunt of satisfaction and his fingers grabbed hold of the cropped hair at North's crown to lift up his head, the other hand damp with perspiration squeezing his jaw hard.

"I'll be back soonest. Off to see a friend of yours. Maybe she can tell us where the money is."

North wrenched his body from side to side, the steel cuffs cutting into his wrists, the chain rattling against the butcher's hook. Honor had realised Peggy was dead, and they had her. Bruno was going to do what North refused to do. They were going to kill her. And he couldn't do anything about it.

No.

Wrong.

He could do something. Kill Bruno. Kill Tarn. Kill all of them.

"I'll give her your best." Searing pain shot through North, starting at his thigh and finishing at the ending of every nerve in his body. Bruno lifted up the knife he had stabbed into the flesh and muscle of North's right thigh. It ran bloody along its length.

"Whoopsy," he said.

He wiped the blade between the ball of his thumb and the pad of his index finger, flicking the blood off before licking them clean. He patted North's cheek, letting the head fall back onto his chest, and North heard the metal taps to the patent shoes cross the wooden floor and the door close behind him.

The blood from his thigh was hot on his leg, as it poured from the open wound. Tick tock. It wasn't wide but it was deep and the loss of blood would weaken him past hope of resistance, past any hope of stopping Bruno.

North's eyes were almost shut. Between the slits, he could see Kyle rubbing the reddened knucklebones of his fist as he leaned against the mirror. North read the impatience in him. The brothers were mumbling to each other. Ignoring the body swinging on the butcher's hook. Kyle wanted to get on with it. He had a dog to feed. Bruno liked them to keep the dog hungry – made for a better watchdog, he said, but Kyle wasn't so sure. Forget the dog. Tyler was having a good day – he'd be happy to play this out for as long as it took.

"Which one of you was born first?"

The twins looked across then at each other, as if considering whether to ignore him or answer. Tyler shrugged, the muscles round his neck moving up and down.

"Me."

North did his best to nod.

"Then you won't mind dying first."

It took Tyler time to process the words, glaring at North, his neck thickening, as his brother moved across to the shadows – electro-pop blaring suddenly from the sound system. They were comfortable in the gym. Familiar with it. Maybe they used it to inflate their already ridiculous muscles. That was all good – the more relaxed they felt, the better.

Tyler moved back over to North, working him like he probably worked the punchbag lying on the floor, his eyes squinting – one-two, one-two, building. North let it happen, willing himself not to go too soon. And then it came – a punch hard enough to knock North backwards. He allowed his weight to carry him back and then forwards, the momentum giving him just enough power to lift his legs, wrap them around Tyler's neck, and squeeze his thighs together, the movement forcing his own blood to gush from his wound, the sensation of denying his attacker the right to draw breath. Roaring as he turned, Kyle leapt for North, pulling at his legs, punching them and his twin, regardless of which was which, in his frenzy to separate the two. North had one chance. He shifted the full weight of his hanging body on to Tyler, as if he were a child riding on his father's broad shoulders, locking his feet together at the small of the back and bringing himself high enough to lift the chain over the butcher's hook and down around the exposed throat in one smooth and crushing move. He crossed his arms so the steel links could get better purchase on the throat, blood coursing through his arms till they screamed, till the tiny bones in the other man's neck gave, the fight for breath stopped, and the body below him folded – North folding with him.

With his brother lost, Kyle scrambled for the Mac 10 by the mirror. North threw himself to the ground, his legs still trapped under the goon's corpse, taking cover behind the boxing bag which exploded as 9mm bullets ravaged its red leatherette length looking for the flesh-and-blood man behind it. Sawdust flew into the air from the bullet holes as North grappled for the dead man's SIG P226. He pulled at the body, half lifting it, the arm swinging wide, and the punchbag exploded again – Tyler's corpse with it – blood and bone splinters everywhere, noise bouncing from wall to mirrored wall. The gun in his hand, North reached round the end of the boxing bag and fired once. Twice.

The first shot took out the mirror behind his assailant, shattering it into a million fragments, each one showing a man dropping to his knees as if in prayer as the second shot found its mark – dead-centre of Kyle's forehead.

North kicked off the remains which had pinioned his legs, and scrambled to his feet. His ears rang from the close-quarters firefight. He picked up the Mac 10 from Kyle's body and checked the magazine. It fired one thousand rounds a minute.

Empty.

The P226 should have had thirteen more bullets in the magazine.

It had two.

One for Bruno. One for Tarn. It was enough.

On a hunch, he reached across to check Tyler for another weapon. He eased the switchblade from the holster strapped to the dead man's ankle and slipped it into the back of his waistband. He stood up then hunkered down again, taking out the knife and cutting into the dead man's thigh. He held his breath as he carved out a huge gobbet of flesh, hot blood dripping from it.

A turquoise and white-tiled corridor lead to a narrow back staircase with an ornate banister. Antique Spy caricatures lined the staircase walls, statesmen and judges ridiculed and popularised. As he rounded the corner of the landing, North stopped in his tracks. An enormous Doberman lay across the threshold of a door. Somewhere in the back of its throat, it growled. Its ears flat against its head, the dog raised itself on its haunches and then stood on all four legs.

His eyes never leaving the black pools of the monstrous dog's, North moved his right hand behind his back to grip the heavy duty plastic handle of the eight-inch switchblade. The dog walked towards him, breathing in his scent through its wet black nose, black slobbery lips pulled back, wrinkling the muzzle and revealing shining yellow teeth.

North made himself stand still and with his left hand threw the chunk of meat into its maw. The meat was gone within seconds. With a sudden bound, the dog leapt, almost knocking him to the ground with its weight, its two front paws against his chest, licking his cheek, the smell of blood and dog breath.

North let go of the knife to push off the dog. She rolled over onto her back, squirming, and he stepped over her sprawling body.

"You, madam, are a disgrace to your profession," he said.

The guard dog got back on her feet and trotted beside him, her body tight against his.

He kept his left hand on her warm, bony head, the pistol in his right.

74

Two bullets. With a mighty kick he booted his way into the room where the screaming was coming from – the gun out in front of him. It wasn't Honor. Or Peggy. Fangfang was tied to the bed, her arms outstretched, her neck in a noose with a long leather cord that lay across the black silk pillow. Bruno covered the struggling girl, the cord bunched in his fist, his other hand across her mouth. He scrambled off the bed, reaching for the bedside drawer, dragging the teenager's head up from the bed till the cord unwound itself from his grasp. North fired the gun at the drawer and Bruno screamed in pain and frustration, snatching his hand away and crashing against the wall. One bullet left. North moved the gun to his left hand and pulled out the knife from his waistband. He cut Fangfang's ties and she scrabbled at her throat to release the pressure of the noose, coughing and gasping.

The Doberman stood snarling at Bruno, cowering in the corner of the room. Not even his own dog liked him. Bruno aimed a kick at the animal's haunch and the dog snapped, slaver hanging from her jaws, teeth grazing the pale pink flesh of the fat man's massive calf – spots of blood rising among the curling hairs.

"Are you all right, kid?"

"They found us – destroyed the computers," Fangfang said ignoring the question as she scrambled into the black leggings and Hello Kitty sweatshirt discarded on the floor. Her voice was husky from the cord. He saw the men force the door, smash the computer bank, screens fizzing and popping, glass shattering, Fangfang's terror.

"I didn't damage the goods, North. I was just softening her up before I brought her downstairs to convince you to talk." Bruno was reasonable, two grown-ups together trusting in the logic of torture. But if Bruno hadn't hurt Fang, it was because he hadn't had time.

He'd had every intention.

"We can deal." Bruno's hands wrapped themselves around his dangling penis – eager to bargain. "I'll tell you it all. Tarn's gone too far this time."

North's smile didn't reach his eyes. "I can't take you seriously, Bruno. Where's Peggy? Is she still alive?"

Bruno's lip curled. He shrugged. He didn't know? Didn't care? Or there was nothing to be done?

The cord had left its mark – a crimson welt around Fangfang's slim neck. It would fade faster than the memories of Bruno. Rage built in North. He promised her he would keep her from harm. The sensible thing was to keep Bruno alive and find out what he knew. But then North never claimed to be all that sensible.

"Look away, Fang."

Fangfang put her hand to her neck and her fingertips touched the pulse there, but she kept her eyes on Bruno – her absolute fury surging through North's own veins joining his. The urge to take Bruno apart.

He sensed the other gun before he saw it.

The Baikal IZH-79 wasn't a big gun but it was huge in Fang's small hand, her fingernails bitten down to the quick, red and bleeding round the ragged edges, and Bruno's bulging, sclerotic eyes fixed on it. He started cursing. He had put down his own gun on the chest of drawers by the door before tying her to the bed. Fang didn't forget.

"I found your medical records, North."

Of course she did.

"A bullet in the brain is pretty sick."

North savoured the compliment.

"Is that how come the Jedi mind tricks?"

When she pored over Peggy's notebook, she'd sensed him. She didn't understand what she felt, only threw out the distraction that was Michael North from her own brain to concentrate better and find out what she needed to know. But she'd logged the intrusion. Fangfang missed nothing.

A weight lifted from North. Dark and heavy and oppressive as North shifted out from it into the light. If Fang had sensed him, then his instinct – his intuition – was real and true.

He wasn't sliding headlong into insanity.

"Complicated it is," he told the girl with the gun, and she giggled, but the gun didn't waver in her hands.

A bullet in his head did complicate life. That much North knew for a fact.

Was it a skill he could use? Or did it use him?

Was it a weapon he could master? Or a force that would overwhelm him?

That much he didn't know. He didn't know a lot of things.

But that didn't stop him feeling a whole lot better about himself.

"Okay, your turn. Tell me – what does Fangfang mean?"

Violence had been the answer for him for years, but the little hacker was cleverer than him. She was cleverer than anyone he ever met. And she didn't have to kill Bruno, because North would do it for her. He might even sleep better for it. In the darkness of a London street, he once killed a man to protect a child and hoped to God he did the right thing. In the darkness of a Mayfair flat, he promised to protect a girl he didn't know. A stranger. But Fang was more than a stranger to him now. She was family.

The Baikal dipped and pointed at the carpet, and in the corner, the naked man's muscles tensed as he made ready to take his chances at what he read as the hesitation of a child.

Fangfang.

"Fragrance of flowers," she said, lifting the gun, her left hand taking the weight of the right around the stock, firing it point-blank into Bruno's face, his brains splattering out of the back of his head, sliding down the overblown slick golden roses papering the wall, as his body slid to the snowy carpet – his legs outstretched – just a little way ahead of them. The noise and the recoil made her step back but she didn't let go. What was left of Bruno's face looked surprised, as if he thought the girl didn't have it in her. Maximum damage. No mercy shown. He'd taught her the rules of war.

The Doberman barked furiously once, then lowered her head and whimpered. It was quiet then, the guard dog pushing her way between North and Fangfang, her body warm between them as the enormous head bent to lick the girl's foot.

Outside – the sweet, pure song of blackbirds.

There were people to whom things happened. And there were people who made things happen. Fangfang made things happen.

"It suits you," he said.

The girl's irises were the dark grey of the winter sky he could see behind her through the bedroom window of a dead man; the barrel of the gun she still held, a third eye – black this time and smoky.

Moving slowly, he reached out to take the gun from her. *Made in Russia* on the slide. Converted from a CS gas pistol to 9mm ammo by Lithuanians. Fired by a tiny Chinese Geordie. Killing a genuine Cockney monster. Fangfang. Dragon killer. The small fingers reluctant to let it go.

When Fangfang's bottom lip came out, it was far enough for him to see the ragged cut Bruno's teeth had left.

"I won't feel bad about him." She nodded in the direction of the sitting corpse.

Telling North. Telling herself. Telling the corpse. He believed her.

North didn't want her feeling bad. In point of fact, he'd rather she never thought of Bruno again.

"Good. Forget him. Forget all of this, Fang. Go work for Google, kiddo."

For a moment, he thought she was about to argue the case, then something in her relaxed. " 'Do no harm'." She made a small, spitless sound of disapproval, retched a little. "I'm taking Mam and Granny Po back to China for a holiday. I'll send you a 'postcard', old man."

"You don't have my address, Fang."

The girl grinned as she turned her body away from the ruin of the attacker she'd shot, her hand finding the dog, scratching behind the pointed ears, the rear end shivering with satisfaction, and the hind leg thumping the ground in approval.

"Sure I do, moron-person."

The study was on the ground floor to the left of the front door. A display of waxy lilies smelling of funerals and grief filled an ornate silver vase on a burnished burr-walnut table dead centre, an immense longcase clock standing sentry. North's eye snagged on the hand-painted bucolic scene on the clock face. Plump villagers celebrating the harvest, sheaves of corn, jollity. Death standing by with skeleton fingers wrapped around a scythe. North didn't register the time. He didn't need to. All he knew was that it was time for Judge Lucien Tarn to die.

Inch by inch, he pushed open the door, his palm flat against the painted wood, the P226 in his other hand.

Tarn stared out of the window at the garden as the rain fell. He must have heard the shot that killed Bruno but gave no sign of it. Across from him, a fire raged in the hearth – logs and papers curling and crimping and turning to ash.

"You're letting in the cold."

In a brocade smoking jacket the colour of clotting blood, the reflected Tarn bared his white teeth in a smile or the grimace of a cornered animal, North didn't know which. But by the time the judge turned round – a brandy balloon in his hand – there was no doubt that it was a warm smile.

"I find myself constantly delighted to see you, North – even now." The judge laughed at his own absurdity, the brandy crashing from side to side against its fragile glass walls.

I trust there'll be no pain.

Behind North, a draught pushed against him, and then fell away again like a breath taken and let go. Fangfang was gone, along with a dog almost as big as her. It was as if she'd never been there. Never killed a man. She'd travel to China. Come back and rule the world someday.

The judge felt it too. North could tell. That someone was leaving, rather than arriving; that there was no rescue from Bruno or anyone else.

"You boys never did get on." There was a note of regret in Tarn's voice. "A regular Cain and Abel. Cain killed Abel because he was jealous that God loved Abel more. I didn't love Bruno more. You were always so much more intriguing, so much prettier."

"Good to know."

"Taking the money was an act of genius, North. Bravo. Everyone was perturbed, which I imagine is how you wanted them. I warned them to leave you be, but money is so very necessary. I'm impressed you managed, though it was naughty and you must know they won't ever let you keep it."

They'd have to find it first, thought North. All of it – not just the two Cayman Island accounts that Fang dropped breadcrumbs to. The other two – his and hers, she wrapped within so many layers of virtual and financial chicanery, North wasn't convinced he'd find them himself. She built her own firewall against the prying of the one-eyed man, blocking their access and playing back recorded files to maintain the outgoing traffic. She told him as much with her empty cans of Diet Coke. "£?u/me" she'd written in steam from ancient coffee that belonged to a dead woman. "OK£1m," he'd replied, then wiped it away with his sleeve. Fang didn't understand – defending herself from criticism with big round eyes as they came down the stairs together.

She took £100m for each of them. She dazzled and he didn't begrudge her.

"When they couldn't dig you out – the thought was you'd slipped away to find the consolation that comes with immense wealth. I very much wanted that happy ending for you."

"I was never one for fairy tales."

"Even so, I put you down as a romantic. Perhaps that's why I thought you had to see Honor Jones one more time to save her from the wolves. But you didn't, did you? You knew we wouldn't be able to resist bringing you in to retrieve the money. Because this is what you intended all along, isn't it, my darling boy? To be standing right where you are with a gun in your hand. So very 'macho' of you."

"Where's Peggy?"

"There's never any point asking a question to which you already know the answer."

"Where is she?"

Tarn sat down in the captain's chair behind the outsized desk. "I liked her." Weary and old. "I'll go so far as to say I admired her, and between you and me I don't admire many women. But she had a brilliant brain. Utterly original."

"What happened?"

"Some throw away remark by that pomposity Bannerman. She went back in and saw the 'corruption' I believe was the word she used. It wasn't any corruption. It was simply that her work was worth far more to government, or indeed to any government-in-waiting, than she could begin to guess."

"And the Board – who else is on it?"

"Of course, you're asking so you can kill them too." A statement rather than a question – the long bony fingers steepled, the legs stretched out under the desk, leather-soled shoes, as if the judge were in chambers. "Very well. A former

Prime Minister, the New Army's Chief of Staff, the head of the Met, two former heads of the security services and a Cabinet Secretary, a newspaper proprietor, several captains of industry, a Duke. The list goes on." Counting them off on his fingers bored him. "There's a note of all the names here. I thought you might still be curious." He picked up a piece of paper North hadn't noticed before and started reading from it. " 'Bulldog' Milton, General Sir Benet St John, Pandora Koch." He laid the list back down on the blotter and sat forward in his seat. Ready to hand down his considered opinion. "But there's no point, dear boy. Were you to go round night after night chopping off their heads, they will grow back. Power is an addiction every bit as bad as your purple pills."

Tarn picked up the brandy glass again and raised it to his lips, a help-yourself gesture to the cut-glass decanter with his free hand – the civilised host – and firelight shone through the brandy, crawling and flickering across the skull which rested on a pile of shiny black envelopes next to it. Something in Tarn's eyes. Malice. Extreme malice.

Peggy and Honor, their heads together, dark and blonde, as the east wind blew on Hermitage Island. Peggy's broad smile. Her bruised and swollen face. Her mouth moving – reasoning. Raising broken hands to gesticulate. The clink of heavy chain links. Bruno moving closer. Her back to the room. Gazing into the night sky beyond the glass. Stars everywhere. Bruno's meaty hands around her slim throat. Reaching out towards the darkness and the light. Unseen galaxies. Breaking with who she'd been. Hearing the birth of the universe and the death of planets as her knees buckled. Understanding all of it.

Peggy lived and died with stars in her eyes. The sockets of the skull were dark.

And North knew. Peggy was dead. No doubts.

Sane. Rational. Trusting himself.

Tarn's thin lips twitched in what might have been a smile if there had been any humour in it.

"I'm forgetting my manners," the judge said. "After all, you've never met." His bony index finger reached out, pointing first at North. His chest. "Michael North – my protégé and faithless assassin." The hand dropped, the buffed nail of the index finger tapping the skull as if to call it to attention. "Do let me introduce – Dr Peggy Boland, my reluctant houseguest and astronomer extraordinaire."

Tarn's palm cupped the bony pate in ownership then slid over it with a faint sibilance.

He lifted Peggy's skull up to his own face to gaze into the sockets, before holding it away from himself in appraisal. "Disappointingly, her cranium was no larger than you'd expect for a woman, her brain no heavier. I hoped it might be. An ounce. Two. Bruno indulged my whim. His family were taxidermists in Whitechapel for generations. He severed the head and boiled the skull. He's not at all squeamish. It's one of the reasons I keep him around. Kept him around, I should say."

Peggy refused to cooperate.

"Dr Boland and I enjoyed several fascinating conversations. In my own defence, I did attempt to reason with her. In point of fact, I pleaded with her to keep working with us. I explained that we aren't doing anything that Russia isn't trying to do as we speak. Or China. We merely got there first – thanks to her. She's less judgemental in death than she was in life." He opened the jaw till it gaped. " 'You're a very bad man'." Then snapped it shut again, cackling.

This was North's mentor – more than his mentor. The judge who jailed him and the redeemer who saved him – recruiting him, and turning him into a weapon to protect the state as he saw fit. To Hell and back with the rule of law.

"Don't look like that, North. Dead is dead. Peggy was a scientist – not a woman for churchyards and mournful vicars. The rest of her is under a white camelia in the garden. I sit out there in summer – it has an excellent view of the night sky."

Honor would have to be told. And he would have to do it. Watch her fall apart.

Hoping she would come together again.

"Of course, Peggy would have lived on the mantelpiece once Bruno worked his kitchen magic on you. He was looking forward to it, and I confess I was intrigued to see that bullet hole from the inside out as it were."

The judge made a violent poking gesture with his stiffened index finger into the curled fist of his other hand. Despite himself, the gun in his hand and the distance between them, the hairs on the back of North's neck rose at the anticipation of his own damaged skull on the judge's desk.

"I'm sorry you have to die young, North. Life is about what you leave behind. Your legacy. Peggy was a young woman, but she understood that, which is why she fought to protect hers. You, on the other hand, leave nothing."

The one-eyed man knew North was inside the judge's townhouse. His watchers witnessed North's capture in the park. They didn't come for him. Didn't rescue him, and he didn't expect them to. The judge was right. He had sprung the trap using himself as bait. A hand-off straight out of Honor's playbook. He found Peggy – at least what remained of her – and he was in the machine. All he needed to do now was shoot the man who knew him better than he knew himself, who'd loved him and now hated him.

"You went too far, Tarn."

"Fathers always disappoint, my darling."

"The Board was about defending the country – not taking over."

"Semantics. We've defended this country and its values the best way we know for more than four hundred years." Tarn's fury was mounting. "Steering her. Guiding her. Doing what had to be done. The rise of Parliament – us. The death of Kings – us. Wars – us. Peace – us. Brexit – us. History doesn't happen – we write it." He laughed, and the laughter was jagged. "The bombs unsettled the populace, made them fearful. And it won't stop there because we have a backdoor into everything thanks to Peggy. A power blackout? Hospitals down? A small nuclear catastrophe? Everything is connected.

"And sooner rather than later, North, there'll be a spark to the tinder and up it will all go. The old politics. Another Great Fire to purge us. All the excuse we need to impose order."

"You're talking revolution."

"I'm talking transition. Look around. Old alliances are over. The world as we know it is gone. The nation-state is threatened by multinational corporations with respect for no one and nothing. By religion. Global migration. Technology. The market has failed us over and over despite its promises. Democracy is dying and people are crying out for change, for strong leadership if they but knew it. One spark, North – the New Army will move and the Board will take charge. And when that happens, this country will rise up again richer, stronger, united whether I'm here to see it or not. *That* is my legacy.

"Do what you've been trained to do, North." From the hallway, there was a whirr and a settling of brass, as the hands of the grandfather clock came together at noon and the first chime sounded. Tarn's voice was a thing of dust. "And do it, knowing I'm proud of you. What I've made you."

The judge was across the room. But North felt the animal sensation of the other man's mouth against his. The lips parting. The hard, muscled tongue forcing his mouth open. The urge to devour and swallow and make him disappear. He shook his head and Tarn's lust broke into a thousand sharp and dangerous pieces. It was time. Overdue. North's finger curled round the trigger refused to obey the neural instruction from his damaged brain.

"Apart from one thing, Tarn. Peggy set you up. The authorities wanted to draw you out in the open and you fell for it."

The judge's face set in a rictus of dismay.

"The smart chip doesn't work. We reprogrammed it. Peggy left behind the coding to destroy it all, and a fourteen-year-old called Fangfang Yu just blew down your house of cards. Everything's connected, you said it yourself. We uploaded your destruction."

"She wanted to destroy it, write its own destruction into the program," Hone told him and they wouldn't let her. But Peggy did it anyway. She wrote the program, and swaddled it in plastic and tarp to keep it from harm and dropped it into the cold North Sea. Trusting her friend to find it. Trusting her protégée to know the right thing to do.

The final chime and the air settled to silence but for the soft crackle of the fire, but outside the wail of sirens grew closer – police cars squealing to a halt outside the judge's house, their revolving blue lights reflected in the drops of rain running down the glass.

North picked up Peggy's skull. The police were at the door. He would leave the judge to his public shame. To sentence and confinement. Out from the anonymity of power and into the bright white glare of accountability and punishment. And what was left of the Board would make sure that Tarn hanged himself on remand. Or died one night of a broken heart lying on a prison cot.

Tarn ignored the ringing of the doorbell, the pounding on the front door, which in turn shook the bevelled window glass in its sash frame. He got to his feet. He wasn't finished yet. "Everything I've done, North, was for my country." His chin was up. "There are always casualties in war. You. Peggy. You are all disposable."

He raised the glass as if to make a toast to himself. Judge Lucien Tarn's verdict on Judge Lucien Tarn was "innocent". He was a hero and a patriot and a member of the Board.

Forever. Britain. Say it isn't so.

North pulled the trigger. The bullet smashed through the brandy glass, the judge's teeth, the soft tissue of the brain, the bone of the cranium, before coming to rest in the padded leather of the chair. It was quick. He owed Tarn that much. And it was lethal. Which was for Peggy.

75

It was a first-class omnishambles-cum-clusterfuck. DCI Slim Hardman was beginning to understand why he'd been seconded to the Metropolitan Police. The judge murdered in his own home. Moreover, a murdered former Supreme Court Justice who was allegedly responsible for bombings and kidnappings throughout the country. A naked corpse with no face in the bedroom. Two dead Muscle Marys in a basement gym which looked like Al Capone shot it up. Traces of human remains in the kitchen. And if the conversation with Honor Jones MP had any truth in it, a conspiracy that would delay his retirement for a decade as he unpicked it and it played out through the courts. He sucked in his stomach in anticipation of the press photographs. His wife would insist on a new suit.

The folder laying out JP Armitage's accounts landed in his inbox yesterday – he might be a good detective but he was no forensic accountant. The forensic accountants though were all over it before he even made it to his car for the drive south. The accounts reeked. Standing next to a one-eyed man who was never introduced, Northumbria's Chief Constable had made it plain – he wasn't asking Hardman to go to London. He was telling him. "You're the man of the moment," he said. "I don't envy you."

Hardman didn't know who sent the folder, and he was willing to bet he never would. It came with no message other than the instruction to ring Honor Jones's private mobile number and an exact time to call. "She'll want to talk," the message said. A message signed with a cross and a nought – a kiss and a hug, his young sergeant translated for him.

All he knew was that life got very interesting after the death of Walt Bannerman. Ever since the arrest of Michael North, who disappeared back into the shadows as if he'd never existed.

"Sir." The white boiler-suited figure held a piece of blood-splattered crested paper between his tweezers. He slid it into a transparent evidence bag as his superior approached, his youthful face pale and serious.

DCI Hardman took in the list of names, all of them written in green ink. Military. Business. The political Establishment.

His wife wouldn't be pleased when he told her the post-chemo holiday to New Zealand to see their boy and the grandkids was off. He was disappointed himself, but he would make it up to her. He'd tell the lad to come home – pay for the tickets and maybe he'd stay.

Hardman took out his phone and snapped the list. When he had a quiet moment, he would send it to Honor Jones. Against procedure but it seemed the least he could do. And he wouldn't want the list "disappearing". He handed back the evidence bag, meeting the studiously disinterested face of the forensics technician with the same equanimity.

"Process it, sonny," he said, turning away. He allowed himself the smallest of smiles as he smoothed the tie over his belly.

76

As North exited the back lane three streets from the townhouse, he looked left and right. He couldn't be sure, but by Soho he knew Hone's people weren't following him. He was free and clear. If he went back to Mayfair, there'd be no trace of any intrusion in the old lady's apartment, there'd be no old lady in the fridge – only yellow sheets and silence. And across the road where Hone kept them under surveillance, there would be no coffee cups, no ash and no spread-eagled corpse bleeding into a Persian carpet. It would be like the one-eyed man were a bad dream.

77

Honor opened the door of her garden flat before he raised his hand to knock on it. No Peggy. When he stepped towards her, she didn't resist, instead there was a small groan and she buried herself in his chest as if she couldn't bear to look at him, or bear for him to see her.

She cried for three straight hours when he told her about Peggy. Warning her before he drew out the skull from the jacket he'd wrapped it in. She screamed anyway. Before she got angry. Ranting and raving, and beating her fists against the walls till they were bloody.

After the anger came silence. Then more weeping. Quieter this time. Peggy's skull between her hands. Sadder and darker in the bedroom she wouldn't let him enter. Before she opened the door again and called for him. Her eyes dark and terrible. Like the worst had happened and would keep happening. Before she moved into his arms, her lips found his, and he comforted her the only way that was left.

"I went into politics because she told me that was how to make things better. It's not enough. If the coup is over with Tarn dead, what happens to the hostages they took?"

He'd been asking himself the same question.

"The Board's pragmatic or it would never have survived this long. The soldiers will unlock the doors and let them walk away. They won't hold onto them – there's no reason to. The moment's over. The Board knows where they live – it'll be made clear that they can come for them and theirs any time if they speak out."

Her elbow took her weight as she leaned in towards him, her crazy-hot breast against his chest, the sheets gathering around her, their starchy white folds emphasizing the satin smoothness of her skin.

"I've got a lawyer looking for Peggy's refugees – Rahim and the children. I've made sure they'll have a home and enough money to live on. It's not much, but Peggy would want it done."

She went quiet again at Peggy's name and the thought passed through North's mind that Honor was settling her affairs.

"I couldn't save her, but I can say why she died. We'll tell the world that Tarn killed Peggy and why. That the Board was behind the disappearances – some among the disappeared will come forward, I'm sure. I'll tell the police everything I know about the bombs – all those deaths. How they used me, and JP's involvement. I don't want there to be any place for these people to hide. There'll have to be an inquiry – more than one. Prosecutions too. The smart chip needs stripping out of whatever it's in and production needs to stop immediately. JP left everything to me, so I can do that myself. The New Army has to be taken apart. And the Board exposed for what it is."

When he met her that first morning at dawn in the park, she trembled at the sight of him. The thought of what he was there to do. Seven days had passed – her hair was shorn and her face older, warier, harder. Unrecognisable from the photographs of the smiling, polished politician Tarn first sent him in the black envelope.

"Aren't you frightened?"

She lay back, her head resting on her crossed arms, and stared at the ceiling. "Should I be?"

"You've seen what they can do. Peggy would want you alive."

Her body didn't move but her head turned towards him. "I've been frightened my entire life, North. That's long enough.

"Peggy sent me a postcard once of something Churchill was supposed to have said. I already knew it. It was based on one of his speeches. 'Never, never, in nothing great or small, large or petty, never give in except to convictions of honour and good sense'. Do you know it? 'Never yield to force: never yield to the apparently overwhelming might of the enemy'. 'Convictions of honour' – I can relate to that."

There would always be a place for the Board in the darkness, North knew that even if Honor didn't. Whatever case Hardman constructed – or was allowed to construct.

Whatever light Honor attempted to bring would shine for a while, maybe even a year or two, perhaps as long as a decade. But eventually it would go out and the shadows come back. Still, for a while at least, there would be light and truth and Honor would be the one to bring it.

He wondered if it would help ease her grief for Peggy. She didn't mourn JP – it was enough he'd been involved in Peggy's disappearance – and North hadn't told her yet of JP's role in the fraud that tipped her father over the edge. Perhaps that was always where fate meant her father to go, and perhaps not.

"How do you cope, North?"

The bullet was part of him. He fought against what it took away and what it brought with it. But, lying with Honor, he accepted what he was – that he could know men and women, and not judge them for their sins.

The index finger of her right hand lay against his lower lip like a reminder to tell the truth.

He liked the touch of it.

It made him want to kiss it. Kiss all of her.

"How do you cope with always being alone?"

You don't miss what you've never had.

But right now, he'd never felt less alone. He hadn't found the words before she spoke again.

"With Peggy gone, I'm just that girl in her bedroom who knows no one is coming, because everybody she loved is gone."

Her eyes were dry but her voice cracked at the word "gone".

North wished there were a way to bring Peggy back for Honor. For her not to hurt.

The problem with loving someone was that either you left or they did, and there was never enough time together.

He always believed love was an impossibility for him, because he never had a pattern to follow. And he knew this much – that it was hard to love someone. But he knew, too, that it was harder not to love at all.

"You didn't stay in the dark, Honor. You unbolted the door and you came out."

But it was too early to talk about tomorrows and families. They both knew that.

And later, when he could speak again and when she spoke too, when they were close and warm, she said: "I'm sorry it took me so long to trust you. All I could think about was finding Peggy and keeping her alive."

It wasn't up to North to forgive Honor – he knew better than most what someone would do to survive.

"She was cleverer than all of them, weren't she – JP, Tarn, your one-eyed man?"

Peggy hooked JP and showed him for what he was, destroyed Tarn's plans to bring down democracy, and did what she thought was right when she was told to do wrong by a cyclops. Yes, she was cleverer than all of them. Peggy fixed things. People. Problems. The unfixable. That's who she was.

Honor's thigh lay against his.

She kissed the forearm he had wrapped around her, her lips soft against his skin. She was done with the big picture for a while.

He once knew a girl called Jess who wanted to fly away to somewhere warm. A smell of orange blossom. Did she catch the plane? Tears in her eyes as she sipped cold champagne, her mother's seat empty beside her in the gloom of the cabin? Pulling up the blind. Flying above candyfloss clouds and facing towards the New World. The rising sun through the window painting over her freckled face with gold. He hoped so.

North had no idea if he had a future with Honor. He had no idea how long he had left, or whether she could forgive him for what he had been. What he did know was that any future with Honor couldn't be a violent one. Her father's violence put paid to that. Theirs was a fragile partnership.

"I dreamed about her the other night," Honor said. "We were young. Younger even than when we met. Small children. She was holding onto me and we were running. Pell-mell along the sand. But we were laughing as we ran, and we weren't running away from something. We were running towards it. Do you believe in dreams, North?"

"I never sleep long enough to dream." Why mention the nightmares?

Her naked back was to him, the spine curling in its own question mark.

"Can you stop killing?" She tried to make the question sound casual but there was a tremor in her voice. The list of Board members Hardman sent through to her mobile, without comment, made for grim reading. North was glad it was Hardman's problem and not his. Tarn was wrong – he didn't want to know the members of the Board so he could kill them. North was leaving their fate to justice. Real justice.

He turned her over, putting his finger against her lips now. There would be a day very soon when he'd have to think about what he had done in the name of the Board, and the men he had killed. He'd have to go through each and every one and judge himself innocent or guilty of their deaths, but today wasn't that day.

She carried on regardless. "Because whatever you've done, you're not that man any more and you know I'm right. You're a good man, North, and I don't want you killing – not for me, not for anything or anyone. However it all turns out."

She kissed him – her soft mouth against his – and a key turned in his chest, unlocking him.

Her eyes were pale green, their rim a darker woodland green and at their heart a sunburst of gold. They searched his face for agreement. She was sadder than he'd ever known her. Hope gone. He read the grief in her for Peggy, felt it, saw it, but couldn't mend, it so he kissed her, his mouth against hers. She took it as an answer to her question. Maybe they had a future and maybe they had this one night before he sailed away on a ketch called Liberty. Either way, the killing was over for him. Eventually she slipped from him into sleep. He steadied his breathing, matching it to hers, willing himself to follow her wherever she'd gone, and it came to him that he did have a soul, but that his soul lived in her. Even if he couldn't form the words yet. He might live to be old – he allowed himself to hold the idea between his hands like a death's-head moth. Or he might die sooner than he should. He once wanted a mother to love him who never did, and he once waited to die because he knew one day he had to. Not any more. Michael North would die when his time was up.

Till then every second ahead sparkled.

He always envied those who slept as easily as they breathed, their willingness to let go, their presumption no predator would come for them in the night. Letting himself into their bedrooms, stepping over their worn-down leather slippers, careful not to wake the wives next to them. Killing men as they slept. It was a mercy – why wake them to terror and the knowledge of certain death? Better to take them in their goose-down dreams. The glass of water undisturbed on the bedside table next to them. He didn't envy the easy sleepers tonight. For now, he didn't envy those who slept because he was content enough to feel her surrendered body against his. Moving closer, he stretched out his length along hers, his thighs tucked under hers, and she sighed, her breath moving the hairs on his arm like a zephyr through spring grass.

78

Surrey

6pm. Monday, 13th November

Bunty Moss let herself into the house with a key she borrowed from a neighbour.

James didn't get home till eight most days. Standing in the hallway, the front door out into the rainy day still open behind her, she rang Pam.

"He'll be so pleased. How's your brother, Bunty?"

It took a heartbeat for Bunty Moss to process the question.

"Long since dead, thank you, Pam."

There was an intake of breath the other end. Confusion.

"I'm so sorry. Let me put you through."

The black-bound Bible was on the hall table. Walsh didn't need it where he was. He'd died with his hand in hers. She didn't know how it got there. If she had to guess, she'd say the young man who came looking for Peggy left it for her. She placed her palm against the cover, and it felt warm to the touch.

"Bunty?"

Her husband's voice. Hope. Desperation. Thirty-five years of loving her.

She could hear too the faint noise of planes outside her husband's office as he wept down the phone. He wasn't a man for emotion in the general way of things. Landing and taking off. The gateway to a nation. Business as usual.

79

The press conference was scheduled for noon. In time to catch the bulletins.

80

Westminster, London

Nearly noon. Tuesday, 14th November

From the grass, she looked for him as the quarter bells chimed, her eyes scanning the crowd, the streets, flicking up to the windows with their bomb-proof curtains – but she didn't see him and he felt no urge to step into the light. This was her chosen battleground. She was safe here. Confident and righteous. As he had known she would, she had to stop looking – there were too many camera crews, too many snappers and hacks around her on Abingdon Green.

She opened her mouth to speak, but a cameraman jerked his thumb towards Big Ben.

They didn't want the noise of the bell tolling the hour corrupting the recording. Twenty-five seconds between the chimes and the hammer to fall against the Great Bell. Expectant. Waiting. Twenty-two. Twenty-one. She could wait that long. Wait for the bell to toll and for truth to be spoken.

North turned away – sixteen, fifteen. She'd warned him not to get in any camera shot. To stand well clear. She'd meet him later. They'd have coffee together in Portcullis House – water the thirsty fig trees. Make plans. He was already starting to cross Abingdon Street at nine seconds, eight. Moving towards the river as Big Ben tolled the hour for the first time and she slid to the ground. Only the frantic shutters of the photographers alerted him. The bell still tolling as the screaming started.

Noon.

"Doctor. We need a doctor." A presenter he recognised from the BBC late-night news was hysterical, kneeling by Honor, her long crimson wool coat muddied as cameramen trampled over it, almost toppling onto the body. Honor Jones was dead. He was two hundred yards away, there were fifty people between her and him, but he knew it. He knew it as soon as she'd fallen, as soon as the first monkey pressed the shutter, before the sirens blared. There'd been no noise. A silencer. The hole pre-cut in the glass of an upper-storey window. The sniper would be breaking down the weapon. Fitting it back into its case.

Already moving. He wouldn't even be breathing hard. It wasn't personal. He was following orders. Her name was written in green ink. *Honor Jones, MP. Extreme security risk.*

It was a high-risk strategy. Even as the first ambulance drew up and the police cars skewed onto the grass, blocking the road – police suddenly everywhere, running, their hands on guns, shouting into walkie-talkies – the professional in him recognised the skill of it. The great and glorious and terrible inevitability.

He stood stock-still – everything else frantic and swirling around him. Around her body. Listening for her. But there was nothing. Only horror and grief and fear, and the sense of something being ripped from him, because he hadn't held onto it with all his strength.

This was on him.

He should have let her be. What did the one-eyed man say? Don't begrudge her the golden ticket. She'd be alive if he hadn't dropped that phone into her pocket in St James's Park. If he hadn't expected her to do the right thing and talk to Hardman. If he hadn't reminded her who she was. The Board silenced her before she could reveal them and condemn them. And the Board punished him. Because he took their money. Millions of it. And in return, they snatched the only thing of any value in his life – the woman he learned how to love. He wanted to walk across the road. Beat back the crowds, medics, police. Lift her into his arms, say her name – over and over – breathe back life into her. But what was gone was gone.

Instead, he pulled the baseball cap lower, pushing his way through the crowds that were coming to stare, and he kept walking. One last look at the melee around her. The phones were raised now. Aloft. Recording. Witnessing. Walking away from Honor. Not too fast. Not too slow.

If you were going to take her out, if it were going to get messy, why wait for her to tell everything she knew? Do the hit. Take the hit and move on. Tarn warned him. *"There'll be a spark to the tinder and up it will all go."* A Great Fire. Is that what she was? Tinder? An assassination so close to a bombing campaign would create hysteria. Tarn's final wounding blow.

Or maybe people weren't so quick to move. Maybe the Board wouldn't have their revolution. Their transition. Maybe everyone's life would carry on and democracy survive. Instead, there'd be the odd documentary. Occasionally, a newspaper would run her picture – maybe one they'd taken today, framed with the clock face behind her as time ran out. She was beautiful, papers like beautiful women – they sell more papers. They especially like beautiful dead women. Beautiful dead women who die with just that hint of mystery attached. She'd be one of them. Marilyn. Diana. Honor. She'd have hated that.

That was what did it. Her scorn. How much she'd have hated to be one of those beautiful ghosts.

"You're not that man any more," she'd said as her soft lips pressed against his in the night, *"you know I'm right."* She believed him to be a good man, and there was a chance she had it right.

"Never yield to force: never yield to the apparently overwhelming might of the enemy". She had lain there naked, quoting Churchill.

It began to rain, and he shrugged himself out of the leather jacket. Passing a bin, he tossed in the jacket and the cap. He started running – slow at first, easing into his stride, the impact of the pavement shuddering up his spine and across his skull. Chasing after Honor Jones. He promised he'd stop killing – she made him swear it on her naked body, and he would. Because he was a man of his word. He would stop killing – just as soon as he found those responsible for the death of Honor Jones, and tore their heads clean off their shoulders.

Note to Readers

Our hero returns in another adventure – *Curse the Day* – in December 2019.

Michael North is grieving after the high-profile murder of the woman he loved. And he's vowed to make those responsible 'curse the day' they were born.

But before he can take his revenge, he has a job to do.

Recruited to protect a genius scientist on the brink of a game-changing breakthrough in artificial intelligence, North is soon in all kinds of trouble. There's bad guys. There's a flesh-eating giant octopus. There's murder, and a great deal of mayhem.

Can North save the world? Can he save the day? Can he even save himself?

If you've enjoyed reading *Killing State*, head over to my website at www.judithoreilly.com and sign up to the newsletter to keep in touch, or you can always follow me on @judithoreilly. I've written a couple of Michael North short stories; I'll happily send you one if you're interested. Do let me know.

And bearing in mind that North is a new kid on the block, if you can possibly make the time, do please spread the word and post a review on social media or simply recommend the book to someone. Reviews make a world of difference and I appreciate each and every one.

Judith

Acknowledgements

Thanks are due to: Laura Palmer, Lauren Atherton, and the fantastic team at Head of Zeus; Patrick Walsh, my agent at Pew Literary who kept the faith; Martin Fletcher; Ellie Wood; and Tim "Hawk-eye" Pedley. My experts, advisers and facilitators include: Professor Carole Mundell and Tim Kaner of Bath University; Professor Tim O'Brien of Jodrell Bank; Dr Karen Bower; Oli Wood and Eric Pinkerton; DCI Andy Mortimer of the Metropolitan Police; Colonel (ret'd) AWG Snook OBE, late PARA; Dr Eamon McCrory of UCL and Philip McGill. Thanks too to Mei Lin; Grahame Morris MP and Karie Murphy; Michael Reilly-Cooper; Dr Malcolm Bates; Nick Mann; Dr Will Elliott and Dr Stephanie Greenwell FRCA. They have done their best to keep me right with the facts. Any wilful misinterpretations and outright mistakes are of my own making.

I originally published this thriller independently. Without the support of the great writers who took the time out to read and blurb my book, and those national newspaper journalists and commentators who reviewed it, I wouldn't have the chance to publish it again it with Head of Zeus. Thank you.

The same goes for Matt Bates who was good enough to buy it and distribute it around our rail network and airports.

I also received guidance and support from: David Morrell (the Father of Rambo); Steven James; Shelley Weiner; Venetia Butterfield; Lisanne Radice; Sophie Wilson; Carrie Plitt from Conville and Walsh; John Ash at Pew; Georgina Aldridge and the team at Clay's; Charlotte Summers; Sophie Atkinson; Stephen Waddington; Iain Dale; Warren Shore; Sorrel Briggs, Ella Paul, Lottie Macdonald, Megan Constable; Jan Frazer; Rob Watts; Andrew Alderson and the legendary Ray Wells. Special thanks are due to Karen Sullivan at Orenda Books for her timely and generous pre-publication advice, as well as to Karen Robinson, Simon Walters and Anne Cater along with her crack team of generous-hearted and insightful book bloggers.

First readers and cheerleaders include: Sue Brooks and Andrew Macdonald; Abigail Bosanko; Angela Barnes; John Woodman; Joanne Robertson; Fiona Ward; Allison Joynson; David Paul; Clare Grant; Fiona Sharp; Helen Le Fevre and Tim Burt; Marie Sedgwick and Grace Coates; Mary and Stuart Manley; and Mary Major. Hey, it takes a village.

In particular, I need to acknowledge Helen Chappell for her brilliant original design and IT skills, as well as her advice on algorithms and probability, and of course her friendship.